Already His

Sandy Raven

Michael has been Elise's future husband since she was ten...
Only he didn't know this.

"I detest smelling salts!" Elise opened her eyes and shoved the offending bottle away from her face, then gave him a frosty glare.

"Then you should not have fainted." Relief flowed through Michael. For a moment fear of losing her had paralyzed him, but when he realized what had happened he'd ordered the coach to stop and called for her maid to help him. God, he was going to hate explaining this to her brother.

"I didn't faint. I *never* faint."

He cracked a cocksure grin. "Right."

"Did I hear my lady? Has she come to?" Bridget asked behind him.

Elise tried to sit up, but he held her down. "Rest. Your maid's just concerned. Yes, she's finally come around," he said to the maid. "Why do you women insist on wearing things like this—" Michael held up the spencer. "—on warm days like today?"

"Because," the servant said, "to appear indecently dressed will bring the wrath of society down onto her head. It's my job to see that she at least appears conventional."

"Did you...?" Elise sputtered, apparently just noticing her sleeveless dress and unbuttoned collar. "How did...?"

"I removed it to aid in cooling you. Don't worry, I didn't take any liberties. I was too busy fanning you with your book." He lowered his voice so Bridget couldn't hear him, and added, "Besides, when that time comes, I want you very much conscious, my sweet." Smiling, he thought, how he looked forward to that day.

Elise muttered something he didn't fully catch, though it sounded like a rant about stubborn men and their misguided allegiance. Michael knew she was well when she turned another frigid glance his way. "Let's be off then," he said. "Woodhenge is still some four hours distant, without the stop for lunch." He held Elise's hand, preventing her from leaving the coach and riding with her waiting maid. "No. You stay with me. She can ride in the other coach."

"Oh! You arrogant cur," she hissed. "I don't *want* to ride with you."

He held his tongue thinking she would definitely want to be with him before this day was over. If only he could restrain his frustration at her insolence. "Be that as it may, you will." He sent Bridget back to her vehicle, and shut the door on theirs. Soon they were underway once again.

Within minutes Elise fidgeted with the book she'd finished. He could tell she was contemplating re-reading the thing to avoid talking to him. He didn't want that. He wanted her ebullience and vivaciousness to fill the coach. He wanted to talk to her, explaining the decision he'd come to, and ask if she'd still felt the same about him, and about a possible future together. Then afterward, assuming she still did, he would laugh with her, hold her, touch her, kiss her.

But if she didn't, he had only twenty-four hours in which to change her mind. And the only way to begin with this spirited minx was to be honest, because that was the one thing he knew she valued beyond measure. She always had.

"Do you remember that night at the Holderman's?" he began, his voice sounding somewhat strange, even to himself. *Maintain control,* his brain ordered his heart. When she nodded, he continued, "Do you remember what you said?"

"I'm afraid I said a great deal that night," she said as she stared out the window. "I cannot remember specifically what it is you wish me to recall."

Michael took a deep breath, almost afraid to begin. "You said, *'Have you ever known something to be so right and true in your deepest heart, without ever knowing how it could be that you know.'* I have not forgotten your words. You spoke from your heart when you said that." She turned to face him, and he thought he saw a flicker of something, an emotion deep inside her she was yet unwilling to give rise to, so he continued, hoping it was the response he'd wanted. "I think I understand what you meant now, because I don't know where this feeling is coming from. I only know that I don't want to lose it."

"May I ask how you came to this conclusion?" Her voice barely contained her emotion. He could see that she wanted to believe him, and he could only continue as he'd began, with honesty.

"On my word, Elise, this... this... whatever-it-is between us caught me very much unaware. One day, you were just Ren's annoying sister, and the next I wanted you and at the same time knew I could never have you. Then I started thinking on *why* I couldn't and every reason came back to one thing—the agreement your brother and I made when we were young, in which we promised each other sisters were off limits. At the time it was made, I worried about your brother breaking Christina's heart. You were never an issue, as you were just a child."

She didn't react to his speech, but he could see she was fighting a smile. Michael removed the loosened cravat completely, as it was growing warmer and more stuffy inside the slow-going coach. He shed his unbuttoned waistcoat, tossing it onto the seat with his jacket, and continued, "Then there was our age difference. In my head, I wasn't seeing you as the young woman you've become, but rather as the little sister of my friend. Am I making sense so far?"

Michael could see the hope bubbling just beneath the surface, but she just nodded mutely. He went on. "That night, at the Holderman's, you tried to tell me the age issue was irrelevant, but I wouldn't let myself believe it. Then *you*, termagant that you are, arranged that evening at the theater with Huddleston and Wilson."

"I've got questions about that..." she began, but as realization dawned, her eyes first widened with shock, then narrowed with skepticism. "How did you know...."

He held up a hand to cut her off. "Later, please. Let me finish. When I asked Ren about allowing someone older than me to court you, he reminded me of a few things and clarified others, basically telling me what you'd said the night of the Holderman's ball—that our age difference would not be an issue with him.

"Once that began to sink in, I started to see that I couldn't allow someone to 'tame' you or break your spirit. It was the one thing about you that always drew me to you. That's what makes you special."

"You followed me the other night," she said. He

loved that tilt she got to her head when she asked him a question. "And you heard Edgcumbe, didn't you?"

He nodded. "I only thought to be there to protect you should you need me. Though you obviously held your own. I should have known you would be fine. You are a strong and direct young woman. Edgcumbe is like a colt still finding his legs, and not what you need, Elise. In a few years time, he would have worn your spirit down and you wouldn't be happy. Neither would he. Then, soon after, he'd seek his comfort elsewhere, be it his club, gaming, or a mistress. And you would continue to grow older and unhappier." He paused and let his words sink in.

"Look at me. Please, Elise." When she did, he spoke again. "That's not what I want for you."

It seemed an eternity to him while she quietly digested his words. True to what he knew of her nature, she asked, "Why are telling me this? Now?"

"Because I want to kiss you again, Elise."

Already His

This book is a work of fiction. Names, characters, places and incidents are the product of the author's imagination or are used fictitiously and are not to be construed as real. Any resemblance to actual persons, events, or organizations is entirely coincidental.

Copyright © 2013, Sandy Raven

All rights reserved. No part of this book may be used or reproduced in any manner whatsoever without written permission except in the case of brief quotations embodied in critical articles and/or reviews.

Cover design by The Killion Group, Inc.
Interior layout by Author E.M.S.

ISBN-13: 978-1-939359-03-2

Published in the United States of America

Dear Reader,

Already His is the second book in my series, ***The Caversham Chronicles,*** and I hope you enjoy Michael and Elise's story as much I loved writing it.

This book is special to me because the heroine and I have one passion in common. Horses.

Note that the type of horsemanship Elise practices in this book likely didn't exist at that time in the form we would recognize it, even though Xenophon had written his book *On Horsemanship* around 350 BC, and Daniel Sullivan (d.1810) had already whispered his way across Ireland. Anyway I cannot, in all good conscience, write something my heart doesn't believe is humane (i.e., the normal horsemanship practiced then,) so I didn't do it. I believe in and practice safe and humane horsemanship, and cannot see any heroine I create doing otherwise. Elise also rides astride which women did do at the time according to my research. It was much more common in the countryside on the mainland, rather than in England itself, and women usually wore breeches of some sort under the skirts of their riding habit. Keep in mind that during this, my favorite period in English history, society believed it was undignified for a lady to ride astride. And when all a young lady had to recommend her were the size of her dowry, familial connections, and her reputation, they usually kept their reputations pretty spotless.

This Summer, the third book in the series. ***Loving Sarah*** returns to the ocean, and you'll find the preview first chapter at the end of this book. It's the story of

Ren's youngest sister who wasn't in London during the events in this second book as she was too young, but she does make an appearance in the Epilogue.

Sarah craves adventure and thinks the three Seasons she's had have been enough. She's ready to settle into a comfortable spinsterhood. But first, there are a few things she wants to accomplish while she's young enough to do so. One of those things is sail across the Atlantic in a race that her brother-by-marriage, Lucky Gualtiero, and his business partner, Ian Ross, are participating in. Knowing she will be sacrificing a great deal by doing it, she stows onto his ship waiting until after the start of the race to make herself known.

Except she didn't make it to the right boat.

I would love to hear from you! So, if you have any questions or comments,

I'm online at:
SandyRaven.com

and on Facebook at:
Facebook.com/SandyRavenAuthor

Sincerely,
Sandy Raven

Acknowledgments

To my natural horsemanship mentor and friend, Janet Schipper. If I could just have an ounce of your understanding of how a horse thinks inside my brain, I'd be a much better horsewoman than I am.

To my DH, Curtis. They say that necessity is the mother of invention. But it's also the maker of a pretty darn good proofreader and copy-editor. Thanks for helping me out. I owe you.

To Gail Shelton. You're the best editor and friend a writer can have.

To my D1. You're the absolute best I.T. Department a mom can have. I'm so proud of you, sweetheart.

To my D2. You get me, and for that I love you more than you could ever know.

To Janet, Marilyn, Beverly and Nita. I have known no finer horsewomen in my life. I am honored to call you my friends.

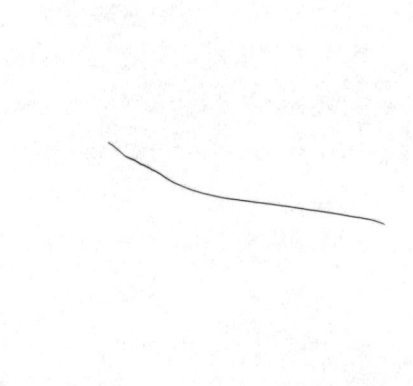

Prologue

Woodhenge (near Goring), Summer 1808

Michael Brightman, heir to the pile of crumbling stone in which he currently found himself, hurried through the narrow corridors, eager to reach the rooms he kept in this, his uncle's home. He thought about his odds of finding a willing wench among the kitchen or laundry staff at that moment, but decided against it. And the village was certainly too far to travel in the middle of his older sister Sabrina's wedding feast, take care of business, and return. Damn his balls, but the past two hours of staring at Miss Stansbury's delectable decolletage—and envisioning his face planted between those luscious breasts—caused an uncomfortable tightness is his breeches that would need relief soon, whether by his own hand, or a willing woman.

He'd prefer the latter, but in a bind his hand would do.

He hurried through the chilly hallway of the family wing and slowed his pace when he heard the muted sobbing and delicate sniffling of a young lady as he passed the priest hole. The medieval tapestry that hung on the wall to his left had been the handiwork of several of his early female ancestors and their ladies, and had been in that same spot for over three hundred years. Only a few knew the true purpose of the tapestry was not in displaying the battle scene which won the first Earl of Camden his title, but rather it served to hide the entry of a secret passageway. The tiny room hid a stairwell leading to an escape route from the castle that not many knew about, so Michael wondered who it was hiding during his sister's wedding feast. The room had been a favorite of his and his sisters when they were children. He and Christina used to play in the secret room, and hide from their nurses when they were young. Thinking on it, he hadn't seen her below in some time, and he just passed Sabrina and his mother, so likely this was Christina. He wondered what had her so upset?

Glancing up and down the corridor and seeing no one, he moved the tapestry and slid behind it. Running his hand along the wall, he reached the open entry to the priest hole which began the escape route his relatives used on more than one occasion when the castle had been attacked.

As expected, he found Christina, in the tiny antechamber to the stairwell, with a solitary taper lit on the table. The room was unchanged since the last time he'd been there, with only one small table and two chairs filling the space.

He stood in the doorway, feeling as though the entire room had grown smaller over the past few years. Michael watched as Christina blew her nose delicately into a linen. His heart wrenched for her, his little sister. "If you had shut the door," he said, "I never would have heard you weeping." He put his hand on her back, wanting to give her his sympathy for whatever was breaking her heart. "Why aren't you below, enjoying the festivities?"

"No reason," she sniveled and wiped her nose. "I'm simply feeling sorry for myself."

"I know you better than to believe that nonsense. You're the least likely girl to feel sorry for herself that I know." He stroked her back gently. "Come now, dry your eyes." Michael tried to sound cheerful, thinking to get his sister back out into the great hall where the party was ongoing. "Tell me who it is that has you in tears and I will make sure the bounder pays for your upset."

"I cannot."

"Absolutely you can. You know I'm not averse to pummeling the face of the Prince himself if he were the one, though I doubt you'd find him to your liking."

Christina dabbed at her eyes with her kerchief and shook her artfully arranged golden curls. "No. It would drive a wedge into your friendship. Even though he was not the only young man standing near me, when I turned I saw no one but Glencairn. I just hope Lord Vance did not witness his actions, because *he* is the man I am most interested in. Glencairn, though of noble birth, will certainly wind up a drunken, debauched rake. If he were to ever marry, he will not make the unfortunate young lady a good husband."

"What did he do?" Michael had to ask, though he was not certain he really wanted to know because he hated the thought of having to call out his friend.

Christina started a convoluted explanation, and in between wiping her tears and blowing her nose, Michael thought he heard her misspeak. "He did *what?*" Michael's ire rose, especially when he realized of whom she spoke. "Glencairn touched you inappropriately? In front of others? Where?"

She nodded.

"Christina, tell me exactly what did Glencairn do?" Before he pounded his friend's face into a bloody pulp, he wanted to be certain of his actions.

"We were leaving the dance floor after a long, exhausting country dance, where Mr. Hampton was my partner, and Glencairn partnered Miss Prudence Chichester. There was such a crowd on the way to the refreshment table as it was the end of a set. Lord Vance was nearby, on my left, and Glencairn was directly behind me. I felt a large warm hand, masculine to be sure, touch me..." she dropped her voice to a whisper, "on my..." she seemed to struggle with saying where Ren touched her.

"Where did he touch you Christina?"

She pushed the heavy wooden door closed, and whispered, "He more than touched my bottom, Michael, he... he *squeezed* it! I have never been so shocked in all my life. That's when I turned around to see your friend standing directly behind me acting nonchalantly, as though what he'd done was of no consequence."

His sister went into another bout of tears, repeating her fear that Vance might have seen what Ren did, and that her chances with him were now forever ruined. Michael wanted to slam his fist into Ren's ugly mug for what he did to cause his sister such distress. He knew better than anyone what a profligate rake his friend was. Michael had to warn him away from ever touching his sister again. At sixteen, Christina was too young and innocent for the likes of him.

Michael had heard enough. He wanted nothing more than to pummel his friend into the ground for taking liberties with his sister, but held his anger in check for her sake. He strode from the room, and went in search of Lord Glencairn, his best friend for ten years, since their very first day at Eton when they were both eight years old. The bounder had touched his sister inappropriately and by damn he would apologize to her.

Michael found Ren in the old castle's receiving room which was the official card room for the evening. He sat with one of his new brother-in-law's relations, Michael forgot the fop's name, and several other young rakes, most of whom were older than they, Lord Vance among them. As Michael drew nearer, his friend met his gaze and gave him a lazy smile, likely influenced by the amount of alcohol he'd consumed.

Ren stood. "Would you like my seat Michael? I'm thinking about asking Miss Chichester for another dance. Hopefully a country dance where she has to skip a time or two." His friend leaned in closer and whispered, "I keep hoping those glorious breasts of hers will come bouncing out of that low cut gown."

Michael had heard enough. He swung first and clipped Ren on the jaw.

"What in hell was that for?"

"I think you know," Michael hissed as he swung again, only this time Ren was able to deflect the blow.

The other guests in the room leaped from their chairs and cleared the floor for the two young bucks to fight.

"Is this about Prudence Chichester?" Ren said as he kept out of Michael's reach. "I didn't know you were interested in her."

He shook his head, swung at Ren again who deflected his strike.

"Are you drunk, Michael? I'll admit to having a few

myself, but not...." Ren swung, Michael ducked and came around, only to feel the force behind his friend's punch to his rib cage.

Michael grabbed Ren and wrestled him to the ground. "Did you touch my sister inappropriately?" He hissed only loud enough for Ren to hear his words. Heaven forbid that action were made public. It could ruin Christina.

"You're either drunk or insane, Michael," the young Lord Glencairn replied as he held Michael down.

But Michael was only momentarily pinned because he shoved Ren hard enough to roll his friend beneath him. Pressing his elbow into Ren's shoulder, pinning him, as he reached out with his free hand and grabbed Ren's wrist. "I'm neither, you ass, and you owe my sister an apology."

The double-ring of young men circling them began to shout and Michael heard one of them call out, "Tell us what the fight's about!"

Michael just grunted, not one to make public his emotions. He spoke in a low tone for Ren alone to hear. "My sister is in tears upstairs. She said you squeezed her bottom coming off the dance floor."

"I did not," Ren hissed, "and I won't apologize for something I didn't do."

Michael lessened the pressure into Ren's shoulder and shifted his weight, which proved a tactical error because he was soon back under his friend. Michael heard his coat tear and thought about the peal his valet would ring over him in the morning. "She's upstairs crying because she said you touched her in a most egregious manner." He struggled for a breath as his friend bore the brunt of his weight onto his chest, pinning him with a leg up. "She's my little sister!"

"Gad, Michael! You'd think I tupped her for the reaction you're giving me." Ren pressed Michael's leg a little higher up and he felt a burning sensation on the back of his thigh as he tried to buck his friend off.

"Don't talk about my...." Michael strained, trying to best Ren and roll them over, "Don't talk about my sister like that!"

"I gave you my word, so I don't... understand why..." Ren grunted when Michael pushed up with the one foot he had on the stone floor, and tried to roll them over. "You'd believe her and not me."

Michael heard material tearing, and wasn't certain if it was his or Ren's. "Did you...."

"I swear I haven't touched your sister!"

"You will promise me you'll never touch her," Michael hissed in Ren's ear.

"Believe me," Ren said, "I have no desire to dally with your sister!" Ren weakened his hold a moment, and Michael rolled Ren under him.

"I want your word on that," Michael said, shoving his knee into Ren's groin for leverage.

"Bloody hell," Ren ground out. "Only if I get yours in return."

"You're a sick sod." Michael strained against the material which held him captive more than his friend. "Your sister's yet a babe."

The sound of shouting finally reached the confined circle of onlookers watching their debased efforts.

"Remember that when we're older and she's on the market," Ren hissed.

"Do I have your word," Michael demanded just before Ren flipped him on his back.

"Do I have yours?" As the words left his mouth the entire room fell silent. It was then that he knew someone, or likely more than one persons of importance, had entered. Persons of enough rank and presence to command the parting crowd to silence.

"Glencairn, get off the floor." In a deadly calm voice, one known to make lesser men's knees buckle, His Grace, the eighth Duke of Caversham, addressed his son. Then he added, "Brightman, the same for you."

Ren wiped the blood from his nose and lip before meeting Michael's gaze one last time before they separated. "Then we're in agreement? Sisters are off limits?"

"Glencairn," Ren's father repeated, "Now."

Michael didn't speak, but met Ren's cold silver gaze and nodded.

Haldenwood, Summer 1812. At the occasion of the marriage of the eighth Duke of Caversham to Lady Amelia Manners-Sutton.

Looking down from her perch in the oak tree near the terrace off her father's office, Lady Elise Halden decided she would run away and join the gypsies. Gypsy children were free to roam the countryside and do as they wished, including fish and shoot their bow and arrows. Gypsy children could ride their ponies whenever they wanted for as long as they wanted. Gypsy children didn't have to obey to the wishes of their nanny, governess or tutors—all of whom prevented her from doing the aforementioned activities as she pleased.

And as of today, she would now have to add a

stepmother to the ranks of *those ordering her about.*

Footsteps on the terrace told her someone was pacing, albeit slowly. She didn't think anyone was looking for her, as no one ever did. Curiosity almost got the better of her. She knew if she shifted her position to look behind her, the tree would move alerting the person on the terrace of her presence. After a few minutes she caught a whiff of tobacco smoke and realized someone had come outside to puff on a cheroot. If she did not move, she could go undetected and be left in peace.

She heard the heavy footfall of a another man step outside, then recognized her brother Ren's voice as he spoke.

"Why do unwed ladies think that the happy occasion of celebrating a marriage is the perfect place for choosing a husband? I had to escape the dancing before one of my new stepmother's young relatives finagled me into a compromising position. I've just turned twenty-two and far from ready to marry."

"I don't know how you were able stay in there as long as you did," the other voice replied, "I felt very much like meat hanging at the butchers." There was a pause as the young man dragged on his cheroot. After he exhaled, he continued. "During our entire dance, Miss Valerie Morton informed me of her age and that she has made her bow."

"Nothing wrong with that," Ren said.

"Oh, but she then listed a long string of accomplishments as though she were applying for a position. She then asked why she hadn't seen either of us at any of the events in Town. I told her I was busy studying and you were often out of the country."

Her brother grunted as he sighed, one of his few outward signs of frustration she'd learned long ago. "The lady with whom I danced, my new stepmother's cousin, though not unattractive is not my type," Elise heard Ren say. "What's worse, she is following me around like a spaniel, complete with big brown puppy eyes." Her brothers voice dropped to just above a whisper as he said, "You know I much prefer the petite blonds with blue eyes and bounteous breasts."

The conversation was getting interesting, so she shifted slightly on her perch in order to better see to whom her brother spoke. She went as far out onto the limb as she dared.

"When the time comes that I must take a bride, I want a lady with spirit and courage." She got a look at the man with her brother and recognized him as one of his friends she'd seen before. Michael Brightman's handsome brown hair and hazel green-brown eyes made her heart flip in her breast. What an odd sensation she thought. "She must enjoy the hunt, fishing and chess. We should converse on topics beyond fashion, romantic novels and housewifely skills."

"There you are." Elise heard a female voice address the two young men. "Come inside, gentlemen. The dancing is about to start again and the numbers are uneven for a reel. We really need you both."

"Yes, ma'am," her brother said.

"Yes, mother," Michael replied.

Both young men left the terrace to rejoin the festivities and Elise felt an incredibly superb idea hatch in her brain. She would have to marry eventually, and so would Lord Brightman. He might be an appropriate match for her, she would have to check. Certainly he was a gentleman with a title and was connected to an earl somehow. And just last week when discussing her own father's upcoming marriage to Lady Amelia with her governess, the dour-faced old woman tried to instill in Elise the importance of marrying within the proper bloodlines.

Elise didn't care about bloodlines, except in the case of the horses in her father's stables.

All she knew was that listening to Michael just now proved to her that they were perfect for each other. As she listened to him list the attributes he looked for in a bride, she realized she fit each and every one of his criteria.

Before the week-long wedding celebration was over, she would convince one Michael Brightman that they belong together and should marry. Their situations were so very similar, as neither was ready to marry. Why, she had to wait at least four more years because she heard Catriona in the kitchen say she was fourteen when she married James the under-gardener. Elise heard this just the other day when the staff was talking about how young her new step-mama was, and how she was soon to present her papa with another babe.

She had to get to her room to think out a plan. As she saw it, the situation was very similar to what Old Ned taught her about horse training. Elise didn't see a difference. She needed to make the horse *want* do her bidding, as the old man always said. And to do that she needed a plan before she climbed onto the horse's back.

"But first I have to get out of this tree," she said to herself. She looked down and decided it was a too high to jump down, even with the green limb bending low under her weight. She also might hit the branch beneath her, and that would hurt something fierce. No, she had to get to the trunk and climb her way back down the way she came. Reaching for a limb over her head to hold onto for balance, she stretched up an arm while at the same time holding fast to the branch on which she sat.

"Oh, fiddle-faddle. Come here." Elise reached out again, this time grasping a cluster of new leaves and then the branch. She felt the seam under her arm tear and swore again. "Maisy will be angry now that I've torn my dress." She'd never hear the end of it from her maid. And if her father found out.... Oh, heaven. She'd likely be punished, and that was after she got spanked.

She tried to keep her hold of the branch over her head while she scooted toward the trunk, but she was unable to do so without ruining the dress further. Grabbing the branch over her head with both hands now, she tried to pull herself up when she heard a crack and felt herself falling, only to have her skirts snag on a branch, stopping her descent.

In the blink of an eye, Elise both thought she would die and realized she wouldn't. She almost wished for death when she realized she wasn't alone. On the terrace, fanning herself, was one of her father's guests, Lord Brightman's mother, Lady Richard. And here Elise was hanging by her skirts from a branch in an oak tree. She supposed it was a good thing that it was her and not a male guest witnessing her humiliation.

The sound of fabric tearing echoed throughout the side garden. Just as Lady Richard reached her, Elise felt the material give and she squealed as she fell the rest of the way down, landing in the arms of the woman, sending both of them falling to the ground.

Elise rushed to get off Lady Richard, hoping she hadn't killed her. When she didn't move, Elise knelt beside her and took her gloved hand in her ungloved ones and pat it, as it was what she saw the housekeeper do whenever a housemaid fainted. She then began to pray as she hadn't prayed since the last time she was about to get caught at something she wasn't supposed to do.

Lady Richard groaned and moved, and Elise heaved a sigh. As soon as the woman opened her eyes, Elise knelt over her and began to apologize profusely.

"Ma'am, I am so very sorry. Please do not.... my father will be so very angry."

"Move aside," said the woman with gray streaks in her ruined coif as she sat up. Elise handed Lady Richard the pearl-encrusted comb that fell from her once artfully-arranged hair, then rose and stretched out a hand. She ignored Elise's offer of assistance and rose on her own, then began to dust off her backside. The lady's aqua colored dress was now in disarray and probably stained as well. Elise apologized again for her behavior, and prayed Lady Richard didn't want retribution for Elise ruining her dress and mussing her hair.

Lord Brightman's mother looked down her nose at Elise, who stood almost as tall as she, and asked, "Who are you, and what were you doing spying on the guests in the house."

"I am Elise Halden and I wasn't spying because I was in the tree before my brother and his friend came outside."

Elise watched as Lady Richard rearranged her bodice, and wondered if she should mention the rip in the back. She decided against it. If the woman was this mad and she didn't know about the tear, imagine how angry she'd be if she did.

"Just what were you doing in that tree, Elise?"

She'd come to the tree to escape the taunts from some of the older girls during the feast, then Michael and Ren had come outside to puff their cheroots and she was trapped aloft. Elise smiled as she remembered the qualities Michael listed when he described the woman he wanted as a wife. The instant she heard them, she knew he was describing *her,* and that they would marry one day because they were perfect for each other. She gathered her ripped skirts and held them in her hands, as she looked up to the limb from which she just fallen to see if she'd left any material behind.

Smiling, she turned to the woman who softened her landing, and replied, "Falling in love, I think."

Chapter One

London, May 1822

"Have you heard the news?"

Lady Elise Halden shot her dearest friend in the whole world a stern gaze and tightened her lips. Unable to move for fear the dressmaker's pins might come out of place, she hoped her friend would catch her expression and hold her tongue. Lady Beverly Hepplewhite's eyes widened as she continued into Elise's room and hopped onto her bed.

Elise looked down to the stitchers working on the hem of her gown. "Excuse me," she said. Holding a rose-colored ribbon in place on her sleeve, she stepped off the stool and addressed her maid and the seamstresses. "Bridget, Madame, will you give us a few minutes please? I'll ring when I'm ready to continue."

Adding a straight pin to the ribbon before leaving, Madame Fuichard and her two assistants quit the room. But not her maid, Bridget. She looked directly at Elise and her friend. "You're due to come out in five days," said the red-headed maid, just a few years older than Elise. "If you do something foolish now, His Grace'll banish ye for sure. An' because I don't have a fondness for the Grampians in winter, I won't be going with ye."

Once the door shut behind her maid, Beverly said, "I was wondering why he didn't come for breakfast. Now I hear he's gone to Woodhenge to make arrangements."

Elise lifted her hands, showing Beverly her inability to hold them steady. "I have never in my life been so nervous as I am now. These horrid butterflies are the result of the entire *ton* believing Michael, *my Michael*, is in need of a bride *now* simply because his uncle has died and he's ascended to the title."

"You can't say it took you by surprise. We all knew this day would come as the old earl has been on his deathbed for the past year," Beverly quipped. "Heaven knows the new Earl of Camden has a responsibility to all those women in his family. After all, he's now the only male and will need to see to an heir very soon."

"His mother and older sister have been pressuring him to take a bride for the past year. Now he *must* wait three months." Elise sighed. "My heart wants to believe he's been waiting for me, but my brain says it's unlikely."

"I've always wondered why the old earl never married," Beverly said. "Was he... you know, light in the instep?"

Elise shook her head. "Heavens, no! It's not common knowledge, but—" Elise checked to make sure Bridget hadn't come back into the room, and continued, "The old earl had a scandalous marriage many years ago. He'd fallen in love with, and married, a young lady who was unfaithful while he was in India on the Crown's business. She then became with child by her lover. Both mother and babe died in childbirth. And the earl, as you know, never remarried." Elise's mind raced at what she could do now to benefit her cause. "This does not help my chances."

"Michael will be in mourning for three months, Elise," Beverly stated. "He'll not start a bride hunt until after that. *That's* when you need to worry about competition."

"In three months I won't have you here to help me think things through because your Papa will be back any day now. Won't he?" When her friend nodded, Elise sighed, feeling as though the whole world was conspiring against her.

"I won't be moving to Land's End, Elise. I'll only be a few blocks away."

She nodded as she caught her reflection in the mirror. "I had so hoped to win him over gradually during this season. Now I shall have to contend with every mother of a marriageable-age daughter, and the daughters themselves, all pursuing Michael for his new title and wealth." Elise studied the dress pinned onto her with a disapproving eye, and sighed with double frustration. "You would think that Michael being my brother's life-long friend would give me an advantage," she muttered. "He'll likely not wish to be in the same room as me."

She stamped her foot, her complete annoyance giving rise to a flourish of unladylike manners. "Damn his uncle for dying last night!"

Beverly gasped at Elise's invective. "The man couldn't very well plan the time of his departure from this world, Elise."

She sat at her dressing table, her shoulders slumping in dejection. "I'm sorry for my selfish tirade. The old earl really was a dear man." A pin stuck her in the waist and she pulled the offensive thing from the dress.

Beverly nodded, "You know, that dress has turned out better than we originally thought." Her friend eyed it closely. "But, something is still missing." She shook her head. "Perhaps after you have your jewels and your mother's tiara on, it will complete the effect."

Elise contemplated her friend's words. The as-yet unfinished dress she planned to wear Saturday was completely conventional, and the latest fashion among her set. It gave her the appearance of a proper young lady. The lady her brother wanted her to be. She did want to please him—all of them really—and make he, Lia and Grandmother proud of her on her special night.

The skirt was crushed white silk with rows of narrow rose-colored satin ribbons ringing the skirt up to the knee. The same colored ribbons ringed the puffed white silk sleeves at the edge. The bodice of rose-colored silk ended just below her less than acceptable bust line. It successfully created the desired effect of a more abundant cleavage than God had provided. A wide band of silk rosettes, precisely three shades lighter than the ribbons, intertwined with satin greenery at the hem of the floor-length creation. More of those same rosettes were sewn into the folds of ribbon gathered on the sleeve, and on the same material gathered between her breasts.

Looking at herself in the mirror with a critical eye, she realized that the dress she once adored, she now hated. The exquisite, one of a kind creation from Madame Fuichard made her look just like all the other girls out on the marriage mart this season. She would be unremarkable among the herd of other chits being paraded about by anxious mamas.

"What am I going to do, Beverly? How *ever* will I

get him to notice me?" She stamped her foot again. "You more than anyone know I have the worst luck where Michael is concerned. Now to be forced to catch his eye while all the other unmarried ladies out there do likewise.... Why, I could never compare! I am not as pretty as they are."

"You are so," Beverly argued.

Elise cut her off, "Not to mention that he remembers every misdeed and prank I've executed on him since I was ten."

"He doesn't know about Attila," Beverly said with a confident smile.

Elise remembered seeing Michael at Tattersalls that day three years ago and laughed. "No! He doesn't know that was us, and it's best left that way." She began to pull pins from the dress, removing all the rosettes as her imagination began to wander. "I knew Attila was perfect for Michael when I started him under saddle. And I was right, for Michael loves that horse." She smiled as she pulled pins from a ribbon and tossed it onto the table. "To this day, the man has no idea I was the one who trained him."

They were silent a moment as Elise continued removing adornments from the unfinished dress. Their eyes met in the mirror, and Beverly asked, "What are you doing?"

"I've been fretting over this for the last hour." Elise pointed at the pile of rosettes and the ribbon from the hem she'd just pulled. "There is far too much frippery on this dress. It isn't what I normally wear, so why pretend I like it?" Their eyes met in the mirror again. "I need a dress that reflects *me*. The old me *and* the new me. Who I have always been, and who I am today."

Beverly's eyes grew wide with excitement. She smiled and nodded. "More important than a just a dress, what you need is to come up with a plan for *making* him take notice of you. Though nothing like you did when you were fifteen. That little act nearly got you killed and it was over a year before Michael returned to Haldenwood."

"I did *not* nearly get killed. I was barely scratched. And I never would have fallen off that trellis if it wasn't rotted to begin with." Elise remembered all too well how fabulous Michael looked when stripped to the waist, baring that magnificently muscled chest and back of his. She had stared, mouth agape at the beauty of him. As she felt the vines ripping away from the stone, and the remnants of the ancient trellis crumbling beneath her, her friend screamed, alerting him to her presence as she dangled from his balcony. He'd come running to the rail and looked down just in time to see her land flat on her back in the freshly weeded flower beds below.

"Perhaps it was a little embarrassing for him, but I was duly punished.... after father ascertained I was indeed well and truly alive." Elise closed her eyes and sighed. "I remember thinking I'd died and gone to heaven." Meeting her friend's blue-eyed stare, she added, "That was before I fell!"

Beverly threw her arms up and flopped back on the mattress. "You've been falling for him since you were ten. One day I'm afraid you might fall too far and get hurt." Her friend turned a worried expression to her and said, "you must, I implore you, endeavor to restrain yourself. The consequences are too severe for us now."

"I shall, I promise, but I need your help devising

some way to make him notice the new grown-up me, and not remember the irritating little brat I was." Elise clasped her hands together in a praying fashion and brought them to her breast. "I so desperately want him to realize that I have waited for him all these years, and I am already his."

"What we need is a plan," Beverly said.

"Yes, you've said that." Elise stared at her short, mousy-brown hair in the mirror, now wishing her hair were longer, her face prettier, her features more feminine, and her nearly non-existent bosom, more full and lush. Anything so he would see her as a beautiful, desirable woman. Michael was so perfect in her eyes that he deserved a charming, ladylike wife. Granted, she could do nothing about her actual looks, but what about her clothes? Could her clothing help portray her in a more desirable light? A tighter fit to the bodice? A dropped waist perhaps?

But more important than her looks and clothing, she understood it was her behavior that must be tempered. To that end, she vowed to continue to work on that part of her personality. It often felt like a sisyphian task she undertook, with the hope that one day Michael might think her worthy.

After several minutes of complete silence while both girls contemplated the problem, Beverly leaped from the bed, startling Elise. "I've got it! Or, at least, I think I do."

Eyes closed, Beverly paced the long hand-tied Turkey rug, rubbing the bridge of her delicate nose with the thumb and forefinger. "What we want is for Michael to see you for the woman you've become, and not as the girl you were. Right?"

"Yes, of course. You said as much a few minutes ago."

"You know me, Elise, everything has to be mapped out, the goal identified and a plan put into motion to accomplish the task."

"Yes, yes, you have always been the planner. But what have you come up with?" God, she hoped it wasn't too unorthodox. With her brother overseeing every move she made, she'd never get away with anything outrageous. If she even tried, Bridget was right, he'd send her to that box of rocks he used as a hunting lodge up in Scotland for sure.

"You must not only behave differently, but look different as well," she said. "Stand up."

Elise did. Beverly walked around her. "You look just like every other chit at every other ball we've been to this past month."

Elise resisted rolling her eyes. She knew that. Hadn't she just been thinking it all morning? Beverly tugged at Elise's short, straight locks. "Granted, your hair is shorter than the other girls', but it is very much the trend now that you and your sister-in-law started the fashion. Why every woman with a backbone is liberating herself of the nuisance of long hair."

Elise smiled at her best friend. "Yes but my hair just sits there, where your hair is fabulous, curling like it does."

"Elise, this will become a mutual admiration session if we let it. We simply must stay on task."

"Right."

"Now, let's start with this dress. It's all wrong. It's a debutant's dress. What you want is something more... womanly. A sheath of a dress. Something that will maximize what figure you do have with less frills and flounce. Something a tad more daring. Are you following me?"

"I believe I am," Elise whispered, staring at the dress in the oval pier glass. "You're right. That is what has been bothering me since I saw myself in the mirror."

"You need something plain, but not white," Beverly said as she continued to scrutinize Elise's figure and dress. "No pastels, either. The only people who wear pastels are little girls and wall flowers."

"I don't think my brother will allow me to make my debut in a scarlet peignoir, Beverly." Just because she'd been daring in the past, she had to remember her goal—to become someone Michael would desire. She wanted to be the kind of woman he would be attracted to, and proud to marry.

"No, I shouldn't think he would. But he needn't know what your gown looks like does he? And what about the duchess, or your grandmother? Will either of them be assisting you on Saturday evening?"

"I suppose I could manage with just Bridget."

"Yes you can. Now about your dress...."

After several more minutes of staring into the mirror, Elise and Beverly concluded the current dress just would not do. So they sketched a design for a new dress. A dress that was sure to catch the eye of every man in attendance. Most hopefully, the new Earl of Camden.

"What if we're wrong?" Elise asked. She realized, for the first time, that this feeling of doubt was foreign to her. If the stakes weren't so high, she'd throw caution to the wind and go with her heart. "What if this backfires? This is my entire future we're placing in the hands of a modiste."

"This will work, Elise. There is nothing in this design that is unorthodox. The dress is not immodest in any way. It is simply... simple. Which allows *you* to shine as the jewel you are. *This*," her friend pointed at their sketch, "Lord Camden, will appreciate. I promise you."

Elise pulled her bell cord and Bridget, Madame Fuichard and the seamstresses returned. Elise showed Madame the sketch and asked if it could be ready by Saturday afternoon, five days away. Madame looked about to faint, declaring the task impossible in the few days before her big ball.

"This is a not a dress fit for a young mademoiselle making her debut to the world. This.... This 'creation' is perhaps something fit for a married woman wishing to court scandal."

"My lady," Bridget stated, "One look at ye, when you come down to dinner in that, and they'll be sending you right back up here to change into another gown." The servant shook her red curls while she studied the drawing. "Ye won't get away with it, I tell you."

Then it hit her. Why not two dresses?

She took Beverly aside and asked, "What do you think about changing gowns? I mean to have one for dinner and another for the ball."

"Well," Beverly mused, "as I see it, your biggest obstacle is your maid. We can't have her leaking our secret. Then, all we need to do is calculate the time it would take to come upstairs after dinner, change, then reappear in the receiving line. We cannot do it without Bridget's help."

Elise nodded then turned back to the modiste.

"Could you do both?"

The modiste looked from Bridget to Elise. "There simply is not enough time to find the material and sew another new dress."

Not about to let her plan be defeated, Elise gave a winsome smile to Madame Fuichard, then added, "I have enormous faith in you and your assistants, Madame. But, if you don't think you can do it, would you be upset if I ask Madame Robillard if she could squeeze me into her busy schedule?"

Madame closed her eyes tapped her pencil on the dresser. Elise could sense the other woman's agitation with her. "I shall pay you handsomely Madame, if you could make this dress also. I truly do not wish to go to another modiste."

"If I do it," the other woman said with some reservation. "I will need to hire two more seamstresses to have just your two orders completed in time." The modiste studied the sketch closely, saying, "The dress appears simple and easy to make, and we already have your measurements. We would need the fabric selection."

Elise clapped her hands together and grinned. "Wonderful! We shall go shopping for new fabric this very minute. Unless Madame has something suitable for this design, in a color to complement my complexion already in her shop?"

The woman returned Elise's smile, either because of the opportunity to double her fee, or because she instinctively loved the idea of being known as dressmaker to this sister of a duke. "It just so happens I received a bolt in my latest shipment from the east. In fact, it is so newly arrived I have not even cut into it. It is a dark ivory silk, the color will be a perfect highlight for your hair, skin and eyes, and because you are so willowy and graceful, you will carry this masterpiece with exceptional flair. There will be none to match you on this night or the rest of the season, Mademoiselle."

"I wish to purchase the entire bolt, as I trust your judgment completely, Madame. Now, if you could create this dress," she held up the sheet of heavy vellum, "for me *alone*, you will have my gratitude, as well as exclusivity as my dressmaker for the rest of the season."

This seemed to please Madame immensely, and she assured Elise she would have both dresses for her to try on in two days.

Later, as the women gathered their belongings to leave the chamber, Elise reminded them of the need for secrecy. The last thing she needed was her brother getting wind of her intention and somehow foiling her plan.

Once she closed the door behind them, she turned to her friend and said, "That went very well, don't you think?"

Beverly smiled and nodded. "I do. Michael will hardly be able to dismiss you once you appear on the landing wearing that dress. His eyes will be riveted on you the entire night."

Early Saturday morning, hoping to avoid the amazingly organized chaos that was the preparations for her ball, Elise and Beverly headed out the front door after breakfast, prepared to go for their usual ride in the park. Unlike other young ladies, Elise and Beverly actually rode to enjoy their horses, not to be seen.

"Thank you, Niles," Elise said, as the butler held the door open.

"Yes, thank you, Niles," Beverly added right behind her.

"It would not be remiss of me to remind you ladies of the evening ahead."

"How *can* I forget, dear Niles," Elise replied, "My stomach is roiling because of nerves as it is. I'm hoping this ride will calm them so I can eat something before tonight."

Niles watched over the ladies as they waited for the grooms to come up with their horses. But before the grooms arrived, a familiar dark green carriage bearing the gold-inlaid Camden crest pulled in front of the Upper Brook street home of the Duke of Caversham. A groom hopped down, opened the door and lowered the steps, and out stepped the man Elise had fantasized about since she was ten years old. At that time, her papa had just married Amelia and her brother was away at school. Often when her brother returned home he had Michael in tow, and that's was how she became acquainted with him. But it was the evening of her father's wedding celebration that she fell in love with him. As soon as she realized she wanted to marry him, Elise did what any little girl would do to force an unwilling young man to come up to scratch—she held his horse hostage by hiding it in another barn until he agreed to marry her.

Michael removed his hat as he ascended the steps. His cocoa brown hair was slicked back as though he was fresh from a bath. Those familiar greenish-brown eyes, set wide on his face under a strong brow, held an amused twinkle this morning. The grin turning the corners of his well-formed wide lips upward was most contagious. Elise's fingers just itched to trace his fine features, including the faint cleft in his chin. Even though he had a tiny 'v' shaped scar on his cheek from some childhood accident, he looked too devastatingly handsome for his own good.

And it bothered Elise that he knew she thought him handsome. Though she hadn't told him so recently, she *had* told him just that in the past. She remembered the day many years earlier, when she'd gone into the barn to find an angry Michael waiting on his horse. She told him he was too handsome to go through life scowling. He said nothing to her, just mumbled at her as he took his horse's reins and left.

Today he smiled. Which irritated *her*. Though in his favor, everything was irritating her on this day, and knew she really needed to temper her thoughts before getting on her horse. The excitable little mare was doing well, and Elise really didn't want to end up on the ground because she couldn't control her own emotions.

Michael's light gray fine wool coat bore a black velvet mourning arm band to match the collar. The fabric stretched across his shoulders as though it was pasted onto his broad back. A silver satin waistcoat adorned with onyx buttons hugged his trim waist. Her breathing stilled as she could almost imagine him unbuttoning them, to relax over a game of cards or chess. What she wouldn't give to have him relax in such a manner with her.

Even in mourning, this man looked every bit the handsome rogue. His buff-yellow nankeen breeches looked as though his well-muscled thighs were poured into them, without a wrinkle in sight. She surmised that his fine boots probably took his valet hours to polish to their mirror shine.

She tried—really, really tried—to appear bored and disinterested in his presence, even so far as feigning interest in the traffic on the street. Elise knew she more than likely was not succeeding.

He came up and greeted them. His smile warm and genuine.

Beverly curtsied and said, "Good morning, Lord Camden."

"Yes," Elise said when she turned to face him, bobbing a quick curtsy. "Good morning, my lord." She immediately turned away, as though staring down the street would bring the grooms out of the mews faster.

He nodded to them. "It is turning into a beautiful day, ladies," Michael replied. "I'd begun to despair after waking to a fog so thick I was unable to see across my garden." He came to stand beside them, and asked, "Out for a ride on this fine morning?"

His proximity made her more nervous, causing her heart to beat faster. Elise's naturally sarcastic tongue blurted out the first thing that came to her head. "No. We just thought we'd watch the traffic pass by in our best riding habits."

Beverly elbowed her and shot her a warning glare. Turning her full smile back to Michael, she said, "You must forgive her, my lord. Tonight's festivities have left my friend on tenterhooks and those she loves most have been the recipients of her stinging retorts all morning. I am hoping this outing will bring back the sweet disposition I know Elise to have."

Elise just stared, slack-jawed at the excuses for *her* behavior pouring from her friend's mouth. She wished it were possible to kick herself for those words—once for thinking them, and once for saying them. Why, oh why, did she always turn her sarcastic tongue on the only man she wanted to impress with her changed ways?

"Yes," Michael replied, giving her a sympathetic smile. "Let's hope this ride rids Lady Elise of her nerves before the evening's big event." Turning to Elise, he smiled. "Just remember to breathe deeply and relax. All will turn out well."

"Easy for you to say. It's not *your* debut!" She did it again, snapped at him when she wanted to entice him. She wanted him to see the new Elise. Why was it so difficult to change? She'd never win him over if she didn't.

"You're right, it's not. But I'm trying to help here, Elise."

"You can't help, when you're part of the problem." Immediately she slapped her hand over her mouth, embarrassed by her words. "I'm so sorry. I shouldn't have said.... Oh, dear." She felt her body tremble and her eyes well with burning tears. She swallowed the lump that rose and words of apology rushed out of her. "I'm sorry, my lord. You would think because of all the preparations we made last year, that I would not be so nervous now. But, since the start of the season, I have felt somewhat left out, attending everyone else's ball when I hadn't had my own yet."

Michael nodded his head. "If I could I would offer to dance with you, but as you know...."

"Yes, I know," Elise said. "Your family is in mourning."

"But if I were not, I would love a dance."

He appeared sincere, and not in his normal teasing

manner. Elise wondered if he were feeling well because he was usually ripe to pick on her when she was in a snit like a moment ago. Not letting this new, compassionate mood of his slip by she said, "I will hold you to that, my lord."

He nodded. "Absolutely do, We can even make it a waltz if you have permission."

"Of course I have permission," she said. But the sarcastic tone with which she'd begun her reply quickly died. "We got it last year just before.... Um, before we...." Elise stopped, remembering that day the family had planned to leave for London and last year's season. Grandmother had taken a tumble down the main stairs, striking her head, knocking her unconscious. For almost a week they held vigil over her, hoping she would awaken. Their prayers were answered when one afternoon she opened her eyes, thus beginning her long recovery. As a result Elise missed her first season.

"That's right," he said quickly. "Grandmother was recovering."

Elise nodded, unable to speak as she was still ashamed at her outburst. And now she had the added emotion of remembering the pain at nearly losing her grandmother.

"All is well now," Michael said with a smile. "Lady Sewell is in prime form, ready to take on the Season with you and your family." He winked at her, causing her to return his smile. "I know the season will be over by then, but in three months we can have our waltz."

The three of them watched as the grooms led the horses forward—mares for Elise and Beverly, and a quiet gelding for the groom following as guard. Michael tipped his head and bid them a delightful ride.

Once mounted and away from the house and the groom, Beverly turned her curly blond head to Elise, her eyes reproachful. "That was better. You started off sounding shrewish, but recovered when he mentioned the family foregoing the season last year."

The mares walked on a relaxed rein toward the park entrance. "Remembering grandmother's accident brought back the fear and emotions from those weeks when we didn't know if she would survive. It still causes me upset."

"Or were you tongue-tied because you were surprised to find Michael being polite to you?" Beverly turned to look at her. They rode through the park's gated entrance, and her friend added, "Remember, you must give him a reason to want to be in your presence, or else all is lost."

"I know you are right. Over and over in my head I go through every scenario possible with him and plan how I would comport myself in that situation. Inevitably, I never do what I rehearsed and my sarcastic mouth just takes over." It was times like this when Elise thought she would drown in her despair.

"Do you remember what Mrs. Pritchard taught us to do in those situations?"

Elise shook her head. With her brain in the barn her entire life, Elise never paid much attention to their comportment teacher. Which was why she was in this predicament in the first place.

Beverly went on. "She said to close our eyes and count to three before we reply. First, you'll appear more intelligent—as though you'd thought your answer through before replying. Second, it will make you appear less like a bounding colt and more the refined lady you should be. And isn't that what we all struggle to portray? Images of serene, intelligent ladies?"

"Not everyone," Elise replied. "I certainly don't see those Corrigan girls attempting to appear more intelligent, and look at all the bucks circling them each night!"

"We should be so lucky."

Elise nodded and they both laughed as they followed the bridle path, keeping their horses at a walk, preferring to wait until they reached the far side of the Serpentine to race—away from the prying eyes and condemning glances of the others taking in the morning sunshine. But Elise's mind wasn't on the lovely morning, or even the Corrigan girls and all their many beau.

"I cannot believe he said he would actually waltz with me when he comes out of mourning." She looked over at her friend and smiled. "I now have three months to perfect my dance."

Elise sighed. She had to change. She had to temper her thoughts, her words, and her actions. It was the only way for anyone to really believe she was different. That she had grown up. Or, as Beverly said, all would be lost, because the new Lord Camden would just marry someone else.

With a slight flick of the wrist, she gave a light tap of her crop behind the girth of her off-side, which sent her mare bounding forward, leaving her friend and her groom staring at her back.

Michael Brightman, the new twelfth Earl of Camden, strode into the dining room at Caversham House, an unusual cheer rising within. Likely because it was a weekend, and there was nothing needing his attention until Monday morning. It definitely didn't have anything to do with seeing the little hellion out front. The fact that she was nervous about the night ahead told him she at least cared enough to present herself in a manner that would make her family proud. Could it be she was growing up?

The little hellion, all grown up. Shocking thought that. Hopefully it meant no more romantic interest in him. He stumbled over the edge of a folded carpet, and caught himself on the door jamb.

Michael laughed at his clumsiness, then smiled and greeted Ren and Lia, as he did most mornings when they were all in Town.

"Good morning Your Grace," he said to the duchess, "you are looking radiantly beautiful as usual."

"I'm sorry about all the disarray, my lord," the Duchess of Caversham replied. "I have been assured all the carpets and boxes from the decorations will be out of the hallway before the festivities begin this evening."

He turned to his old friend and said, "And you look... just as you always do these days, like you want to strangle someone." Michael proceeded to pile a plate high with eggs, kippers, and bacon, then took a seat across from the duchess and next to Ren. "So, who is it you want to kill this time?"

"My sister perhaps? She's been pain in my backside this past week."

"Leave her be, husband," the duchess warned. "Her behavior is to be expected considering tonight is *her* ball. Since the season began, we've attended everyone else's parties. Tonight is *her* night."

Michael knew what a strong-willed chit Elise could

be when her mind was set on something, so he had to sympathize with his friend on this. Except she was off this morning. Like a slightly lame horse, where you can't tell exactly where the thing is bothered, she was just... off.

"She was looking rather piqued just now," Michael commented. "Hopefully an invigorating ride will settle her." He swallowed a mouthful of food. "You can tell she's nervous. She's snapping like a shrew, and.... Wait, she's always like that." He winked at Ren. Michael actually found the whole discourse refreshing. Elise's discomposure, while not something he'd laugh at, was out of the ordinary for her. So the stress of the night's festivities was starting to wear on her. At least he was able to calm her before she mounted the mare. He'd hate to see her injured or worse because she wasn't paying attention while riding her horse. Elise didn't ride tractable, quiet horses. No. She trained as she rode, so she rode horses that would be problems for most riders.

But the good thing about tonight was Elise was now on the marriage mart. Soon she would be locked away in the country at some poor fop's estate, bearing offspring to continue that man's lineage.

He remembered his mother's departing words yesterday, and it only served to pressure him to fulfill his duty now that he had the title. He was, after all, the last male in a family of eleven women. She reminded him of the fact that the title would not just go into abeyance, it would, in fact die with him if he didn't see to finding a wife and begetting his own heirs.

Still, Michael smiled. Lucky for him he had a three month reprieve to mourn his uncle before starting his search for a suitable bride. He wondered if this paragon of ladylike virtue, if she even existed, would mind if he continued his tradition of breakfast with his friends before work.

"Like I said before," Ren replied, "I can't wait to hand her off to some unsuspecting chap and get her out of my hair. She's put more gray on my head this past year than I ever gave our father."

"Husband!" Her Grace chided.

"Oh, you don't mean that and you know it," Michael said with confidence. "The gray hairs part might be true, but handing her off to some young, dunder-headed prig? That's not what she needs. Elise requires someone who will appreciate her spirit and charm." He lifted a forkful of egg to his mouth. "Not some spineless ninny or worse someone who will break her to his will like a horse to saddle."

Where did *that* come from? Why was he defending Elise? Looking out for her well-being? The disconcerting, gnawing feeling he'd experienced just now struck a chord in him. An irritating one, at that. He was not going to feel sorry for the girl. She sat a horse better than he, and was almost as good a shot with a pistol as he. Why, she was probably even a decent card and billiard player as well. He already knew she played a fair game of chess and backgammon.

She was a sporting lady. Not one of those simpering women one was compelled to feel sorry for. The chit was, and always had been, a nuisance—fancying herself in love with him since she could string a sentence together. So numerous were the times she had placed herself in his path either to annoy him or, as she grew older hoping to catch his eye, that he could not count. Though in all honesty she hadn't done so in several years. At least not since her grandmother had moved in with them and Ren married. Her grandmother, her brother's wife, and her house guest, Lady Beverly Hepplewhite, all seemed to be very good influences on Elise. And Michael had to admit he hadn't seen much of her since she started on this horse project of hers.

Yes, she would make some horse-mad fop a decent enough wife. And with a dowry as ample as hers, she'd be betrothed before the season ended.

"If I didn't know any better, I'd think you were talking about yourself," Ren stated, matter-of-factly as he met Michael's gaze over the rim of his coffee cup. "But we do know better, don't we?"

Michael turned his attention to the egg and sausage on his plate, determined to explore this peculiar feeling later. "Most certainly, Your Grace. I don't need any added troubles under my roof. Have enough as it is, what with my mother and now my sisters pushing all these women at me—everything from barely-out-of-the-schoolroom misses to widows older than I." He shook his head for emphasis. "I certainly don't need your hellion sister sharpening her claws on my fair heart." He sipped his coffee, and looked up into the sympathetic face of the duke. "No, my friend, the safe route's the one for me."

"Ha! That'll be the day, you rapscallion." Everyone turned to the doorway when a silver-turbaned Lady Sewell entered the room leaning on her cane. Michael and Ren stood as the duke's elderly grandmother came to take her usual seat to Michael's left.

"Good morning, my lady," Michael said as he placed a kiss on the older woman's wrinkled cheek, and assisted her to her chair. A footman brought her a plate with her usual breakfast, then cut her ladyship's ham steak for her, and stepped back from the table.

"Camden, when your three months mourning are over you had best have a future wife in mind."

"I thought I'd marry you, darling," Michael said. "After all, we get along smashingly and I've never had a whist partner as sharp as you."

"If I could give you the heir you need, I'd take you up on it." The woman's blue-gray eyes sparkled with mischief as she forked a fluffy piece of egg.

"If it wasn't considered bad form, you would have every one of my dances tonight, my lady." Michael said, as he realized their conversation was causing his friend to squirm in his seat.

"I told Elise last night that if I were a young miss again I'd not settle for anything less than a man who's kiss made my lady parts quiver and my brain turn to mush." His Grace choked on his coffee, as his duchess serenely scooped the yolk from her egg cup as though the ribald dialogue was a normal occurrence. "Ah Camden.... If I were a few years younger, I'd make you my third husband."

The servants would later say amongst themselves that they all heard His Grace choke on the mouthful of food he'd been about to swallow. A footman stood poised to run for the family physician in case his presence became necessary—which, thankfully, was not.

Chapter Two

"Oh, Elise," Beverly whispered, her voiced tinged with a hushed reverence, "you're beautiful! You're the living image of a nymph, or siren. The image is inspiring of...."

"Scandal," her maid said flatly. "It's goin' to cause a scandal, I say. And this family has never had the likes of the one you're about to bring down on it."

"Bridget, you will please refrain from your pessimistic diatribe." Elise fidgeted on her stool, as she considered the worst that could possibly happen. She decided whatever her brother might do to her tomorrow, however he might punish her, it would all be worth it if tonight went well. Because this was the moment she's dreamed of for as long as she could remember. She wanted to see the expression on Michael's face when she reappeared to take her place in the reception line. She hoped beyond all hope that he appreciated the effort she'd put into looking her best, albeit unlike any other young lady of their set.

Her hands trembled as she attempted to unclasp the sapphire necklace she'd worn with the rose and white dress. "I must hurry and get in the reception line with my brother and Lia." She stared at the simple gown and knew the image she wanted to portray differed greatly from the one reflected back at her. She lowered the necklace to the dresser top, and began to think. She then removed the drop diamond and sapphire earrings, then the tiara, which didn't sit on her head quite right anyway. "Better," she mumbled, "but not perfect."

Elise rummaged through her jewel chest for another pair of earrings, then put on the more simple pearl drops. She met her friend's gaze in the mirror. "Beverly, may I borrow the wreath you wore in your hair at Lady Herrin's masque? I know your father brought it to you from his travels in Europe, but if I promise to be careful with it, may I?"

Her friend's eyes widened as a smile grew on her face. "Oh, that would be perfect," her friend whispered before she exited the suite and went across the hall to the one she used while they were in town. She returned within a minute, and said "I just met Her Grace in the hallway and stopped her from entering your room. She said to hurry as they have started receiving guests."

Carriages continued to pull forward in front of their house on Upper Brook as they had for the last ten minutes, their wheels and horses' hooves drowned out by the sounds of tittering women's voices and the deep-tenored laugh of their male escorts. With each passing moment of the last hour, even as she pushed her favorite dessert around the plate, Elise had debated whether or not she should change into this gown. But the awed reaction of her dearest friend as she placed the thin wreath of delicate gold and white silk flowers in her hair validated her decision to go forward with her plan. She was more determined now than ever, to go downstairs with her head held high and flashing her most honest, dazzling smile, and win the heart of the man who'd held hers for nearly all her life.

"No young lady in your position should appear so inappropriately dressed," her maid said as she placed the last hair pin in Elise's borrowed headpiece.

"For the last time, Bridget, there is nothing inappropriate about my gown or my appearance." Practicing her smile on her maid, she added, "And there's nothing you can say to make me feel less than perfect tonight."

Michael stood amidst a group of friends gathering at the base of the wide, curving staircase. Discussion centered around the latest doings of the parliamentary session. He occasionally inserted the appropriate comment here and there to pretend interest, but there was no use denying the fact that he really didn't know what the devil they *were* actually talking about. His thoughts were elsewhere at the moment.

When the Duke and Duchess had taken their places in the receiving line, which was noticeably absent one particular debutant honoree, he'd taken his position here, at the base of the steps and waited. The little minx was supposed to be in the line with her grandmother, brother and sister-in-law. Her Grace was giving the excuse to those coming through the line that Elise was feeling nervous. Which wasn't an untruth as he could attest to from this morning.

But, Elise was up to something. He sensed it. And that was the reason he stood in just this spot. It had nothing to do with the company that gathered around him, but everything to do with the fact that the proverbial female thorn in his side had to come down these particular steps and make her way to the reception line behind him.

He noticed his friend's forced smile as Lady Charnwood held him captive, likely filling his ear with her opinions on reform. As the older woman spoke, Michael caught his friend's eye intermittently glancing to the top of the steps. Finally, Lady Charnwood moved on and His Grace leaned over and whispered to his wife, and the Duchess excused herself from the line. Michael made way for her as she walked past him and the other gentleman with a smile and a nod, to make her way up the steps. It was obvious to Michael that Ren had sent his wife upstairs to check on what was keeping Elise.

When she returned mere minutes later, he saw her whisper into her husband's ear. Though His Grace nodded at his wife's words, Michael knew his friend well. The strained smile on his face hid Ren's ire. She had best not pull a prank and embarrass her brother and sister-in-law on this night for they had gone above and beyond the norm for her come-out. To disrespect them by making them receive her guests was beginning to irritate *him*.

A collective intake of breath sounded from several guests waiting in the line that extended out the front door of Caversham House. When Michael saw their gazes raised to the top of the steps, he turned. All conversation in the hall below halted, and every well-coiffed head turned to the landing as Lady Elise Halden appeared. Drawing his gaze upward, he felt an invisible blow to his gut.

Standing at the top of the steps she paused and met his gaze, a radiant smile breaking across her face. A woodland nymph come to life, she was as ethereal and enchanting as all the stories of maidens of the forests he'd ever heard. Atop her head was no debutant's tiara, but a delicate wreath of tiny gold and white flowers which accentuated the effect. A gold ribbon curled forward to caress her collarbone. Her filmy gold silk shawl slid casually down her arms, baring an expanse of creamy skin. The man who took her to wife would a fortunate man indeed.

His mouth watered.

He had to shake the erotic image from his mind. Reminding himself that this was his best friend's little sister. The same sister he swore he'd never think of in this manner. The same minx who climbed a trellis to reach his balcony and watch him dress, only to fall into the flower beds below when she'd lost her hold. Michael was here as Ren's friend, to wish the young lady well in her husband-hunting endeavors. Not that *he* was interested in her as anything other than *his best friend's sister*. Perhaps if he reminded himself of that often enough, the salacious thoughts running through his head would do the honorable thing and disappear.

She smiled the knowing smile of a young woman who was certain of her beauty and worth. He watched as she met the crowd's censorious stares, with her own smiling countenance, her gaze daring any one of them to even hint that she'd done anything inappropriate.

Michael was certain some of the ladies in attendance had waited with bated breath to see what Elise would wear, or do, so as to gossip about her behavior over morning calls the next day. And gossip they would, for this gown highlighted Elise's uniqueness in a most fitting way.

But the men also had waited to see the duke's notoriously unconventional sister. While waiting,

Michael overheard several of the unattached young bucks say they were excited she was finally available for them to court.

Thinking back just ten hours, in the dining room at breakfast, Michael had prophesied that Elise would be betrothed before the end of the season. Knowing the chit in question—and her brother—watching this should prove to be most entertaining.

Michael almost felt sorry for all the other debs coming out this year because Elise never did anything with mediocrity, but with a brilliance and enthusiasm that far out-shone the rest of her fair sex. In all his days, he'd never known any woman so brave as to buck convention and be true to herself as he knew Elise to be. The hem on the simple ivory dress was cut well above the ankles on both sides, while the front and back ended in a point that touched the ground between the lady's feet. The design revealed more ankle than was the norm for a ball gown.

Glimpsed from the side when she walked were transparent stockings, a sheer match to her dress, again hinting at more flesh than was appropriate for a young, unmarried lady. Still, the outright simplicity and lack of adornment on her gown, and the fact she wore no jewels but tiny, delicate pearl drop earrings, completed the nymph-like image. Whether her intent was to cause a sensation, attract the attention of every single male from twenty to eighty in attendance, or to sow seeds of jealousy amongst her competition, she succeeded.

Michael could not envision any other woman wearing such a gown and looking as exquisite as Elise. Her graceful, willowy form carried the fitted dress like a glove. It hugged her tight as a corset down to her waist, and from there fell smoothly down to the unconventional hemline. For a moment he wondered how such a sleeveless, strapless creation remained on her body without slipping down—especially as Elise hadn't the ample bosom most men desired.

What the hell did they know anyway.

When she reached the bottom of the steps, Michael barely managed a smile and a greeting. He wanted to shout out to the entire room, *Look! See what a lovely young lady this termagant has blossomed into!* Taking her gloved hand into his, he managed to say, "You are radiant, my lady." He placed a kiss atop her knuckles. "More beautiful than if you'd chosen to adorn yourself with frills and diamonds."

"Thank you, my lord, but that doesn't negate the fact that I feel much like a head of cattle at auction," she said, that devilish twinkle unmistakable in her gold-flecked amber eyes. "Available to the highest bidder, or in this case the oldest, most noble title."

Michael threw his head back and laughed, breaking the tension between them. Her brother stared at her, his expression resolute, lips thinned, trying to mask his rising ire. Michael said, "Or one led to slaughter unless you comport yourself appropriately from this second forward." He held out his arm and Elise put her hand on his, and Michael led her to the reception line a few feet away. Behind her, Elise's friend Beverly followed.

Leaning in close enough for Michael to catch a whiff of her faint lavender scent, she whispered, "And, as I've recently been reminded, any candidate for husband must also be in possession of wealth comparable to my own, or His Grace refuses to entertain the man's offer."

He swallowed hard and collected himself. "Ah, so

pirates and highwaymen need not apply?"

She turned a dazzling smile up to him, unsettling him like a green boy. "Unfortunate for them, but no. They wouldn't make it in the door."

She greeted her brother and sister-in-law and took her place between the Duke and Duchess of Caversham and immediately began greeting the guests as the line began to move again.

After the last of the guests passed through the line, they were finally able to enter the festivities. Alone with Lia and Ren, Elise took the opportunity to apologize to her brother and sister-in-law for her tardiness to the reception line, and the change of wardrobe. "Thank you for not getting upset." Elise whispered as she took Ren's left arm, unable to look into his eyes for fear she would find disappointment in them over her choice to change gowns.

Her brother looked down with hardened steel-colored eyes. "As my insightful wife has advised me, I am picking my battles." Lia peeked her head from her brother's right side and smiled, letting Elise know all would be well.

Only then did she sigh, relieved to have that behind her.

Her brother led their party toward the open ballroom doors, Michael, Beverly and her grandmother having gone in some time ago. They made their way through the rose-and-ivory-decorated room, the crowd parted for them until they'd made their way to the dais flanked by white flowers of different varieties on a rose colored linen. A footman arrived with a tray and she lifted a champagne flute and sipped.

"Excellent strategic move, child. Dressing down rather than wearing all those gaudy stones," her grandmother whispered. "And a second dress for a debut will be all the rage now. Mark my word." The gold-turbaned Lady Sewell tilted her head and raised her monocle so as to better examine the bodice of her dress, then raised her gaze back to Elise's. "You've no cleavage exposed. How do you ever hope to make the sale, if you don't let them have a peek at the goods?"

Elise and Beverly choked on their drinks, and Lia smiled serenely as her brother turned away murmuring something to no one in particular. Elise leaned over and kissed her grandmother's cheek, thanking her for the compliments, and her grandmother added, "Sit deep in the saddle young lady, for you're in for the ride of your life starting this very night!"

No sooner had the words been said, several young men appeared and began chatting with her and Beverly. Talk was mostly over mundane things, like the new play opening and Lord Colson's new phaeton. But while the men spoke of races and the amusements they were all familiar with, Elise's mind began to drift.

How she wished she could dance with Michael on this night. Earlier in the day he'd said he would waltz with her when his mourning was over. She couldn't wait for the day they could dance it together. For now though, she had to get through this first dance, the one with her brother. She was sure he intended to give her yet another a stern warning about her behavior.

When the orchestra struck the chords of the piece she'd chosen, Ren offered his arm, leading her onto the floor. Taking her right hand in his left, and placing the other lightly on her back, he whirled Elise around the floor in the dance she waited over a year to perform.

"Was there something lacking in your upbringing," her brother said so casually as to belie his true feeling, "that has caused this complete lack of respect for convention?"

Elise turned her gaze to his, and smiled. "No, Your Grace. I simply felt that in order to present myself in a manner more true to my real self, I needed to dispense of the trappings and frivolities that other *girls* hide behind. Society says that as of tonight I'm no longer a girl, but a young lady ready for marriage. I intend to make that point very clear this evening." *And hopefully bring a certain someone up to scratch*, she wanted to tell him, but thought better of it. If her brother knew her thoughts, he'd never believed she'd changed at all.

"I hope that for once in your life you can find it in you to hold such comments to yourself," he said. "It would do no good to have every rake desperate for your fortune knocking on my door. Their suit would be refused before they had the opportunity to warm a chair across from mine."

"Which is as I wish," she said with all sincerity, "since I plan to marry for love alone. So do not worry that I will encourage the attention of anyone unworthy of me."

When their dance came to an end, they walked back to their seats as the rest of the guests crowded onto the floor. Her sister-in-law was deep in discussion with two matrons, both of whom had several marriageable-aged daughters of their own. As she approached their group the other women turned their backs to her, shutting her out from their discussion. This reinforced her determination to remain composed and unperturbed in the face of the derisive comments she was sure to hear from the women of *le bon ton*. She went past her sister-in-law, to stand next to her grandmother. Elise smiled as the two women left the dais, their conversation with the duchess over.

Curiosity filled her as she leaned over and asked why the two so suddenly decided to leave their company.

"I find I am having to defend your choice in gowns," her sister-in-law said, her voice tinged with anger.

Regret filled Elise and she was about to apologize to her sister-in-law, when Her Grace added, "I merely stated that, as I observe the others of your set here in this very room, your gown is more modest in *decolletage* than most. The fact that yours is absent a three inch strip of material at the shoulders is inconsequential, the fitted bodice accentuates your slender shape, and if the curve of an ankle is going to incite a man to lustful thought and deed, then he isn't a man we would have aligned with our family. I also reminded them that you are an extremely beautiful young *lady* with the good fortune as not to require trinkets, frills and such to impress and attract any suitor your heart desires."

Her sister-in-law had defended her! Elise felt a tight knot rise in her throat, and she fought the urge to cry. She hugged Lia fiercely and thanked her. "I wanted to appear separate from the crowd, because I'm *not* like the others. I'm *me* and wanted to present and reiterate that fact to all."

Her sister-in-law hugged her back with equal enthusiasm. "If anyone so much as dares to taint you with gossip pertaining to your gown or decision to not to wear gaudy jewels to weigh your slender beauty down, they will have to answer to me, I promise."

"I couldn't have said it better myself," her grandmother said, raising her champagne flute to her rouged lips. She winked at Elise. "Notice the old heifers didn't dare say a word to me about your marvelous dress. I would have said the same as Her Grace, except perhaps not quite so politely."

"Grandmother," Elise said softly, her veneer of false composure close to cracking, "Mrs. Pritchard once said that I should endeavor to say nothing if I had nothing nice to say."

"Balderdash. Go around criticizing the debutant honoree, and you might find yourself uninvited from other events of the season," her grandmother said with just enough force in her voice to be heard by the two matrons who stood nearby.

Lia saved the moment when she said, "It seems the young bucks want a turn about the floor with you. Go, have your fun, and don't worry about gossip. Your grandmother and I shall protect your reputation. Besides, no one would go against me or risk my wrath. For some reason I have garnered a reputation as having a terrible temper, when really they should be more concerned with Grandmother's tongue and not my temper!"

Elise turned and as she did so, bumped into the first of her dance partners for the night. The Honorable David Sinclair caught her by the waist to keep her from falling, his hand lingered slightly longer than was appropriate.

"Lady Elise," he said, then bowed low. "I came to ask if I may have this dance."

"I had promised it to someone, sir. I am very sorry," she said.

"Since the unfortunate gentleman is not on hand to have the pleasure of dancing with you, I offer myself up." Mr. Sinclair smiled, but the effort never made it to his eyes.

Elise looked around for the dark-haired gentleman with the eggplant colored coat she'd originally promised the dance to, and when he failed to appear, she acknowledged he likely was in the card room and had forgot his promise to her. It happened to her all the time. She looked up into Mr. Sinclair's Nordic good looks, and nodded her head and smiled.

For the duration of the dance, she forced herself to pretend she didn't notice the way his blue eyes roved over her body in a covetous way. She got an uneasy chill when his hand lifted hers as they paraded through the parallel lines of other dancers. When the reel was over, she thanked him and turned to go back to where Beverly waited. But his hand reached for hers, and he attempted to keep her on the floor as the musicians began a new piece.

The brashness of his move wasn't lost on her, but she didn't want to cause a scene. Elise really did want to make her brother proud of her. Also, her deepest wish was for Michael to see her now as a desirable woman—not the hellion who would walk away from the floor leaving her partner staring at her back for his impertinent assumption she would favor him with a second dance.

Sinclair's hand lighted on the small of her back. With the slightest pressure, he urged her to take her place in leading the procession forming behind them in the first steps of a polonaise. Just as she was about to go with him, she heard a familiar voice from behind her unwanted partner.

"Sir, I believe this dance was mine."

His voice, deep and sure, sent a thrill up her spine. Michael had come to rescue her. He risked gossip doing this. Elise felt her heart beat a little quicker and her entire body grow warm. She turned to face Michael and he bowed to her. Sinclair did the same and stepped back.

It wasn't a waltz, but Elise was thankful Michael had come. Mr. Sinclair's intent on keeping her out for a second dance was unwanted on her part, and she didn't know how to refuse him without causing a scene.

"My pardon, Lady Elise," Sinclair said, through a forced smile. "I had hoped to be in your company a moment longer." He turned to Michael. "My lord, I entrust her to your care." He bowed once again before departing.

Elise stepped into Michael's arms, the only place she wanted to be since coming down the stairs. "Thank you."

"You looked like you needed rescuing." He smiled at her when she looked up into his hazel eyes.

"I cannot thank you enough," she whispered. "But you cannot do this again, Michael. People will think you had no respect for your uncle." She followed his smooth flow as he accompanied her in the parade across the floor, his strong hand guiding her.

"The matrons might gossip, but the young ladies will all be jealous of you, mark my word."

"What makes you say that?"

"This is my only dance tonight," he replied. "Unless

you need rescuing again."

Inside, she trembled. Elise couldn't help the joyous feeling that came over her whenever she was in his presence. But this? This was what she'd always wanted. She prayed he felt at least *something* beside indifference toward her. And as if her prayer had been heard by the Almighty himself, her answer came in his next sentence.

"You've grown into a lovely young lady, little minx. Have you changed your ways as well to match?"

She felt blood rush to her face as she tried to remember what it was Beverly said earlier this morning. Wait three seconds before answering, so as not to appear coltish and ill-mannered. After what felt like an endless wait, she finally said, "You will soon see, my lord, that I have indeed matured inside, as well as out."

He navigated their turn, as the couples began to pair off and go in different directions. She and Michael paraded on one side of the dance floor with half the dancers, and the other half went the opposite direction. He said, "One of the things I have always admired about you Elise is your courage and honesty. At times I feel I've known you so long I can read you. You didn't want a second dance with Mr. Sinclair, did you? I could sense that you wanted nothing more than to leave him on the floor, didn't you?"

"In the past I might have done so," she admitted. "But am learning to temper my actions. I am not the girl I was. I'd like to think I have grown up. Where I might not have cared before, I truly do not wish to hurt a gentleman's feelings. Ever."

"Have a care, Elise. There are more like Sinclair out there. Rakes who know how to woo a woman out of their fortunes."

She bristled at his words. "I assure you I did not encourage him."

"I know you didn't encourage him. My eyes never left you as the two of you danced. It looked as though you could barely tolerate his touch."

She settled, thankful he noticed her discomfort."You're very observant, my lord. Even though he is pleasant enough, there is something about him that I cannot quite put my finger on. Or perhaps it was just his presumption that I would be willing to stay on the dance floor with him. His actions bothered me such that it nearly provoked me to the point of walking away from him."

They raised their arms for the couples on the other side to parade under them, then they took a turn gliding under the arms of the other dancers. Michael whirled her around as their dance came to an end, the music crescendoing to its finale. When he stepped back from her, she found her body missed his touch and nearness.

She smiled as their gazes met. "I had a wonderful time, Lord Camden. Feel free to rescue me any time you see me such a situation again." He nodded, then led her from the floor to a group of her friends. Silently he bowed, then he turned away and strode from the room.

Elise noticed Beverly holding court in the corner between the dais and the wall and headed toward her. And, as usual, young men of all ages found Beverly utterly charming and delightful. Elise never aspired to attract the bevy of gentleman admirers that her friend did. She only wanted one admirer. The same one she'd wanted all her life.

"My God," Michael breathed as he reached the solitude of an empty retiring room upstairs. What was happening to him? He'd meant to tease Elise earlier today when he'd seen her on the steps, but couldn't when he realized her nerves were stretched tighter than a harp wire. That had been the first clue that something was wrong with him. He'd never before held anything above tolerance for the little hellion who'd been an embarrassing thorn in his backside all those years. And now look at him! Compliments, kindness and servitude toward that termagant.

What had changed? He'd seen her in ball dresses before many times since the season began. He'd even seen her bare feet and legs as they dangled from a tree limb last summer, when he'd gone to Haldenwood to bring important contracts for Ren to sign during Lady Sewell's recovery. It had been one of those idyllic warm spring days when the sun shone bright, beckoning all it touched to bloom.

Well, it seemed a certain flower did bloom—right before his eyes—and he'd missed it.

She'd certainly caught his attention tonight. A nymph. A natural beauty unadorned by frippery and jewels. She, in all her simple elegance, *was* the gem. If those bucks down there didn't understand that, they didn't deserve her.

Where had *that* thought come from? In the past he never would have considered Elise in the same category as a gem, never in a million years.

Until tonight.

Now, he found he didn't like the idea of sharing her with anyone. What in hell was happening to him?

"No!" he whispered into the silent room. *Not that.*

Dread weighed heavily on his shoulders. Whoever would've thought.... Certainly not he. And definitely not Ren.

"Oh, Christ!" He remembered his friend downstairs. His best friend, the man who'd grown up with him, and attended Eton and Oxford with him. The best friend who cried in his study the night he returned from India and discovered his father and pregnant stepmother died in a suspicious carriage accident.

How would he explain this to Ren? What about the very public brawl in the middle of Sabrina's wedding all those years ago? And the promise they'd made to each other? Granted, they were eighteen years old and in university at the time, when he and Ren had sworn sisters were off limits. Ironic now because Michael proposed the promise to protect his own sister, and it was he who wanted.... God, why in the name of all that was holy did he have to want her?

He could never tell his friend he wanted to abrogate the promise they'd made to each other. He simply could not hurt Ren in that manner. And it would hurt him if Michael continued this little flirtation with his sister. Because, even though he was loathe to admit it, Ren wanted nothing more than to see his sister happily settled with a worthy man, and have a family of her own. Ren knew Michael's every sin and vice—most of which were committed while in the company of his friend—thus eliminating him from the category "*worthy.*" He and Ren were also into their thirties now, thus making Michael too old for the likes of Ren's newly-launched *younger* sister.

Then there was matter of her annoying infatuation with him all these years. As a child, Elise had followed him around Haldenwood when he visited, wanting to read sonnets and poetry to him, play cards with him, or ride with him.

As she grew into a young lady, so too did her infatuation with him grow. In order to preserve the friendship with her brother, he'd thoughtfully and purposefully avoided being caught anywhere alone with her, afraid what she might do. But now he wanted nothing but to be alone with her and find out what could happen.

He stopped his racing thoughts. This was too perverse. This type of thing only happened to the characters in those sleazy serialized novels some women read. Not to upstanding members of the nobility like himself.

His mother would not approve of Elise for those same reasons he found her desirable. She often reminded him that high spirited ladies were also the ones most likely to succumb to a rogue or rake, and least likely to make a stable wife. As an example she always reminded him of his uncle and his unfaithful wife who died bearing another man's child.

Which only reinforced the fact that toying with the notion of marrying Elise was pure foolishness, for all parties involved were sure to suffer. If this nonsense were allowed to play out, the final outcome would be a wedge in the one relationship that meant more to him than any other. He didn't doubt it for a moment, because Ren loved his sister and would die to protect her honor. And he, Michael Dennis Brightman, now the Earl of Camden, wanted nothing more than to do all manner of *dis*honorable things with that same young woman, most of which had to do with getting that lithe, young body of hers entwined with his on a bed behind locked doors.

For her own good, he needed to cease this flirtation with her before she took his words and actions to heart and held out hope for something he could never give her. Her brother would never agree. A new resolve fell into place and straightening his waistcoat and cravat, he strode from the chamber and back to the ball. He had enough to do with trying to find the bride who would fill his nursery. He didn't have the time or energy to help Elise find the groom who would help make hers.

So, why couldn't he shake the feeling that they should be filling one together?

Elise watched Michael's departure from the room and smiled to herself. He *had* noticed her, and he *did* desire her. It was evident in his touch and in his every word to her as they danced. She couldn't wait to get Beverly alone and tell her how thankful she was to her, her dearest friend, for helping her plan this evening and win her future husband's heart.

Nothing could dim her spirits now that she knew it was only a matter of time before he declared himself. She would, of course, accept his suit and finally wed the man she'd dreamed of marrying forever. But until then society dictated she dance with as many of these other young men as she could before falling into exhaustion. She would sit out every waltz until she and Michael could dance one together, which would have to wait until after his mourning. After they'd left the dance floor, he fled the room, she thought to join her brother in the card room. Then Lia told her that Michael had remembered something urgent that needed tending, so he made his excuses and begged forgiveness before his early departure.

After Michael had gone, the rest of the night was unremarkable. Elise did nothing to embarrass her family, and held herself with the grace and dignity that befit her station as the oldest sister to a sitting duke. Fortunately, she was spared having to dance again with The Honorable David Sinclair, who clung to the fringes of her collected bevy of gentleman. Though, as the evening wore on, she realized Sinclair wasn't quite the ogre she'd at first assumed him to be, and in actuality was quite intelligent. Nor did he appear to be threatened by a woman who enjoyed discussing politics and philosophy.

But she still didn't want to dance with him again. Something in his touch filled her with a coldness, resonating through her in an unpleasant manner. It made her go out of her way to avoid touching him the rest of the night.

So after hours more of dancing, smiling, chatting, and hiding her yawns behind her hand or her fan, Elise and Beverly went up the stairs, to their respective chambers, too tired to review the evening's event, promising to do so as soon as they woke in the morning. She wished Michael hadn't left so soon, and wondered if she'd done something to cause him to leave right after their dance.

Elise's final memory before falling asleep was the look of appreciation and desire in Michael's hazel eyes, first as she descended the staircase, then later as he partnered her in their dance. She smiled to herself in the darkened room. Total happiness was within reach.

The next day's gossip sheets would declare the debut of Lady Elise Halden a resounding success, and the young lady herself labeled an *incomparable* and a *diamond of the first water,* the likes of which had not been seen in the London social scene in years. Her trend-setting gown, which at first was thought to be too daring for a gently-reared young miss was hailed as more proper and practical than some worn by other ladies of the same class and age. Proper for her modest decolletage, and practical for her ankle-baring hemline which prevented the lady herself and her many dance partners from tripping on excess material.

Chapter Three

Snuggled under the eider down quilt on her bed, Elise tried, really tried to make herself fall asleep. She'd been awake all night, anticipating her next meeting with him. But now bright summer sunshine streamed through her open drapes, and the sounds of birds singing cheerfully in the garden below drifted in the open window drowning out the sounds of the street. Smiling to herself, she knew it must be an omen of a bright future.

Footsteps in the hall hurried toward her room. Recognizing them, she immediately bolted upright, and ran across the room to open the door before Beverly even knocked. She flung her arms around her friend, who arrived in her night robe and slippers, obviously fresh from bed herself. They squealed and jumped up and down, then danced around the room in girlish vivacity. Minutes later they fell back onto Elise's bed, breathless.

"Did you see the way he looked at you? He was positively smitten!"

"Do you think so? I'm afraid to hope, that after all these years...."

"I watched him as you entered the room and his eyes never left you." Beverly leaned up on an elbow and held her gaze. "At times he'd look around to make sure no one was watching him, but then his gaze would always return to you. When you walked by him, coming to the dais after the dance with your brother, you smiled, he smiled, and when you passed by his eyes caressed your backside. Whenever someone came up to chat with him, if they got in his line of sight he'd skillfully shift his position so that he'd have you back within view. In particular, he watched you closely as you danced with Mr. Sinclair."

Rolling onto her stomach, she faced her friend. "Oh, Beverly, he said some of the most flirtatious things to me while we danced. I hope he's forgiven me all my youthful schemings. I couldn't bear it if he thought I hadn't changed."

"Well," her friend replied, "that's yet to be determined. But judging from what I witnessed with my own two eyes, I don't think Lord Camden is seeing you in quite the same light as before."

Bridget entered the room, carrying a tray of tea and breakfast for both girls. "I figured you was in here and thought you might want something to eat too."

"Thank you, Bridget." Elise sat up and took a piece of ham. "Whatever would I do without you?"

"Well, seein' as I don't plan on goin' anywhere, you'll never have to know, now will ye?"

Elise swallowed her bite. "Do you know if my brother and sister-in-law are up yet?"

"They're breakfasting in their chamber and the morning papers are in the room with them."

Beverly and Elise shared a worried glance. Her maid kindly relieved them of any fears when she plastered a smile on her freckled face. "They're sayin' you're a huge success, my lady."

Beverly expelled a long-held breath. "Really?"

"Oh, my," Elise said. "That's wonderful news!" Elise then looked at Bridget and chided, "See? You were worried for nothing." Elise smiled triumphantly.

"Well, like I told Mrs. Steen," her maid said, "the season ain't over yet. You've still got time to fall on yer face."

"I won't, Bridget. You'll see. I will make everyone of you proud of me." Taking another bite in a most unladylike manner from the slice of ham she held between her fingers, Elise mumbled through a full mouth, "Most especially Lord Camden."

Once breakfasted and dressed, the two young ladies went in search of the duchess. They found her seated at her desk in her morning room and greeted her as Niles left the room.

"He brought more cards." Lia waved her hand over the stack. "This pile only gets bigger and bigger. We'll have to decide which events to attend and which to send our regrets." The Duchess continued to flip through the cards saying, "And the flowers! Have you looked in the front drawing room yet? It smells like grandmother's hot house in spring." She handed Beverly a note, saying, "It's from your father."

Elise sat in the chair before Lia's desk. "Where is my brother? I wanted to thank you both for last night."

"He and Michael were to meet after breakfast at that place... Ah... *come si dice? A salone para....*"

At Elise's look of confusion, Her Grace tried to clarify, "That place where civilized men beat on one another. Ah... *uno ginnasio?*"

"Oh! A gymnasium," Elise replied, finally catching her meaning. "They've gone to Gentleman Jim's."

"Yes, that's it," Lia said. "A gentleman's gym!"

"I hope Ren isn't too hard on Michael. After all, I only danced with him one time and *he* came to *my* rescue." She wanted to add that she didn't want her brother pummeling her future husband, but held her tongue.

"My father will be here Friday!" Beverly squealed with joy, before she lowered herself into a chair. Tempering her speech to more ladylike tones, she continued. "He sends his regards, and has reminded me once again, to thank you both from the bottom of his heart and my own." She looked up from the handwritten pages and smiled. "He says that in every letter, you know." Beverly lowered her gaze and continued to read her father's correspondence.

"I'd begun to worry that he might not make it. I'm so glad he will be here," Elise said, genuinely happy for her friend, even knowing it meant an end to having Beverly live with her. Because of his position as an attache for the government, Lord Hepplewhite was gone a great deal and for long stretches of time. Beverly's mother died when Beverly was a child living in India with her parents. After Lady Hepplewhite's death, her father hired a succession of nurses and nannies to care for his only child while abroad. When she turned thirteen, her father returned to England and purchased a home near Haldenwood. But Lord Hepplewhite was called away again, and he thought it best to leave Beverly in England to receive "a proper polish and launching," as he'd called it, and left Beverly with a succession of governesses, as she had no relatives with whom to reside. After her last two governesses left to marry, Ren, Lia, and Grandmother, all offered to have Beverly stay with them, since the two girls were such close friends.

Beverly continued to read her letter, and Elise thought there was no friend more dear to her. Elise owed her friend the world because she willingly chose to postpone her own come-out when Elise decided to remain at Haldenwood after her grandmother's fall last year.

Her friend folded the pages and returned them to the envelope. "He's asked that I meet with his man of business and make the necessary arrangements to increase staffing and such for the Mayfair house." She looked from Elise to Lia and back, and fairly trembled with excitement. "My father is finally coming home to stay."

"That is wonderful news, Beverly," Elise exclaimed.

"I can hardly believe he will be here in less than one week," Beverly said, very relieved her father would make it in time.

The door to the morning room was open and all three ladies heard the sounds of her grandmother's cane, then her voice as she grumbled to a house maid about following too closely behind her. When she'd entered the room, she addressed Lia. "I must have a word with you dear."

Lia gave her full attention to Grandmother, and Elise saw her brow furrow with concern. "Ma'am?"

"Who is it that set these house maids to following alongside me? Ever since I arrived, they hover so closely I'm going to blow over if they so much as breathe on me."

"I shall speak to my husband, and see if he will relax the constant protection." Lia looked over to Elise, then back to her husband's grandmother. "Ren wants to protect us, but doesn't understand how confining it feels to us women."

Elise stood and gave her seat over to her grandmother. Her Grace turned to Beverly and finished the prior conversation by saying, "Given that you have only a few days, you will need Mrs. Steen to help you. She's a gem when it comes to staffing a home. I would be lost without her."

"Thank you, Your Grace," Beverly said. "The house has been closed since the last tenants moved out after Christmas. It will take a small army to ready it for occupancy again."

"I'm sure it will. And remember, tomorrow morning we have your fittings scheduled, Beverly."

"Yes, ma'am."

"Also, here are more replies," Lia handed over the late arriving cards. "Keep your list updated, so we can make our seating arrangements for the dinner closer to the day of the ball."

"Yes, ma'am." Beverly came around the desk to hug the seated duchess. "I do appreciate everything your family has done for me." Elise noticed her friend's blue eyes swimming in tears. "When I was a little girl, I never dreamed I'd be able to have all this—your friendship, this ball...." Beverly visibly fought to control her emotion. "I wouldn't have it were it not for your generosity."

"It's nothing," Lia said to Beverly as she held the younger girls' hands. "You've been with us almost since the day I came to this country. You are like family to us. My husband has great esteem for your father, and I am not doing anything your mother would not have done were she still alive."

"Yes, I know," Beverly said. "But I still appreciate all you and His Grace are doing for me. I will be forever in your debt."

"Seeing you married well is the only repayment we require dear." Lia looked at Elise, then back to Beverly, and said, "If the way the season has gone thus far is any indication, you will both make splendid matches. *Sono certo*."

Elise wished she could be as certain as Lia. Her idea of a splendid match is the only match she'd ever wanted—a match with Michael.

A knock on the door preceded Niles, who stated that Lady Elise and Lady Beverly had visitors in the yellow salon. The Ladies Royce and Stone had arrived and were waiting on tea.

"So it begins, dear hearts," Lia said. "Have a good visit. Should you need me, send a footman. I must finish Luchino and Sarah's study plans for the coming week while I have a moment. If the ladies are still here when I am done, I will come down."

Elise's grandmother leaned on her cane and raised herself from the chair. "I will come with you and see what those two mischief-makers are up to. You two can accompany me down the stairs as long as you don't smother me like the housemaids do."

"I would never smother your ladyship," Beverly said.

At the bottom of the steps Elise, her grandmother, and Beverly entered the yellow salon to find Lady Stone and her widowed sister Lady Royce seated on the

Chippendale chairs near the window overlooking the side garden. Elise asked Niles to please check on the tea tray then greeted her guests. The older ladies, twins who rarely parted from each other's company, had been dear friends of her mama's in their youth. Both stood as godmothers for she and Ren, and as such had a special place in their hearts—even if Elise considered them both sweet busybodies.

This morning both women, identical in their tartan dresses, smiled simultaneously. Lady Stone spoke first. "I'm sorry we were unable to stay long last night, my dear, Lord Stone was feeling unwell."

Her grandmother sighed. "Herbert is such a dramatist," she said as she sat on the sofa opposite the ladies. "I told my cousin not to eat the honey and goat cheese hors d'oeuvres." She shook her plum-colored turbaned head, adding, "Silly man deserved every gastric distress that befell him because he wouldn't listen to me."

Elise hoped to diffuse the situation before it escalated. She leaned forward and said with honest sympathy, "I hope this morning finds him much improved, my lady."

"Yes he is, dear." Lady Stone smiled at Elise before turning to her grandmother and sighing with exasperation. "It's his gout troubling him again Beatrice, and he explained it all to you while we were at dinner, but you seemed more concerned with getting extra berry sauce on your pork roulade than with what Herbert was saying. But that's neither here nor there." Lady Stone looked over to her and Beverly on the sofa. "Louisa here," Lady Stone motioned to her sister, "stayed the duration and reported exactly what the gossip rags are touting. Your party was *the* event of the season. His Grace must be very proud. With your good looks and dowry, you'll land yourself a coronet before the end of the year, I don't doubt."

"I hope he is proud of me, Lady Stone, but as you know, the season is just into its' height, and we have two months yet. It's doubtful anything will come of my first outing, and I should think I'd want to take my time finding a husband. One can never be hasty in a decision of this magnitude."

"Quite right, my dear," concurred Lady Royce. "A young lady of your station must be careful not to allow some penniless handsome devil to pay court to you. Absolutely no good will come of it. But I'm sure our godson will see to it that you select wisely."

The tea cart arrived and the maid served. When she left, Elise said, "He's already given me the lecture ma'am." She stirred her tea with as delicate a hand as she could manage to portray the ladylike image that was so necessary to achieve her goal. "I will heed his warnings, I assure you."

"So," began Lady Royce, looking directly at Elise, "who have you set your cap for then? Camden?"

"Because if it is," added Lady Stone, "you've a long row to hoe young lady. It's not likely he's forgotten your antics of the years past."

"Then there's his mother," Lady Royce added. "She'll be a hard critic to win over. Lady Richard has often said she would like a quiet, girl of good reputation and temperament for her son."

Elise's heart dropped like a rock into her gut. She knew Michael's mother would be an obstacle. Elise would have to win over Lady Richard with her newfound maturity, or the woman would never accept her as her only son's wife.

Her grandmother set her cup on the saucer a little less delicately than she should, causing all heads to turn her way. "His grace has threatened to banish her to The Box if she so much as sneezes in Camden's direction," her grandmother interjected.

Elise's cheeks burned with high color, she was sure. Her grandmother was supposed to love her, not humiliate her!

"Well that's no punishment," Lady Stone scoffed. "It's beautiful and rugged year-round up there."

Her grandmother shook her head and gave Lady Stone an exasperated glare. "How soon you forget Louisa, that was my childhood home. It's the Grampians. In winter it's frozen, desolate, and mind-numbingly boring."

Elise needed to get a handle on the direction of this conversation before any rumors started and Lady Richard caught wind of her continued desire for her son. She prayed fervently she could put a stop to the gossipy relations in her midst. All she needed was for these two busy-bodies to spread tales during the rest of their calls as to whom Elise had set her cap for. And, as the morning had just started, this was likely the first stop on their rounds for the day. She lifted her chin and after taking the final sip from her cup, she replied in as uncaring and dispassionate a voice as she could manage.

"No, I've been over Camden for several years. He's nothing more to me than...."

Beverly recognized her discomfort as Elise stumbled on her words and took over. "Oh, he's nothing more to her than a dear friend of the family."

The ladies turned their attention to Beverly. Lady Royce began with her questions for Elise's friend. "And have you set your sights upon any young man yet?"

"With her looks, Louisa, she can get any man she wants." Elise's grandmother said about Beverly.

"Didn't you see the way the men flocked around her last night Eugenia?" Lady Royce asked.

"With her blond curls and blue eyes, she'll be betrothed before the season is over," said Lady Stone.

"Well then, it's a good thing Hepplewhite will be home soon. He'll be just in time to walk her down the aisle," her grandmother said with her smooth, sarcastic wit.

Beverly looked over at the ladies across from them and said, "I doubt I could attract even a church mouse, for I have neither the looks nor the fortune Elise possesses. Which suits me fine because I've always dreamed of making a love match." Her friend nervously wrung her hands together while under the scrutiny of the elderly matrons. "You see, Ladies, during this season, and with the opportunity I have had these past two years to reside with the Duke and Duchess, I've realized *not* having a fortune can be a good thing. This way I will know my groom-to-be is marrying me for me."

"Girls," Lady Stone said, "you will soon learn that it isn't the fortune or lack thereof that will get you a husband who will shower you with both affection and attention. It's how you comport yourselves publicly and treat him in private."

The rest of the visit was spent discussing which activities and events the girls were planning to attend. The elderly ladies nodded their heads approvingly, and soon bid Elise and Beverly farewell.

No sooner had the Ladies Stone and Royce departed, when more callers arrived. And after that, they went for a quick ride in the park. Thus the day was spent, until such time they had to retire to prepare for the night ahead. And even though Elise was thoroughly exhausted, she wasn't about to miss the Everly ball. From what she'd heard, Lord and Lady Everly threw a grand fete every season and she wanted to look her best—just in case Michael chose to attend.

The ballroom of the Everly's London home was ablaze with light from the magnificent trio of chandeliers overhead. Yellow roses, late daffodils and lilies filled the room. Elise followed her brother, sister-in-law, and grandmother through the open door, with Beverly at her side. After greeting their hosts in the receiving line, her brother saw a few of his friends, all married gentlemen, and after giving his wife a discreet kiss on the cheek, he headed back to the gaming room—no doubt to play cards while the wives and daughters held court in the ballroom above them.

Elise and Beverly followed grandmother and Lia as they all made their way through the crowd which parted for them thanks to either Lia's rank or grandmother's cane, she wasn't sure which. As she moved through tightly-packed ballroom, it felt as though the eyes of the entire *ton* were on her. If the entirety of the guests at the Everly ball thought she'd be so daring every night as she had been the previous night now that she was officially out, they would be wrong.

Conventionality prevailed this night, as Elise appeared in a pale green satin evening dress with a patent net overlay. Delicate lace gathered her hem into pleated scallops and traced the seams in her modest bodice. With a string of tiny emeralds grazing her collarbone, and the larger ones dangling from her ears, she was feeling almost as confident tonight as she had the night before.

They nodded and greeted several guests they knew, and even a few they didn't. She and Beverly greeted a group of friends, and promised to return momentarily. They then followed Lia and Grandmother onward to the matrons seated near a bank of windows for the breeze if offered. Beverly lifted two cups of punch from the tray held by the footman and handed them to Elise, then took two more for Lia and Grandmother.

"I'm so glad you came, Your Grace," one of the guests said, as she came up to their group as her sister-in-law assisted her grandmother into a chair. When the woman saw she had Lia's attention, she dipped into a curtsy before the duchess, then greeted her grandmother. "Lady Sewell," the woman said.

Elise knew Lia was still uncomfortable with the attention she received when out at events, but also that it was one part of her new life that she would, with time, become accustomed to.

"Lady Marchmont," Lia said, "I would like to introduce you to my sister-in-law, Lady Elise Halden and her dear friend, Lady Beverly Hepplewhite."

The pinch-faced, beak-billed woman nodded and forced a smile, and raising her hand she called forward her daughters to introduce them to Lia. Two equally pinch-faced girls came forward, they could not possibly be more than sixteen years of age.

Beverly then handed the punch cups to Grandmother

and Lia, and after introductions were made all around. Lia gave the slightest nod that Elise took as their cue to be off. She and Beverly walked over to a group of their friends, some of whom they'd seen only hours ago in the park, and began chatting until the orchestra returned from break.

From nowhere it seemed, Sinclair appeared to take a place next to her and joined in their conversation. Elise tried to pinpoint what it was about him that caused her to be on edge when he was around. Any young lady in the room would be lucky to have Mr. Sinclair's attention as he was fair of face and form. Impeccably groomed, he dressed in the very latest color and fashion, his clothing was expensive and tailor-made to his broad chest and narrow hips. His disposition was kind and he enjoyed conversing on some of the same topics as she. He seemed well-educated and intelligent.

But he wasn't Michael. The man her heart hungered for.

When a new piece began, he turned to her. "My lady, may I have the honor?"

For a moment she'd thought to beg off and escape to the retiring room, but it would be beyond rude to decline his offer of partnering her. And as much as she wanted to, she just couldn't refuse him. To do so would not help people believe she'd grown up. Nodding and placing her gloved hand on his arm, he led her gracefully through the crowded dance floor, one hand lightly on her waist, as he partnered her in a country dance, where his expert moves were everything a gentleman could aspire to, and as his hand warmed under hers, she began to relax.

After a minute, he gazed down at her, his blue eyed

expression serious. "I wanted to ask if I might pay a call tomorrow."

"Of course you can call, sir." She smiled at him, wanting to give him the same opportunity she would any other appropriate young man who showed interest in her opinions. "We can continue our conversation on the merits of educating the poor. You seem enlightened in so many areas of reform, perhaps I will be able to convert you yet."

"Perhaps," he replied. She looked up into his expression and saw his grow soft. "If I wanted to ask you for a carriage ride in the park, would you be so inclined?"

"As long as you get permission from my brother, and my groom is present, I don't see why not."

Sinclair nodded in agreement and as they continued to dance his blond hair fell onto his forehead giving him a quaint boyish charm. She chided herself for her earlier observation of him. He seemed sincere and harmless. She thought maybe she'd not given him enough time to relax and become himself in her presence.

When their music ended, Sinclair returned her to their group, then left to get them a beverage. While he was gone, another gentleman asked for her company in the next dance. Seeing Beverly move onto the floor with another partner, Elise nodded and allowed her new partner to lead her onto the floor.

When she returned to her group of friends in the corner she saw Sinclair waiting, holding two flutes of what appeared to be champagne. His handsome face had a fleeting dark expression, but as soon as their eyes met it changed and softened again. Was there anger directed at her dance partner? Or had she mistaken the look she'd just witnessed? He seemed much more relaxed now, but for a moment she swore his eyes shot daggers at the unfortunate young man in front of her. She thanked her partner and he bowed before leaving for the card room.

Sinclair smiled and handed her a glass. Elise thanked him, took a sip of the contents to see how bubbly it was before taking a healthy swig because she was so thirsty. Her companion smiled and chuckled. "Would you like more, my lady?" he asked.

She closed her eyes, letting the liquid flow into her veins, relaxing her. "No thank you, this is quite sufficient." She watched as Beverly remained on the floor with her partner for yet another dance with the same gentleman. Her friend knew the unwritten two dance rule as she'd reminded Elise of it often enough, any more than that and she'd be as much as declaring her betrothal.

"Who is the man dancing with Lady Beverly?"

Sinclair squinted, as he focused on the throng of people on the floor. "That is Sir Terrence Marlowe. He's my cousin, but more importantly I consider him a friend."

Elise lifted her eyes to his. "I just want to make sure my friend is not falling for the wrong sort."

"Your concern is unnecessary. He's as gentle as a lamb." He lifted her gloved hand, and placed a kiss on her fingertips. "As am I, my lady."

From somewhere behind her, a familiar voice said, "Sinclair." Sinclair nodded his greeting to the man her heart wanted above all others.

"Camden," Sinclair returned, still holding Elise's free hand.

Turning to Elise, Michael said, "I've been asked, by your brother, to look in on your well-being. Are you having a good time, my lady?"

Elise could hardly breathe. How could he expect an answer from her? Withdrawing her hand from Sinclair's grasp, she smiled up at Michael. "Of course, I am. Tell His Grace he needn't worry."

"He'll be greatly relieved." Michael continued to stand guard over Elise, causing Sinclair to shift nervously in his midst.

When Beverly and her dance partner returned, Sir Terrence greeted Michael and left to get the ladies some punch. Sinclair remained at Elise's right, Michael on her left. Beverly and another young lady whose name Elise couldn't remember struck up a conversation next to Michael. For several long minutes, an awkward silence fell over Elise and the two men. She downed her champagne and placed the empty flute on a passing tray.

The musicians began the strains of a waltz and as a crowd of more dancers headed to the already packed floor, Michael moved to in front of her and bowed. Elise wasn't expecting a dance with him. Last night was an uncommon occurrence as he'd rescued her from an unwanted dance partner. Her heart began to race at the thought he'd ask her again. Heaven help her, but Lady Richard would think she was corrupting her son.

"Would you care to take a stroll around the room, Lady Elise?"

Forgetting that Sinclair stood next to her, she lifted a trembling hand and took Michael's extended one. They hooked arms and he placed hers on his forearm, then rested his other over the top. The warmth from his hand seeped through his glove and hers, calming her nerves.

This man always evoked the most pleasant sensations in her.

She glanced over at him as they strolled around the edge of the room. He was handsomely attired, as always, in his black trousers and coat. As he always wore black, much like her brother, the markings of his mourning were not plainly visible. She noted his polished gold buttons had been exchanged for the onyx ones, and he wore the black velvet armband over his sateen coat sleeve. His snowy white cravat was tied in an intricate knot, with an onyx pin held the creation in place.

He looked wonderful. And miserable.

She wondered if men ever felt trussed-up like the proverbial Christmas goose, as women often did. As she herself *usually* did.

His hand purposefully over hers, Michael led her straight through the crush of people, to the far side of the room and away from Sinclair's prying eyes. He didn't stop until he'd taken her through the open doors leading to the veranda.

"Where... are you... taking me?" she stammered, confused at his actions. "We'll be missed."

"Not in that crowd." He turned a corner and kept going, dragging her along, past other privacy-seeking couples, until he found a secluded area between doors that seemed to satisfy him. When he turned to her, his hazel eyes glowed with what she thought was anger. For the life of her she couldn't understand what she'd done to cause his upset with her.

Even though he was beautiful when he was mad, she much preferred his smiles and sweet words to this darker emotion. The color in his cheek and the taught set to his chin made her want to reach out and touch him, to smooth the worry away, though to do so publicly might encourage his wrath.

"Did I do something to displease you, my lord?" she asked. "You appear angry. Is it with me?"

He seemed to struggle with his emotion and words before he spoke, and when he did they were clipped and tense. "Do you always drink your champagne so quickly. Do you not understand what alcohol does to a woman's inhibitions?"

"It was one tiny flute, Michael, and it was flat. It could hardly cause loosened inhibitions, could it?" She turned to walk away from him, but his hand snaked out to grasp hers.

"Have a care not to let the likes of Sinclair monopolize so much of your time. You'll drive away other, better-suited admirers and perhaps taint yourself with a reputation which you'll not find easily erased."

"Whatever do you mean?"

He appeared to consider his words before speaking. "Just that men know things about other men, that are best not mentioned in front of ladies."

"Oh, he seems harmless enough," she replied in all honesty. "He's been most kind, and attentive."

"Mark my words, Elise, he is not the sort with whom you'll want your name attached."

"Thank you for your warning." She turned to re-enter the room before anyone noticed she was gone. "But I'm able to choose my own friends."

He grasped her wrist, stopping her. His hazel eyes cold and possessive. "I thought you said you didn't enjoy his company?"

"That was last night. I find tonight's reaction to him rather the opposite." She lifted her hand and began to tick off her reasons on her fingers for Michael's benefit. "Firstly, he isn't at all bad looking, and I thought so last night as well. Secondly, he does not treat me as a child to be reprimanded for some imagined slight." She met his leveled gaze. "And thirdly, he listens to me and my ideas regarding education reform. We discuss topics that interest us both. Topics outside the latest fashions and gossip. And arguments." The last was added specifically to remind him of his annoying habit of taking her words and making them weapons in his squabbles with her.

"So you see, much as it pains me to admit I might have been mistaken, I believe I may have been with regard to Mr. Sinclair." Her voice sounded odd to her own ears, tinged with regret.

Without ever laying a hand on her he turned her, pinning her against the facade between the open doors of Lord Everly's library. His great mass had pushed her until she felt the cool stone wall behind her. His eyes now sparked with an angry fire, pinning her more effectively than had he physically restrained her. Something flashed in those eyes, an emotion she'd not realized he held toward her until now.

Jealousy.

Her heart raced then leaped as she recognized it. Her breathing became shallower then stopped as he leaned toward her, his lips coming dangerously close to her own. Her whole being shivered in anticipation when she realized he intended to kiss her. Unconsciously she licked her lips.

But instead of pressing his lips against hers, he

leaned in close and whispered into her ear, "I will only say this once more, Elise. Be wary of Sinclair. He's in desperate straits and is in need of the biggest fortune he can land. And you outrank him, so on both those accounts, I know your brother will not approve his suit."

Frustrated with his teasing actions, she felt compelled to remind Lord Camden that he held no power over her. "My brother has said I could marry for love Michael, and I will. I care not for a title and my wealth can sustain myself and whomever I choose as husband comfortably for the rest of our lives."

"Not if the man you choose is a bad gambler, or a man already mortgaged to his teeth to the cent-per-centers," he hissed.

Finished with his vituperative warning, he lingered where he stood, so close to her his nearness caused her pulse to gallop unchecked. Elise trembled. In anger? Or excitement?

"Have you ever been kissed, Elise?" His voice sounded raspy as he whispered next to her ear.

She couldn't trust herself to speak, afraid she might say something to break the moment's magic. He had to know she'd never been so intimate with a man. Kissed? She'd long prayed for the day he gave her her first kiss.

"I thought not," he said raggedly, lifting his gaze from her lips to meet hers. "I shouldn't do this." His lips were so close she could feel the warmth of his breath on her cheek. "But I can't help myself."

Michael's lips grazed hers, lightly at first, then more firm. He slanted his mouth on hers, moving over her softness. One hand on either side of her head, effectively pinning her beneath him, he coaxed her with the gentle touch of his tongue, to open for him, and she did, not knowing the impact her sweet innocence had on him.

All at once, he wanted to both give and take. He wanted to plunder and conquer, while pleasuring and loving. He wanted to mark her as his, yet at the same time encourage her adventurous soul.

He lifted his mouth to take a steadying breath. Mistake. Reality slammed into him when she uttered one word.

"Again?"

He stared at her, with what he was sure must have been a look of complete and unequivocal amazement. Why was he doing this? Virginal misses fresh-to-market were to be avoided at all costs. And most especially *this* virginal miss! Good God, she was Ren's sister. The termagant whose infatuation of him these many years had been the bane of his youth.

She must have mistaken his expression because she ducked under his arm and started to run. He caught her easily, turning her to face him, and for the first time since her father and stepmother died, he thought he saw a tear perched on the hellion's lower lash, and he was the cause for it. He'd upset her when that was not his intent.

God help him, he didn't even know what his intent was.

"I'm sorry for that," she whispered, her eyes downcast. "I am trying to change. Every moment of every day I have to remind myself that I must behave like the lady everyone wants me to be rather than the person I am."

"It's I who must apologize. I knew better and yet I still kissed you."

She lifted her head, and her eyes widened as realization dawned on her and she laughed heartily. Quickly catching herself before others began to stare at them, she dropped her voice. "By God, you're right!" she whispered, "I'm *not* the one at fault. It is *you* who knew I was untried, and *you* kissed me anyway. That being the case, I must thank you for that first lesson. Now I shall have to practice my new skill often so as to become more proficient because you obviously found me lacking." Slipping from his grasp, she strode into ball room just as the dance ended, looking to all who watched like a couple finishing a dance.

When they reached her group of friends, Michael leaned toward her and whispered for only her ears, "You were not... lacking, I promise." He looked around to see if anyone paid them any attention, when he thought it clear, he whispered in her ear, "Practice with anyone but me, and I shall have to take you over my knee, little minx." With that warning made clear to her, he quit the room and rejoined the men below. He suddenly felt like throwing some darts.

Michael didn't understand what was happening between them, or why he'd done what he had. He only knew that kissing Elise felt right. And it scared the wits out of him.

Her Grace would later impart to her husband in the privacy of their bedchamber, that his sister had a wonderful time dancing with many *beaus*. When he asked if she thought there might be anyone who met the criteria he set for a possible suitor to his sister, the duchess replied, her brown eyes dancing with merriment, "I believe so. Yes."

Of course when asked who the man was, the duchess apologized to her husband, explaining she feared revealing his name might jinx a possible budding romance.

Chapter Four

The next morning, Michael strode up the steps of Caversham House with renewed determination, especially since crossing paths with Sinclair on the footpath in front of the duke's residence. Last evening he'd decided to use every resource at his disposal to prevent the likes of him ever winning Elise's hand. Admittedly, he hadn't known the man until two nights ago, though the name had sounded familiar. His initial feelings of unease grew into deep concern once he remembered where he'd heard of Sinclair.

Now, with the information he had, he was sure Ren would see the risk of allowing the degenerate anywhere near her.

Niles took his hat and cloak, Michael thanked him, then inquired, "Is His Grace in his office?" At the servant's nod, he said, "I'll see myself in."

He found his friend seated behind his desk, chin resting on his twined fingers, contemplating some matter of grave import. If it was what Michael thought, he thanked the heavens he'd arrived when he did.

Ren's gray-eyed gaze looked weary. "Did you see who just left?"

Lips tight, he gave his friend a curt nod. "May I ask what he wanted?"

"Permission to court my sister."

He gave a sardonic little laugh before replying. "Then you might be interested in what I've learned about the man."

"I know he's in debt up to his ears and needs to wed an heiress. He confessed as much only a moment ago. But he's smitten with her he says, and is under the impression that Elise is agreeable to his suit. Because I've told her I would consider a love match, provided it were with the right man, I feel obligated to find out what her feelings are regarding Sinclair."

"What did you tell him?"

"That I would think on it. In the meantime, he plans to return later today to take her for a ride in the park." Ren leaned back in his chair, throwing his booted feet onto the corner of his desk. "So, what did you learn?"

"After you hear what I'm about to tell you," Michael began, "you'll not allow Sinclair anywhere near her." He brought a chair to the side of the desk and sat. "As you've said, he's in debt to the usual tradesmen, has no land of his own, and has quite a few vowels with some pretty disreputable money-lenders. But that's not the worst of it."

His friend's gray eyes turned cold, as he grew alert to another possible threat. "Go on."

"Have you ever heard of *Dominatus Rex*?"

The duke quirked a brow filled with serious concern. "No. What about it?"

"They're a group of men, mostly younger sons, from some of the best families." He shook his head in dismay, remembering how revolted he was when he'd first read the reports from the investigations of previous cases in which these men were involved. He knew Ren would want to keep his sister safe from them. Hell, *he* would do whatever was necessary to keep her safe from their kind.

Michael continued. "They are young men with all the benefits of a gentile upbringing. Yet they practice cruelty on young women to achieve sexual gratification. Their most obvious crime is rape, but they do not exclude torture. Their preferred victims are virgins, and it is not unusual that the girls are shared among the guests at weeks-long elaborate orgies held in the country. It is important to note that the girls they choose are never willing, to these degenerates it's the fight that arouses them. So they seek strong-willed, independent-minded young women."

Ren removed his feet from his desk and sat upright. "Is Sinclair affiliated with them in any way?"

"He's a member. But I don't consider that the worst part."

His friend shot out of his chair. "Not the worst part!" Ren began to pace the room. "Tell me everything you know about him."

"There was a case a couple of years ago—you may have been away at the time—where Sinclair was betrothed to the eldest daughter of a well-off merchant, the contracts were signed, the dowry had been settled on him, and it looked like the happy couple were about to wed. The date was set, they'd started reading the banns and such." Michael rose and poured himself a cup of coffee as he watched his friend wear a path in the carpet. The attorney in him took over, speaking dispassionately of the facts, yet angered that nothing could be done to the guilty party.

"Here's where the story gets strange. A colleague of

mine was contacted by the father of the bride-to-be a week before the wedding. He wanted Sinclair investigated because his daughter started behaving oddly. Where initially the young lady had not feared Sinclair, and was a happy, blushing bride-to-be, she now deeply feared her betrothed. She begged her father not to be forced to marry Sinclair. Upon questioning the young lady, my colleague discovered Sinclair had violated the girl terribly. It seemed that after using her for his own pleasure, Sinclair had ordered the young lady to pleasure his friends as well, while he watched. He threatened to take the lady's younger sister and use her in a similar fashion in order to gain the bride-to-be's continued cooperation.

"When Sinclair got wind of the investigation, he arranged to have witnesses walk in on his bride-to-be and another man. He said the girl lied about his part in the tale she told. Sinclair then cried off the marriage and by law was allowed to keep the girl's quite sizable dowry."

"The bloody cur," Ren swore.

"With men such as he, pleasure comes from the domination—taking away the independence and spirit of the woman. I'm sure that's what attracted him to Elise in the first place. Lord knows she's got both in abundance. His need for funds and her considerable dowry and inheritance make her an even more appealing target."

While he sipped his coffee, Michael swore to himself that he would not allow Sinclair or any of his ilk near Elise, whether his own relationship with her went anywhere or not. She was special to him, even if only as Ren's sister, though last night's kiss had perhaps upset what was an amiable relationship with Elise in his mind. Now there were a myriad of confusing emotions running through his head regarding this little minx, but he couldn't focus on any of them until the threat from Sinclair was resolved.

"He obviously went through those funds quick enough." Ren paused at the window, staring onto the street. "He must need to refill his coffers. I'll be damned if he'll do so at my sister's expense. I don't want him near her, Michael, and shall tell him as much. If he so much as comes into the same room as she, he'll find himself considering a one-way passage to Australia."

"I knew you'd feel the same as I do. Now we have to convince your sister that she's not to encourage him in any way."

"I hope Sinclair isn't who Lia meant when she said Elise might have someone in mind already."

Michael's eyes grew wide. "She said that? Really?"

His friend nodded, causing an odd sinking sensation in Michael's gut.

"If it is, and Elise knew we'd had him investigated, then warned him off her.... She'd be so vexed, it would set her mettle up and she'd probably go against my wishes just to be contrary," Ren said. "No, this is best handled without her knowledge. I'll take care of him when he returns this afternoon for his drive in the park with Elise." His friend resumed his pacing. "I'll need your help getting her out of the house so they don't cross paths."

Michael tried to think of an excuse to make her want to leave with him, since he didn't think she would after having promised to ride with Sinclair.

Michael had an idea. There was a task he could use

her help with—something no woman could resist. With that in mind, Michael said, "I'll beg her assistance in selecting a gift for Mother's birthday. It's in ten days and I haven't got a present for her yet. So I will take her shopping."

"Once you have her out of the house," Ren said, "make sure you don't get back until well past the hour she agreed to meet Sinclair."

Michael nodded. This was the opportunity he'd needed. Taking Elise shopping would give them time alone so he could apologize for his behavior the night before.

Elise lifted the cashmere shawl and wrapped it around her shoulders before checking her appearance in the mirror. Tucking a short lock behind her ear, she left her room to see what Michael wanted. Part of her hoped he wouldn't mention the kiss because she really didn't want to be reminded that she was awkward and inexperienced. Of course, the bigger part of her wanted him to kiss her again and teach her everything she needed to know to please him.

She nodded to the footman as he opened the door to the drawing room. Michael stood by the window, staring out onto the street below. The olive nankeen breeches fit his powerful legs as though they'd been painted on him. His dark blue coat, which sported the black velvet armband, fit in much the same arousing fashion. She'd always thought him handsome, but he seemed even more so lately. His dark brown hair feathered back off his face, as though he'd just run his hands through it. He met her gaze and smiled.

"Good morning, my lord." She tried to force herself

not to smile, to no avail. She adored being near him. Smiles rose of their own accord. "To what do I owe the pleasure?"

"I was hoping you might help me. It seems I've forgotten to purchase a gift for my mother's birthday next week, and could use some advice on what to get her. To that end, I invite you to come shopping with me."

"I'm sorry. I cannot," she said, hoping her disappointment was evident in her tone.

"Why not? Is it because of your friend, Beverly? If so, she's invited along as well. I could use the advice of more than one young lady."

"No." She shook her head. "Beverly and Mrs. Steen had an appointment this morning." She felt in a quandary, undecided what she should do. She wanted more than anything to go with Michael and have the opportunity to be alone with him again. Yet, as much as she wanted to go, she was afraid she might once again make a cake of herself, asking him to kiss her.

His voice lowered to a raspy whisper. "Is it because of last night?"

"That's not it at all." She glanced at the ormolu clock on the mantle, desperate to change the subject. Every time she recalled their kiss she was reminded of her foolish behavior in begging him to kiss her again. "I've promised to ride with someone at three o'clock. It's almost one now. I'm afraid we would never be back in time."

"You will. I swear on my honor as a gentleman." He extended a cavalier bow. "It shouldn't take long to select a gift. It's just that I can't think *what* to get her."

She thought a moment. On the one hand, she really

did want to go with him. But on the other, what if she did and didn't return in time? It would be unconscionably rude of her to break her plans with Sinclair. What then? She could make her most sincere apologies to Mr. Sinclair, and hope he'd forgive her and ask again. Or perhaps not ask again. It really didn't matter. Michael was the man she wanted, not Sinclair.

Her mind made up, she smiled sweetly. "Only if you promise to have me back home before three, will I agree to go."

"I promise." He returned her smile. They really should give out awards for acting, he thought, for he'd clearly win. Without a doubt.

"Then, in that case," she said, "let's be off quickly. So I can be back on time."

She looked magnificent this morning, dressed in a modest yellow carriage dress with a smart bonnet that tied under her chin, and a fine cashmere shawl. An odd sensation, like a stab of jealousy, coursed through him when he realized she'd chosen her dress not for him, but for Sinclair.

He spent many hours last night, contemplating his behavior at the Everly's. He remembered their kiss and the soft innocence of her lips. It alarmed him to think that if he'd had the chance, he'd have taken her further. He'd actually wanted his best friend's little sister—wanted her in a most possessive way. If the situation were reversed, he'd have thought his friend a degenerate. He almost felt as though he was, especially when he thought of the years she tormented him with her girlish infatuation.

For heaven's sake, he'd watched her grow from nearly a babe!

But there was one thing he knew was certain as hell—she'd wanted that kiss as much as he did. All night long he'd tried desperately to deny that he'd kissed her for his own selfish reasons, but in the end he could not. He'd wanted to kiss her, to feel her lips come alive under his. He'd wanted to stir the passion in her to see if she was receptive to him. When she'd asked for a second kiss he grew nervous and uncertain for the first time in his thirty-one years.

He'd awakened after a fitful rest, then went to the office and began making inquiries into Sinclair. And now, here he was, handing her into his phaeton while a Caversham groom held the horses. Once she was situated, Michael went around to climb up next to her. Taking up the reins and whip, he smoothly guided his matched liver-chestnut pair into the traffic. He glanced over to Elise who was eyeing his team, and asked, "Where to?"

"I don't know, this is your shopping expedition."

"What I meant was, did you have any ideas?"

"Michael, I haven't seen your mother in years and I certainly do not remember her well enough to predict what type of presents she may or may not like."

"You're a lady."

"Thank you for stating the obvious."

"You're welcome." He sighed, not wanting to argue with her this day. "Surely you must have some idea of what ladies like, or else why come with me?"

"Because you're up to something and I've yet to figure out what it is."

If it weren't for getting her out of the house so Ren could deal with Sinclair, he would never have volunteered for this divine torture. "I should turn this team around and let you off at your brother's again."

"Don't do that, I'm watching your horses. I like the way they move."

"Elise, I was not jesting when I said I needed help with a present. My mother's birthday is in ten days." She was silent, as though she'd not heard him at all as she studied the team he was driving. "I should bring you to her party just to prove I'm telling the truth."

"You'd do that?" Smiling brilliantly, she turned her laughing amber-eyed gaze to him.

For that smile, he'd tolerate her insouciant behavior. And more. "I just might."

"Well, in that case," she said sweetly, "we'd best get her something absolutely perfect. I've found the most wonderful presents aren't necessarily expensive. Sometimes a simple gift, chosen with the recipient in mind and given from the heart is what is most treasured."

He considered the suggestion, but again drew a blank. Jewels or some other such trinket was what he'd originally had in mind, and that might make a good start.

"Absolutely magnificent," she commented. "There's no sway to their pace. Where'd you get them?"

"My uncle had a passion for horses as well. The barns and fields around Woodhenge are filled to capacity with the results of his efforts. His personal office is filled with stud books and extensive pedigree charts. Everything is quite detailed. You'd have to admire the man."

"I never knew," she said, amazement obvious in her voice. She settled back into the seat and turned wide eyes to him. "Has Ren told you about my project, the one I've been working on these past few years?"

Michael nodded.

"Next year I should have several mares and geldings ready to sell. They are all under saddle and training daily at home. The mare I'm riding in the park this month will be for sale soon, though I did not breed her. I plan to bring them to town to finish their training just before selling them." She beamed with pride as she spoke of her horses as though they were her own offspring. "Next year's sale horses are the first of the crop I got when I crossed a few of my Arab mares with a Spanish horse I purchased that has a marvelous ambling gait. The result is a flashy little park horse, bred for a lady's comfort in the saddle."

"Ren mentioned something along those lines. How do you plan to advertise and market them?"

"By riding them in the park. Both Beverly and I. Then we shall spread the word that one or two are for sale, and rely on word of mouth." She sobered when she remembered the time. "So, where shall we start?"

"Start what?"

"You see! I knew you were up to something, Michael. You cannot even remember we are shopping for your mother's gift."

"You make it easy for me to lead you in a jest," he replied. "How about we start at the jewelers? Perhaps a cameo or broach...."

More than an hour later they still had not chosen a gift either wanted to give his mother on the momentous occasion of her fifty-fifth birthday. Item after item was rejected. He listened as Elise remarked on piece after piece as the proprietor displayed them. In her opinion, everything was either too gaudy or too common. One time she even remarked to the embarrassed man, "Come now Mr. Reed, I can name three other matrons with exactly that same broach. It's not unique enough to be a gift to a woman of her stature."

Michael appreciated the fact that she took her task seriously, for this was a real dilemma, not something he created to keep her from her planned excursion with Sinclair. Had he not required her assistance, he had every faith that Ren would have kept her locked in her room if necessary.

As they left Mr. Reed's establishment, she mused, "I'm sure your mother already has a great deal of jewelry, and anything we purchased today would become just another 'piece' in her collection." She looked in the window of the next shop and the next, as they waited for the groom to bring up his phaeton.

"Then perhaps something different," he replied. "Larger, maybe?"

"What did you have in mind?" she asked, open to suggestions to consider.

"A mantel clock, a crystal vase, silver candelabra?"

With Elise seated on the cushioned bench next to him, he expertly maneuvered his team into the afternoon traffic. "No, those won't do. But if you could please take me home, I shall think on it tonight and we can resume our search tomorrow."

He turned his team into Regent's Park and slowed his horses to a sedate walk. This seemed to irritate Elise who appeared eager to return home before Sinclair arrived. That she was taken with another man bothered him. Of course she had no idea what the cad was about and with any luck she never would.

"I'd hoped we might have a minute to talk," he said.

"I wanted to apologize for last night."

"Apology accepted," she stated, her frustration evident in her tone. "So there's no need to continue this drive."

An open barouche came toward them, slowed and Michael recognized a friend of his mother's, Lady Thomaston and her daughter, Lady Clarence, and the younger woman's two daughters. Both women were widowed, Lady Clarence only recently relieved of her mourning colors. Smiling broadly, the older woman waved to them and he cued his team to halt.

"Good afternoon Lord Camden," both women said. Turning to Elise, Lady Thomaston added, "And to you too, Lady Elise."

Michael nodded his greeting, and Lady Thomaston extended her sympathies with regard to his uncle, then began extolling the virtues of a drive in the park and how fresh air was important to one's health. "I used to tell Lord Thomaston these same words, but he would never listen to me. And of course, neither did my son-in-law, else my daughter would not be a widow now, would she?" He agreed with her, which he realized too late he never should have done, as this only encouraged further chatter.

He smiled and held his tongue with a politesse hammered into him when he first began to study law. The fact that Clarence died in a duel over another man's mistress was well-known. That his widow chose to recreate history perhaps for the benefit of her grandchildren was her business. And he didn't know if more fresh air would have done old Thomaston any good because that man died of a fever on his sugar plantation in the Caribbean.

"Lord Camden," said Lady Clarence, "Mother and I would love to have you come for tea one afternoon."

"That would be lovely," he replied. "Though I shall have to check my schedule before I can commit to a time and date. Send a note to my secretary, Mr. Overmeyer."

"Of course, my lord," said Lady Thomaston. "We are at your convenience."

"And we'd love to have you, Lady Beverly and the Duchess come to tea as well, Lady Elise," the older widow added. "Also at your convenience."

Elise smiled at the women and nodded. "I should check with their schedules as well, you understand."

"Of course, we understand," said Lady Clarence.

Elise laid her hand on his sleeve and turned pleading eyes to him. Taking the hint, he bid farewell to the women and cued his horses forward once again.

When they were a safe enough distance from the ladies Elise said, "Those poor girls. They looked positively humiliated at the behavior of their mama, who was fawning over each word from your mouth."

"Jealous?"

"Never," she shot back. "Though, you could stand to listen to your own advice." He gave her a curious look, to which she replied in a teasing voice, "You should be careful my lord, there are women out there who would want you only for your title and fortune."

He threw his head back and roared with laughter, which unfortunately drew stares from those curious equestrians and pedestrians beginning to crowd the park. Michael hated calling attention to himself, though Elise seemed to have no problem doing so.

"Do you think a carriage dress could be cut any

lower and still be called a dress? Really. Someone should warn her to cover her chest so she not catch her death of cold with so much flesh exposed." With a huff, she turned in her seat to look straight ahead. "I kept waiting for her to lean forward a bit more to see what might spill out." He chuckled, she looked over at him and continued, "You must admit, she was practically salivating over your every word, Michael."

"Lady Clarence is a friend of my sister's," he replied. "She's a widow, with two young daughters. Just like any other young widow, she's desperate to marry again."

As soon as Elise realized they were traveling further into the park she said, "Please, Michael, take me home. I've promised to ride with someone."

"After we talk about what happened last night."

"There is nothing to talk about." She sneaked a peak behind them to the groom who rode in back. Then she said in a dispassionate and flat tone, "You kissed me, Michael. You know you were the first gentleman ever to do so, but realistically speaking, you're hardly going to be the last. Grandmother says...."

"Do not," he implored, "for the love of all that's conventional and proper, take anything Lady Sewell says to heart. She's an old woman who would stir up trouble just to watch the debris settle."

"She is not," Elise defended her grandmother. "And as I have determined to marry for love alone, I want—as every intelligent woman should—to compare kisses to make sure I find the perfect mate for me."

"I'll be damned if you're going to go about testing each young buck to see if you like how his lips feel on yours!"

"Come now, Michael, you're not my brother. You can hardly exert that sort of influence over what I do."

"The hell I can't. I'll tell Ren, and...."

"If you did, then you'd also have to reveal that *you* kissed me. How do you think he'd react to that?"

She had a point. He very well couldn't order her brother to lock her away because he had already kissed her—obviously disturbing him more than her. As the path neared the canal, Michael pondered what she'd said as he spied movement near the edge of the field. He saw two children, a little girl and a little boy, carrying a small wooden box between them, then set it down near the bushes. The girl lifted the cloth covering the top of the box, then the boy turned the box over onto its side. The girl was crying, so he pulled his team to a stop to observe.

Michael saw that Elise also noticed the children. They both watched as the girl sat on the grass in front of the crate and began to coax whatever was inside to come out. Two furry little orange kitten heads appeared and behind them a tiny black one. Michael saw that all was well and cued his team to resume their walk.

"No! Please Michael, stop!"

"Why? They're just releasing some kittens. If they were going to drown them I'd say something, but it doesn't appear they're in any harm."

"Stop right this instant! Can't you see how upset that little girl is? And those are kittens, Michael. Babies! They cannot possibly fend for themselves. They look barely weaned."

"Very well, but they go to your stables, not mine." He pulled the team off the path, set the brake to the phaeton and handed the reins to the groom. After dismounting he walked around the back of the vehicle to help Elise down, only to find that she'd already made it part way to the children. Carriages began to slow and watch he and Elise as they moved closer to the bushes. He knew this did not bode well. People were sure to talk about the incident, and never would anyone come close to the truth of it. It didn't bother him, but it might Ren.

"Hullo dearlings," Elise greeted the children. "What have you got there?"

"These are our kittens," the little boy, who appeared to be about nine, said solemnly.

"Well if they're yours, why are you turning them loose under the bushes?" Michael noted that Elise wasn't being accusatory, but sounded instead like a curious child herself. He was sure she did so to put the children at ease.

"Our mum says we can't keep 'em, 'cause we have 'nough cats," the boy said. "An' everyone knows kittens grows up to be cats."

She turned her attention to the crying girl, the little thing barely out of nappies, holding onto two of the kittens and petting the third in her lap. "Why are you crying then, sweeting?"

"My kitties."

"I know they are, and they're very cute kittens, too," Elise replied.

"She don' want ta turn 'em loose. She's 'fraid they'd get eaten by monsters."

"There's no such thing as monsters, you know," Elise reassured the little girl. "In fact, in all my years, I have yet to see one. And I'm pretty old."

Michael watched Elise lower herself next to the little girl on the grass. "They're awfully cute kittens. Mind if

I pet them?" When the child nodded, Elise stretched out a hand and began to pet the feline head closest to her. Within moments two of the three kittens were climbing onto Elise's yellow carriage dress, but she didn't seem to mind at all. Most young ladies of his acquaintance would not have sat upon the ground or allowed the sharp-clawed little creatures to venture onto their expensive clothing.

Not Elise. She was the opposite of every other young lady he knew. Her gentle mien with the children raised his opinion of her even more. She would make the right man a fine wife and good mother to his children. And if he were honest with himself, Michael had already begun to picture her lithe, naked form in his bed. The resulting discomfort each time it happened was the price he had to pay for thinking of his best friend's sister in such an improper manner.

"I'm sure you're thinking this is a good place to leave them, and it might be if they were just a wee bit older," Elise said sweetly to the children. "I'm thinking that because these are still babies, they might need a mummy. Just as you two do."

Both towheaded little ones nodded in agreement.

"What if I could be their mummy and take them home with me? I'd give them a good home in our barn with lots of mice to catch and they'll have ever so much fun there."

The little boy smiled and puffed up pridefully. "Their mum is the bes' mouser in all London! They'd be perfect for the job, milady. Don't ya think so, Meggie?"

The little girl's mouth spread slowly into a smile and she nodded her head in agreement, stray curls falling free of her cap.

Elise beamed, happy at rescuing the little felines. "Wonderful! Have you by chance named them yet? You'll have to tell me, for I'd hate to confuse the little dears by changing their names."

"This'n 'ere's Blackie." The girl handed the very shy black kitten to Elise. "An' this is Tiger and the other orange one is Naughty."

"He hasn't done anything yet to be naughty," Elise replied.

"No, silly!" the boy said. "That's 'is name. Naughty."

Elise giggled. "Oh, I'd love to know how he came about that name."

"He pusses his brothers away when it's time to eat," the girl said.

"Thank you for telling me. I'll have to see to it that he has his own dish, then." Elise gathered the three kittens and replaced them in the little crate.

"Would you like to learn how they fare, dearlings?" Both children nodded their heads. She looked at Michael and asked, "What time do you have, my lord?"

He removed his pocket watch and flipped the lid. "Ten minutes after three o'clock."

Elise raised an eyebrow, then gave him a half-crooked smile and he understood. She had missed her appointment with Sinclair, which had been his intention all along. But she wasn't as upset as he'd thought she'd be. Turning back to the children, she said, "Meet me back here in one week, at precisely three o'clock, and I shall tell you how they are getting along. Agreed?"

Again, the children nodded.

"Michael? Will you help me?" she asked.

He extended his hand and she handed him the crate. Her amber-eyed gaze danced in merriment. "Hold that while I rise."

He watched her rise, unaided, a willowy lass swiping grass from her skirts. They then bid the children goodbye, with Michael carrying her new pets back to his phaeton. Placing the box on the bench, he assisted her up, and went around to sit next to her. As he drove his team back onto the path, he asked, "Why did you tell them you would meet them in a week?"

"Because first, it reassured them that the kittens they care so much about are going to a good home. Second, I do plan to be here next week and I'm willing to bet that by then they will have forgotten about the kittens. If I'd suggested tomorrow or even the day after that, there will not have been enough time passed and they might still cling to the pain of losing their kittens."

Her logic astounded him. Michael had never seen her manage children before, and that she cared what caused a crying working-class babe upset, sent a warm feeling to his heart. He was learning there was so much more to Elise than he'd ever suspected.

"What do you plan to do with them?"

Without hesitation she said, "We shall give the two males to your mother for her birthday and I shall keep the female."

"Kittens? Are you sure?"

"Absolutely," she replied. "They're perfect." Elise spoke at him as though he didn't know women.

He wanted to remind her that he knew women well enough. He had two sisters and five nieces. He'd also had several mistresses before. So he knew the fairer sex enough to know that an animal wasn't high on their list of gifts they'd want to receive. Women wanted baubles. Baubles and trinkets.

"Michael, all little girls have a soft heart for fuzzy warm creatures."

"Did I mention my mother is turning fifty-five? She's hardly a little girl."

"She was a little girl once and I doubt she's changed so much that she'd refuse these adorable kittens."

Damn her, but she was more than likely correct. And he didn't understand why he hadn't thought of a pet before. She was right. His mother did like animals and he remembered her having several cats as he grew up.

"I'm learning much about you, Elise. And it's all so very different from what I've known of you all these years."

"We all grow up at some point." Then she turned mischievous amber eyes to him and said, "An' everyone knows kittens grows up to be cats."

He smiled, chuckling at her imitation of the young boy. "I do have another question. How do you know which one is female and which two are male?"

"Well, aside from the fact that I looked to confirm as I held them, orange cats are usually boys. And because this female is black, I'll keep her. She'll be more vocal once we separate her from her litter mates, and as she gets older."

"You seem to know a great deal about felines." Even to his own ears he sounded smitten, and that just wouldn't do. He had to remember this was his best friend's *little* sister. Until he could work up the courage to bring up the topic with her brother, she was off limits.

"I should," she replied. "I have thirteen of them now."

"Thirteen cats, and this one is black. Are you afraid you're setting yourself up for a run of bad luck?"

"I don't believe in such superstitions. A woman must make her own luck if she's to get what she wants in this world."

Lady Elise Halden, Michael was learning quickly, was a breath of fresh air in this stifling society of theirs. If he didn't watch himself, he might actually fall hard for this sister of his friend.

"Did I mention," she began, "that nearly all thirteen of my cats are female?"

"No. Why is that?"

"Because they're the best hunters."

Michael threw his head back and laughed heartily.

The next morning's gossip columns all reported that a certain unmarried earl had been seen in the company of the unmarried sister of a certain duke and that the two appeared to be having a wonderful time in each others' company. The column ended with speculation as to how long it will be before the earl in question took this unmarried lady to bride.

Chapter Five

Upon the return of Michael and Elise to Upper Brook street, a good hour past the time they'd agreed to, Michael went directly to Ren's office.

"How did it go?" Michael asked, taking a seat opposite his friend.

"After I told him I was refusing his suit and warned him off my sister, he became somewhat incensed, demanding a reason. So I told him I knew about his previous betrothal and the circumstance surrounding the dissolution of the contract.

"Then I asked him about his extracurricular sport. He denied it at first, but when presented with the proof you provided me from the father of the girl, and the reports from his former staff, he became defensive. I'd swear I saw a desperate, dangerous glint to his eyes. I told him I didn't care one whit about his sexual peccadilloes as long as they don't involve gently bred young ladies, and as long as the women involved were willing and left their beds uninjured. That upstart bounder had the nerve to tell me I was 'too gallant' with the type of women they chose to play with. Then I warned him I would be watching them now, and one wrong move would see them all imprisoned—or worse—for assaulting our fairer sex."

Michael digested what his friend just said. "She needs to be guarded at all times. Elise cannot be allowed alone, in case he should do something rash, either in desperation or retaliation."

"I agree, which is why I've already sent for Cartland. You remember him, don't you? I used his firm a couple of years ago when Lia...," Ren coughed through the hitch in his voice. "When she went missing."

Michael nodded as he lit a cheroot. The man's firm was the best in town. Michael had used him several times on his more important cases, and could swear the man had connections from the bowels of hell itself, to his own noble ranks. "She can't know she's under guard or she'll do something imprudent—like evading her protectors."

"Yes," Ren conceded. "She can be a stubborn little hellion when told she 'must' or 'cannot' do something."

"You're forgetting, no one knows this better than I." Michael thought of several instances when as a child Elise had been ordered by her father or stepmother not to follow him around when he'd come to Haldenwood to visit. It was all to no avail. She'd followed him anyway. Sometimes she was caught and punished and other times he could have sworn someone watched him, but could never prove it was Elise.

His friend gave him a wan smile, then exhaled the smoke he held. "Thankfully, she seems more interested in the abundance of young bucks making the rounds this year than hounding you. I gave her a very stern lecture about comporting herself in a ladylike manner, as befits her station, else she'd get sent back to Haldenwood, or worse, I'll send her to The Box, and there would be no other seasons for her." As Michael hooted with laughter, Ren continued, "I think I got my point across."

"About tonight," Michael said, "are we going to the Holderman's? It's expected to be a crush, as usual."

"I believe so, though I'm not sure yet. Marcus hasn't been feeling well, so Lia and I may not attend. But Elise and Beverly have been looking forward to it since the invitation arrived. If we do attend, I will have to avoid the card and billiard rooms. I will play the courteous, attentive spouse and entertain my wife and her friends—all the while watching over my sister."

"Nothing serious with my godson, is there?"

"According to Prescott, he's teething. But you know me, old man. When it comes to those I love, I'm ever cautious." Ren chuckled. "Lia thought my bringing the doctor around was premature, but damn it, Marcus is my son and if I want reassurance from a physician, then I shall have it."

Michael tapped the ash of his cheroot into the ashtray, and resumed his relaxed posture. "Though I fully acknowledge the fact that I have a responsibility to provide an heir, I don't know that I'm ready for the ups and downs being a husband and father entails." He flicked at an invisible speck on his coat sleeve. "I rather liked my nice, orderly existence without the added emotional complications. When the time comes to marry, I shall find someone who doesn't disturb my composure or try to rearrange my orderly routine."

"That person doesn't exist, I tell you," Ren replied. "Find someone who will challenge you and upset the routine, man. I highly recommend it."

Michael coughed, thinking there was a young lady upstairs who did just that, but taking her to bride was out of the question. "I don't disagree, Your Grace. What is most important is finding the balance of biddable wife and divine temptress," he said as he rose to take his leave.

"That is the challenge my friend," Ren said, following him to the door.

"Until tonight then," Michael said, immediately wondering if he should take the evening off and work on the stack of contracts that needed review.

"Until tonight." Ren confirmed.

That evening, as Elise prepared for the night out, she mulled over in her head how she would explain to Sinclair her absence when he'd called earlier. She decided that, instead of fabricating a tale of some minor crisis, she would simply tell him the truth. Doing so was easier on the head, not to mention the heart.

She was disappointed that he didn't show up, and that he didn't send a note explaining his absence. It would have been the gentlemanly thing to do. But she didn't have long to think further on it as Beverly entered the room with a radiant smile and twirled around to reveal the gown she'd selected to wear.

Ice blue silk with dark blue flowers embroidered in a scalloped ring around the hem, the color highlighted her fair complexion magnificently. "Beverly, you're absolutely beautiful. Have I ever told you how much I envy you your blond curls and blue eyes? Not to mention your abundance of cleavage," she added while looking down at her own imperfection.

"Here we go again..." her friend began. "I'm beginning to think you're fishing for compliments."

"Not so! Have you ever noticed that when we are out together, it's your looks that attract men to come chat with us? Of course, I hold my own during the conversations, but I have no illusions as it concerns my average looks. My eyes are set too far apart, my nose is too wide, and my mouth far too big."

"You're also too skinny, and your hair is too straight." said her grandmother as she entered Elise's room.

"Yes, I know, Grandmother, but I can do nothing about any of it."

Both girls laughed at the truth in her statement.

"All those features you described fit beautifully on *you,* darling girl." Her grandmother waved her cane impatiently, saying, "Come, it's time to be off. We have only one gentleman with us tonight as your brother has decided to stay in after all."

Elise exchanged a look with Beverly before linking arms with her dearest friend, and stepping out of her room and into the waiting night.

Shortly after Michael arrived at Caversham House to pick up the ladies, he and Ren stood in the drawing room discussing the security measures surrounding the ladies. "There will be three guards at the Holderman residence, one in front, one in back, and one inside. I've added another groom to the coach. They are all armed."

"How did you get a man inside at Holderman's?" Michael asked. "Is he a footman?"

"No. Cartland has a gentleman working for him. The man is a former spy for the crown and the second son of a lower-ranking noble. His name is Mr. Stephen Carroll. My secretary is now securing an invitation to all events we will be attending for the rest of the season. The man will come and introduce himself to you. Introduce him to the ladies as your friend. Do the same for him as you would for any other peer we come in contact with.

"The ladies know nothing of the increased security. I'd hate for them to worry, and as I told Cartland, this is likely for just a few weeks, to make certain Sinclair is respecting the boundaries I set him." The men heard the chatter of the women as they came down the stairs. Ren added, "I cannot ask you to refrain from the gaming, but I would be forever indebted to you if you'd keep an eye on them for me."

"There's no fun in stripping those dilettantes of their fortunes." Michael pulled at his cuffs, and straightened his coat. "I'd rather have the challenge of besting you out of a few shillings, than taking vowels from amateurs."

"Same for me," Ren laughed, then took a sip of his brandy.

The ladies' voices drew closer as they came down the stairs, and Michael noted his friend's concerned expression. "Don't worry," he said, "I shall keep her in my sight at all times."

"Right. Well, that's about all I can ask, isn't it?"

Both men watched as Lady Sewell, Elise and Beverly entered the room. Michael's breath caught in his chest when he saw her, an airy vision in pale green silk with ivory lace accents. The scoop neckline revealed a modest amount of cleavage. A large pear shaped diamond fell from the center of a perfectly matched set of pearls to settle invitingly into the hollow just above her breasts. Diamond and pearl drops graced her delicate earlobes and a tiara of pearls and diamonds rested on her short brown hair. The image she presented was one of true sophistication and elegance. As always, her amber eyes sparkled full of life as they met his gaze.

The only thing he could think was *how could this have happened*? The hoyden who dangled from a trellis, who'd swung from tree limbs over head as she spied on him endlessly as a young man, had morphed from her cocoon and emerged a magnificent butterfly. A beautiful butterfly. His heart hammered in his chest and he felt rooted to the spot as Ren stepped forward.

How was he going to explain this... this... *change* in his feelings to Ren?

His friend cleared his throat and Michael's gaze snapped to Ren's. "Ah, yes," Michael muttered as he came forward to greet Lady Sewell.

Ren did the same and after kissing her cheek, she said, "I spoke to Lia in the hallway just before knocking on Elise's door. She said to tell you that Marcus is sleeping for now. I told her she should nap as well because the babe will be up again soon enough."

They placed the ladies' pelisses over their shoulders. Catching a faint whiff of Elise's delicate lavender perfume, Michael wished he could linger near her, wished he could touch her. He fought the urge because of the presence of her brother.

There couldn't be a repeat of last night's folly. He had to avoid putting both of them in such a situation again—at least until he could work out what these emotions were he was experiencing. It wasn't fair to Elise, nor Ren, and it was putting a strain on his self control.

Michael assisted the ladies into the carriage bearing the Caversham crest and the driver cued the team into traffic. Soon the conversation continued from the foyer.

"Sometimes I think my brother worries excessively about us. It feels smothering at times."

Lady Sewell came to her grandson's defense. "Be thankful he cares, dear. There are many who do not. We all know men who have left the raising of children to staff, dictating rules from a distance."

Michael nodded. Turning to Elise he said, "We are taught as boys that honor, keeping our word, and protecting what is ours, whether that is our family or our possessions, is everything to a man. Your brother is just doing what his father did before him, and what he will teach his sons to do as well."

It was the truth, but Michael would never reveal to the ladies that there had been times of very real threat to their family in the past. Ren had successfully hidden the facts of their father and stepmother's deaths because he didn't want Elise to think of her cousin as a murderer. And now there was this threat of Sinclair looming over them. Michael knew his friend very well, and he knew that he would worry for Elise until she was safely wed and settled in the home of a new protector, her husband.

By the time they arrived at the Holderman's mansion, their mood had lightened and all were in good humor. This served them well for the line to disembark and enter the stately home was horrendously long.

Michael dread the night ahead. He hated the thought of having to watch over Elise as she danced and courted her many suitors, and considered this his due penance for stealing that kiss the night before. The kiss he couldn't forget. The one that both of them had avoided discussing. He really did have to clear that up with her soon. Michael didn't want her to believe that kiss meant as much to him as it did. If Elise knew the power she held over him.... He was afraid to speculate where such knowledge would lead. She was the type of girl who take the knowledge and use it to her best advantage, twining his heart around her long, delicate fingers.

The ballroom was filled to capacity by the time they entered and a waltz was underway. It seemed to Michael that all eyes turned to stare at their party when they were announced. Once he ascertained that Sinclair was not in attendance, he left the ladies to seek out their acquaintances and have their fun. He stood on the far side of the ballroom, near the open terrace doors, and did as he'd promised his friend—stood sentinel over Elise.

A tall and lean well dressed young man, no more than twenty-five, came to him in the corner of the ballroom. His dark hair and eyes were likely considered good-looking by the ladies. Michael wondered who the un-jaded fresh-faced lad was, and what he wanted. Probably an introduction to someone he knew. He gave the man a slight smile, acknowledging him.

"Lord Camden," the young man said, "I am Mr. Stephen Carroll, I work for Mr. Cartland."

Michael lifted a curious brow. "Are you certain you have the experience necessary, Mr. Carroll?"

A hardened glint flashed in the younger man's eyes, but his expression remained poised, collected. Michael was impressed. "I assure you my lord, I am more than qualified." Lifting a flute from the tray as a footman passed, he continued. "Now, as I am only just arrived, may I ask who is the young lady I am to keep watch on?"

Michael kept his skepticism to himself, knowing he would also be with Elise as she attended functions, pointed her out in the crowd. "She's the tall one in mint green with ivory lace, short brown hair." He didn't want to say he thought she was the most beautiful young woman in the room that night, but he certainly thought it.

"Thank you sir. I shall make myself known to her. Would you care to make the introductions, or should someone else. According to His Grace, he believes she might balk at having a guard, so she'll not learn of my position from me, nor my partners outside."

"I thank you, Mr. Carroll," Michael said. "It is perhaps best to find someone else. Lady Elise is rather miffed with me at the moment, and might suspect something if I were to make the introductions. Do you know anyone here from among your set, that could make them?" At the man's nod, Michael gave a relieved sigh. "Good. Then let's hope the evening is quiet, sir."

Soon after Mr. Carroll began to weave his way into the crowd, several of Michael's peers came to join him and they discussed the mundane trivialities they usually did at events of this sort. Several times he was asked why he didn't make for the gaming rooms and he replied with the banal excuse of either enjoying the view from where he stood, or not being in a mood for games. It wasn't until after he'd said them that he realized they weren't excuses at all.

"I say Camden, is the rumor true?" Lord Randolph, a paunchy man some years his senior, held a respected position in Parliament.

"Depends on the rumor, I suppose," he replied. "What have you heard?"

"That you're on a bride hunt," the older man said, and quickly added, "I realize you're in mourning, but...." The man seemed uneasy with the topic. "if the rumor were true, I have a daughter with the face and voice of an angel."

The gentleman on his right coughed a fit and his poppycock of a friend slapped him on the back, as though to revive a dying man.

"I certainly would *not* say I'm on a hunt," Michael replied. "My uncle, though ill for many years, has only been in the ground a week. By my calculations I have two months and three weeks left to mourn the man." When he saw that Randolph was puzzled by his words, he asked, "Who is it that is saying I'm on a 'hunt?'"

"My wife heard through Lady Ennisdale, who heard it directly from Lady Knebworth. Since then, my lady wife has been pressing me to make an introduction to our Caroline."

"My sister," he grumbled. Damn her meddling soul. When he saw Sabrina next week, he would be sure to ring a peal on her ears about minding her own affairs. Suddenly the looks he and Elise received today while out made sense. The stares, the waves, the greetings he'd thought were given because of the lovely social butterfly in his company, were actually intended for him. Those title-hungry mamas couldn't give a fig for Elise, they'd wanted *his* attention. The only reason he hadn't been set upon by the charging hordes, must be because he'd just arrived fifteen minutes ago. Word of his arrival had likely just made the complete round of the room, and Randolph was the first brave soul to venture forth with a request for an introduction.

It looked as though he was in for a tedious night. He wondered how long this news had been working its way through the *ton* gossip vine. "Randolph, when did your wife heard this news?"

"She came to me two days ago in a winded frenzy. Wanted to know how well I knew you, then quickly imparted the gossip. Of course, I told her I was not going to go out of my way to foist our Caroline on you, but that should the moment arise...."

As the man droned on Michael thought back. If he hadn't left Everly's early last night, he was sure to have been hounded then. Today he'd been too busy to note until now the odd reactions he'd received. This also explained the mountain of cards and invitations waiting for his attention on his desk. They'd all arrived—every single one of them—in the last few days. Suddenly, the pieces of the puzzle fell into place, and he now understood. He had to call off his mother and sisters.

Taking a glance at Elise, noting her deep in conversation with a group of young people, and with Sinclair nowhere to be found, he pushed away from the wall. As long as he kept her within sight, he should be able to move around the room.

Meeting the girl would do no harm. He might even find her interesting. Thus accepting his fate and knowing Lady Caroline wouldn't be the only debutante foisted on him this night, he said, "Let's go meet your daughter, Randolph."

Elise spied Michael's handsome form as he spoke with the Randolph girl. A stab of jealousy pierced her heart. She realized she couldn't possibly be the only one who was interested in Michael for a husband. With him now in possession of a title older than her brother's and a fortune nearly as large, it made him a very attractive target for those meddlesome, matchmaking matrons with available daughters. She quashed her jealousy and decided to enjoy the evening, at least until she could come up with a plan.

"My lady, would you like to dance?" asked a gentleman she'd been speaking to a few moments earlier. Mister something. Curran? Carroll? Carlyle? Turning what she'd hoped was her most radiant smile to him, she nodded and allowed him to escort her onto the floor.

During the entire dance as she whirled around the room, her gaze always returned to Michael. Hopefully it wasn't too obvious to her partner. He was rather nice. If she could only remember his name.

But it really didn't matter. After that dance came another with a different partner, and another after that. She soon tired and escaped the floor as her escort left to get her a punch. Outdoors, the air was much cooler with a slight breeze coming off the river. She stayed well within the light of the ballroom, but far enough away from the doors that she got the moment of privacy she desired.

From the moment she knew she was in love with Michael all those years ago, her heart had never wavered. Michael's kiss last night gave her the spark of hope she'd yearned for. During the ride through the park that afternoon, she knew he meant to tell her the kiss meant nothing to him. But earlier tonight at the house his hands lingered on her shoulders when he'd placed her wrap about her. Then during their carriage ride here she felt him hold her protectively when the carriage hit a bump. His actions led Elise to think she could possibly be wrong, and that perhaps he *did* care.

Seeing him now with Lady Caroline Randolph was

like a burning, painful blow. The other girl was beautiful, demure and feminine. She was everything Elise wasn't.

"Might I give my lady a refreshment?" Michael's familiar voice rang through her with welcome delight.

She turned her gaze to meet his, and gave him a weary smile. As she took the glass he offered, she said, "My last partner... um...." She dropped her voice to a whisper. "This is embarrassing for I cannot remember the young man's name. He went to fetch one for me."

"The young man that just left?" If Elise didn't know better she'd think that Michael was laughing at her. "Mr. Carroll?"

"Yes. He's a superb dancer and quite handsome as well." She looked up at Michael. " Do you know him?"

"Only casually. He's a second son I believe. His father is a minor baron from Kent."

"Yes, he said he was from Kent," she said. "He seems rather nice."

"Your brother would never agree," Michael said, reminding her, "He has no title and no fortune. All he has to recommend him is his familial connection."

She stared at him, her brow furrowing. Concern colored his voice as he asked, "What's the matter? You seemed to be having a good time in there. You hardly sat out a dance during the orchestra's last set."

She sipped the punch he'd given her, thankful for the relief to her parched throat. "Nothing is the matter. I'm just tired and confused, that's all."

"Tired I can understand. But confused? Might I inquire as to why?"

She had to be honest with him, because in the end it was what she desired from him. "Yes, but...." She looked around to make certain they weren't being spied upon before continuing, "I don't know if you can help me."

"I'm certain I can," he offered. "There's no problem so large I wouldn't attempt to eliminate it for you."

"What if *you* are the problem?" she said in a voice just above a whisper.

"Ah, I see," he replied.

She wondered if he really did. "Well, I'm glad you do, because I surely don't."

"Elise," he began, "I wanted to talk to you about this earlier today, in the park, but then we were sidetracked with the kittens, and.... Well, I want to apologize again for my boorish behavior last night. It was wrong of me to...."

"No. It wasn't. It wasn't wrong of you, and I wish you would stop apologizing. I just want you to kiss me like that again. And again and again and again."

He groaned and raked a hand through his thick mane. She sensed his unease with her revelation. It looked like he would rather be anywhere but where he was, that was how uncomfortable he looked. She turned away from him, and looked out over the Holderman's manicured garden.

"I'm sorry. I should never have said that. One day I hope to master keeping my tongue. It's a virtue I've lacked since first learning to speak." Out of the corner of her eye, she saw the traces of a smile tinge the corners of his lips. She felt the color rise in her face as she realized that he of all people knew of her inability to hold her thoughts. "Of course you know that."

"All too well, my lady." His profile was beautiful against the glow of the chandeliers spilling out from open doors. "Though I never found your openness and honesty an undesirable trait."

"Do you see? Herein lies the problem, my lord. We're dancing around this thing... this relationship if you will, that we are each perceiving differently." She hoped his continued silence meant he was actually considering her words. "I think you know where I stand. I can't possibly make it more clear than I have for all these years. And, before you ridicule me, I *have* taken my brother's words to heart, and tried to temper my emotions, hold my tongue, and all manner of other things I'm supposed to do. I do this to show you all that I have matured out of some school-girl infatuation."

She looked up at him and asked, "Have you ever felt strongly about something? Or known something to be so absolutely right and true in your deepest heart without ever knowing *how* it could be that you know it?"

He gave a slight nod as he stared off over the rail behind her.

"That's how I feel. And try as I might, I cannot come up with a way to explain it to myself. I just live with it and will likely continue to do so." She leaned over the balustrade, feigning attention at something on the lawn below. She spoke to him in a voice so low she barely heard herself, "Except each day gets more and more painful."

When he still did not reply, Elise realized he didn't hold any affection for her other than a brotherly sort. "Of course, now that you know all this, you'll no doubt hie yourself back to your office or whatever hole you hid in the last time and I won't see you again for months and months." The knot in her throat grew more painful, and her voice cracked as she spoke, but she had to speak her mind. She knew no other way.

"Elise, you are my best friend's little sister." The tension was evident in his voice. "I'm afraid what I feel for you cannot be...." He struggled for the right word. "Cultivated. I would lose the esteem, and thus the friendship of your brother, for he would certainly think me dishonorable for feeling the things I do about you."

A tiny glimmer of hope began to flicker in her heart. "Then you felt it too, last night."

He nodded curtly, his expression grim and resolved. "But I will have to deny myself—and you as well—for my devotion and promise to your brother must take precedent over what I've come to feel for you."

"But why? What promise? Explain it to me so I can understand," Elise demanded. "Is it the age difference? If so, just look around us! Men marry younger brides. My brother is one of them. He's the same age as you and Lia is just a year older than I. Surely *he* will understand. Papa was old enough to be Amelia's father yet they loved each other very much."

Michael shook his head. He was fighting this. It was obvious to even the blindest person. And she was tired of battling him. Even Napoleon knew when he'd lost the war. "Well, then," she whispered. "I've tried."

She took two steps back toward the ballroom, stopped, and turned to face him again. "You'd best return to the anxious mamas and their perfect daughters, for every one of them thinks you're making plans to fill a nursery."

Elise plastered a smile on her face and went back to the party. She would force herself to at least pretend to enjoy the remainder of the evening no matter how much she hurt. Throughout the night the squeezing pain in her breast grew, several times threatening to force her to tears. But she would not allow herself to cry here. Tears were something she reserved for the solitude of her bedroom. When she was alone.

Lady Beatrice Sewell, upon seeing the saddened state of her grand-daughter *and* the distressed state of Lord Camden after their return to the ballroom, vowed—if only to herself—to do everything within her power to bring these two people, who obviously loved each other a great deal, together.

Even if the gentleman in question was a stubborn dunderhead.

Chapter Six

Elise felt as though her head had been split in two by a woodsman's ax. Burying her face beneath her pillow to keep the sunlight from penetrating her eyelids, she tried one more time to summon the energy to rise from her bed. The day had to be well on toward noon, and still she couldn't bring herself to face her family. By now Michael would have come to have breakfast with her brother as was his habit on days when they worked. With the quiet mood she'd been in when they arrived home, Ren was likely to ask her questions. And if her responses didn't match her grandmother, Beverly, and Michael's responses, there would be even more questions and then another lecture on her behavior.

It was too much to deal with right then. Her eyes felt swollen and her nose was surely reddened from all the indelicate and unladylike blowing she'd done overnight. Unless she desired to be frightened, she dared not look into a mirror.

She heard the door whisper open and soft footsteps move about the room. It was likely her maid. The footsteps neared the bed and backed away. Elise was sure Bridget thought her still sleeping. She just wanted to be alone so she could figure out how best to proceed with the inevitable line of questioning, so she feigned an unconscious state hoping her maid would leave the room.

"I know yer not sleepin'," Bridget said.

Elise grumbled under the pillow.

"How do I know, ye ask?"

"Mmmm."

"Because there's two more kerchiefs on the floor. And I picked up the last half dozen before I left here an hour ago." The maid huffed. "I wonder if there are any left in the drawer."

Elise threw the pillow off her head and shielded her eyes from the light. "Is it possible to get some peace, quiet and dark?"

Bridget understood and closed the curtains. "The best thing for that headache of yours is to drink some tea and put a compress on yer head."

"It's not what you think. I may have caught a head cold."

"As ye say," Bridget fluffed Elise's pillows behind her back and folded her bed covers to her waist.

"I don't think it's a good idea to go downstairs. I wouldn't want to risk giving it to anyone."

"As ye wish." The maid repeated as she handed Elise a bed robe.

"Oh, you think you know it all, don't you! I have a head cold. Really, I do!"

"You don't have to convince me," Bridget went into the dressing room, then returned with a folded wet hand towel. Handing Elise the cool rag, Bridget then brought her a cup of tea and set it on the table next to the bed.

"If you so much as hint at anything other than my having a head cold belowstairs, you'll be sending us *both* back to Haldenwood. Because if my brother learns the real reason for my distress he'll send *me* back there, and *you're* coming with me!"

"Humph! That might be preferable to watching ye make a fool of yourself over his lordship. So long as ye don't bring shame down on the family, I'll hold my tongue. My loyalty is to His Grace and His Duchess."

"I am *not* making a fool of myself over Michael. He...." Elise caught herself and for once, held her tongue. "Oh, never mind." She placed the compress over her eyes and for the first time since she'd climbed into bed in the wee hours of the morning, she didn't want to cry.

She wanted to vent her burgeoning anger now. But the maid wasn't the one deserving of her wrath. That was reserved for a certain peer of the realm, a man who'd admitted he was attracted to her but regarded his relationship with her brother as more worthy of allegiance than exploring the possibility of a romance with her.

No wonder she felt ill. In the matter of minutes, he had raised her hopes by admitting he had feelings for her, then squashed them by telling her nothing could come of it.

Men were a confusing lot. Wherever did they come up with the idea that women were fickle? She'd never wavered about anything in her life. In fact she was the most decisive person she knew.

Her head really did hurt and she decided it would do her good to spend the day in bed. Telling Bridget she would see no visitors today lest they catch her cold, Elise dismissed her.

Minutes later, Beverly entered. "I'm not afraid of a head cold." She sat on the edge of the bed, studying

Elise's features. "You look horrid. I'm available should you wish to talk about it."

"It'll do no good," Elise replied. After ascertaining there were no others in the room she continued, "Talking about it won't change my situation." She plopped back onto her pillows and replaced the compress to her puffy eyes.

"I saw the two of you disappear onto the balcony last night, and when you returned you had a saddened look about you. I don't think anyone else noticed, but no one else knows you as I do. And Michael seemed distant, yet watchful the rest of the night."

If her friend saw her disappear and Michael follow her, then others might have as well. So Elise told Beverly everything—from the kiss at the Everly's to the conversation at the Holderman's. "He admitted to feeling something for me, but because of his devotion to my brother, he's unwilling to pursue it further." Tears began anew. "Ugh!" She swiped at the drops rolling down her cheeks. "I hate crying. It makes my head hurt."

"Me, too," her friend sympathized.

Elise dropped her head back onto her pillows. "I have to give up any dream of a match with the man I've loved forever."

"No." Beverly said as she shook her head. "What we need is another plan. He can try to fool himself into thinking there is nothing between you, but I have seen how he looks at you."

Elise wanted with all her heart to believe her, but she was the one he'd rejected last night. Not Beverly. Even now Elise heard the words as clearly as if he were right there repeating them in her ear.

Already His

I will have to deny myself—and you as well—for my devotion and promise to your brother must take precedent over what I've come to feel for you.

"It won't work," Elise said, tears clouding her vision. "His resolve is firm."

"Not so firm that he's oblivious to you. You cannot *see* what I do because it's your heart that's involved. But I see the way he watches over you. He's *not* indifferent to you! Elise," she whispered in case someone entered. "He *kissed* you! And that is not indifference!" Beverly stood and patted Elise's hand. "I'll come up with something. The first plan brought us this far. He's noticed you and admits to having feelings for you. Now we have to bring him to heel."

Elise removed the wet compress and stared into Beverly's eyes. "He won't allow himself to fall in love with me. Don't you understand?"

"We'll just have to see about that," her friend said. "Now, I have to go to my house with Mrs. Steen and supervise preparations for Papa's arrival Friday. By the time I return, I will have come up with a strategy for landing your lord. Meanwhile you rest and try not to worry overmuch. Everything will work out. You'll see."

After Beverly left, Elise spent the entire day moping about her rooms. She read from a book of poetry that had her in tears nearly every other page. Lia came to visit and Elise had successfully convinced her sister-in-law that she might be safer keeping some distance as she didn't want to give Lia her head-cold. After her luncheon tray was removed, her grandmother came to visit, but wasn't buying her tale.

"A lady should be careful not to spend too much time out on the balcony after dancing," her grandmother warned. "One never knows what they might catch. It could be a head cold or...," her grandmother sat next her and put a wrinkled and weathered hand on hers. "My guess is it's a broken heart."

Elise almost cried because her grandmother's voice was so full of concern for her.

She shook her head. "Truly, I have a case of the sniffles."

"Well," her grandmother said, "when you get over your sniffles you should see to making Camden jealous. That tactic works practically every time, you know. It was how I landed Sewell after your grandfather passed away." Elise looked at her grandmother with surprise tempered with skepticism. "What was I supposed to do? I was still a young woman who wanted affection in my life and he was a handsome man who stimulated my brain—" She had a far-away look on her face as she smiled, as though remembering her love. "—As well as other parts of me."

Elise wiped her eyes and blew her nose. "As I told Beverly, it will do no good. His loyalty is to Ren. He also mentioned a promise, which evidently plays a part in his decision."

Her grandmother stood and leaned on her cane. "Think about what I said, my dear. Camden could use to be put in his place by the threat of someone who might be a serious competitor for your hand, not some spineless namby-pamby."

Elise stood and wanted to hug her grandmother and give her a kiss for understanding, but the older woman backed away. "Just in case you do have a cold, I shouldn't want to catch it you know. I've decided to go to the theater tonight with Louisa, Eugenia and

Herbert."

Later that evening, Beverly came into her room as the upstairs maid removed her tray.

When the door was shut, Beverly burst out, "I have it! I have been thinking about this all afternoon."

"What do you have?"

"Plan B!"

"Whatever it is, it won't work, I tell you," Elise said. "While you were gone, my grandmother came to visit and thinks I should try making him jealous."

"Your grandmother and I are of one mind because I came up with the exact same idea." Beverly poured herself a glass of water and drank. "And I'm certain it will work, but if you don't really *want* Michael to...."

Curiosity got the better of Elise. "Let me hear what it is before I agree to anything."

"Well, first you need to spend a few days recovering from your 'illness.' After all, as they say, absence makes the heart grow fonder."

Then, Elise's dearest friend in the world, laid out a battle plan so brilliant as to make Napoleon himself envious.

Two days later Elise was still "unavailable" for visitors. Word of her illness spread and became exaggerated among their set—an unexpected result of her temporary isolation. Notes wishing her well and bouquets of flowers now decorated her chamber, as well as the various receiving rooms below stairs.

On the third day, Ren sent a message asking if he needed to call in Prescott to see her. She told him thank you, but no. She'd already begun to feel better and perhaps might be well enough in the morning to meet the family for breakfast. Hopefully by then she would have firmed her resolve to follow through with their scheme. Because her heart still wanted the man it has always desired.

Michael began to get concerned over Elise's continued hermitage, even wondering if she was truly ill. By the third morning, he was ready to demand to see for himself if she was indeed recovering from some serious malady. He'd almost been tempted to reveal to Ren his suspicions about her 'illness,' but to do so would bring questions about his own sentiments, and he hadn't had the opportunity yet to broach this subject with his friend.

No, that wasn't quite right. If he were honest with himself, he'd admit he hadn't worked up the courage to broach the subject, unsure what his friend's response would be.

When he entered the dining room on that fourth morning of her reputed illness, he nodded to Ren, and was relieved to see Elise sitting across the table from Lia with Beverly seated to her right. "Good morning, all." He poured himself a coffee, took a seat next to the duchess, and motioned to the footman that he did not desire a place setting. "I see the patient has recovered. We'd begun to miss your cheery presence."

"Thank you for your concern, my lord," Elise replied. "I much appreciated your note and flowers. As you can see I am well recuperated and ready to continue my usual activities."

From anyone but Elise, he would have believed in the earnestness of her words. But for some reason he felt he should be skeptical. She was never this polite to him, especially this early in the morning. Michael didn't see Lady Sewell at the table and inquired as to her health.

"Grandmother has taken breakfast in her rooms already," Elise said, "as she has plans with friends this afternoon."

"As I was telling everyone before you arrived, my lord," said Lia, "I must attend the Eggleston's ball this evening." The duchess resumed cutting her breakfast ham. "Clarissa Eggleston is a dear friend of mine and I would like to show my support for her daughter's *entrée*."

"As you wish, Your Grace." Michael looked over at the two misses across from him, and asked, "Will you two be going as well?"

Beverly looked from Elise to Michael. "We haven't decided yet. I'd hoped to go to the theater. A new play is opening tonight, and Elise and I have been invited."

Elise nodded. "Yes, I'd like to see it as well, as I've had enough of balls for now. I find the crowds of people and the resulting over-warm ballrooms hold no appeal for me." She met his gaze. "And worse yet, when a lady attempts to revive herself with fresh air on the balcony she's met with all manner of scoundrels."

The little minx! She'd just called him a scoundrel. Michael only hoped her brother didn't speculate about whom she spoke. He didn't like the idea of Elise attending a function without him being present. He felt the need to stand guard, but if they were properly escorted and chaperoned, he couldn't very well invite himself along.

His Grace lowered the Morning Post and asked, "With whom will you be attending?"

"Viscount Huddleston and his friend, Captain

Wilson," Elise replied. "We danced with them at the Holderman's before I became ill. Afterward, our conversation was very engaging. They sent us an invitation to the theater, and we accepted. Both gentlemen seem very sincere and honorable."

Michael lifted a brow in question. "Isn't Huddleston older than we are? And what about this friend of his, do we know him?"

"Christopher is a year or two older, I believe you're right," Ren replied. "And his friend Captain Wilson is Reginald Wilson. One of the younger sons of Baron Wilson of Parham. Decent chaps, both. Like us, they've been friends forever. I don't recall ever hearing anything negative about either man. I believe Grandmother is friends with Wilson's mother."

"Good," Elise surmised, "You'll not object, then?"

Michael watched as Ren shook his head, then said, "I don't think so. Who will be your chaperon?"

"Captain Wilson's widowed sister, Mrs. Anne Leonard," Elise said.

Michael knew the woman. A bluestocking with pet projects that mirrored Elise's, she'd fit right in with Elise and Beverly who champion educating the poor. There was nothing dubious about the lady's reputation, thus he couldn't dispute her chaperonage in any way.

His Grace looked at his sister, "Yes. Well, I only ask that you come home after the theater, and not follow the crowds to the various parties afterward. Nothing good happens at that time of night."

Both girls nodded, and turned to smile at each other, and Elise said, "Thank you, brother."

Ren nodded and Michael couldn't help but think that Elise had something up her sleeve. She almost always did. And this felt too suspicious for her not to be planning or plotting something.

"Yes, thank you, Your Grace," Beverly said. "What about you, Lord Camden?"

Michael set his cup down on the saucer. "I haven't decided yet. I may spend the evening at home for once catching up on paperwork. You wouldn't know that I'm in mourning to see the pile of invitations sitting on my desk. Too, I find myself weary of the constant social whirl. If it isn't one event, it's another."

"I quite agree," Elise replied. "Why it's amazing you men get anything done at all this time of year."

Her subtle imputations were not lost on him. Also, he knew exactly why she chose to accept that invitation to the theater from Huddleston. It was to make the point to him that her brother would not be disagreeable to a friend of his, and a man of similar age, marrying his sister. She was systematically invalidating each one of his rationales.

Elise chattered on while stirring her chocolate. "I also think it was that whirlwind of social activity that contributed to my catching that horrible head cold."

"No doubt," Michael droned with affected boredom before casually taking another sip of his coffee.

"The things we must endure to fulfill our duties and obligations to our status," Elise declared. "I swear I am already thoroughly exhausted of the season and we are only a month in. Already I cannot wait to return to Haldenwood and my horses." When she finished her chocolate, she set her cup down and excused herself, and Beverly soon followed.

It took him only minutes, but Michael understood her game now. The little vixen. She knew he has an affection for her, and she thought to make him jealous.

"Ha! Jealous?" Michael whispered as he took the ribbons of his team and cued them into traffic. "I've never been jealous of anyone."

Until now the voice in his head told him.

"That went rather well," Elise noted upon returning to Beverly's rooms.

"Yes, quite. Though you must try harder *not* to take your jabs at Michael in the presence of your brother. His Grace will notice sooner or later, and you don't want to risk his wrath."

"You're right, but I'm still very angry with him." He kissed her. She didn't kiss him. He was the one who stepped over the line first, and she could not help but think that he would not have done so if he didn't feel at least something toward her.

"Be angry when you're not in the same room as your brother. That's all I ask. If he should catch wind of what we're about, you're back to the country and I'm stuck here with my father after Saturday's ball. How can I help you then?"

"You are right, as usual," Elise replied. "But do you think he surmised the reasons I chose the theater tonight with Huddleston and Wilson?"

"Without a doubt. He's not a successful barrister because he's dense, that's for certain." Beverly returned her attention to the stack of acceptance cards to her ball before her on the *secretaire*. "Now, would you like to send a note around to Sinclair, telling him you've recovered and would like to see him? I know I was not mistaken about the glaring looks Michael gave you when you danced with him."

"No. The man failed to show up after saying he would and had I been home, he would have left me waiting for him with no explanation as to his disappearance. I should be angry with him, but instead I feel... nothing."

"Perhaps he had good reason for not coming around."

"*And* for not sending a note?"

"Point made," Beverly stated.

Just then a knock on the door brought news from a footman that gentleman callers were in the morning room below asking if both young ladies were at home for visitors. "Tell them we will be down momentarily," Elise replied.

"This is good," Beverly said once the door was shut. "More competition for the commitment-leery Lord Camden."

Michael and Ren lingered over another cup of coffee after the dishes had been cleared. Her Grace excused herself to write a letter to her brother and Ren's littlest sister, still in the country.

"You're certain this Huddleston and his friend aren't despoilers of innocents?" Michael wanted to make sure that they weren't protecting Elise from Sinclair, only to turn her over to someone worse. He'd heard of the Viscount, never anything shady or disreputable, but it bothered him that he didn't know the man. When he arrived to his office he would have his secretary check with the usual debtors to see if Huddleston was current on his accounts. A lot could be learned about a man when you knew to whom he owed money.

"Certain," Ren replied, leaning back in his chair.

"The viscount is from the north somewhere, and is the quiet type. I think he'd prefer his hounds and the lure of a good hunt to the social diversions of Town. If I remember correctly, he's quite a good hand with a horse, which is something he and Elise have in common. He served in the cavalry and like you, recently came into his title and is feeling the pressure of securing his legacy. Wilson's father bought his commission and the captain has an excellent reputation for turning a coin on the exchange. The man turned his instinct for survival on the battlefield to surviving—no, thriving—in the financial markets. I've taken his advice on one or two investments and you and I both made a tidy little sum as a result. Both men were near the top of their classes at Oxford and neither is destitute. If either man made an offer for Elise, I'd be hard-pressed to refuse him." His Grace reached for his cup. "And both girls could do much worse, as we witnessed with Sinclair."

"You've done your homework already, it seems." Michael hoped he was successful in hiding his aggravation. Ren was right, both girls *could* do worse. It still didn't sit right with him. It should be him with Elise that night and every night. Him. Not Huddleston. Not Wilson.

Unless his friend relieved him of their mutual vow he could do nothing to give Elise hope. At least until *he* worked the courage up to make an offer for her himself.

"I didn't have to, really. I know both men."

"Doesn't the age difference... disturb you?"

"Not really." His friend scanned the room to make sure they were alone. "I'll admit, at first it did, then I discussed it with Lia. She said much to lessen my unease and after mulling over what she said, I've concluded she's right. Considering that a man isn't really ready to marry until he's in his prime, say thirty years, and a woman's prime child-bearing years are in her late teens to about thirty, the age differential is to be expected. Besides no young buck is mature enough to make a good husband. Think on it, Michael, were *we* ready to be husbands and fathers at twenty or even twenty-five?"

Michael shook his head.

"There you have it. Also think about this—it will take a *man*, a strong man with the patience of all the saints in heaven combined, to handle Elise properly, not some young pup."

Michael wanted to ask if Ren would feel the same way if *he* were to consider taking Elise to wife, but thought better of it. Now if only Michael could forget the way her lips felt beneath his and her delicate scent of lavender in summer. And the way she smiled at him as though *he* were the reason behind the smile, the secret behind the sparkle in her amber eyes. He had to get out of here before he said something he might regret.

"Well, I shall be off," Michael popped up out of his seat, and stated with more cheer in his voice than he felt in his heart. "The office awaits and I've lingered too long over breakfast."

"But you didn't even eat," Ren said. "Are you well? Don't tell me *you're* coming down with that head cold as well."

"I assure you I am well. Just not... hungry this morning."

He bid his friend farewell, and during the carriage ride to his offices he realized if he didn't say something to his friend soon, Ren would likely give his sister in marriage to another.

Then again, even if he did want to tell his friend he wanted to court his sister, he couldn't. He was in mourning and where at first that fact was somewhat of a shield protecting him from the annoying invitations and requests for introductions to every damn available chit in the *ton*, it was now a major annoyance. Now, he had to watch Elise dance and smile and laugh with every young rake who asked her.

He attacked the mountain of correspondence on his desk with vicious efficiency. His afternoon meeting with a client didn't go as well as he'd expected and his frustration with his clerk became so evident as to merit an apology to the man. Before he accidentally offended any other employees, he decided to take himself home along with a stack of important papers requiring concentration.

Stepping out of his carriage at his home in Hanover Square, Michael saw Lady Randolph and Lady Caroline standing at the curb of the footpath, waiting for their carriage.

"Lord Camden," the older woman, Lady Randolph greeted. Michael thought her hat abominable with summer fruits arranged in a small cornucopia, resting off to the side. As he spoke, he could hardly tear his eyes from the sight. "How wonderful to see you again. We have just come from tea with your neighbor, Lady Ennisdale," she said.

"How... pleasant." Michael drolled, wondering what his neighbor was gossiping about now. Likely she had him betrothed to someone, after all, the gossip sheets had him with a new woman once a week.

Then a thought came to him. He had to make certain Elise was safe with Wilson and Huddleston, and what better way to do that than from within the theater?

He looked down to Lady Caroline's upturned face to see a bored young lady wishing she were somewhere—anywhere—else right then.

"Lady Caroline, do you enjoy the theater?"

The handsome Viscount Huddleston, and the equally dashing Captain Wilson led Elise, Beverly and Captain Wilson's sister to the ducal box at Covent Garden Theater. Elise allowed herself to be escorted by the captain, after Beverly stated a preference for the viscount earlier in the evening while finishing their toilette.

"The Viscount is nearly the perfect man for me Elise," Beverly said. "He's an avid horseman who also has an appreciation for opera and theater. You know that last immensely raises him in my esteem. It is so difficult to find a man who truly appreciates the stage, and opera in particular."

What no one outside the Halden and Hepplewhite families knew was that Beverly had a most beautiful mezzo-soprano singing voice. If it weren't for her extreme shyness at performing she would surely be the *ton's* songbird. But Beverly could never perform for an audience for she'd freeze and be unable to sing a note. Thus she only sang in the privacy of her room or when she thought no one was about.

Elise spared herself the excruciating humiliation of playing an instrument or singing because she knew she didn't do either well. Her piano instructor had once commented, "I'm afraid there isn't enough money in all of England that could force one to sit in a room and listen to your ladyship play." From that moment on, she never again laid her fingers on the ivory keys, which suited her just fine. She'd rather have been spending those long tedious hours with her horses anyway.

Elise suggested that they sit in the ducal box as her brother and sister-in-law were otherwise entertained this night. Knowing the box had a better view of the stage than the Viscount's rented box on the level above them, it just made sense to suggest it.

Beverly nodded, her elegantly coiffed curls bouncing in agreement, saying, "That is a very good idea, Elise. Though only if the rest of our party doesn't mind." Turning to the captain's sister, Mrs. Leonard, Beverly added, "You really can see more of the stage and hear the music better from there."

As the footman opened the doors to the Caversham box, the sight that greeted Elise simultaneously infuriated her and made her heart skip several beats. Seated in her brother's large box were Michael and the beautiful Lady Caroline Randolph, with her mother, Lady Randolph, seated in front of them near the rail, her opera glasses already in hand peering down upon the crowds filing in below. Refusing to allow his presence to shake her, she caught her breath and counted to ten—quickly—before greeting them. Mrs. Pritchard would have been proud.

"My lord." She nodded to Michael, who had an exaggerated, if not purely comical, look of surprise on his face. She was going to kill him, Elise told herself as they entered her brother's box. Looking over to the beautiful lady at his side, Elise greeted Lady Caroline as well.

"Perhaps we should go to our box, Lady Elise," Huddleston offered.

"Not at all, Huddleston," Michael replied. "There's room here for all of us." Michael motioned for a footman to bring more chairs. "We'll move to the left, and your group can have the remainder of the box. I would have gone to my box, except it's been let this season." Michael looked from Huddleston to Wilson, then Elise. "I so rarely use it."

"And you chose to come to the theater tonight, of all nights! How fortunate for us" Elise was going to kill him in the morning if he showed his face at breakfast.

"I thought you were staying in tonight and working, Lord Camden," Beverly said.

"My clerk was able to help me breeze right through that mountain of briefs."

She and Beverly moved forward into the box and greeted Lady Caroline and her mother, then made the introductions to their party, including Mrs. Leonard. "We didn't think you had theater plans tonight, my lord."

"I wasn't sure what I would be doing when we last spoke, but I had the good fortune to bump into Lady Caroline and her mother while on my way to an afternoon appointment." Elise watched him turn a radiant smile to that young woman's divine visage. "Of course when she mentioned there was a new play opening tonight, I thought it would be a delightful way to spend an evening, and Lady Caroline the perfect, most delightful guest to accompany me. His Grace has often said I could use his box so naturally I assumed it was free since they were going elsewhere tonight."

Elise wanted to strangle him. He knew damn well

she and Beverly were coming tonight. The bounder was toying with her. But why? He'd made his decision, and broke her heart in the process. She'd not fall for whatever game this was that he attempted to play with her. Turning a smile of her own on the Captain, she said, "Have I thanked you yet for the invitation, sir? We—Lady Beverly and myself—adore the theater. Don't we?" Elise looked to Beverly for help making the entire situation seem less awkward.

"Yes, indeed." Beverly and the Viscount took their seats in the front of the box, with Beverly seated next to Lady Randolph and Mrs. Leonard. Lady Randolph continued gazing at the goings-on below them with rapt attention, Elise didn't think the older woman would be bothersome to Beverly or she would have offered to sit next to both chaperons so Beverly could enjoy the performance. This left Elise and Captain Wilson to sit behind them, which meant she sat next to Michael and Caroline. And as fate would have it, she had to take the seat to his right, stuck between the captain and Michael.

She twined her hand in the captain's arm, and asked, "Have you seen this play before? Or did you perchance read a review? I've never heard of it. I think it may be a new one." God, she hated making small talk, and the captain was very quiet. It was taking everything she had to draw him out and converse with her. Admittedly she was nervous with Michael so close, but she knew propriety dictated that she focus her attention on her escort for the evening, not the blackguard seated to her left.

The gas-lights dimmed and all conversation in the hall did as well. The heavy curtain lifted and the production began. Elise watched the characters on stage, giving no mind to their performances. She couldn't follow along with the story at all because of *his* presence, and she realized at that moment, how she handled herself this evening was likely the most important thing she would ever do. If she did anything that could be construed as humiliating to the family or Lord Camden—especially as he was with a young lady—her brother would ship her north. Banish her to the banks of the river Dee and that crumbling pile of stones her ancestors called a hunting box.

Of course Michael was beyond handsome tonight—as usual—and dressed in trousers, the latest male fashion. His companion was gowned in a peach silk and tulle creation, adorned with tiny seed pearls on the bodice. The outfit complemented Lady Caroline's skin and hair beautifully. If Elise could just get beyond the fact that she still loved him, she'd have to say that they made a striking, handsome pair—his dark good looks and cosmopolitan flair alongside her classic features and delicate grace, his affable personality and her demure sweetness.

When they reached the intermission, Michael, Captain Wilson and Lord Huddleston went to fetch refreshments. Beverly, Anne Leonard, and Lady Randolph exchanged pleasantries, forcing Elise to do the same with Caroline. It wasn't a simple task. Elise casually brought up the merits of using gas to light the theater instead of candles, and Caroline's only comment on the matter was that the gas smelled. Elise complimented her on her peach-and-white satin hat with its three small ostrich feathers that curled smartly around her ear. The girl gave Elise a pretty little simpering look, and said, "Mama says it frames my face nicely."

At that moment, she gave up trying to chat with the girl. Michael deserved someone vacuous like her as his wife. Caroline didn't appear the type who would ever contradict him and gave the impression of a marionette waiting to have her strings pulled.

Elise excused herself, then whispered to Beverly of her need to visit the lady's retiring room. The footman opened the door for her and when she stepped through, ran straight into Michael's solid frame, knocking his punch onto her chest, staining the bodice of her gown with the pink, fruity concoction.

It took all she had not to ring a peal on him, but she bit her tongue. And not for the first time tonight. He apologized, quickly handing his now empty cups to Captain Wilson, and pulled a kerchief from his waistcoat pocket, handing it to her as she continued to walk away.

"Where are you going?" he asked.

She ignored him as she pushed her way through the crowd. If she hadn't needed the retiring room before, she did now. Punch trickled down between her breasts. As much as she wanted to, she very well couldn't dry herself in front of all the patrons of the theater. To do so would be uncouth, and since the gossip pages were already going to have fun reporting on this as it was, she would not give them anything else to anger her brother.

He caught her elbow and stopped her. "I asked where you were going."

"To try and clean this mess up," she hissed at him. Once started, she couldn't stop. "You've effectively ruined my evening. Not just with this." She gestured angrily at her ruined dress. "But by your unwelcome presence." She glanced around hoping no one paid attention to her, but spied the reproving glances of several matrons. She groaned. "And just *why* are you here? You knew I was coming tonight. Haven't you done enough to me already, that you must hound me wherever I go?"

"I haven't begun to do half the things I'd like to," he whispered.

"Stop it! You're the one who said there could never be anything between us. So why won't you listen to your own words and act accordingly? Quit trying to confuse us both." She shoved her elbow into his ribs as she pushed past him to enter the retiring room. "Excuse me."

When she returned to the box, she discovered Michael standing by the door with her pelisse. The second act had already begun, so the two of them stood alone in the tiny anteroom of the box.

"I thought you might want to cover the dress. Or we could leave if you wish."

"I cannot leave Beverly with Viscount Huddleston and Captain Wilson. Even with Captain Wilson's sister with them, it would ruin her. So thanks to you, I'm forced to remain in this wet gown the rest of the evening."

"I've apologized already for that."

"Who said I accepted?" She snatched her pelisse from his hands and put it over her own shoulders, shrugging away from his attempt to assist her. "None of this would have happened if you weren't here, you dolt. You knew I was coming. Why did you come here? Tonight of *all* nights?"

"Because I had to see, to make sure, that the two

men you were coming with were worthy of you."

"It is none of your concern, Michael," she hissed as she nodded her head to the footman letting him know she was ready for him to open the door.

"If you haven't accepted my apology yet," Michael whispered into her ear from behind, "you soon will."

As she entered the box, to her amazement, she saw Captain Wilson, her escort for the evening, seated in their box next to Caroline Randolph, heads together whispering and laughing as though they'd known each other for years.

Like Elise and Michael.

"I'll explain later."

She glared at him, not sure whether to slap him or thank him.

Society watchers in attendance at Covent Garden that evening were all agog over the fact that a certain earl entered with one young lady on his arm and left with a completely different young lady. The information was quickly noted and within minutes was on the way to the *Times'* and the *Post's* gossip writers.

Chapter Seven

"Well, that was an interesting turn of events was it not?" Beverly said the next morning as they breakfasted in Elise's room.

"Yes." Elise buttered her toast. "And I think he planned the entire thing."

"Come now, Elise, Michael couldn't have possibly planned bumping into you. How was he to know you'd be leaving the box as he entered?"

"He might not have planned spilling his drink over me, but he had something concocted along that line." She ripped off a vicious bite from her slice of bread. "I'm sure of it," she said through a full mouth. There was nothing he could say to change her mind. Michael knew she'd be there, and he inserted himself into her evening plans.

"I asked Huddleston about Wilson and Lady Caroline, and it turns out the two have known each other ages." Beverly stirred sugar into her tea. "It wasn't until recently that he'd thought to pursue her. Her father refused his suit last year, telling the captain that his wife thought to get a title for their daughter." She met her friend's gaze and sipped. "Caroline is, after all, an only child."

"Beverly, Caroline is a nice girl. But she hasn't a

single thought of relevance in her head. Admittedly, she is quite beautiful, but for how long can looks keep a man attracted to a woman?" Elise cut into her ham, and forked a piece.

"I don't know... until they fade perhaps?"

Elise thought a while, then shook her head. "No. Judging from what I've seen of successful marriages, I've observed that it's those unions where the woman is educated beyond needlepoint and watercolors that are the happiest. Think on it. Don't you agree that it's when a man does not have decent conversation at home, it's *then* that he seeks fulfillment in another woman's company?"

Beverly chuckled. "Somehow I don't think it's conversation a man is getting from his mistress."

"No, of course not. But, the inability to hold dialogue on topics of interest to the man is a direct factor in causing that man to seek more... preferable companionship. Why, it's the very reason the demi-monde exists. Think about the women of that set. They're always patronizing some art form, political cause, or some such. Some even admit to being blue-stockings. Now I ask you, why do *you* think the men are attracted to them? Not all of them are pretty."

"Because the men can get what they want with no strings attached," Beverly said, "unlike in marriage."

"Ah, but the women get what they want as well. For some it's trinkets, clothing or a home. For others it's that male voice to lend credence to, or help them promote, their own liberal ideas."

"You really have thought this through, haven't you? You're not, by chance, thinking of joining them?"

Elise wanted to laugh at the genuine concern evident

in Beverly's eyes. "Of course not. It was merely an observation. That's all."

"Good. Because I'd hate to hear what your brother might do to you if you said to him you wanted to begin holding literary readings, or worse—sponsoring philosophers or poets."

"That will never happen. Don't worry."

A knock sounded and a housemaid appeared, stating that His Grace wished her presence in the dining room. The girls exchanged worried glances. They'd chosen to breakfast in Elise's room specifically to avoid her brother until they could arrive at some explanation for what occurred last night. She was sure Michael had already informed Ren that *he* had accompanied Elise, Beverly and Huddleston home last night. Now her brother was going to question *her* about what *she* had done to precipitate the events.

She held no illusion as to her brother believing her innocent. In his eyes, she was still the same Elise and *always* was the one culpable for *any* incident regarding Michael. Hopefully Michael would be downstairs. Not because she wanted to see him, but because he could help clear her of any wrongdoing.

"Big brother beckons and I don't think he means to wait until I've finished eating." When Beverly set her napkin on the table and moved to rise, Elise put up her hand, stopping her. "You needn't come. It's me he's angry with. And it wouldn't do to have that anger spill over onto you. Especially since tomorrow night he's hosting your ball. Let's keep you in his good graces."

Elise entered the dining room to find Ren and Lia seated, having already breakfasted and enjoying a cup of coffee. Except her brother didn't appear to be enjoying anything at the moment. Before him, spread on the table was a newspaper. Her heavy heart plummeted. She couldn't take another step.

"Sit!"

Of all the many chairs surrounding the long table, Elise took a seat next to her sister-in-law for two reasons. First, Ren couldn't reach her there to strangle her and, second, she hoped Lia would provide support in managing her brother's wrath.

"Would you like to read the gossip column?" He pushed the publication toward her. She recognized this tone of voice, tinged with barely restrained anger. It was one she was familiar with.

She shook her head. "I don't have to. I was there. I know what happened."

"Would you care to explain to *me* what transpired? You left here with one escort and returned with another."

She told him exactly what occurred, hoping it would soothe his temper. She was mistaken, and correct in her earlier assumption that he'd hold her responsible.

"I'm telling you the truth. I had nothing to do with it. First—" She ticked off the count on her fingers for emphasis. "—*he* showed up in your box after *knowing* Beverly and I would attend the theater with Huddleston and Wilson, for we discussed it at this very table yesterday morning. Why is that?"

She lifted another finger. "Second, about the punch. It was an accident. I had no way of knowing he was behind the door. Third, it seems Captain Wilson and Caroline Randolph have been secretly carrying a *tendre* for each other for quite a while, but neither Michael nor myself knew of it."

When Elise returned her hands to her lap, Lia grasped them under the table. Elise was thankful for her support as Ren rarely thought Elise innocent whenever mayhem occurred.

"Husband," Lia began, "in light of these facts, you can hardly reach the conclusion that Elise had a hand in this."

"Forgive me, but her track record with regard to any incident involving Michael has given me cause to doubt her." He glared a warning to Elise. "And rightfully so."

"I know you do not believe me, but I had nothing to do with last night's events."

Ren pushed back from the table and rose. "I'm going to reiterate once more just so you don't forget. Do *not* presume to bring scandal onto our family. You'll not like Scotland in the winter."

When she entered her room afterward, Elise was met by an anxious Beverly. "That went about as I expected." Elise threw herself onto the bed. "Ren thinks *I* initiated last night's debacle and has once more warned me about scandal. He threatened, yet again, to send me to Scotland."

"I take it Michael was not present to corroborate the facts."

"No, and I don't think Ren's spoken to him this morning."

"Well," her friend began, "we need to re-think our plan."

Clutching the pillow she grinned wide, and rocked with unspent, excited energy. "No, Lord Camden has now noticed my existence as a woman. Your plan is working beautifully. Now, let's see.... What are we going to do today?"

Michael entered the ballroom at the home of Lord and Lady Purvis and was immediately inundated with greetings and invitations to meet daughters, sisters and other various female relations of both friends and strangers alike. He didn't want to appear rude, but he kindly sidestepped each trap and wended his way through the crowd to stand near a group of acquaintances while his eyes scanned the attendees for a familiar willowy, short-haired brunette with amber eyes.

He spied her on the dance floor, her graceful form dipping and swaying to the country dance played by the orchestra. In a gown of palest pink, she was the young nymph that haunted his dreams of late. When she turned and he got a glimpse of the daring neckline of her dress, he froze. Surely her brother didn't allow her to leave the house looking like that. If so, he would have to have a talk with his friend.

Then he remembered. It wasn't his place. He'd made no claim to her. Yet.

His eyes followed her through the dance and watched as she curtsied, thanking her partner, and immediately returning to her group in a corner near the entrance onto the veranda.

Cartland's man on the inside, Mr. Carroll, sided up to him and leaned on the other side of the same column Michael held up. They both faced the ballroom floor, the object of their attention some twenty feet away from the edge of the floor, in a semi-circle of too-young, aspiring rakes. "The lady has danced every single dance since she arrived, except the waltzes." The investigator glanced over at Michael, who met his gaze for a moment then turned back to watch Elise. "Do you know if she has permission?" The investigator did the same, but spoke to him in hushed tones. "I don't want to ask her if she hasn't received it yet. As tall and graceful as she is, waltzing with her would like waltzing on a cloud." Michael grunted. "She might be high above me, but when you're in her presence she doesn't make you feel it. She is truly an unique and rare jewel among the paste. Is she not?"

"Carroll, you have a job to do." God, this was all he needed. Another besotted pup to shove away when he claimed his prize. But only if he grew the backbone needed to approach his friend.

The investigator chuckled. "If I didn't know that you were one of the men who'd been cleared from being suspect, I'd report that you were one to keep the lady from. Especially with the covetous way you look at her as though she were the last morsel on the dessert tray."

Michael pushed away from the post, mumbling, "At least she remembers my name." He didn't think Carroll heard. In fact, now that he'd said it, he realized it was best he hadn't. Michael didn't want to antagonize the man who was supposed to protect the woman he wanted as his wife. He strolled around the fringes of the ballroom, greeting friends and speaking with dowagers—his mind always on where Elise was at any given moment.

Around her were at least a half-dozen men, young bucks and old rakes alike, hanging on to her every word, eager to perform her every whim when she asked. Someone handed her a lemonade from a passing footman's tray and she smiled radiantly to him in thanks.

He'd be damned if he would approach her and

become one of the fawning fops gathered around her skirts. His only reason for attending, he reminded himself, was to see that she remained safe. No rule said he had to do that within ten feet of her.

Beverly leaned over and whispered to Elise, "He's here and he's noticed you. Keep up the good work."

"Where is my grandmother?"

"Seated near the punch table with several other dowagers."

She nodded and replied to something a gentleman near her said, hoping her comment sounded appropriate. For all she knew, she could have just agreed to marry him. Looking again at his bulbous nose and goat-like smile she decide that wouldn't do at all. She simply had to pay more attention to the conversation lest she say something she'd regret.

Elise shifted her position such that she was facing Michael and could just barely spy him over the left shoulder of the man conversing with her. Out of the corner of her eye she would occasionally catch a glimpse of Michael when he moved, his black evening attire making him appear panther-like in the brightly-lit ballroom. From where he stood at the edge of the room with his crowd of friends she could occasionally meet his gaze and whenever she did she'd pretend to ignore him. And even though he did not dance, she did. Often.

Remembering the embarrassment he caused her the night before at the theater, and watching as he held on to a young lady's hand a good bit longer than necessary for an introduction, Elise realized two could play this game. She closed her eyes a moment and took a deep breath. Then she faced her admirers with renewed charm.

Elise hated to lose.

Lord Edmond bowed, "My lady, I believe this dance is mine."

Elise hoped her smile reached her eyes as she laid her hand on his and allowed him to lead her into the crowd on the floor. And so it went. Dance after dance. Until the evening finally ended for the two young ladies and Lady Sewell.

At home, before climbing into her bed, she said a prayer that she was doing the right thing. Because for the first time in a week, Michael hadn't come to greet her, hadn't even acknowledged her presence all night. All she had to rely on were Beverly's assurances that he had, in fact, never taken his eyes off her.

The next morning brought a flurry of activity once again to Caversham House. Footmen moved furniture, flower deliveries were made, and upstairs, Beverly finished packing her belongings for the move to her father's townhouse. Lord Hepplewhite sent a note to his daughter informing her of his arrival in town and with a squeal and dance, Beverly begged to be off to meet with him, promising to return in plenty of time to ready herself for her momentous evening. This left Elise quite alone for the first time in months.

She sent word to have her mare saddled, thinking the morning a beautiful one for a ride through the park. Donning her favorite habit and gloves, she topped her head with a stylish hat sporting a dyed ostrich feather plume.

Waiting in the foyer for the horse and groom, she spotted Michael leaving Ren's office. She wanted to dive into another room to wait for him to depart, but it was too late. He'd seen her as well.

"Good morning, Elise. Off for a ride?"

"Yes, I feel the need for fresh air and sunshine." She hoped she sounded bored enough to dissuade him from joining her. He was handsome as usual this morning, and she hated him for it, but there was something else about him she couldn't quite put her finger on. Then she wondered at how—or more precisely with whom—he'd spent his evening after leaving the Purvis' ball. A twinge of jealousy toward the possible other woman gnawed at her.

"Good. Good," he said. "Enjoy the day, then."

With that, he was gone. Out the front door, up on his waiting horse before she could shut her gaping mouth. What? No biting sarcasm in return? Was he feeling well?

She didn't have long to ponder those questions because the groom arrived with her mare and his own gelding. He handed her up into the saddle and followed her into the park at an appropriate distance. Once she rounded the far side of the Serpentine, she cued her mare into a steady canter and relished the breeze on her face.

Elise had to prepare herself for the very real possibility that he would never love her as she loved him. He had kissed her and found her kiss lacking, and probably didn't know how to let her down without hurting her. Ignoring her was his way of doing the deed.

Damn coward.

Elise turned off the bridal path and jumped a log here and there before slowing down and turning for home.

She needed a change of scenery. When she returned to the house, she would ask Lia if it would be appropriate to quit town for Haldenwood after Beverly's ball tonight—for at least a week, preferably two. She really was tired of this social schedule young ladies were expected to keep and missed her horses at home. In the letter she'd received yesterday from their stable manager at Haldenwood, three of the four foals that were due from her new mares had been born over the past two days. She wanted to see them, and check on the progress of the horses in training.

A spark of self-doubt caused by Michael's actions the night before threatened to spread. Going home for a few weeks would be the coward's way out of an uncomfortable situation. If she went home to Haldenwood she would be running away from the pain, of watching Michael court another, perhaps even Lady Caroline Randolph. Rather than facing those emotions head on and coming to terms with his indifference to her, she would be running.

As her brother's friend and business partner, Elise would be forced to see Michael, and occasionally hear her brother speak of him, even if he married another. It was pain she must learn to abide whether she lived at Haldenwood or—heaven forbid—was exiled to The Box, which according to her brother was so far from Aberdeen there were no humans for miles.

"Lady Elise!" A male voice called from behind her.

Elise turned around to see Sinclair coming toward her, his team of pacers winded and breathing hard. She stopped her mare off the path and allowed him to catch up to her. She wondered if he was now ready to apologize for not showing up for their ride earlier that week.

"Mister Sinclair, how good to see you." She dropped a glance to his horses. "Exercising your team I see."

Sinclair looked at her somewhat sheepishly and continued. "I must explain what happened and apologize for not taking you on our appointed ride the other day." Elise looked back at her groom resting some twenty feet away, and relaxed. She turned back to Sinclair. "You see, I went to speak to your brother that morning and—" Elise thought he looked both sad and embarrassed. "—and his grace would not give me permission to take you for a drive. In fact, he warned me away from you."

Elise was surprised at this, not only because Sinclair appeared harmless, but that Ren would do this without telling her. He had to have had his reasons, but out of courtesy he should have told her as he knew she had been waiting on him that day.

Sinclair turned to her with his handsome visage sincere with regret.

"I didn't want you to think that I never showed for our appointed ride. The truth is I'd been told not to return. As I have abided by his grace's warning, when I saw you I felt I owed you this explanation as I do hold you in high esteem."

"Mr. Sinclair, while I respect my brother' authority as my guardian, I make my own decisions regarding whom I consider my friends.

His face brightened, as he smiled. "I would consider myself beyond fortunate if you might consider me your friend. Especially as I would value your opinion, and any pointers you have on training my new team.

"I would be glad to offer you assistance with your

horses," she said. "How can I help you?"

After discussing the issue he'd been having with his team, Elise and Sinclair settled on meeting in the park the very next day so she could drive his team and see how they went for her in the harness. Of course she would have to keep this a secret from her brother. He'd likely be cross with her. But perhaps after one or two sessions she could confess to Ren, and hopefully he'd see Sinclair as she did—a harmless rake who wanted her help with his horses and maybe even a friend.

Once she'd returned to Caversham House, she dropped her stirrup, brought her leg over the pommel and slid down without assistance. She stroked the mare's neck before handing the reins to the groom and thanking him. Inside, she asked after the duchess and her grandmother and was told they were with the Ladies Royce and Stone in the yellow salon.

Not wanting to disturb the ladies, she went up to her room and began her reply to the stable manager, inquiring as to the health of the new foals, their mothers and the one mare yet to drop her offspring. As she finished detailing the increased nutritional rations for the mares she asked that as soon as the last foal was born, he put the four mare-foal pairs out in a pasture to themselves with perhaps an old gelding or two and keep a close watch on them.

When she handed the letter to the footman, he'd mentioned that Lady Royce and Lady Stone had departed and that Her Grace and Lady Sewell were in the yellow salon if she still wished to speak with them. Elise thanked the man, then sought out her grandmother and sister-in-law.

She sighed as she took a seat next her grandmother.

"Miss your friend already, do you?" Grandmother asked.

"Yes. I got quite used to her being here with me."

"It's to be expected." Her grandmother sympathetically patted her hand. "After all, Beverly's spent the past two years with us. She's a darling young lady and I love her as I would one of my own grandchildren."

Elise nodded, looking from her grandmother to Lia, unsure of how to ask for what she wanted. "I'll miss Beverly, but I wanted to ask you something unrelated."

"Go on," her sister-in-law prompted, her voice tinged with concern.

"Would it be considered impudent if I were to ask to leave for home in the middle of the season? I find I'm not cut out for this type of schedule and am exhausted. I was thinking to rest a few weeks at home, then return."

"Funny you should mention leaving town," grandmother began.

"We've been invited to Woodhenge for Lady Richard's birthday celebration," Lia finished.

"For certain, you three should attend, but my presence isn't required, is it? I don't know the lady well, and could spend that time recuperating with my horses at Haldenwood. I have three new foals on the ground, and a fourth due any day now."

"The invitation included you, but if you really want to go home, then I could talk to your brother. I don't think he will object. In fact, I doubt he'd force you to come with us, considering your history with Michael."

"Yes. He will never let me forget my past." Elise took a deep breath. "It pains me that Ren doesn't believe my version of the other night's events. And that he still thinks *I* instigated it all."

"Michael has since corroborated your story," Lia said. "Your brother isn't angry any longer."

"He hasn't said as much to me." Her brother hadn't even sent a note of apology, much less come to offer one in person. He must find the act distasteful, always thinking he was right.

"I'll speak to him for you. Meanwhile, consider coming with us to Woodhenge." Lia gave her a somber smile. "You might find that it'll make for an interesting and well-received turn of events."

"Whatever you're both thinking, it won't work. Michael isn't the least bit interested in me, and has told me as much. He only sees me as Ren's little sister." Elise pushed down her tears, refusing to allow them to flow. "He said he values his friendship with Ren too much to risk it in a relationship with me."

"Nonsense," Grandmother argued. "It's obvious whenever the two of you are in the same room that he cannot take his eyes off you. I've watched his miserable hide these past few days." Elise smiled, finding her grandmother's words an encouragement of sorts. "My thinking is that a week at Woodhenge might just be what's necessary to spur things along."

"Do you really think so?" Elise asked.

Both Lia and her grandmother nodded. "Grandmother has pointed it out to me as well, and I agree with her assessment. He's watches you with longing in his eyes. As though he's...." She watched as Lia searched for the right words, *"come se dice... innamorato di te."*

"That has been my fondest wish for as long as I can remember." Elise looked at them both with hopeful skepticism. "You know this goes against Ren's wishes, don't you? He's threatened to send me to The Box on more than one occasion."

"Your brother is too rigid and unyielding for his own good," Grandmother said.

Lia chimed in, "Especially where you and Sarah are concerned. You know he loves you both very much. If he seems uncompromising, understand that it comes from having to take over the responsibilities of gaining a dukedom *and* raising his siblings. So while he is your brother, he's feeling more like a father in this regard. It's as though he's trying to see you settled as your father would have done."

She hadn't thought about it in that way, but she was right. To her, Ren was a brother, not a guardian, though that became his role upon the death of their father. She could understand his blurred sense of responsibilities. But that didn't take care of Michael, and the fact that both her grandmother and her sister-in-law wanted her to attend a party where she had a feeling Michael would attempt to make a fool of her.

"I'm not certain my heart can take another squashing," Elise said.

"If Camden so much as says a cross word to you," Grandmother said, "I shall pound him into the ground with my cane."

"And if he gets up after that, I shall tear his heart out with my bare hands," Lia said.

Elise looked at both women then wiped a tear before daring a smile. "Why are you helping me?"

"Because lovers belong together," her grandmother said.

"And sometimes they need a little help," added her

sister-in-law.

Later that evening, in Beverly's suite, Elise hugged her best friend in the entire world and said, "Good luck, my lady." When Beverly began to tear up, so did she. They didn't have long to be melancholy for of course Bridget was there to snap the two girls back to reality with muttering something about a new trend starting with girls wanting two dresses for their debut now—one for dinner and one for the ball.

"Your father is down there waiting for you, my lady," Bridget stressed. "The receiving line is forming. You have to go!"

"She's right, if you wait any longer the flowers in your hair will be wilted before you take to the dance floor."

"I'm nervous," Beverly whispered.

"I know you are," Elise said. "If you weren't, you would have reminded me that the flowers are silk." She led her friend by the hand to the door, where the maids opened them wide, and Elise said, "I'll go down the back steps, and wait for you in the ballroom once you're done with the receiving line."

When the door shut behind Beverly, Bridget handed Elise her fan and tucked a stray strand of hair behind her ear. "Try and behave yourself tonight. For yer friend's sake, if not yer own."

"Why does everyone think that it's *me* who's always the cause of trouble?"

"Perhaps because ye have a history for it."

She signaled the maid to open the door and Elise quit the room and made her way down the back stairs. Elise didn't want to impose on Lord Hepplewhite, or Ren and

Lia, as they greeted their guests. She rounded the corner to the main floor foyer, and saw Michael standing alone at the base of the steps, looking towards the front doors at the guests entering the receiving line. He appeared to be looking for someone. She wondered who it was he waited for. Perhaps he'd invited his friend from the night before.

The closer she got to him the more she realized how exceptionally handsome he was tonight, dressed in a midnight blue formal coat with his mourning arm band in place, taupe trousers, polished black shoes, and an expertly starched and knotted white cravat. The onyx tie pin peered from within its folds and when he turned, the stone caught the light for a moment, appearing to wink at her. The color of the stone and coat made his eyes appear more green than brown tonight, and more handsome than any other man she'd ever met.

But it didn't matter. He'd said there could be nothing between them and no matter what Lia and Grandmother tried to do next week, she was holding fast to her heart because she knew better than to believe anything might come of it.

"Good evening, my lady." He gave her a little bow as she neared.

"Good evening, my lord." That much she said in a normal voice, in case others overheard. For Michael alone, she hissed, "Would you be so kind as to *go away?*"

"I'm afraid not."

"Michael," she said as she scanned the foyer to make sure no one could hear her, "my brother has threatened me with banishment to the wilds of Scotland unless *I* leave *you* alone. It irks me that he's never nearby to see that it's *you* that will not leave *me* be. Like the other night at the theater. You knew I would be there and with whom. Still you chose to attend and sit in my brother's box, with of all people Lady Caroline Randolph. Who can compare to her? She's perfect." Awareness washed over her as she realized what he'd done that night. He'd compared the two of them while side by side. The arrogant knave. He disgusted her. Elise didn't know why her heart longed for someone so cruel. With a huff and a dismissive toss of her head, she strode to the ballroom leaving him behind her.

"Whatever you're thinking, you're wrong." He caught up to her. "One day I'll explain it all."

"Save your explanations. I really don't care." She stood at the entrance into the ballroom, pasted on what she hoped was her most brilliant smile, and walked in. Michael was hot on her heels, still hissing something at her behind his own forced smile.

"The hell you don't." He reached for her hand and placed it on his arm, flashing a wide grin to those witnessing their entry. "You care so much, you're hurt, when you shouldn't be."

Elise was beyond aggravated with him. Not only was Michael behaving irrationally, but she realized it was too late to pull her hand from his as there were now some two hundred pairs of eyes turning their way. "I assure you I neither require assistance down these steps," she hissed through the smile plastered on her face. "Nor do I want your escort into this room."

"Too bad." His hand firmly planted over hers, he led her into the ballroom. "It's done." And for show, he bowed and kissed the air above her gloved hand then smiled.

She snatched her hand from his grasp, and through that same false smile of her own, said, "Go and find yourself a bride and get to work on that nursery." She turned her back on him and headed for the safety of her grandmother's company. Surely he'd have the good sense not to pursue her among the turbaned set. But before she left him, she had to get one thing clear to him. "I am forever out of your hair."

Some in attendance at the ball in honor of Lady Beverly Hepplewhite said that it appeared that Lady Elise had given the cut direct to the new Earl of Camden. If they only knew the truth of it. Because if there was any part of that earl that Lady Elise wanted to cut, it was his heart—straight out of his chest.

CHAPTER EIGHT

Michael watched Elise walk away from him with a determined stride, her back so straight and chin so high as to almost appear absurd. The hell she was out of his hair, he thought. Michael decided it was time to put himself out of his misery. Or deeper in it if he listened to some of his friends.

It was time to speak with Ren.

Last night it had annoyed him to see her hold court over a group of young bucks who could never appreciate her zest for life. He wanted to both control that passion and encourage it at the same time.

While unable to sleep in the wee hours of the morning, he'd devised what he thought was the perfect plan. Sending word to his sisters that he wanted to host Mother's birthday party at Woodhenge, he closed both letters with a post-script stating that they could stop meddling now. His decision was made.

The not-so-subtle message should state loud and clear to his interfering kin that his countess had been chosen. Of course, his choice would raise the eyebrows of his mother and sisters, for they knew of the romantic infatuation the child Elise had had on him. They'd even been witness to some of her antics.

His mother might be a problem. Not that he sought

or needed her approval of his choice for bride, but he would like for her to be happy with his selection. After his uncle's funeral a few weeks earlier, she reminded Michael that a scandal chased his uncle from London, and that he needed to choose an appropriate lady who would be an asset to the title and make him proud. She must not be someone high-strung or flighty in nature. Thus, without even saying her name, she intimated that Elise would not be a good match for him for she'd used those same words to describe the duke's sister on several occasions.

Because of her childhood infatuation with him, his avoidance of Elise over the last few years had been necessary for his sanity. Keeping his distance from her protected not just himself, but also Elise. If she would climb that trellis, who knew what else she might try to gain his attention?

And where he questioned her sanity back then, he now questioned his own. What brought him to this point? The point where he now returned her feelings?

How ironic it was that now *he* had to pursue *her*.

He spied Elise as she made her way through the crowd to hide behind the skirts of her grandmother. He'd let her have her fun. From his years of observing the fairer sex, he'd deduced that all ladies needed to experience the power of bringing a man in. So he'd play her game.

For the time being.

He watched her from the shadows as she danced and chatted with her friends. The lovely Lady Beverly Hepplewhite's debut was turning into quite a successful event. When Elise disappeared through the doors onto the terrace on the arm of some young gentleman, a jealous streak raced through him. He maneuvered toward the open doorway through which they'd exited. If she cried out for help, he'd only be a matter of several steps away.

Or so he'd thought. He followed the laughing sound of her voice and that of the young man, as they strolled down to the darkened corner of the terrace. He watched as she took the young man in question by the hand and led him toward the duchess' private garden. *The impertinent minx.*

His mind screamed to protect her, but how could he when she was going beyond the lighted terrace? Taking the stairs down onto the lawn, he traced their footsteps into the garden, careful to remain a short distance away.

When he arrived within hearing distance of their conversation, he heard her describing the virtues of the species of tiny roses climbing the trellises, and then do the same with the larger blooms. It all appeared innocent enough, until the young man's voice turned serious.

"My lady, it is my most sincere wish that you have developed an—" Michael could swear he heard the boy's voice squeak. "—an affection for me. And, if such is the case, I would like to ask your brother for permission to court you. We needn't marry anytime soon unless, of course, you desire a hasty union. Which would be very welcome on my part, I assure you."

"Lord Edgcumbe," Elise began, and Michael knew from the tone of her voice, she was about to let the boy down. He smiled. "As flattered as I am by your declaration of affection, I feel I must be honest with you and tell you that I regard you as a friend, and nothing more. Besides you really don't wish to tie yourself to me. Everyone will agree that I'm too shrewish and independent-minded for my own good."

"Well, I had hoped that those qualities would be tempered by marriage to a man strong enough to tame you."

"Ooh, ouch." Michael winced, then fought an eruption of laughter, knowing what was to come. "Not smart Edgecumbe," he whispered.

"Tame me?" Elise's voice rose to the fine quality of a subtle shriek. Michael was losing the fight to remain silent. "Oh, sir! That was a poor choice of words! I'm no animal to be tamed, and you've barely witnessed my shrewish tongue! That said, to preserve my dignity and your addle-brained arse, I believe I'll take my *untempered* self and return to the house."

Michael ducked behind a statue, standing in its shadow, waiting for her to make her exit from the garden. She trod off in a huff, her beautiful gown and jewels disguising the hoyden hiding beneath. As she passed she muttered something about all men being alike.

How untrue, he thought. Just then Edgcumbe stepped forward and noticed his presence. He appeared mortified at having his rejected declaration of affection witnessed by anyone.

"Don't worry, Edgcumbe," Michael said to the lad, who looked to be barely twenty-one summers. "She's been giving me fits now for years. And she's right, you know. As a frequent recipient of the dark side of that lady's shrewish tongue, I can confirm she's not for you." He stared at her back, smiling as she entered the doors to the ballroom. "No. She's the queen of shrews and as such, needs a match with the king of fools."

He left the young Edgcumbe behind to lick his wounds and followed in Elise's wake.

Upon reentering the ballroom, Elise accepted the first dance she was invited to join. Perhaps she had been a tad naive, now that she thought about it. Edgcumbe's interest wasn't really in the roses her grandmother grew, he'd wanted to get her alone so he could profess feelings for her. The whelp barely knew her. Never had she given him reason to think she felt anything other than amity for him.

She smiled and thanked her partner and returned to the relative safety of her sister-in-law's side. Ren and Michael, she was sure, were in the card room, likely raking in as much coin as their opponents cared to risk.

A familiar voice came from behind her, so low it almost whispered, and so close she felt the warmth of his breath on her neck. Her body trembled and her heart stopped as she recognized his scent, his presence behind her. "Dance with me, Elise." At one time this was her fantasy. This would have been her dream come true. But tonight it took everything in her to try to ignore him. She had to remember this was the same man who had kissed her just last week, then cavalierly said there could be no future for them because he would honor a promise to her brother over a chance at love. She straightened, glanced to Lia to make sure she was still conversing with the matron to her left, then turned her head and shot him a glare. "You know you want to," he said with a devilish grin.

"You're in mourning, remember. Besides, you have no idea what I want Michael. If I had my way, I'd strangle you myself then hang you from the highest tower."

"You wound me, my lady. May I ask why you wish me so... dead?"

"Your actions will surely get me banished from town by my brother. Now go away!"

"He can't send you anywhere I can't retrieve you." He leaned in close and took her hand, the simple act causing her insides to tremble. "Come with me Elise. Now."

"Why are you doing this?" she hissed.

"I'm not quite sure why," he said honestly.

"Well, until you know, leave me be." She took two steps away from him.

Instead of doing what she'd asked, he caught her elbow and led her behind the orchestra's screened backdrop, and through a hidden door which opened into the servants workstation. He continued through the connecting narrow hallway, until they emerged in the library. The door closing behind them just in time, as Elise heard two footmen pass by chatting as they carried trays of beverages.

"Michael," she protested. He ignored her, still pulling her along behind him. His actions tonight were truly going to cause her banishment. He knew Elise wouldn't put up a fight. Not because of any fear of what her brother might do, but because this was Beverly's night, and Beverly didn't deserve such behavior from her.

They went through the library doors onto the family's private terrace, around the corner from where she'd just been minutes ago with young Edgecumbe, well beyond the flaming torches lighting the main terrace outside the ballroom. There he pulled her into his embrace and led her in the remainder of a waltz Elise recognized. It was one of the shorter waltzes, but that didn't matter. If her presence was missed in the ballroom, it would bring gossip down onto her. Damn him.

"Do you *want* to ruin me?" she demanded.

He gave her a wicked smile, one barely visible in the minimal light spilling out from the house. "Not in the way you think." He twirled her around and brought her back into hold. "Will you come to my mother's birthday celebration?" he asked as he moved them gracefully around the table and chairs.

"I haven't decided," she replied, curious to see if he really wanted her at his home, or if he was playing the gracious host. Not that she didn't believe her sister-in-law and grandmother, but Michael did have a recent history of uncertainty when it came to his desires. "I am exhausted because of this hectic schedule we've kept, and I thought to perhaps go home for the week to rest." She scrunched up her nose as they danced. "I have a lingering sniffle still." She hoped God would forgive her the tiny lie.

"You can rest at Woodhenge. I assure you it's large enough to find solitude wherever you wish."

"No," she repeated, refusing to look at him.

"Then who will give mother her kittens?"

"You can, they are your gift to her."

"No. The kittens are your gift. My gift to my mother is something else altogether."

"Oh?" She lifted a brow, curious as to what he'd found to purchase for his mother. "What did you get her?"

"I remembered something you said the other day,

about the most perfect gifts not necessarily being something you buy, but one that comes from the heart." He whirled her around. "And that is all I will say on the subject. If you wish to know what I'm giving my mother, you'll have to attend her party."

Elise pretended to struggle with indecision. She was going, even though she knew time with him in such a close confine would make her fall even more helplessly under this spell he was weaving. The entire week her brother would be watching her closely, and if he so much as thought she was annoying Michael, he'd make good his threat to send her to Scotland.

Elise turned a smile up to him and said, "I'll come. But only if I have your word that you'll do nothing that will get me banished."

"You have my word," he said with all sincerity.

"For some reason I'm having difficulty believing you," she muttered as she looked up at him, never missing a step.

He chuckled, and the deep sound resonated within her. "I see I must prove myself to you."

He turned her with a great flourish as the last faint strains from the orchestra were coming to a close. "We'll see about that," she snipped. Stepping away from his hold she said, "Tomorrow I must ride in Regent's Park at three o'clock to meet with the children, as it has been one week. Would you care to come to see that I am right about them not showing up?"

"I believe I shall."

Michael bowed to her in the solitude of the private terrace, then took her hand and led her back to her grandmother and Lia's side.

"Your Grace," Elise said, when she saw a lapse in

her conversation with the matron, "Would you happen to know where my brother is?"

Lia leaned forward to say for Elise and Michael's benefit alone, "In his office. I believe he said he needed to find something at the bottom of a bottle of whiskey."

Her grandmother hooted with laughter, and behind her Michael coughed, catching Ren's humor. People around them began to turn their heads and look toward their party. "Perhaps I'll go help him find what he's looking for." He bowed to both ladies and nodded to her before leaving to find her brother.

Early the next morning, Elise went to Beverly's room to talk with her before she left for her father's home. Hearing voices and movement within, Elise knocked once, the door opened from within and she ran straight into her friend.

"I was just coming to look for you," Beverly said, retreating back into her bedroom. "I thought you might still be asleep."

"How can I sleep knowing you're moving out today?"

"As I've said before, I'll only be a short drive away."

"Right. Well, did you have a good debut, my lady?"

Beverly hugged her tight. "Yes! It was an amazing night. And before I forget, Caroline Randolph has more than fluff between her ears. She's amazing with numbers, statistics, probability, and such. And that's what she and the Captain have in common. Did you know she's the reason her family is solvent today. She took over her father's investments when he proved unable to turn a coin. She met Wilson when she needed a man to make her trades on the 'change. It's really quite a romantic story. I think you would like her."

"Well, then I misjudged her," Elise said truthfully, "and for that I'm sorry." She plopped in a rather unladylike manner onto the chaise before the hearth. "I saw Lord Huddleston paying particular attention to you." Elise looked at Beverly with hopeful anticipation for her friend, for Huddleston was considered to be an excellent catch. "Was it welcomed attention on your part? Did your father like him? Do you have plans to see him again?"

"Yes, yes, and yes! He really is a dear, and is sincere in his affection for me." Beverly took Elise's hands in hers. "He's asked my father if he might court me, with the inevitable outcome being marriage, of course. Father said yes, but only after discussing Huddleston with your brother."

A smiling Elise wrapped her arms around her friend and nearly began to cry. "I'm so happy for you Beverly. Really I am. My brother said Huddleston loves the hunt as much as we do. That and the fact that he's horribly rich, very handsome, and titled makes him a perfect match."

"I hear the household is preparing to away for Woodhenge. Are you going as well?" Beverly asked as she carried a stack of kerchiefs to her trunk.

"Yes, though it is only because I've been bested. Michael will not tell me what his gift is to his mother. He says the kittens are my gift to her, and that he's gotten his mother something else, and he chose this gift by taking my advice. Now he has me extremely curious."

"May I confide *my* observations of last night?" Beverly asked.

"Of course! When have you ever had to ask permission?"

"Well, you've got him on your hook, Elise. He couldn't take his eyes off you the entire night. He's smitten I say. Now all you have to do is be yourself and you'll have him eating oats from your hand."

"What makes you think that?" Elise very much wanted Beverly to be right in her assessment.

"I saw him come in from the terrace right behind you. I assumed...."

"You're mistaken. I wasn't with him. Edgcumbe wanted to see grandmother's roses." At Beverly's look of skepticism, she quickly justified herself. "I really did think he was interested in the garden." Realization dawned on her with flaming embarrassment. "Oh, goodness... then he heard...."

"Heard what?" Beverly asked.

"Michael must have heard Edgcumbe propose marriage."

"What?" The shock and disbelief on Beverly's face almost caused Elise to break into laughter. "You're joking!"

"That's what I told Edgcumbe," Elise said somberly. "Only I didn't know Michael was nearby. He must have heard the entire exchange."

"Oh, I'm willing to bet he did. This is perfect! Elise, don't you see, Plan B has landed the fish."

"I don't see how you come to that conclusion, but I do plan on enjoying myself at his estate. Supposedly the previous earl had an excellent stable."

"As soon as you return to Town, I want to hear all the details because I think there is a great deal more to this. He's luring you to his estate for a reason, Elise.

Think about it, his mother and sisters will all be visiting while you are there. Lord Camden has something planned. I'm sure of it."

"No," she replied. "He's been a good friend to my brother since their childhood. We're just going out to celebrate his mother's birthday." Elise could only dare to dream that he might consider her as a bride, but she didn't hold out hope. He'd already said there could be no future for them. Then again, last night his behavior was wickedly seductive, asking her to dance the way he did, sent shivers racing through her body. And this was after he'd overheard Edgecumbe's proposal.

Perhaps Beverly was right. The idea held some merit. One usually wanted what one could not have. Elise just had to make herself less available to him.

They spoke more about the previous night's ball, and soon it was time for Beverly to leave. After she gave her thanks once again to her host and hostess for their patronage, she bid a tearful goodbye and climbed into her father's carriage and left for Mayfair.

Elise checked the time and ran to her room to change for her ride with Sinclair today. She'd told him she would meet him at ten, and it was nearly that now. She called for a groom and a quiet gelding, not knowing what she might find with Sinclair's horses, and her geldings were preferable to have in a training situation than the unfinished mare she'd been working with.

She found Sinclair resting his team in a shady spot near the Serpentine. That in itself told her he at least cared for their comfort. When she approached, the horses didn't appear to be breathing as hard as the last time she saw them.

"Good morning, Mister Sinclair," she greeted as she

rode up to his phaeton.

"Good day to you Lady Elise," Sinclair replied, and tipped his hat in her direction. His team began to come alive as she rode up, expecting to work again.

"You have a nice-looking team there, can you tell me what you know about them and if you don't mind, I'd like to drive them. While I do, you can either wait here or ride my groom's horse." She smiled and motioned back to her groom who rested, mounted on his horse, some twenty feet away. "So, tell me what issues you are having and I will see if I can help."

After a few minutes of discussion, Elise took the reins of Sinclair's team as he held her horse and waited. She drove his phaeton twice around the track and realized the problems were caused by a lack of familiarity, being that the team were a recent purchase.

Elise pulled up to where Sinclair stood and drew the team to a stop. She handed the reins to her groom as she pulled the brake and climbed down unassisted. She turned to Mr. Sinclair with a smile. "Your new pair are a nice match. One has more training than the other. Given time, they should do just fine for you. Your veteran horse on the right is very steady and forgiving, not flustered by distractions and whatnot, and the younger horse on the left looks to his partner for reassurance. That's good. Your gelding on the left is softer in the mouth than your veteran on the right, which also makes a good placement in the hitch as most people are heavier-handed on the right."

"I am left-handed, my lady," Sinclair said.

"I hadn't noticed, sir." Elise thought about it a moment, then continued, "Then try switching their position in the hitch to see if that helps. You could unintentionally be heavier in the younger horse's mouth. If you're constantly preventing him from doing what you're asking by holding him back, then telling him he's misbehaved for not doing it, then who is at fault?"

"You could be right. I hadn't considered something as simple as left-right positioning."

"I'm not sure that is the only problem you're having, but start with that, and after I return from the country, we will chat again. Sometimes a tiny change can make a world of difference for both the horse and driver." He nodded, telling her he understood. She added, "relax and loosen your hold on your reins a bit. If you hold it tight, then the horse will think there is something to be frightened of and work themselves into a nervous lather. That is why you had to exercise them so hard—to wear them into quiet submission."

"Ho, there, Lady Elise! How jolly good to see you again." Elise turned to see a young man she'd just recently met, Mr. Carroll, riding up on a big black hunter that was nicely balanced and muscled. Not unlike his owner, she thought.

"Why Mr. Carroll, how are you," she said as he neared. "I was just helping my friend, Lord Sinclair with his team. He's just recently purchased them and was having a little difficulty with the younger of the two." She took the reins of her horse as Sinclair went around to take the reins of his team from her groom.

Elise made the introductions, and the two men gave a polite, if terse nod of the head in greeting. She mounted her horse with her groom's assistance, and arranged her skirt before taking the reins from the groom.

"I'd heard you were a fair hand with a horse," Mr. Carroll said. "It's rare to find a woman with such knowledge."

"Yes, well, I've loved animals since I was a child," she said.

"Lady Elise, I shall be on my way," Sinclair said.

"Think about what I have said, and if you'd like we can meet after I return from the country."

Sinclair nodded. "I will do as you say, my lady, thank you." Sinclair climbed into his phaeton and gathered his reins. "I look forward to our next encounter." His eyes slid over to Carroll's then back to her. "To follow up on the team's training of course."

Elise smiled at Sinclair who's team was already in motion. "You are welcome, sir. You can tell me of your progress then."

Sinclair tipped his hat toward her. "Good day, my lady," he said, then cued his team to a smooth trot.

Mr. Carroll looked at her through an apologetic grin, and said, "I hope he didn't leave on my account."

"Lord Sinclair is very polite and shy. Not the outgoing sort. It must have taken a great amount of courage to ask a lady for help. I was happy to oblige him."

Mr. Carroll nodded as he watched Sinclair's phaeton round a bend in the track. "Well, Lady Elise, I'll not keep you." He looked over to her groom and nodded. "Good day, my lady. I hope we shall see each other soon."

"Good day to you too, Mr. Carroll," she said, then cued her horse for home. She had just enough time to have luncheon before she was to meet Michael for her second ride of the day.

She and Michael had gone through the entire Regent Park twice looking for the children, and after not finding them, Elise said, "You see? It is as I thought. They are not here." She gave him a smile and tapped her mare with her stick and cantered off.

Michael caught up with her and slowed them down. "You will make a fine mother one day Elise. I meant to tell you as much after seeing you with those children last week."

She wanted to tell him, *I don't want children if I can't have yours,* but knew it would be too shockingly forward, even if it was the truth. Instead she said, "Thank you, Michael. I do hope to be blessed with many children one day."

They walked their horses side by side, not speaking but enjoying the quiet companionship until they reached Caversham House.

"What are your plans for the evening, my lady?"

"I believe we are staying in and preparing for our trip tomorrow."

"Then I shall see you for dinner," he replied.

Elise debated taking dinner in her room that night, but decided against it. Michael was up to something and she wanted to find out what. He was being far too solicitous toward her of late. And that was not normal for Michael. And with the family leaving for his estate in the morning for Lady Richard's birthday, Elise wanted to know what she'd be walking into. When he followed her into the house and went toward Ren's office, Elise climbed the steps to her room. Once there she called for a bath, then opened her chiffarobe and tried to decide on a gown for dinner.

Monday morning dawned warm and humid, with the sun making a valiant attempt at burning off the overnight fog. Elise breakfasted in her rooms, having overslept from spending a sleepless night too excited for the coming week ahead. She entered the dining room and greeted her sister-in-law cheerfully, asking if everything was alright. Her grandmother, and brother's absence were noted.

"I think it is now," Lia said, never looking up from her coffee cup. "I wasn't so sure a few minutes ago."

Elise thought the reply odd and took a seat across the table from her. "What is keeping us from leaving?"

"Your brother and Michael went into his office about thirty minutes ago. At first I thought I heard yelling, then a crash. I went to see what had happened. When I approached the closed doors, I heard laughter, so I came back here to wait."

Lady Sewell's maid appeared at the corner of the table and curtsied to Lia. "Ma'am," the girl said, "Her ladyship has bid me to inform you she is not feeling well. She says not to change your plans, but to leave without her and she will follow you tomorrow." When she'd finished she bobbed another quick curtsy and when Lia nodded, the girl left the room.

Lia lifted her fine china cup and finished her coffee, returning the cup to the matching saucer before standing. "I'll go check on her, and collect Marcus and his nurse."

Elise nodded. "Do you think Ren is canceling the trip?"

"No," Lia said. "I heard laughter. So whatever the issue was, they seem to have worked it out."

"Fine." Elise said, "I'll just go back to my room and

read until we're ready to leave."

Just as she spoke the words her brother and Michael entered the dining room, both men smiling. "That won't be necessary," Ren said. "You and Michael go ahead. Lia and I will follow along in the morning with Grandmother and Marcus."

Elise did not miss the look of surprise and bewilderment that crossed her sister-in-law's face.

"That's quite all right," Elise said "I'll wait until tomorrow and leave with the rest of you."

"I would rather you have Grandmother with you," Ren said, glancing at Lia and nodding. "Since she is not feeling well this morning, the two of you go on ahead." Her brother turned his gaze on her. "You'll be fine." He then looked over at Michael, giving him a hard stare. "She will be unharmed. You gave your word."

"I am wounded, Your Grace," Michael said through his smile.

Lia opened her mouth to speak, but Elise jumped in. "I'm sorry. No." Elise shook her head for emphasis and moved to stand behind Lia's chair, as though her petite sister-in-law could physically protect her. "I will not. Perhaps at one time I might have agreed to this, but not now. I am *wise* to him." She continued to shake her head. "It's a ploy. He's repaying me for all my years of tormenting him. He's repaying me by ruining me. Making it so no other will marry me, or worse—do something so scandalous that I get permanent banishment." She implored her brother, "Please, don't make me go!"

"Husband, do you think this is wise?" Lia asked as she reached a hand out for Elise.

Ren turned a reassuring smile to his wife. "It will be

fine," he told Lia. Then he turned back to her. "Elise, he's not going to do anything—" At this Ren glared at Michael. "—besides show you Woodhenge." His expressions softened when he returned his gaze to her. "His sisters and mother should be there already, so you'll have appropriate chaperons once you arrive."

She turned and glared at Michael. "You did this. I don't know how, but you did this. Just like that night at the theater. You're behind this." Taking her basket of kittens she marched out down the hall without a look back at either of the two men.

Michael smiled to his future brother and sister-in-law, happy Ren agreed to the one day head start. "Isn't she beautiful when she's angry?"

"She's still my sister and until you're wed, *I* am her protector. Don't make me sorry I did this. You're my best friend and though it might pain me to do so, I'll call you out if you hurt her."

Michael hugged Lia and shook his future brother-in-law's hand, and said, "My coaches will be here in the morning. Again, I thank you, both."

"You have the one day you requested. Make the most of your time."

"You'll find your sister a completely different woman when you arrive tomorrow," he promised.

"Just make sure she isn't *harmed,* am I making myself clear?"

"Very clear, *brother*." He headed toward the door, turned around and gave his friend a smile. "I like the sound of that. *Brother*. I've never had a brother before, you know. And there isn't anyone I'd want for a brother more than you."

Ren smiled back at him.

"Until tomorrow, then." Michael followed Elise out to the waiting coach.

He climbed into the vehicle and found Elise with her nose in a book, refusing to acknowledge his presence. He made himself comfortable in the seat across from her and knocked on the roof. Instantly, they were off. Nearly an hour later, she was still ignoring him.

"Would you care to stop and stretch your legs, my lady?"

Nothing.

"Well, I would like to stop and stretch mine." He tapped on the roof and, minutes later, the heavy traveling coach rolled to a smooth stop. The coachman opened the door and lowered the steps. Elise looked up at him momentarily then returned to reading her book. Michael stepped down, walked around the coach and into the woods a moment. When he heard the other coach in their caravan nearing, he hurriedly righted his trousers and went back. In the other vehicle was Elise's maid, riding alone. Thinking it best Elise not know this, lest she invite the woman to ride with them, he climbed back inside and tapped on the roof, getting them moving again.

"It'll be some six hours before we reach Woodhenge," he said. "I'll provide you ample opportunity for comfort breaks, should you choose to take them."

Still no reply. Because of the oppressive heat he removed his coat and freed the buttons on his waistcoat. Sitting back, he closed his eyes and rested his head against the velvet squab. He needed to catch a quick nap. Lord knew he hadn't had much sleep recently. A certain amber-eyed vixen had been haunting his dreams.

Elise finished her book and dropped it onto the seat next to her. She fidgeted in growing discomfort, but was too proud to ask the sleeping Michael to stop for her. As if sensing her situation, he opened his eyes and pulled his pocket watch from his waistcoat.

"It's been over two hours," he said. "Are you finally ready to stop and stretch your legs?"

She didn't reply. She hated him for what he had planned for her. His motives had become crystal clear to her this morning. This was how he was going to be rid of her. He'd do something to make her the scandal of the season, then she'd be forced to leave town in shame. She was determined not to have any part of his scheme. She resolved to comport herself in a manner above reproach, ignoring and staying as far from him as she possibly could. Which was damn near impossible to accomplish in the confines of a slow moving traveling coach.

"Fine with me," he replied. "I could go for another couple of hours. It'll get us to our destination sooner."

She gave a frustrated snort and banged on the roof herself. When the vehicle had stopped moving, she grabbed the strap and positioned herself to bolt from the door the moment it opened.

As soon as the steps lowered, she raced into the woods to relieve herself. As she was righting her drawers, she heard his footsteps following behind her. "Stop! Don't come any closer," she pleaded.

"I only wanted to make sure my lady wasn't thinking of fleeing my company," he said. "That's all."

"Oh, I'm sure," she muttered under her breath. "Probably hoping to spy me in my drawers, or worse."

"It's the truth," he said with a chuckle, "whether you care to believe it or not."

"You're not supposed to eavesdrop on a lady when she's relieving herself. It's uncouth." She rearranged the skirts of her chemise and favorite peach-and-cream-colored poplin carriage dress, wishing she could remove her spencer. The day was getting warmer as it went on and she was beginning to feel uncomfortable in the coach, even with all the windows open.

She debated with herself on whether or not she should remove the article of clothing. When she neared their coach, she saw Michael squatting in the grass watching over the two kittens. He was such a soft-hearted man, at least when it came to animals and small children, though he was nothing of the sort where she was concerned.

"Ready?" he asked, looking up at her.

"Yes," she replied. "Where is the other coach?"

"Behind us. Not to worry. It's moving slower because of the additional weight."

"I wasn't worried. I just wanted to get another book to read."

"They'll catch up with us in about an hour when we stop for lunch. There's an inn ahead that's known to have a decent cook."

She climbed into the coach ahead of him and took the basket of kittens he handed up to her. Resting the basket on the floor between the seats, she prayed he would hurry so the vehicle could get underway again, pushing what little breeze was available through the windows.

He climbed in, the doors were closed, and he signaled the driver. They started forward at a walk rather than a trot, to allow the other coach to catch up. Of course, this did nothing to help move air through their conveyance in a comfortable manner. Elise fidgeted in her seat.

"Do you need to stop again?"

"No."

"Then why are you so flushed and fidgety?"

She wondered whether she should tell him. Being a man, he'd of course tell her to remove the offensive bit of cloth and allow the breeze to cool her. But society dictated rules—not just of fashion but also mores—be strictly adhered to by ladies of her tender age and social standing. And one of those rules was not removing clothing in front of a man not your husband.

"Michael, I'm feeling very warm. I need either more breeze coming through these windows or I must remove this spencer before I faint from the heat."

"Remove the spencer," he said. "It's as simple as that."

When she didn't move to unbutton the jacket, he asked, "Did you need help removing it?"

"No! It's just that...." She trailed off, knowing if she told him her concern, he'd laugh at her. The old Elise wouldn't have given a thought to removing the spencer. The old Elise regularly bucked convention and skated that fine line between propriety and scandal.

But that was the old Elise. Then a thought shot through her head, causing her to bolt upright in her seat. She hadn't just been placating her brother by telling him she'd changed. She really had. Astounding! Who would have guessed?

"Elise you're going to have to remove the spencer before I remove it for you. You're looking rather pale."

Those were the last words she remembered hearing.

Not all the servants were accustomed to seeing such tender caring from a man toward a woman. But Tom, the Caversham coachman, swore it was how their Duke acted toward his Duchess. Then he smiled, knowing His Grace's sister was in very good hands.

Of course, Bridget muttered under her breath about the *two* of them bringing scandal down on the family after she witnessed the Earl of Camden removing the spencer from Lady Elise's unconscious body.

Chapter Nine

"I detest smelling salts!" Elise opened her eyes and shoved the offending bottle away from her face, then gave him a frosty glare.

"Then you should not have fainted." Relief flowed through Michael. For a moment, fear of losing her had paralyzed him, but when he realized what had happened he'd ordered the coach to stop and called for her maid to help him. God, he was going to hate explaining this to her brother.

"I didn't faint. I *never* faint."

He cracked a cocksure grin. "Right."

"Did I hear my lady? Has she come to?" Bridget asked behind him.

Elise tried to sit up, but he held her down. "Rest. Your maid's just concerned. Yes, she's finally come around," he said to the maid. "Why do you women insist on wearing things like this—" Michael held up the spencer. "—on warm days like today?"

"Because," the servant said, "to appear indecently dressed will bring the wrath of society down onto her head. It's my job to see that she at least appears conventional."

"Did you...?" Elise sputtered, apparently just noticing her sleeveless dress and unbuttoned collar.

"How did...?"

"I removed it to aid in cooling you. Don't worry, I didn't take any liberties. I was too busy fanning you with your book." He lowered his voice so Bridget couldn't hear him, and added, "Besides, when that time comes, I want you very much conscious, my sweet." Smiling, he thought, how he looked forward to that day.

Elise muttered something he didn't fully catch, though it sounded like a rant about stubborn men and their misguided allegiance. Michael knew she was well when she turned another frigid glance his way. "Let's be off then," he said. "Woodhenge is still some four hours distant, without the stop for lunch." He held Elise's hand, preventing her from leaving the coach and riding with her waiting maid. "No. You stay with me. She can ride in the other coach."

"Oh! You arrogant cur," she hissed. "I don't *want* to ride with you."

He held his tongue thinking she would definitely want to be with him before this day was over. If only he could restrain his frustration at her insolence. "Be that as it may, you will." He sent Bridget back to her vehicle, and shut the door on theirs. Soon they were underway once again.

Within minutes Elise fidgeted with the book she'd finished. He could tell she was contemplating re-reading the thing to avoid talking to him. He didn't want that. He wanted her ebullience and vivaciousness to fill the coach. He wanted to talk to her, explaining the decision he'd come to, and ask if she'd still felt the same about him, and about a possible future together. Then afterward, assuming she still did, he would laugh with her, hold her, touch her, kiss her.

But if she didn't, he had only twenty-four hours in which to change her mind. And the only way to begin with this spirited minx was to be honest, because that was the one thing he knew she valued beyond measure. She always had.

"Do you remember that night at the Holderman's?" he began, his voice sounding somewhat strange, even to himself. *Maintain control*, his brain ordered his heart. When she nodded, he continued, "Do you remember what you said?"

"I'm afraid I said a great deal that night." She stared out the window, avoiding eye contact with him. "I cannot remember specifically what it is you wish me to recall."

Michael took a deep breath, almost afraid to begin. "You said, '*Have you ever known something to be so right and true in your deepest heart, without ever knowing how it could be that you know.*' I have not forgotten your words. You spoke from your heart when you said that." She turned to face him, and he thought he saw a flicker of something, an emotion deep inside her she was yet unwilling to give rise to, so he continued, hoping it was the response he'd wanted. "I think I understand what you meant now, because I don't know where this feeling is coming from. I only know that I don't want to lose it."

"May I ask how you came to this conclusion?" Her voice barely contained her emotion. He could see that she wanted to believe him, and he could only continue as he'd began, with honesty.

"On my word, Elise, this... this... whatever-it-is between us caught me very much unaware. One day, you were just Ren's annoying sister, and the next I wanted you and at the same time knew I could never have you. Then I started thinking *why* I couldn't and every reason came back to one thing—the agreement your brother and I made when we were young, in which we promised each other that our sisters were off limits. At the time it was made, I worried about your brother breaking Christina's heart. You were never an issue, as you were just a child at the time."

She didn't react to his speech, but he could see she was fighting a smile. Michael removed the loosened cravat completely, as it was growing warmer and more stuffy inside the slow-going coach. He shed his unbuttoned waistcoat, tossing it onto the seat with his jacket, and continued, "Then there was our age difference. In my head, I wasn't seeing you as the young woman you've become, but rather as the little sister of my friend. Am I making sense so far?"

Michael could see the hope bubbling just beneath the surface, but she just nodded mutely. He went on. "That night, at the Holderman's, you tried to tell me the age issue was irrelevant, but I wouldn't let myself believe it. Then *you*, termagant that you are, arranged that evening at the theater with Huddleston and Wilson."

"I've got questions about that..." she began, but as realization dawned, her eyes first widened with shock, then narrowed with skepticism. "How did you know...."

He held up a hand to cut her off. "Later, please. Let me finish. When I asked Ren about allowing someone older than me to court you, he reminded me of a few things and clarified others, basically telling me what you'd said the night of the Holderman's ball—that our age difference would not be an issue with him.

"Once that began to sink in, I started to see that I

couldn't allow someone to 'tame' you or break your spirit. It was the one thing about you that always drew me to you. That's what makes you special."

"You followed me the other night," she said. He loved that tilt she got to her head when she asked him a question. "And you heard Edgcumbe, didn't you?"

He nodded. "I only thought to be there to protect you should you need me. Though you obviously held your own. I should have known you would be fine. You are a strong and direct young woman. Edgcumbe is like a colt still finding his legs, and not what you need, Elise. In a few years time, he would have worn your spirit down and you wouldn't be happy. Neither would he. Then, soon after, he'd seek his comfort elsewhere, be it his club, gaming, or a mistress. And you would continue to grow older and unhappier." He paused and let his words sink in.

"Look at me. Please, Elise." When she did, he spoke again. "That's not what I want for you."

It seemed an eternity to him while she quietly digested his words. True to what he knew of her nature, she asked, "Why are telling me this? Now?"

"Because I want to kiss you again, Elise."

"Is that all?"

"For now, it will have to be." He didn't want to think of filling a nursery with anyone but her. He wanted children with her courage and spirit, to bring them joy as they grew old together. "Your brother has given me twenty-four hours to see if your feelings might still be the same as they were before."

It felt as though minutes ticked by, and still she hadn't said anything. He had never put his heart on the table before, for a woman to cherish or destroy, and her continued silence made him grow more and more fearful that he was, in fact, too late. Unable to take the deafening quiet any longer, he asked, "Are they... the same? Or..." His words hung in the space between them. Michael was hopeful he hadn't missed his opportunity. "Is it too late?"

She shook her head, mouthing the word, 'no.'

His heart sank. He'd revealed his truest and deepest feelings for her and because he'd taken too long to sort through his emotions, it was too late. He wanted to plead his case or shout at her for being foolish, but instead raised his hand to signal the driver to stop.

Before he could tap the roof, she spoke, her voice straining with emotion, "No. It's not too late." He watched as she blinked back tears in her amber eyes. "They're still the same as they've always been, and the same as they will always be."

Michael collapsed back into the squabs, deeply relieved. Finally, a happy future lay before him—and with a most unlikely young lady. He exhaled a shaky breath, and rubbed his hands on his thighs. "Good. This is good," he muttered, suddenly unsure of himself and how to proceed. Whenever he'd thought about a wife in the past, she was always faceless. Nameless. Someone he thought he'd yet to meet. And that someone had been right in front of him all along. The complete opposite of what he'd always said he wanted.

"Michael?"

He heard an unnatural tremor in her voice. In all the years he'd known her she was never unsure of herself. "Yes?"

"Kiss me again," she said softly. "It's what I've wanted since the first time you kissed me."

"I know, minx." He took her hand and drew her onto his lap. "And when you asked me to kiss you the other night, it scared the devil out of me."

Wrapping his arms around her, holding her close, he thought he felt her tremble. Though it could have been him, so powerful were his feelings for this slip of girl who'd never given up on him, or on her own heart.

He lowered his head and set his lips to hers. She was soft, so soft. She was freshness and innocence embodied. She was as sweet as the first day of spring and as passionate as a sultry summer day. Never had so simple a kiss affected him so, effectively turning his world upside down. Suddenly everything he thought wrong now felt right.

Backing away, he rested his chin on the top of her head and took a deep, shuddering breath to control his ardor lest he frighten her. He had to remember to go slowly with her. She was untried and unused to this.

"Michael?"

He met her gaze. "Yes, minx?"

"It's what I've always imagined."

"I know it is, minx."

He held her that way, close on his lap as he stretched out on the seat, for the duration of the ride to the Royal George where they planned a luncheon and change of horses.

When they disembarked the coaches, Michael smiled and winked at Bridget, who clucked then muttered something unintelligible under her breath. If Elise knew her maid, it more than likely had something to do with scandal. Lord knew, she was ever preaching to her about the repercussions of improper behavior.

Removing her hand from Michael's, Elise stepped over to her maid and grinned so broadly her cheeks hurt.

"Everything is going to be fine, Bridget. You'll see. My dream is finally coming true."

Bridget reached into the baggage coach and retrieved her embroidery. "Has he proposed then?"

"Well.... Not in so many words," she replied. "But we both know that is the final outcome."

Bridget looked at her skeptically, and said, "I'll believe it when I see the announcement in the Post. Not a minute before." Still unbelieving, her maid shook her mop-capped head, red curls peeking from the sides near her ears. "And I can't believe His Grace gave his approval, what with your grandmother feelin' under the weather an' all."

"I'm certain he's given his approval else I wouldn't be here. After all, Ren does love me, much as he says I'm a thorn in his side. And, as my brother said I could marry for love, I'm willing to bet he's allowing us to find out if that's what Michael and I feel for each other."

"And what if Camden tastes yer charms and finds them not to his likin', what then?"

Elise looked around the yard to make sure no one was listening. "You make it sound so illicit... so improper."

"Well, it is! And think on this," she warned, "if'n he's not wantin' ye after he's had his fill, then yer goin' to be left nursin' a broken heart. I know. I've been down that road."

Michael came up just then to lead the women into the private dining room that was readied for them. Elise took her seat across from Michael and Bridget sat at a small table near the door, her ever-vigilant maid playing the role of duenna in the public facility.

The sumptuous fare was quite good considering the location. Elise probably ate more than she should have, but was making up for not having much breakfast. She fed the kittens some scraps from her plate, then let them romp in the grass for several minutes before putting them back in the basket for the rest of the trip.

After they were underway again, Elise stretched out lazily on the seat next to Michael, her head on his chest. "How much longer?"

"Nearly three hours more." He tightened his hold on her when the coach hit a rut.

Before long the good food, full stomach and rocking coach began to take its toll on Elise and her eyelids were getting heavy. "Are you comfortable? Would you mind if I napped?"

"Go ahead, minx." He kissed the tip of her nose. "I'll wake you when we get close."

"I'm happy, Michael." She gazed into his hazel eyes, a tired smile forming.

"I am too, Elise," he replied tenderly. "I am too."

He held her that way for hours, relishing the feel of her against him. In the silence of the coach, his thoughts finally began to fall in place.

Love was but a fleeting thing—something one wished for and if they were lucky enough to experience it, they should cherish it, for love was never lasting. He knew this first hand. Both his mother and older sister lost the loves of their lives far too young, and neither remarried. His uncle lost his wife in childbirth many years earlier and also never remarried, which is why he now held the title.

His younger sister had told him that she never missed an opportunity to tell her husband how much she loved him when he was home. And when he was called away to exotic locations kept secret from her because of national security, she wrote him daily and told him of her love, because she too knew having it was rare and special.

Michael couldn't say this was love. At least not yet. He knew he wanted Elise like he'd never wanted a woman before. He knew there was a strong attraction between them. And he cared more deeply for her than he ever had for a woman. But he wasn't sure that he wanted to label those things *love* yet.

Both he and Ren knew the responsibilities that came with their positions and one of those was the duty to marry appropriately and produce the next generation of leaders for their country. A love match would be ideal, but in the absence of that, there had to be an affection for the other person. He wanted a marriage that was something more than an alliance for the sake of merging lands and wealth, or creating offspring.

Michael envied Ren his happy union and he wanted the same. Over the past few weeks, and especially this last week, the idea of a future with Elise warmed on him. Truly, he hoped it was possible to forge such a future with her. The elemental traits he deemed necessary certainly existed—she was of noble birth and was pleasing to the eye and loin—had those traits not been there, he would never have proposed this arrangement to her brother.

Yes, he found Elise very attractive, desirable even, and he admittedly looked forward to the physical aspects of marriage. Too, he felt both a certain protectiveness and possessiveness where it concerned her. The thought of another man touching her, and doing those things he wanted to do with Elise made him physically ill. Could he have these feelings were he not in love with her? She was high-spirited, true enough, but she was also very intuitive and intelligent. Perceptive and sometimes subtly manipulative, she always kept him thinking. He would forever be on his toes where she was concerned. She also made him laugh, as she had in the Duchess's rose garden with young Edgcumbe. He couldn't imagine her wit and tongue being silenced by a man who sought to control or break her.

He thought of his uncle and his warning of loving the wrong woman. God help him if he were wrong to fall in love with her. He stood to lose not only a vivacious, delightful young woman who'd wormed her way into his heart, but the friendship of a man who was as close to him as a brother. In the end, the possibilities for him and Elise far out-weighed the prospect of living without her in his life. Marrying Elise was the right decision.

At his mother's birthday party, he would announce their engagement to the family.

Elise snuggled closer to Michael, inhaling the sandalwood and spice scent of him. Breathing deeply, she decided he was very comfortable to rest on. So comfortable she'd lost track of the time while she napped. She wondered how close they were. Turning her head, she looked up at him and saw him staring down at her.

"My sleeping beauty awakens."

"I'm no beauty, but yes, I've awakened."

"You underestimate your charms, minx."

"Don't Michael, please. I've long ago realized that my looks are unconventional. I'm too tall, too thin, and do not possess the desirable assets of other women. I can't tell you how I've prayed for—" She paused unsure of how she might sound to a man. "—more of this and less of that."

"You're you. I think you're perfect, and that's all that matters."

She didn't want to debate with him on this topic. He couldn't change her mind. Shifting her position, she realized she needed a break to stretch her legs and answer the urgent call of nature. "Michael?"

"Yes?"

"How far are we now?"

He set aside his papers, looked out the window then down at her. "About twenty minutes."

"Can we make that twenty-five?"

He smiled and nodded as he tapped the roof.

True to his word, twenty five minutes later, they turned onto the long drive to Woodhenge. The estate, he told her, had been in his family for more generations that he could remember. The title, he said, had been in his family over six hundred years, and parts of the house were nearly that old. He began to support maintenance on the estate when it became obvious his widower uncle could no longer do so alone.

"Uncle inherited a crumbling estate and very little funds. He married for love, his wife bringing nothing in the way of dowry to help the coffers. He had a small horse breeding operation where he'd experimented with cross-breeding for a superior carriage horse. So many farms were breeding racers and hunters that he felt there was a niche to be filled in specializing in light and heavy carriage horses. The pacers that pulled my phaeton in the park the day we saw the children with the kittens—those were his. I'll show you around later, and you can study his breeding charts. It's all very interesting."

"Those horses come from the same stock I'll see this week?"

He nodded. "Uncle imported certain horses from the continent and crossed them to our native carriage stock. The result is what's in our barns."

Elise looked up when they rounded a bend onto a wider gravel drive. Woodhenge appeared ahead, an ancient limestone sanctuary with crumbling towers on one side, connected to a more modern, perhaps Tudor, stone residence. Stately and impressive it looked near the size of Haldenwood, only much older. It rose four stories in the center with three-story wings extending off the gleaming facade like a haven in the setting sun.

Never having been here before, she was enchanted by its charm. "Michael, this is beautiful," she whispered in awe.

"Thank you." Pride sounded in his voice. "The land has been in our family since the Invasion. William the Conqueror gifted the land to a faithful retainer who built his castle on the site. All that remains of that original structure are those crumbling towers and the sanctuary." He pointed off to the left side of the circular drive, about eighty yards in the distance. "Other relatives have added to it through the centuries. Although I have no desire to add to the residence, renovations are currently underway throughout. Sections are closed off to guests for the work. I hope it won't inconvenience anyone."

Their caravan pulled into the drive just below the curving, terraced steps, and three little girls came running down to greet them. A woman—their mother perhaps—stood near the doorway. Elise suspected this was one of his sisters, though she was unsure which. She hadn't seen either since her father's marriage to Amelia when she was ten years old.

They rolled to a stop and Elise shuddered. She was sure to be bombarded with questions. How was she to answer them?

"There's nothing to worry over, minx." He rubbed her back reassuringly with his left hand, as his right hand held hers. "It's just my second sister Christina and her brood. I don't see him, but I wonder if her husband, Lawrence, is with her."

A footman opened the door, and lowered the steps. Michael exited first, then extended his hand to her. Once her feet hit solid ground, the three little girls rushed forward and hugged him.

"You're here! You're here!" they shouted.

"I said I would be here this afternoon."

"Good," said one curly headed blond, the oldest of the three, "because Mama won't let us ride our ponies unless you or Papa are with us, and Papa isn't here yet. Can we go riding now?"

"Emily, what did I say?" Their mother gave the child a warning as she came down the steps, and the little one reluctantly backed away, muttering something inaudible under her breath. Her two younger sisters laughed. Seeing this interaction is what made Elise determined to have several children in succession. She hated that she had no siblings to play with as child, which is what led her to spend all those hours in the barn with the animals.

"Michael," the woman hugged her brother, placing a kiss on his cheek. "How good to see you finally. You're a horrid brother that you never come out to visit us."

"If you didn't live in the ends of the earth, I might visit more often."

"Plymouth isn't all that far," his sister replied, then turned a smile to Elise.

Elise spied a glimmer of merriment and welcome in her eyes and relaxed. Michael's sister appeared younger than him. She was a tall blond, unlike him, and very much still an attractive woman at almost thirty.

"You look familiar...." his sister began.

"Christina," Michael interrupted, "this is Lady Elise Halden, Caversham's sister." He turned to her and said, "Elise, this is my sister Christina, Baroness Vance."

There was no mistaking the surprise evident in her expression, as she realized Elise was the one and same hellion who'd tormented her brother for all those years. Michael took Elise's hand and brought her closer to his side, placing his arm around her shoulder, the unspoken meaning of which was not lost on her or the Baroness.

"Christina is my sister closest in age to me. She's almost two years younger."

Michael and his sister shared a smile and a knowing look.

"How do you do?" Heaven help her, Elise thought to herself, she sounded simple-minded.

Then as the Baroness looked from her to Michael, she burst out in laughter. Elise looked down at her traveling dress, wondering if perhaps she'd buttoned the spencer incorrectly. Then she realized the laughter wasn't directed *at* her. It was more of a release of mirth and excitement.

"This will be more interesting than I'd suspected," the Baroness said to no one in particular. Then, as though suddenly remembering her manners, she took Elise's hands in hers, and said affectionately, "Welcome, Lady Elise. Welcome to Woodhenge."

Michael gave his sister a warning glare. "Christina, I trust you will see to Elise's comfort for the duration of her visit."

"For as long as I am here, Brother." She turned a genuine, warm smile to Elise. "Should you require anything at all, just ask. I will do whatever I can to make your stay more enjoyable."

Just then a tiny hand tugged at Michael's coat, demanding attention. He leaned down and lifted the littlest girl, who looked to be about four years.

"Well now, who is this? It cannot be Sophia." Michael looked at Christina and back at the girl in his arms. "For my Sophia was but a babe when last I saw her. This must be... Olivia?"

"No!" the child cried, shaking her head of blond curls.

"Emily, then?"

"No!" Elise watched as the little one giggled and squirmed in his arms.

Michael gave the infant an overstated look of shock. "Sophia? Really? Well, you certainly have grown into quite the young lady, my dear. Before you know it, we'll be hosting your come-out."

"Not before mine," the oldest shouted.

"Mine either," said the middle child.

Little Emily tossed her curls, and feigned an air of

superiority. "You always have to agree with whatever I say. Can't you think for yourself, Olivia?"

Emily's target put her hands on her hips, stomped a foot and huffed. "Mama, she's being mean to me!"

The Baroness closed her eyes, took a deep breath, and made all the introductions with the children, and afterward attempted to usher everyone inside, so the servants could begin unloading the baggage. Elise reached into the coach and brought out her basket of kittens. When she lifted the lid and allowed the kittens out onto the lawn to stretch their legs, the girls squealed in delight.

"You've got three new best friends," the baroness said to her.

"Are they for us?" Olivia asked. "Uncle always brings us treats, don't you Uncle Michael?"

"Can we keep them?" asked Emily.

"I want this one," chimed in Sophia.

The Baroness looked helplessly at Elise. "Children, these are Lady Elise's kittens. You cannot want her to part with her pets. Just as you wouldn't want to part with your goose, Olivia. Or your dog, Emily."

"Well, while she's here, we'll take care of them. Can we?"

Elise laughed. She leaned over and petted the head of Tiger, in Sophia's lap. "Well, it's supposed to be a secret, but I guess since your grandmother isn't here, I might tell you, but only if you promise not to say a word."

All three girls nodded. "We promise!"

"This is Tiger," she said, then pointed to the other kitten in Emily's arms. "And that one is Naughty. They are your grandmother's birthday presents from me. I want to surprise her when she opens her basket Saturday."

"We won't say a word," Emily said, then looked to both of her sisters. "Will we?"

"We won't tell."

"Thank you, then, for caring for the kittens during this week. I'm sure they'd love to have some children to play with. Just be careful not to get them too tired. They're still babies and need lots of sleep."

Michael watched as she managed his trio of nieces just as easily as she managed the two children in the park. He looked at his sister who shared an approving smile.

"How did *this* happen?" she whispered. "I want to know all the details."

"It just..." Michael shrugged his shoulders. "It just did." His gaze never left Elise's slender form as she crouched next to the girls.

"Are they boy kitties or girl kitties?" Sophia asked.

"These are little boys," Elise replied. "And as everyone knows, boy kitties are more affectionate than girl kitties. So I hope your grandmama will adore them as much as we do."

Michael wanted to tell Elise that this boy kitten had a great deal of affection for her. Thinking on it, perhaps he would do just that later tonight.

Baroness Vance spent the afternoon in her room writing a short letter to her sister, Lady Knebworth. In this missive, she stated that she'd just met the next countess and approved of their brother's choice. She added a post-script as well, telling Sabrina she would never in a hundred years guess who the young lady was.

Once she sealed the letter, she sent a courier to Bath with instruction to place the note in Lady Knebworth's hands personally.

Chapter Ten

Later that afternoon, after she had unpacked and had some tea, Michael sent word asking Elise if she would meet him in the library and perhaps take a walk with him. She'd changed from her traveling dress to a summer day dress of fine muslin and felt more suitably attired for the unusually warm weather they were experiencing. As she entered the foyer, she wondered where the library might be. A gray-haired liveried footman stood near a doorway, so she asked, "Could you tell me where I might find Lord Camden?"

The man nodded and moved with a slight limp down the hallway. "Follow me, my lady. I was to bring you along when you came down."

Elise was happy to see that her family wasn't the only one who kept on elderly retainers in service if that was their wish. The trend of having only handsome young footmen was a rather shallow one she thought as she followed the elderly footman down a long hall. The man stopped and knocked on a door, then opened it after they heard Michael bid Elise enter. She thanked the servant, then stepped past him into a long, dark paneled library with several reading tables, each with comfortable, deep chairs positioned around it, and three separate alcoves with sofas and chairs arranged so that each cluster offered privacy of conversation within the grouping. Michael stood near the enormous fireplace with wood stacked for the evening fire if it became necessary. He had one booted foot on the brass tinderbox and one elbow resting on the mantle. When he turned his lazy smile to her, she wanted to pinch herself to make sure she wasn't dreaming. She hoped that looking at him would always take her breath away.

She noticed he had changed into his country attire and was wearing tan breeches with a plain white shirt and unbuttoned waistcoat, having dispensed with the formality of his jacket in this warm weather. He looked comfortable here in this setting, the embodiment of a country gentleman. No artist could have painted a more perfect setting for this man. Her heart gave a lurch inside her chest.

If only, her heart sighed. He felt something for her he said, asking for time to figure out what it was. She wondered if it were possible to help persuade him in his discernment? But if she did, would he resent her if, at the end of the week, he decided they did not suit. That was reason enough not to manipulate the situation.

"I hope you're finding everything to your satisfaction." His smile broadened as she neared. "Is your room comfortable?"

"Very," she replied. "Not even Bridget can find anything to complain about."

"High praise indeed."

"Indeed." She suddenly felt as foolish as a fresh-from-the-schoolroom miss, without the wit about her to converse adequately. Where was her tongue now? Did it just disappear with his declaration of feelings—such as it was. "I seem to have lost my words."

"Me too, minx."

"Why, I wonder? Until this morning, I had no problem communicating with you." His cynical hazel-eyed gaze melted her. She conceded, "Oh, all right, granted, it was more like ranting, raving, and nagging. But still, I was never at a loss for words."

"True." He held out a hand to her and she went to him. Leading her to a table with open ledgers, he said, "These are my uncle's breeding charts and pedigrees, but before you delve into them, perhaps you might like to go out to the barns with me and see some of the horses yourself. Also, I thought we might ride in the morning—if you'd like."

"I'd love to." He then led her out the open French-style doors and across the lawn, following a path around the side of the house and down a terraced lawn. Three long buildings lay ahead. Layed out in a large U-shape and built of brick with slate roofs, the buildings were set near each other, yet many yards apart, forming a large stable yard in the center.

"I like the arrangement of the barns." As they approached, she noted the efficient and organized layout. "It's convenient and safe enough in case of fire. You wouldn't have all your livestock in one building, and the structures themselves wouldn't collapse, only the roofs."

"You've a good eye. For that's exactly what happened to my uncle when he first started out—a fire burned the original barn down to the stones. It devastated him. Hay is kept in a separate barn, a safe distance away, and only enough to feed is carried in each night."

He introduced her to his head groom and his stable

manager. Both men welcomed her, and answered her questions. Elise found both men to be very knowledgeable. Soon they were leading forward the stallions, discussing which traits each tended to pass on to their get. In the next barn they saw the mares, some with foals at the side, and again they talked about the select conformation and traits they bred for. In the third building, they saw the end product—two and three year olds. At this stage in their maturity, a horseman with an educated eye could see what well-bred animals these were and estimate with some accuracy how they would finish out.

"Make no mistake, these are not riding horses. They're bred for a ground-covering pace that can be sustained for hours, but not necessarily a smooth one. They're meant for carriages."

"But the pair you had in the park, their backs didn't sway as one would expect with a pacer," she stated. "Are those two intact?"

"Unfortunately, no. They were gelded to make them more manageable in town. Why?"

"Why else does one need a stallion?" She gave him a sly grin. "I was hoping to breed them. As I see it, men have been breeding ladies riding horses for centuries. I thought it was time a knowledgeable lady took matters into her own hands and developed a mount that was pleasing to the eye, comfortable to ride, yet could keep up with the pack in a hunt. So, I've decided to recreate the old-style palfrey, only with more substance and bone than a delicate or hot breed."

"War horse palfreys?" When he began to laugh, she stopped him with a stern look.

"Not at all!"

"A hack, then?"

"I very much dislike that term," she said. "Especially for a horse that is calmer in temperament than the hot-blooded Irish racers that are so popular these days. In truth, more often than not those horses are unsuitable mounts for a lady. Not only unsuitable, but uncomfortable as well. You men don't have to ride perched in a sidesaddle taking all the jarring in the body. You ride astride with a foot in each stirrup using your knees to absorb the motion of the animal in your legs. As society will not allow us to do the same, I thought I'd do something about it."

They returned to the library, and began their discourse of the merits of breeds and cross-breeding of which Michael knew very little. Elise thought it sweet that he pretended interest enough to listen, and did not seem to think any less of her as a lady for her plain-speaking on the subject. More importantly, she'd found her words again. This she could converse about without sounding like a nervous school girl. For *this* was her realm.

After the tour of the barns and gardens, Michael promised to show her the various fields and pastures on their rides during the week. The sun hung just over the western horizon and they turned toward the house. Elise stopped in her tracks, wondering how he was going to explain her presence to his family.

As though sensing her nervousness, Michael said, "You have nothing to fear. You'll see, it will be a quiet week with family."

Elise wished it were as simple as that. Later, she entered the drawing room where Michael said they would gather before dining and found him alone, his sister and her little ones nowhere around. She'd rushed through dressing for dinner for fear of being unforgivably late. Elise drew closer to where he stood near the terrace doors, wine glass in his hand as he stared out upon the graying light of the evening garden.

"I got caught up making some notes and lost track of the time," Elise offered.

"Not to worry. Christina is not down either." He raised his glass to take a sip of his wine.

Just then a footman arrived with a tray, she lifted a glass and sipped the unknown liquid which turned out to be punch. All for the better, she needed to keep her wits about her.

Michael looked at her with soft hazel eyes, which appeared more brown than green in the evening light. He smiled, the subtle act sending a thrill running through her. "What were you making note of?"

"Listing the physical traits of my mares and those of your stallions we saw today." She sipped her punch and debated if she should tell him more. He seemed genuinely interested, so she went on. "I'm thinking of breeding my mares to a few of them, but I want to see your studs move again. This time not on a line like today, but free moving in the fields, under saddle if they are broke to ride, and in the harness. One of the main things I look for is whether the horse is naturally heavy on the forehand, I want a horse that uses his back end properly, and when they are on a line they can be trained to hide that flaw."

He cocked his head and looked at her curiously. "Funny, I remember that old groom you have saying those same words a few years ago at Tatts when he was there looking for some mares."

Elise lowered her eyes. Her entire body grew hot as she felt the shame clear to her toes. She hoped he didn't make the connection that she and Beverly where with Old Ned that day in Hyde Park Corner three years earlier. "Old Ned taught me everything I know. It's only natural that some of his ideas made sense to me and I continue to put them into practice." She sipped from her cup and finished her drink. Then an awkward silence hovered over them. She needed to change the subject so he didn't remember that day with any more detail than he already did.

The footman came for her glass and she refused another. "I wonder where everyone is?" She sounded too chipper, even to herself.

"My sister must be chasing children to bed."

"Not anymore, brother," said the Baroness as she glided into the room, taking the cup the elderly butler filled for her. Michael's sister grinned, her eyes warm and friendly. "The girls wanted to take the kittens to bed with them. At first I wouldn't allow it. Kittens should sleep in the kitchen. But in the end, the girls won out. Sophia had already fallen asleep with one kitten clutched in her arms. I didn't have the heart to disturb her or the kitten."

"Just so you know, those kittens were *her* idea, not mine," Michael teased, pointing at Elise.

"Mother will adore them," the Baroness said reassuringly. "She has a soft-heart for anything furry."

Dinner was announced, and the three of them moved into the dining room. The long, medieval-style table held scars from hundreds of years use, but it was polished to a high sheen and looked to be lovingly maintained. The chairs on the other hand appeared only a mere one hundred years old, having more curves in the back and legs. Michael's sister sat to his left, and Elise to his right.

"I don't seem to remember Mama liking my furry mice when I was a child," said Michael as the footmen delivered the first course and the butler began to fill their wineglasses.

"That's because you were foolish enough to bring them into the house. If you'd left them outside, she'd never have known about them and they likely wouldn't have wound up inside Lady Montague's belly."

At Elise's gasp, Christina clarified, "Lady Montague was mother's cat. A most foul-tempered creature if ever there was one."

"Let's change the subject, shall we?" Michael said. "We don't need to talk about my pet rodents' mortality as dinner is being served."

"All right. So, brother, why the change of plans for mother's birthday? Sabrina and I had matters well in hand for the party to take place at her house in Bath."

"I realized that Ren hadn't been here in many years, and his bride never. He hasn't seen the changes to the place and I wanted to show him my improvements. You know that sunken Turkish bath was his idea. He has one at Haldenwood, complete with hot running water."

"I went to have a peek at it." Christina turned to Elise. "He told me about the bath's construction in his last letter. You should see it, Elise. It's not complete, but the painted tiles are laid and the workers are installing the pipes for hot water. When my husband arrives, I hope to get him to have a look. Hopefully I can convince him to build one for us as well."

"Of course," Michael replied. "Where is your

husband? Off on a mission for the Crown?"

"He wouldn't say. He's been secretive of late, so I assume so. I did send word for him to come here instead of Bath. I expect him later in the week."

"When did you arrive?" Elise wondered how long Michael had planned this change in arrangements and why?

"Michael wanted me here immediately," the Baroness replied. "The girls and I arrived last night and fell directly into our beds. It had been a very long day of travel." She looked at Michael and said, "Your driver grumbled that we would never arrive with all the stops we made."

Interesting, she thought. So this was a last minute change, and to ensure his sister was here at the necessary time, Michael sent his own driver. Elise wondered what prompted this alteration in plan. "When are your mother and sister arriving?" she asked.

"Later in the week," Michael replied.

"Oh, they'll be here sooner than that, I think," his sister said, suddenly finding her plate most interesting.

"I see." Michael's voice clipped, even taut.

"When are your brother and sister-in-law coming, Elise?"

"Tomorrow morning," she replied in between spoonfuls of soup. "Ren had some business to attend to that prolonged their leaving."

"Are they bringing the baby?"

"Yes." Elise grinned. "He's such a good baby, and growing so fast that if they left him behind for a week, they might find him ready for school upon their return."

"So true," Christina said. "I can hardly believe Sophia is five years old now." She turned to Elise, beaming with pride for her children, and said, "It seems like only yesterday, when my oldest, Emily, was born." Looking at her brother, she added, "Speaking of the girls, I promised them you would take them for a ride in the morning."

"Absolutely."

Course after course, their dinner passed in companionable conversation. Stories of their childhood provided insight into how Michael had become the man he was. And Elise had to admit, if that were at all possible, that she loved him even more after today.

She definitely saw a different side to him. One that was unreserved and more open. Well, around her at least. His previous demeanor toward her was understandable as she truly had been a pest in her youth. A topic she very much appreciated went untouched as the evening wore on. She had to remember to thank Michael for not bringing it up.

When dinner was over, they retired to a small adjacent parlor where they might play a hand or two of cards before bed.

"No thank you, I think I shall retire," said Christina, "I still haven't recovered from my grueling day yesterday. Also, your nieces awaken very early. So I'd best recover some of my normal energy."

They each bid his sister good night, and after she left, Michael lowered himself onto the sofa next to Elise and drew a deep sigh.

"Whatever brought that on?" Elise asked.

"I believe she's sent word to my mother to appear sooner than planned. I wonder what she's cooking up. And, before you tell me I'm imagining things, just this morning I received a letter from my mother stating she,

Sabrina and her daughters all planned to arrive Thursday. As I requested."

"Perhaps she simply wanted help with the arrangements for the party. You never did tell me how many people you invited."

"This is a very small affair. We shall host just family—my mother, my older sister Sabrina, her daughters, and Christina with her family. Mother and Sabrina are both widows as you know. Christina's husband, Lawrence, should arrive before Friday. You've met Christina's three girls and Sabrina has two daughters as well: Phillipa is thirteen, named after Sabrina's husband, Phillip, and her youngest Cornelia, is eleven. Phillip died at Waterloo."

Elise nodded, remembering that Lord Knebworth passed during the war. "I'm sorry for your sister's loss."

"We all were. Phillip was a brave and good man. After his death, mother moved in with Sabrina down in Bath to help her with the girls. They seem to all get along very well together, and I see to it they never want for anything. Knebworth wasn't as fortunate as some of us, but he was a good man, brave captain, and loved Sabrina and the girls."

"I just realized something. Your mother has no grandsons."

"Yes, I know. It's a fact she reminds me of with each letter she writes and each time I see her." He stood and went to a game table, opening its drawer and withdrawing a deck of cards. "Shall we?"

She shook her head. "I'm rather enjoying our conversation."

"As am I, but—" He appeared uncomfortable, tugging at his cravat and collar. "Even with the sun having set, it hasn't cooled enough to be comfortable tonight."

"Michael remove the cravat," she asserted. "Yes, it would be scandalous if we were in town, but here there is only you and I, and you have all but announced your intentions to my brother so I see no reason you have to keep that absurd noose around your neck to please people who are not here."

"Thank you," he whispered. "The jacket must go as well. I'm suffocating." He then removed his jacket and tossed in on a chair, untied his cravat and removed it. Lastly, he unbuttoned the top button of his shirt. "I might as well get comfortable." Then he smiled, and Elise was thankful to be seated, or her legs would surely have given way beneath her, so powerful did that simple, appreciative smile strike at her core.

"Would you care for something to drink? A dessert wine perhaps?" He moved to the sideboard and eyed the selection. "My uncle left me an excellent collection in his cellar."

"That would be nice. Is there something light and sweet? Or just port?"

She watched as he scanned the contents of the sideboard. "Ah," he said, holding up a bottle and reading the label. "You are in for a treat." He poured two glasses, and carried them to the sofa, handing her one. "This is an ice wine from Bavaria. It's made from grapes that are intentionally left on the vine to over ripen. Only when they have a certain fungus on the skin are they harvested." He watched her sip from her glass.

"It's very sweet and not too heavy. I like it."

He sat on the opposite end of the sofa, his back leaning against the armrest, facing her. She'd never seen him so relaxed before, even when playing cards with her brother at home. "Timing is critical in harvesting these grapes. The fungus must appear on the skin of the grape at the same time the first frost is predicted. The grapes are then collected after the first frost. The locals in this region of Bavaria call it an ice wine, because the grapes are harvested in the middle of the night, while still frozen."

Elise watched with rapt fascination as his lips touched the rim of the crystal glass he held, and as he sipped. She wanted to kiss them again, to see if his kiss was as wonderful as she remembered, and to taste the flavor of the wine from them. She closed her eyes to shake the image and return to the present. When she opened them and looked at him, she caught the look in his gaze that told her he knew what she was thinking. Feeling.

Through his smile, he asked, "So, what shall we discuss, minx?"

Relaxed, she leaned against the sofa back, and smiled as she took another tiny sip. "I don't know," she replied. Then she thought out loud, "Why do you call me that?"

"It suits you. And I've thought of you as such for so long that it's just natural, I suppose. If you'd like, I shall stop."

"I'm not sure," she said once she'd taken a sip of her wine. "It has some memories attached to it that I'm not fond of. Memories I'd really like to forget."

He laughed, her candor refreshing. "I don't mean it in an uncomplimentary way at all. Please believe me."

Elise swore there was a glimmer of merriment in his hazel eyes. She swallowed deeply. "I'm glad," she whispered. She could only pray he was willing to forget her past mischievous exploits and see her for who she'd become.

"Shall I call you something else? Do you like Kitten?" His gaze took on a devilish gleam. "Or vixen?"

Elise chuckled. "I like kitten. It's harmless and cute."

"Ah, but you're not helpless like a kitten," he said. "Nor are you mean enough to be a vixen. Perhaps I shall call you 'my pet.'"

"Fine!" She didn't intend to say it as loudly as she did. Tempering her voice she added, "You can continue to call me minx. I suppose I should be grateful you don't call me harpy or shrew."

He laughed again, and when he was done, he asked, "How do you feel?"

"Good." She took a deep breath, then a sip of the delicious wine. "Very good, I think." They were playing at verbal seduction, she thought, and he was quite skilled at it. Time stood still for her when he looked at her the way he did. She wished she knew how to proceed because she very much wanted to, though she could never tell him. If he knew of this strong desire she felt for him he might think her forward or flirtatious. Or, heaven forbid, less than virtuous.

"I wish I knew what to do." The words slipped from her mouth before she could stop them. Immediately regretting sounding like a simpleton, she raised the glass and took a sip to keep from speaking so foolishly again.

His eyes softened. "So do I, minx. So do I.

Elise coughed as she swallowed the wine. When she'd settled, she said, "We must not be talking about the same thing because I was counting on you to know about....." Her cheeks burned and not from the wine. She was embarrassed at where her thoughts were going, or that he might know of what she was thinking.

Standing, she replaced her wine glass on the sideboard, intending to excuse herself for the night, before she said or did something she might regret. When she looked back at him, she found Michael standing mere inches from her, his hand reaching for hers. Unable to control her own body's movement, she leaned into him and raised her lips to his.

She was rewarded with his arms enveloping her, sliding down her back to hold her close. Elise touched him and felt the warmth of his body against hers. His bare hands roved over her back, and when they reached her equally bare arms it sent heated rivulets of passion coursing through her. He broke the kiss, and unaware of the consequences she tilted her head back for a breath. Only to feel his warm mouth come down on the exposed flesh of her neck. She moaned, her pleasure encouraging his further sensual onslaught. She felt Michael's tongue flick out and trace a path on the side of her neck, causing her to shiver in his embrace. His kisses left her breathing ragged. She couldn't think. Couldn't feel anything but the passion between them.

"I know what you meant," he whispered, his chest rose and fell as would a man who'd run for miles after a horse. Did *she* do that to him? "And I don't think I will have a problem satisfying you when the time comes."

She sighed as she looked up into his darkened eyes. "Michael, I don't want this to end. Not tonight. Not ever."

"It cannot go much further than this—not tonight."

"But can we stay together for a while longer? After

your family and mine arrive, we will have no time alone."

He nodded, then brought her with him to the sofa. Positioning himself with his back on the arm rest and swung his feet up on the seat. This brought her to lie casually over him, and she let herself melt into his form as she pressed her lips to his. His hands molded her body close, and through their clothing she felt his hard body tremble. Suddenly she had the insane desire to taste him, all of him, so she kissed him deeper, touching his firm lips lightly with her tongue.

He tore away breaking the kiss, his eyes wide. She thought she'd done something inappropriate. "I'm sorry. I didn't mean to shock you. It won't happen again."

He chuckled, causing relief to wash over her. "Where did you learn that, minx?"

She smiled. "I read it in a book once and have been waiting ages to *'taste the nectar of your lips,'* or the other one, *'delve into the honeyed recess of your mouth.'"*

"They actually write that bawdy drivel in books young ladies read? When I return to work, I shall have to introduce a censorship bill to protect the modesty and chastity of our future generations."

If it weren't for the laughter in his voice, she might have thought him serious, and that would have truly raised her ire. "You wouldn't! Think of all the... *inspired* young ladies out there who will be disappointed if they could no longer read of Lady M's flirtation with Lord N. Why, a full half the population of this country would revolt. We would riot!" She stared into his amused hazel eyes, with her serious ones. "Think on this Lord Camden. If you did such a thing, you can bet that I'd be leading the charge on Parliament. I and every one of my friends. Why...."

He put his hand behind her neck, drew her down and kissed her. Elise stretched her fingers out across Michael's chest and felt his muscles quiver as they roamed over him. All the while his mouth slid over hers. She felt his thumb caress her jaw, coming to rest on her chin, and with the slightest of pressure, he opened her up to him, and Elise couldn't believe the response his action elicited in her. All of the sudden her entire body grew warmer and she felt an intense desire to get as close to this man as she could, in ways she knew were scandalous outside of marriage. A strange stirring in her womb grew, causing her core to grow moist. She trembled again.

Her tongue reached forward and touched his, and his hands pulled her hips closer to him. His arousal was becoming evident as he held her this way, and suddenly she knew. She wanted to meld with him, become one with him, to feel him on her, over her, inside her.

Being with him felt... glorious. All of her life it seemed, she'd known it would be this way with Michael. She didn't know how she knew, she just did. Something inside warned her to be careful of what might happen. But the bigger part reminded her that *this* was what she'd always wanted. *He* was the man she'd dreamed of, the man she'd shed innumerable tears over, for more years than she cared to remember.

She rested her head on his chest, struggling to collect her breath and her thoughts. His strong heartbeat pulsed beneath her cheek as she inhaled his masculine woodsy scent. She wanted everything with him. She wanted him in every way a woman could have a man. Now.

"I want...." Her voice sounded labored, strained, even to her own ears. She cleared her throat, and tried again. "I want you. Michael, I want you, but I don't know what to do."

"I want you too, minx" he said softly, his warm breath dancing in the hair behind her ear. "I do."

"You want me?" Elise looked into his eyes and thought she saw her love returned. It left her with a little trepidation, almost as though she needed to be pinched. She could hardly believe she finally won the affection and love of her heart's desire.

He smiled, and in the dim light of the room, she saw her affection for him mirrored in his warm gaze. "Yes. As crazy as it may seem to everyone else—hell, even to me—I want you, too."

"Then help me, Michael," she pleaded. "Show me how to love you."

"Not yet, minx." He shifted her over to the side and straightened slightly. "We cannot just yet."

Confusion grounded her soaring spirits. He wanted her, yet he was rejecting her when she offered herself to him. "Why?"

"Because we have much to discuss."

"Can't we discuss it later?" Her heart was pleading with him not to reject her when everything was finally so perfect for them.

He shook his head. "You have no idea how difficult it is for me to do this, but we must maintain all the proprieties. For the time being. Things, events, have to proceed in order, so that gossip does not taint you, darling."

"Do you think I have ever cared one whit about gossip?"

"I know you don't, but I have to, and I promised your brother I would protect you and care for you."

Deflated, she rested her head on him again.

"I've thought this out, Elise, and if you will listen to what I propose, you'll see the soundness of it." When she didn't respond, he began, "You need to complete your season unencumbered. Much as it pains me, you must know for certain that *I* am the one you want to tie yourself to."

"I can't believe I'm hearing this."

"Let me continue, please."

She closed her eyes and gave him a slight nod. Even though patience was never a trait she possessed in much quantity, she knew she had to at least hear his reasons, as much as it hurt her to do so.

"In August, we will publicly announce our plans to wed, and we can be married shortly thereafter. Either by special license or have the banns read and have a traditional wedding. Whichever you choose."

"But that's months away! Michael, I want you now, today, this minute. How can you make us wait that long?"

He gave her an odd look, almost as though he appeared pained. "Uncle may have been ill for years, but he's only been dead a few weeks. My family is still in mourning, and proprieties must be observed. There are others to think of here. By mid-August, my family will officially be out of mourning. I thought to have a small celebration toasting our engagement in London. We can marry immediately after if you'd like." Upon seeing the look of disappointment on her face he added, "A couple of months is not that difficult to manage. And I promised your brother that I would not harm you during this time. Understood? So, despite to what you think you want, we will wait until after the wedding to share a bed."

He was rejecting her because of her brother. Turning away the offer of making love with her, when it was the only thing her body and her heart desired. "Damn him!" She raised off him, stood and began to pace the room. "Damn him, and damn you as well for your loyalty to that tyrannical, dictatorial brother of mine. Will you allow him to dictate to you after we wed?"

"He is not dictating anything to me, Elise. I arrived at this arrangement on my own and informed *him* of what I intend. But, your brother is no fool. He saw what was happening right before his eyes. He just couldn't believe what he was seeing. Why do you think he allowed us this opportunity?"

She knew he was right, had even suspected as much. He came up behind her and turned her to him. And suddenly she knew. The desire in his eyes told her. He was holding himself back for her.

"I know you feel this way now, but one day you'll see the wisdom of what I ask *of us*. It's only two months, Elise. We can manage." His stressed words confirmed that this was no easier on him than it was on her.

"I'm frustrated and angry. Partly with you, but mostly with myself." She swiped a tear, and sucked in a deep breath and held it, forcing the rest of them away. "I'm ashamed of myself that I forgot you are in mourning. I am also angry with you, Michael. You have come to this conclusion without consulting me at all. It seems that you and my brother arranged everything this morning. And *now* you see fit to dictate your plans to me, not earlier in the carriage, not while we were walking through the barns, but now.

"Michael, you have given no consideration as to how I would feel about any of this. In your usual authoritative manner, you dictated and expected me to blindly agree. Well, I don't." She quit pacing and thrust her hands on her hips, wanting to explain to him further why she was angry, but her emotions were becoming so jumbled inside that all she could see was his rejection. Rejection, and choosing to live by this silly code of honor. He wanted her as well, she could feel it, yet he would choose honor over their desire.

She would not cry. Would. Not. Cry.

"I... I..." She stuttered. Something she hadn't done in years. "Goodnight." As she turned to flee the room her eyes were beginning to swim in tears and she tripped over a chair. Michael was at her side in one leap, keeping her from falling.

"You think it's easy for me?" He held her close, her back to him. She felt him press his lips to the top of her head as she melted into him. "Since realizing I want you, I have had to justify my change of heart not only to myself but also to your brother who is your guardian whether you like it or not." His hands roved upward from her waist, to cup and mold themselves to her breasts. "I want you so badly I hurt." Her skin shivered as his hot breath moved down to her ear, then her neck which she stretched to give him easier access to her naked flesh.

He took her hand and pressed it on his engorged member. "That's what you do to me, and I can do nothing about it. So you're not the only one left with unfulfilled desires." Elise felt a tremor of fear and excitement course through her to pool in the area between her legs. She knew about the act of mating as it pertained to her horses, as she'd witnessed it many times before. With animals it often was a violent act, where the mare sometimes got bit and the stallion kicked.

But this didn't feel violent at all. It felt wonderful, brilliant and... illicit, which gave it that air of arousing wickedness. She wondered if it would be the same powerful and life-affirming event she'd witness in the stallion barn at home.

"I'm sorry. I don't mean to bring you discomfort or pain." She attempted to run from him, flee the room for the safety of her own so she could cry.

"Don't go like this, Elise." He wiped a tear with his thumb and she rested her head in his hand. "I don't want you to leave upset."

"Michael, I need you. I feel...." She couldn't tell him what she felt because he might think her depraved and wanton. Unworthy of him.

"Tell me what you feel," he whispered as one of his hands reached lower to cup her where she ached. "I will try to help you."

She shook her head, afraid of confessing the sensations he elicited in her.

"Tell me what you want Elise." His hand moved over her and her bottom backed into his erection like a ready broodmare. "I cannot give you what you do not ask for."

"I ache." She panted, unable to catch a deep breath. "Inside, Michael. Please, I want you inside me so badly I ache."

He groaned, and turned her in his arms so she faced

him. "As painful as my condition is, I will not lay with you until we are wed." She opened her mouth to protest, but he stopped her. "On that I will not compromise, Elise." She started to pull away from him, to leave him, but he wouldn't let her go. "But I *can* give you the release you're so desperate for, without entering you. Is that what you'd like?"

Unable to speak, she nodded her head. "My body wants whatever you're willing to give."

As he held her gaze, he led her back to the sofa, laid her down on it, and covered her body with his. He took her lips in a kiss he intended to be sweet and coaxing, instead she opened for him and offered herself to him unreservedly and with an intense passion that belied her innocence.

She tasted of sunshine and lavender and the combination drove him insane with desire. She burned through his veins like a fire through a tinder box, threatening to ignite his very soul. He skimmed one hand down her skirts, over the slender leg beneath, to the hem. Then he slowly slid the muslin up to find pantalettes that buttoned below the knee. Roaming upward toward her hip and waist, he reached the ribbon that held the garment in place and with a gentle tug, he had the waist band loosened.

"Raise your hips," he said, wishing to rid her of the offending garment keeping him from giving her what she wanted. When she did, he removed her drawers so it would be easier for him to pleasure her. He slid the soft material down over her stockinged legs, and to protect her modesty, did all this without raising the skirts above her knees.

All he wanted to do now was to touch her. To rouse her to passion with his mouth, bringing her to the pinnacle of ecstasy while pressing into her with his fingers. He wanted to feel her tight passage grip him as she climaxed.

But he had to go slow. For her sake. Even though she had a passion that rivaled that of a wanton mistress, he knew she was still an untried virgin. He wondered what madness had come over him that would make him agree to such foolishness, for his restraint took effort of supreme proportions.

Michael kissed her lips again, this time tasting the wine she'd had. It was sweet and earthy. Like her. He loved the soft little mewling sounds she made as he moved his lips and tongue down the column of her throat feeling the racing pulse throbbing there.

His heart beat faster because of her, and that she felt the same amazed him. Elise reinvigorated in him the desire for sex he'd thought himself past prime for. Especially as his last mistress left him almost two months earlier saying he was boring. It had been a cut to his manhood, and he'd since been without a woman these past weeks.

Before Elise, sex was about getting the release he needed and paying his mistresses' bills to keep them interested in satisfying him. But this feeling? This was unlike anything he'd ever experienced. Ironic that, until recently, he'd had some of the most talented and eager mistresses his money could buy, and he'd never before cared so much about a woman's pleasure as he did now—with Elise. This had to be love, or he wouldn't be about to pleasure her knowing there was only a fist waiting for him when he got back to his room.

The lavender scent of her soap enticed him, and while he kissed the soft skin of her neck, he eased the bodice down to expose her small, perfect breasts. Glancing up at her, he saw her eyes were closed and she appeared to concentrate on the sensations he caused for her.

Her tight, pert nipples beckoned his mouth. So as not to frighten her, he placed soft kisses at the tops of her exquisite breasts, then rest his cheek over her heart, feeling it race beneath him. She was frightened, he could feel it, but knowing this woman as he did, he knew she was more curious than afraid. Michael moved to take one sweet, ruched tip between his his lips where he circled it with his tongue and drew on it softly. She groaned as he moved to the other and did the same.

He wished he had her sprawled naked on his bed, and that these damnable garments weren't between them. One day, he told himself as his hand traveled down over the curve of her hip, the layers of material keeping his hand from feeling the fire in her skin. One day soon he'd have her as he wanted to have her.

As he suckled he slid his hand up the inside of her leg. When he reached the skin above her stockings, she sucked in a breath.

"Michael?" She looked at him with a mix of desperation and confusion.

"Do you want me to stop?" His thumb stroked the tender flesh of her inner thigh, hoping to persuade her to let him continue. He wanted more than anything to ease her desperation tonight. And he couldn't wait for the day he would show her what they could do together.

"No. I want to know...." Her head fell back and she moaned when his fingers found her curls.

It worked. Her legs fell open for him, and as his mouth loved her breasts, his fingers parted her flesh, and found the slick, aroused treasure hidden within.

She was so very wet, ready, and wanting him. If she were any other woman, he would free himself from his breeches and take what she offered. But she wasn't just any other woman. This was Elise.

He wanted to savor her, wanted her first climax to come from this most intimate kiss. It would be his gift to her for agreeing to wait to consummate their relationship. If he weren't in mourning, and if he didn't want to give her every young girl's dream wedding, he'd get a special license and marry her tonight.

He broke the kiss and lowered himself to her breasts again, and after loving them for just a moment, he moved lower still. When he pushed her skirts up, she gave a soft squeal.

"Shh... You will enjoy this, Elise. I promise." He nibbled and traced his lips up the tender flesh of her thighs, her musk intoxicating him more than a bottle of the rarest wine. His fingers parted her and he placed his lips on her tender flesh.

Shocked, Elise tried to back away from him but his hand held her in place. She cried out on a breathless whisper, "Michael!"

"Shh, minx," he said. "Relax for me."

He began to stroke her with his tongue forcing a moan from her. Her soft voice energized him, and when her body began to tense under his hand, he slid two fingers into her and felt her grip bear down on them. God, how he wished he were inside her. He hated waiting, but there was a lifetime for loving each other ahead of them.

Then he felt her whole body quiver, and Michael broke away, continuing to stroke her with his thumb as his fingers moved within her, and he watched the gloriousness of her as she climaxed.

Awareness of her first orgasm blossomed in her beautiful eyes like a tree coming into new leaf in the spring, vibrant and lush and full of exciting sensations. It was all hers. And she was all his. She would never share this with another.

Tremors shook her slight frame, as wave after wave of pleasure coursed through her and he ceased moving his fingers, holding her. When she backed away from his hand, he watched as she tried to slow her breathing. He raised himself over her and kissed her, then held her close for a long while until she recovered enough to speak.

"Oh, Michael," she whispered. "That was... beautiful."

He smiled in the candle-lit drawing room. "I thought so too, minx," he said trying to calm his own racing heart.

As the young couple left the parlor and wend their way up the stairs to seek their beds, a faithful old retainer standing in the shadows of the upstairs portrait gallery smiled at their backs. This, he would tell the rest of the staff later, was the next Countess Camden, come home to Woodhenge.

Chapter Eleven

The next morning, Elise was up before the rest of the household stirred. Not that she'd slept much. All night she'd relived the extraordinary events of the past evening. She'd hardly slept a wink reliving the sensations, the emotions, the utter magnificence of the act they shared. When Lia arrived, Elise would have to ask if she could speak to her privately. Her sister-in-law had mentioned before that if Elise wanted or needed certain information, Lia would be more than happy to share with her what she knew.

Elise hoped if such information went so far as these intimacies.

As she remembered the evening she again grew angry with herself. She was beyond embarrassed to have forgotten his family was in mourning. In her selfishness she'd pressed him to marry as quickly as possible because of *her* feelings for *him*. She should have remembered his family was mourning the old earl. How could she have said what she had?

Oh, heaven! Elise remembered Michael's gentle touches and intimate kisses and blushed. She'd always prayed that one day Michael might love her one day. But now she knew beyond all doubt that he loved her. If that wasn't love she didn't know what was.

Those were the thoughts racing through her head as she headed down to the stables under the brightening sky. She intended to find a spirited horse and tear across the fields in pursuit of answers. She always found answers on horseback.

Elise strode into the main barn, looking for a groom. Spying one lad mucking a stall, she introduced herself and, after he got over the initial shock of her breeches, boots and fitted riding jacket, she asked him about the available mounts. She told the lad she wanted something with spirit, perhaps in need of schooling. The boy led her to a stall with a big gray filly who stood quietly tied and appeared freshly groomed.

"She ain't been worked yet," the freckle-faced lad said. "I was just abou' to get 'er tacked and work 'er."

"Wonderful! I shall school her."

He looked at Elise and asked, "Ye sure ye want te? She don' know much."

Elise put her hand before the filly's nostrils and let the animal sniff. She then stroked the filly's forehead, then chest, moved to the side, over her neck, and up to her ears. When the filly didn't flinch at her touch on her ears, Elise smiled.

"Good girl," she whispered. "We shall have fun today, you and I." She continued running her hands along the animal's body, wondering about her barn training. The mare appeared well-handled and gave her feet readily. She didn't appear to have any swelling or deformities that might preclude a vigorous workout, so Elise turned back to the groom, and they began to discuss the mare's training to date under saddle. She asked for the mare's bridle, and when the lad handed it to her, she asked for a different bit. Elise preferred something easier on a young horse's delicate mouth for schooling. What the filly needed was guidance and training, not punishment for misunderstanding cues.

The young mare snorted, then pawed the ground in anticipation of exercise.

While she was fitting the bridle to the gray, the lad returned with a lady's saddle. Elise had him take it back. "I won't need one," she said, buckling the cheek piece. "I'll start with her in the paddock and once she's responding to me, you can open the gate and we'll go out for a run."

Taking the reins, Elise led the mare to the center of the paddock where the horse wouldn't get the feeling of being cornered, which could be scary to a young animal. After working with the mare a few minutes on some of what Elise thought to be the basics, she lifted the reins over the horse's head. Then grabbed a handful of mane and rein, and started tugging, getting the horse acclimated to the pressure. She jumped up and down a few times at the beast's side, and once she'd determined the mare was ready, stood at the sloped shoulder, and threw herself over the mare's back, laying over her as the filly began to take a few steps. Elise spoke calmly to her, and with pressure on the reins, asked her to stop. When the horse quit moving, Elise dropped the reins, maintaining hold of the filly's mane. Elise dropped to the ground.

"No one has been on your back like this, have they?" She cooed to the filly. "Well my sweet girl, you are in for a treat."

She repeated the procedure for several minutes, until finally she threw her leg over the animal's back. Once she'd adjusted her position, she cued the mare to walk forward. The horse took a hesitant step, then two, each time stopping when asked. Elise beamed, thrilled at the animal's quick learning.

"Lor! Would ye look at that?" A second boy arrived at the rail to watch.

"Shh. The lady asked that we not move sudden-like or talk too loud," the first boy replied.

Within minutes Elise had the horse turning left and right, walking and stopping, then trotting and stopping with only the barest shift in her seat and leg pressure. The animal had a nice, comfortable trot. Elise wanted to canter now but the paddock was really too small, so she motioned to the lad to open the gate. Three boys now stood at the rail, watching. She asked the mare to walk through, and out into the yard. The mare bolted through, heading for freedom. Elise stopped her quickly by pulling her into a tight circle before the horse gathered too much forward momentum, then brought the mare back into the paddock. They spent more time walking and stopping, walking and stopping. When she was ready, she asked the lad to once again open the gate. This time, rather than walk through the gate, Elise continued to walk and stop in the paddock, while the gate remained open. Only when Elise thought the mare would behave would she ask the mare to walk through, slowly and obediently.

"Just because the gate is opened does not mean you have to bolt through it. It is far more polite for a young lady to gracefully walk through the gate. It is as my finishing governess tried to instill in me," Elise chuckled as she pat the horses neck. "Ugh. I can hear that woman now. Though in this regard she was correct." She pointed the mare in the direction of the gate and cued the mare to walk in a nice relaxed pace.

Beautiful, Elise thought as she made it through the gate without the horse bolting out into the open. The animal was turning out to be more responsive than she'd first understood from her talk with the stable lad. She stopped and started the mare several times in the stable yard, then once in the open field, she did it again at the walk and trot. On prompting her into the canter, the mare gave several bucks, not understanding what her rider wanted. Elise sat through them, pushing her forward with her seat and soon the horse moved into a wonderful rolling gait. With proper training, the gray would become a lovely hunter once she matured.

Wanting to feel the wind in her face and hair, Elise asked the mare to move a little faster as she let the animal have her head.

Unable to lie in bed any longer, Michael dressed and went to the stable to arrange for mounts to be readied for the promised ride with the children. It was still early, and he doubted Elise or the children were up and about yet. He decided he'd get his ride out of the way, then work on some paperwork before they breakfasted. He had to keep busy or he'd think about last night. Again.

Strolling through the main barn, he didn't see anyone about and wondered where everyone was. Normally there would be lads mucking out, bedding stalls and conditioning leather—all the chores of maintaining a proper stable. He heard voices behind the barn and followed the sound, and saw the lads all watching a rider far off in the field. When he reached the fence rail of the practice field, he stopped and watched the training session along with the others. He noted the skill with which the rider managed one of the young horses. The lad had amazing balance for such a gangly youth, and said as much to the hands nearby.

"That's no lad, my lord," said one youth. "That's a girl! And she's really good. You should've seen her swing on that mare's back from the ground, then sit the fits the mare threw at her. Just wrapped her legs about the filly and held on like one o' us!"

Michael's breath froze in his chest. He only knew of one 'girl' who could or would do such a thing. *Damn her hide.* What was she thinking? She'd break her neck! All he could do was watch as she galloped across the fields, leaning forward over the mare's neck, her long legs wrapped around the beast, racing the wind.

And winning.

She slowed to a canter and turned the mare easily, changing leads several times with cues from her seat and legs. As if she sensed his presence, she looked directly at him and smiled a broad, radiant, beatific grin. Slowing to a trot which she sat with the practiced ease of a riding master, she led the mare to the rail.

"Good morning!" Her eyes sparkled with excitement. "The day promises to be wonderful."

"Get down from that beast right now," he said with barely controlled rage. She could so easily have come off the horse, been horrifically injured, or even killed. He'd been afraid from the moment he recognized it was her on the mare.

"And good morning to you, too, Elise," she replied, her grin changing quickly to a sneer. Then she continued to mock him as she imitated his autocratic voice. "I see you've started out your day in your favorite pastime. Tell me, Elise, how does the mare go?"

"Don't get impudent with me, Elise," he ordered, wanting nothing more than to take her over his knee. "You could've broken your neck. Or worse."

At the booming anger in his voice, the filly began to step sideways away from the fence. "Temper your voice, Michael, you're making the mare nervous. And, no I couldn't have gotten hurt. This spirited mare is wonderfully responsive and a joy to ride."

"You could have fallen."

"And so? I would have fallen. I know how to fall, Michael. I've done so more times than I care to count."

"Get off that horse."

"I will when *I'm* ready. Not because *you* want me off or the *horse* wants me off, that's for certain. It wouldn't be good for her training." She walked the mare forward, then backed her away from the rail, turned her away and cued her to canter across the field again. Then she disappeared onto the trail leading into the woods.

He called for a boy to bring him his gelding and to be quick about it. Within minutes, he was following behind her. Hopefully she had the sense to slow down. He didn't see her, and his heart hammered inside him as he looked ahead for some sign of a fallen rider or riderless horse. There was none.

When he reached the wooden bridge crossing the creek, he stopped. Elise stood at the creek with the mare's reins in hand, allowing it to drink. He leaped from the saddle and went to her, crushing her to him, to reassure himself she was indeed in one piece.

She turned her face to his and opened her mouth to say something. He silenced her with a bruising kiss. He intended to punish her, to teach her not to take lightly his feelings, especially when it concerned herself. But when her free hand wrapped around his neck, he became the one reprimanded. When she returned his fear and anger-filled kiss measure for measure, he understood. The things he wanted to discipline her for were the very qualities he adored about her—her passion for living, and her unconventional independence of spirit and mind.

He was falling in love with her. And that was why he was so frightened for her.

His hand roved lower and when he felt her bottom covered in leather breeches, he remembered this bit of unconventionality, too. Breaking the kiss, he looked into her face and stated flatly, "You are never to ride out like this again, understood?"

"No, Michael, I don't understand," she retorted. "Do you mean me taking a horse from your barn without asking you? Or not using a saddle? Or is it my wearing leather breeches? Because I have a very good reason for all of these, if you would care to hear them."

"I don't want to hear any excuses you may have. You are not ever to do these things again. You could have killed yourself."

"Michael, I've been riding since I could walk. And riding *astride* for nearly as long. These breeches are made to my specification for exactly what I do. They provide better grip on horses' backs than a saddle does. The horses seem to like it, too. They feel my seat and leg cues more clearly, thus understanding comes easier. I've found when training a horse, the most common mistake the human makes is not being clear in his or her requests. Once the horse understands what I am asking,

I reintroduce each cue from the saddle and their learning proceeds in a less complicated, more natural way."

He stood there, stunned speechless. "I never knew...."

"Michael, you've ridden horses I've trained at Haldenwood. Your chestnut in town, Attila, I trained him for *you,* Michael, because you'd shown interest in him."

That was the horse Ren had refused to sell him because he'd originally wanted it for his own. While his friend was in Morocco, the Caversham groom had sold him the horse, saying his master decided to sell the horse before he sailed.

He groaned with sudden realization. "That was you with Old Ned at Monument Corner the day of the sale."

It wasn't a question, rather an observation made several years too late. Elise just nodded. As she did, his heart fell. Understanding slowly dawned and it both relieved him and angered him. Relieved that she obviously was more skilled than he'd ever known, and angered because this information was kept from him, though he understood why Ren did so. If the society matrons knew this about her, it could ruin her. Ladies simply did not ride astride, most especially without the use of a saddle.

Michael remembered how quiet and obedient Attila was, and gave up, deflated, his last argument nullified.

"Michael, Ren will tell you, that I'm good at what I do. In fact, I'm surprised he never has."

"Perhaps it's because he thought to protect your reputation."

"Poppycock! No one pays a bit of attention to me or what I do. Why, I believe that until Marcus' christening, half the *ton* didn't even know I existed."

"You've been allowed free rein too long, Elise." His voice sounded weary, even to himself. He feared first for her safety, then for her being shunned by society. "Now you must think about your future and the future of our children. Your eccentric ways need tempering. I'm not saying you have to stop doing the things you love and being the vivacious young woman you are, but...." His voice was strained. Pained even. "I know what it is like to grow up in the shadow of scandal. It isn't something I'd wish for our children."

Elise's brows came together as she squeezed her eyes shut. In the silence, Michael could see she struggled with some decision, as she was quiet for a moment. She heaved a deep, shaky sigh before turning those beautiful golden-brown eyes up to him. "I might be willing to concede to some of your points, but only while in town. When I am at home, in the country, I will continue as I have. It's what I *do*, Michael. I don't *know* anything else. I'm easily bored indoors. I'm hopeless at the pianoforte, I've tried. I also cannot sing or paint watercolors. And if that isn't enough, my embroidery skills are wretched." She wiped at something on her cheek and sighed. "So I suggest that if those are qualities you seek in a wife, then you need look elsewhere, because I can't fulfill your requirements."

If he ordered her to not to ride astride or wear breeches, she would only disobey him. With a sigh, he said, "Never in town and only when I am with you. Agreed?"

She was silent, refusing to acquiesce. Well, he didn't care if she agreed or not. He was doing this for her own good.

"Also, please refrain from this behavior while my mother is here. I want her to think you a perfect countess—not judge you as too young and impulsive."

A rumbling in his stomach reminded him they'd missed breakfast. "Let's get back. I'm hungry."

Rather than ride, they walked back to the barns, giving both of them time to collect themselves before running into the children or his sister.

After they breakfasted, Elise and Michael took the children for a ride in the field behind the main barn where she'd ridden earlier. Elise was surprised to learn that the two older girls had their own ponies at Woodhenge, a gift from their Uncle, with little Sophia holding fast to a promise that he would get her a pony of her own as soon as her mother said she was old enough. When Sophia realized she would not be able to ride alone today, but only seated in front of her Uncle or Elise, she began to cry and ask to go back to the house. Her sisters were willing to let her leave, rather than include their youngest sibling. So Elise shared a secret with Sophia, then took the little one by the hand and went back into the barn. They returned a few minutes later with an aged gelding devoid of saddle. Elise had also removed her skirt, and was again in her breeches.

"Once I'm up, lift your arms to me, Sophia."

Michael trotted up, intending to stop her, afraid his niece would get injured.

"Nonsense, I've done this for years with my own sister, and Lucky too," she said. "Watch her, Michael. Her face will light up when she believes she's the one in control of the horse. Believe me, she'll enjoy herself so much, we'll have a hard time getting her off the horse.

Even better, her sisters will be envious."

"If she falls, Christina will...."

"My arms will be around her, and I will be in control of the horse the entire time," she reassured. "Now, please do your part and keep the other two away from us for a few minutes."

She felt his eyes bore into her as she swung onto the gelding's back, then easily lifted his niece, setting the child in front of her. She spoke to Sophia and as she did, she walked the horse around in small circles. Once the girl was comfortable, Elise handed the reins over to Sophia and allowed her to 'steer' the horse.

What Sophia didn't know and couldn't have known, was that Elise was in control the entire time, effectively using her body to guide the horse in the directions Sophia wanted to go. After twenty or so minutes, she even had Sophia drop the reins and hold her arms out to her side.

The child giggled as she learned to keep her balance without Elise holding onto her. The little one was a wonderful pupil, she thought. One day, she and Michael would have children and she'd teach them the same way she taught Sarah, Lucky, the other children at Haldenwood, and now Sophia.

They went to the far end of the field where Michael rode with Sophia's sisters. Elise met his gaze and returned his smile. His look sent a warm shiver coursing through her. She thought of the night before and decided she couldn't wait for the day she could ride like this with their sons and daughters.

"Look at me, Uncle! No hands!" The child held her arms out and so did Elise, mimicking the actions of the little one in front of her.

Michael knew that at any moment the animal could spook and they might both be hurt, which was the root of his worry. Horses at best were controlled energy on four feet, at worst uncontrollable and dangerous killers. They were livestock one used to get from one place to another, sometimes in a fashionable manner.

During the past few hours, he'd learned what an excellent horsewoman she was, and his respect for her was growing, still he worried for her safety. Now that he realized he cared for her deeply, he didn't want to think of the possibility of losing her.

He hated this helpless feeling as he realized he was falling in love with her.

And it was love, without a doubt. The foundation was there. He was attracted to her as he'd never been attracted to a woman before. His respect for her grew by the hour. Not just as an equestrienne because it was obvious she was talented just from witnessing what he had this morning. But he respected her as a woman, one who was strong enough to stand up to him and to her brother. She was a woman accustomed to doing the conventional in an unconventional way, to traveling her own path to happiness, never deviating from what she loved most, and did so uncaring of what others thought of her.

She was untouched by the pretensions of society and hadn't learned how to feign the look of interested boredom so often seen in the women of his crowd. Her genuine mien, always honest and straightforward, never left you to guess where you stood with her. And he loved that about her. He didn't want her tainted by the artificial games played by those considered his peers.

Mother. His mother would arrive soon. He didn't

know when, for Christina hadn't said. But mother, along with Sabrina and her girls would soon descend on Woodhenge and he hoped to have Elise prepared for them.

He watched her come toward them, her arms now wrapped around Sophia. His niece held her arms out to her sides, showing off in front of her older sisters. But he didn't concern himself with what the children were thinking. He watched Elise, the graceful way she sat this horse, and the one from this morning, as though each mount were an extension of her.

"Hello." Elise stopped the horse and dismounted, leaving Sophia sitting atop its back.

He motioned to the stable lads to come forward as he dismounted his horse. "Hello yourself, minx," he said as he handed his horse off to one of the boys, and another began to lead Sophia around the field.

"You looked far away. Might I hope I was in those thoughts?"

"You were, my lady." They watched the girls ride in the small corner of the field, keeping an especially close eye on Sophia, though they were never out of reach of the girls should they need help. "You handled the children very well and my respect and admiration for your skill has increased ten-fold."

Her cheeks pinked, and she lowered her gaze. "Don't be the blushing miss now! You've proved to me how wrong I was this morning. I acknowledge your incredible skill."

She scraped a booted toe in the dirt. "Thank you."

"You're welcome." After a moment's silence, he said, "Elise, we are soon to be joined by my family and yours. Some of these people we love will have a hard time understanding what has occurred between us."

"Like my brother."

"No. Worse. My mother." He hoped his mother accepted Elise as his choice for a bride. She was the person he most feared not accepting Elise into the family.

"I see." She glanced his way then turned back to the children. "What does she know about me? About what I've done in the past?"

"I've never told her about your antics, but somehow she always found out. She was friends with your mother, and she's stayed in contact with your godmothers all these years. Perhaps in their letters they informed my mother of your continued affections."

"Wonderful," she muttered. "She's never, ever liked me you know. Ever since...." Elise leaned back against the stone fence, and closed her eyes, wondering if he knew what had happened. "Ever since I fell out of the tree and landed on her."

"What?"

Shifting uncomfortably, Elise couldn't face him so she stared at her foot as the toe of her boot scraped dirt. "You should probably know that I was the one who knocked your mother down, ruining her dress at Papa and Amelia's wedding. Of course I ruined my own as it snagged a limb and ripped. If your mother hadn't broken my fall I could have been seriously injured. I was pretty high up."

"She never said it was you," Michael whispered as she nodded. "And I always assumed the child of a servant bumped into her and ran off in fear."

"I told her who I was. She was very cross with me Michael, and rightfully so. Though I apologized profusely, she still told Papa, who swatted my bottom then punished me for a month afterward. I was not allowed to leave the nursery at all. I could not ride, could not fish...."

"Oh, but you did. You even hid my horse from me the morning a group of us were going into the village to shop."

Elise turned a bright shade of pink and looked away. "They could never keep me in if I didn't want to stay punished. Please understand Michael, this was after I'd heard you tell Ren what you wanted in an ideal wife." Elise covered her face with her hands. "Even then I felt you were describing me."

Michael watched the children riding, and the groom leading an indignant Sophia, who insisted she could ride by herself now. He smiled, wanting several just like her one day. "After the trellis incident, Mother suggested that I stay away from Haldenwood for a while, to give you time to grow out of your girlish infatuation." Elise groaned. "She means well." He turned to face her, hoping to make her understand his mother's position. "While she wants me to be happy, the specter of an old scandal and what it did to my uncle is not lost on her. My uncle loved an unfaithful woman. She cuckolded him while he was on the continent. He never got over it, nor spoke of it the rest of his days. I'm afraid she might see our relationship as a mirror of that one."

"I am not her, Michael," Elise insisted, "and you are not your uncle."

"If mother were to see you as I did this morning, her opinion would not change. In face, it would only worsen." He spoke frankly, adding, "I don't want her to think I'm taking an impulsive, over-indulged hoyden to bride. Elise, you are so much more than that. I know this. Please, let mother see the compassionate, intelligent woman you've become, not the child you were. It will go a long way toward making our future a peaceful one."

She leaned up and pressed a quick kiss on his cheek, and Michael could have sworn his heart stopped a few beats. Elise backed away and looked up at him from a safe distance, in case the children were watching them. "I will do as you ask because I love you, Michael. I have always loved you, and always will."

"Thank you," he said.

"I am surprised anyone who knew me could imagine that I would be unfaithful to you. Much as I've tried to keep it a secret, everyone in my family knows that you have been my heart's *only* desire my entire life." He wanted to wrap his arms around her and kiss her, but couldn't because of the children and stable staff within sight. "I just wish it hadn't taken you so long to feel the same way."

"Elise, if I'd done anything any sooner, I'd be one of the worst sort of lechers." He relaxed, feeling more optimistic about their arrangement. Leaning back against a stone post, he pulled a long blade of grass from next to his booted foot and put it in his mouth. "I still feel... *odd* about this. Though I'm sure in time I will get over it."

Elise heaved a sigh and started walking toward the gate. As her breech-clad bottom swayed, she looked over her shoulder at him and said, "Nothing about last night felt odd to me, Michael. In fact, it felt very right and beautiful. So I suggest you get over this reservation your having. And soon."

He groaned as he felt his cock stir. Michael strode after her, catching up to her as she called for the children to come in. "Believe me, I am doing my best to get over it as quickly as possible." They waited at the gate for the children to come through on their ponies. Michael met her gaze. "Your brother will be here soon. He'll want to talk to you."

Elise nodded, not looking at him, fearful it might call attention to their conversation. She spoke in hushed tones when she said, "I'm sure he does. You don't have to fear that I will claim you seduced me, because I feel I'm the one having to do all the seducing Michael. I wish..." She lowered her voice as the children grew closer and resumed walking toward the barn. "Sometimes I wish you wanted me as much as I want you."

He sighed, then muttered something under his breath. The chatter of the children caught up with them, leaving him unable to respond. They walked the children on their ponies back to the stables and handed over the animals to the grooms. Elise stepped into the skirt of her two-piece riding habit, buttoning the side. As she'd told him that very morning, having done this for so many years, she gave in to necessity and had specially constructed habits made which allowed for ease of attachment and removal of the skirt. Her brother had only one request when he'd discovered she rode astride. She was never to appear outside Haldenwood in such a manner. It would cause gossip and scandal. And heaven knew, Ren dreaded gossip and scandal more than anything.

Elise and Michael walked to the house with the three girls. They both noticed Sophia walking like the pony was still under her. Smiling, Elise called out to her, "Don't worry Sophie, you'll only be sore for a day or two."

The older two begged for similar instruction and Elise promised to do so at some point during the week.

Michael groaned and ask that she please get approval from Christina first.

Elise had Bridget order a bath prepared for her while she napped. As she changed out of her riding clothes, her maid said, "Was he so totally scandalized by the sight of ye ridin' around like a lad that he's changed his mind?"

"No, Bridget," she replied, "he hasn't changed his mind. In fact, he said his esteem for me and my skill grew when he saw I knew what was I was doing." She slipped her chemise on and lay on the bed. "I'm glad, too. For, although I would hate to live without him, I would if he ordered me not to continue my riding, training and breeding."

"Get yer rest, m'lady. I've a feelin' ye've got a long evenin' ahead."

When Elise woke from a short nap, she learned her brother and sister-in-law had already arrived and Ren waited downstairs for a meeting with her. She bathed and dressed quickly, leaving the room with her short hair still damp. Finding him alone in the study, she entered and returned his warm smile.

"So, I take it you are in agreement," he asked.

"Of course," she said through her smile. "I cannot wait until he is out of mourning, so we can make our announcement."

"Good," her brother replied, seeming a bit

uncomfortable with what he wanted to say. "He is a fine man, Elise. He will make you a good husband or I would never have approved.

"He is also my friend," Ren added, "and I ask that you not play games with him. Do not marry him if you do not think you can care for him—" He cleared his throat before finishing. "—in... that way."

"I assure you, Your Grace, I care for him, *in that way*."

Her brother visibly relaxed. "Good. Good." He nodded. "Then you got your love match after all."

"I did," she said through her smile. "Thank you."

"Although I will say, I didn't think your sentiments lay in that quarter any longer. It seemed to me you were becoming more open to the possibility of finding a match elsewhere. Especially after the verbal daggers you've thrown at him lately."

"There has never been anyone else for me. I've known it since I was a child."

"And that's another reason this is hard for him—he's seen you grow up. He must get used to seeing you in a different light and that won't come easily. Take this time he's giving you to show him the woman I know you to be."

"I will."

"Does he know about your riding? I've never told anyone the depth of your involvement with your horses. I did it to protect your modesty and reputation. You never know how some in Society will react when they learn things of that sort, especially if the young lady is unwed."

He was protecting her, just as she'd thought. "I assumed you would have told Michael. Nevertheless, he found me out this morning." She told him about her ride on the young mare and then later with the children.

"As a proper guardian, I know I should say something along the lines of 'I hope he can curb your hoydenish ways,' but I cannot. For Lia has mentioned that she would like you to teach her to ride as you do."

She smiled. "We can start tomorrow morning if she'd like. Woodhenge has an excellent stable, and I'm sure a pair of my breeches will fit her, except for the length of leg."

Ren grinned broadly, pride beaming from his entire countenance. "I'm afraid she won't be able to start lessons for at least seven or eight more months."

Elise's eyes grew wide and she smiled before hugging her brother. "Congratulations, Your Grace. Does anyone else know?"

He shook his head. "Just you and Grandmother."

"Splendid! Another nephew or niece for me to spoil."

His Grace, the Duke of Caversham, stared at the slender form of the young woman walking out of the study at Woodhenge. Once the door shut behind her, he whispered, "Father, that's one down and one to go." He tossed back the rest of his Scotch and whispered a quick prayer of thanks that he had a few years to prepare for Sarah's debut.

Chapter Twelve

That evening, Michael, Christina, Ren, Lia, Elise and her grandmother gathered in the study to await the dinner bell. Christina, being closest to Michael and Ren in age, related some of the childhood pranks of the two. Elise began to see a side of Michael and her brother she never knew.

"Are you saying the fight was for no reason?" Elise heard Michael ask. "That it was Vance and not Ren?"

Elise saw Michael's sister laugh and nod her head. Then Ren burst out laughing. "I told you I didn't do it, but you wouldn't believe me."

Seated near the window, her grandmother said to Ren, "You had a reputation as a horrible rake. Why would anyone believe you?"

As Christina continued regaling them with tales of Michael's youth, and of growing up in London, Elise began to get a portrait of a young Michael from the time before he'd met Ren. He'd been an adventurous child, like her, but where she hadn't been restricted by title and position, only social mores, Michael had been taught about responsibility and duty from an early age, having lost his father when he was still in short pants. She supposed she'd been fortunate that she'd lived her entire life at Haldenwood. Life in the country seemed so much simpler than that in London.

At home she'd been free to run and ride through the fields and orchards, climb trees and skip stones on the lake and creek. She'd been allowed to wade barefoot along the shore of their lake in summer, fish, ride, and in general be the little hoyden her brother called her. Raised in London, Michael didn't have as many opportunities to do some of the things a normal boy should have done before going away to school.

When the three began to discuss old friends, Elise went to where Lia and Grandmother sat, and privately congratulated her sister-in-law on her new condition.

"Ren told me earlier, but only because we'd been discussing riding and I told him I would be more than happy to teach you. You do know that my brother could just as easily teach you, because we had the same instructor. I just spent more time playing with my horses than he did. For him, riding was a mode of transportation and a horse a piece of livestock. For me, being alone for so long in that big house, with Ren off at school and Father gone to London for his term each year, my horses were my friends. There were no other companions for me when I was young. Which very much frustrated my nurse and then my governesses. I think Papa was relieved when an appropriate playmate moved to the village. Little did he know that Beverly was in much the same state as I. We became thick as thieves—without the thievery."

"You have a natural gift with horses, everyone who's seen you agrees," her sister-in-law said.

Her grandmother began to chuckle under her breath. "Just look at him," she said, "He can't be in the same room with her without looking as though he might devour her."

Elise felt a blush creep up her neck as the already warm room suddenly grew hot. A footman entered the room and spoke to Michael. He turned to the group and announced, "Mother is here. Their coaches have just turned onto the lane."

Christina's eyes got wide and she mumbled something about them getting here fast, then hurried from the room saying she would see to adding more places to the table.

"I'll bet they left within hours of receiving Christina's note," Michael said. "If so they will have been traveling hard all day." Michael came to Elise's side. Her fright must have been evident, for he tried to reassure her as best he could. "Don't worry. Just remember what I said. Mother just wants to see me happy. You're the woman I chose. She will be happy for us. Now just be yourself and I'm sure she'll find you as charming as I do." He kissed the top of her head and rubbed her back as she leaned into him, hoping she could win over the woman who would soon become her mother-in-law.

The sound of wheels crunching on gravel sent everyone to the porch to welcome the new arrivals. Elise stood with her grandmother, Lia and Ren, while Michael stepped down to help the footman with the door and steps. He extended his hand and assisted the first guest.

His mother hadn't changed much in appearance, except maybe for more gray in her dark brown hair. She stood nearly as tall as Christina, with a similar build. She kissed her son's cheek. "I remember coming here from Town was so much quicker. Bath, for all it's restorative properties, might as well be on the other side of the globe." She moved up to the porch to greet Ren, kissing his cheek as well.

Ren introduced Lady Richard to Lia, then she greeted Elise's grandmother, then her. At that moment Elise wanted more than anything for the limestone steps to open up and swallow her whole.

"You're the little hoyden in the tree, are you not?" The older woman gave her a thorough once-over, staring at her down her elegant, delicately sloped nose.

Elise shrank at the reminder and nodded, while Lady Richard scrutinized her further.

"Well, at least part of what the gossips say is true," Michael's mother said. "You are not unpleasant... to look upon. And this is a vast improvement over our first meeting, is it not."

Heat suffused Elise's entire body and she was certain her face burned red as she remembered falling out of the tree and knocking the woman down. God help her, she wanted to cry, and Elise never cried in public. Ever.

She didn't know why Lady Richard's words hurt as much as they did. True, no one had ever called her beautiful, graceful or ladylike. Well, except for Beverly, but they told each other these things because that's what best friends did. And Lia, because she was her sister now and that's what sisters did.

Michael told her she was beautiful the night of her ball, but Elise was sure it was mandated somewhere in the compendium of perfect etiquette, that all men must, by law, tell the debutant being feted that she was beautiful. It wasn't as though he meant it *in that way* as her brother had asked her earlier.

Just once she wanted to be found worthy. Thus, she

wanted approval from the woman who held influence over the man she loved, and it didn't appear she'd get it. The woman had already found Elise lacking, not good enough for her son.

Still she managed to speak without humiliating herself. "Thank you, ma'am. But I wouldn't believe the gossips. I've learned that much of what they say is untrue."

"I think perhaps in this case they were right." The older woman patted her hand while her gaze drifted over to her granddaughters, making Elise feel almost as desired as a pet spaniel. "I wouldn't worry about landing an offer. You'll have one by the end of the season for your connections alone. I'm sure."

Michael had finished assisting his sister and nieces by this time and came to introduce her to his sister, Sabrina, Lady Knebworth, who appeared much older than Christina. "Now I know why I haven't been here since my wedding," Lady Knebworth stretched and adjusted her shawl. "It's truly the middle of nowhere. Why, we haven't seen a residence for miles." The woman looked at Elise and gave her a knowing little grin, as though they were in on a surprise. She wondered then what Michael had told his sisters about their relationship.

Michael grew straighter and his chest swelled with pride. "Uncle loved this place, and I'm starting to understand why." He practically radiated joy when he looked at Elise and said, "It's a serene and relaxing place to come when Town gets too hot or hectic."

Sabrina greeted Ren, met Lia, then turned to Elise. She took Elise's hands in hers and smiled, then leaning forward, she pressed her cheek to Elise's and whispered into her ear. "Pay no attention to mother. In her opinion, not even Princess Charlotte was good enough for my brother. On the other hand, Christina and I think you are just what he needs."

Elise felt another blush creeping up, and she could only nod as words failed her.

After introductions to Michael's nieces, both of whom appeared to be in that awkward stage of adolescence, everyone moved into the house. Christina appeared alongside the butler, who announced dinner.

Throughout the entire meal the families caught up with each others lives and chatted about the current social climate and events, both in Town and in Bath. Elise listened and responded when called upon, usually when asked something about the other young ladies in Town, current fashions, and if there were any gossip as yet regarding betrothals.

"The mid-season speculation is that Miss Georgianna Emmerson is secretly betrothed to Mr. Edmund Parnell of Derbyshire," said Elise, when asked by Michael's sisters about Town gossip. "Her father, Mr. George Emmerson, has said he will not entertain Parnell's suit because he is up to his ears in vowels. Meanwhile, Miss Georgianna is acting as though that is not enough of a deterrent for her. She's told her father and several of her closest friends that Mr. Parnell's uncle, Viscount Whitsell-Dumfries, is leaving him twenty-five thousand upon the Viscount's death, though it is his older brother that inherits the title."

"Mr. Emmerson has every right to question that man's interest in his daughter." Her brother spoke as an authority on the matter. "No one wants to marry their children off to ne'er-do-wells. If the buck is living on borrowed funds now, do you imagine his habits would change once he has the Emmerson girl's dowry and later both of their inheritances?"

"Likely not," Michael replied.

"Men like that never change," Lady Richard said. "A young lady would do well to heed the advice of her elders in such matters."

She disagreed of course, but held her tongue. Michael's mother remembered her in an unflattering way. Elise wanted to prove to the woman who would soon be her mother-in-law, that she was not the same girl she was before—an incorrigible hoyden with no care for rules nor fear of repercussion. And she only had a few days in which to accomplish it.

The days leading up to Lady Richard's birthday celebration flew by. Elise spent the mornings riding, one day all the way into the village with Christina, Michael and Ren to shop. In the evenings they played games with the children in the garden or on the terrace. Lady Richard relished the time she could spend with Christina's little girls, whom she did not see often. On Friday, Christina's husband, Baron Vance, who'd been away on an assignment joined them, giving Michael and Ren another male cohort in the house.

Lady Knebworth's daughters, Phillipa and Cornelia, who'd impressed her at first as extremely shy young girls, soon relaxed in her presence and were delightful as well as very intelligent. Elise invited the girls to ride with her the following morning, but learned that neither girl rode—an astonishing revelation to Elise who couldn't imagine never being on a horse. In probing further, she found out that each girl had been frightened away from the animals as young children, and their mother had never encouraged them to return to the barn to confront their fears. Elise offered, that when the day came they wanted to attempt conquering their fear, she would gladly help them.

On Saturday afternoon, the day of Lady Richard's birthday party, she gathered Christina's three little misses and gently reminded them that after dinner she must give the kittens they'd come to love to their grandmother. All three took the reminder well, with little Sophia saying that their mother and father had agreed to let them have kittens once they returned home.

Elise bathed and prepared herself for the evening ahead. She had Bridget ready her favorite evening dress of white muslin striped with gold satin, with a handmade Belgium lace hem. She placed two tiny carved, delicate mother of pearl combs on the sides just above her ears, to hold the hair off her face.

Her hands trembled as she pulled her gloves on. She'd never been so nervous in her entire life. Even though she felt Lady Richard might be indifferent toward her, she sincerely hoped the woman liked her gift of the two kittens. If her choice of gifts didn't go over well, it might have deeper repercussions than merely the kittens coming back to Haldenwood with her.

This was the mother of the man she was going to marry. She would be grandmother to the children she bore her son. It was more than just important that his mother welcome her into her family. To Elise, it was critical. Her future mother-in-law could make her life pleasant if she accepted her, or miserable if she did not.

If Lady Richard objected, as much as it would hurt, Elise would not marry Michael.

She was confident that his sisters had already done so. His mother's was the only opinion she'd yet to discern. In the few moments alone with Michael these past days, he said he hadn't spoken with his mother yet regarding her, and for Elise not to worry because everything would work out.

When Bridget was done with her hair, Elise set the kitten that slept on her lap down on her bed with its brother and said, "Remember, when I send for them, please bring them down right away. It wouldn't be fair to the little dears to keep them cooped up in the picnic basket until Lady Richard is ready to open her gift." Her maid nodded in return, and Elise went down to meet the family for dinner.

Upon entering the parlor, Elise noted her tardiness, as did everyone else in the room. Her cheeks burned as she walked across the room, embarrassed to be the last to arrive. She spied the gift table in the corner of the room, decorated with a large vase of fresh flowers and bearing the boxes of presents for Lady Richard. Elise felt awkward not placing a gaily-ribboned box along with the others.

"I'm so sorry to be late," Elise added, and for Lady Richard's ears, "Forgive me, ma'am. I was... putting your present together." Behind her, one of Christina's daughters giggled.

Lady Richard glanced from Elise to Michael, who shrugged his shoulders in a gesture of feigned innocence. "You have piqued my interest, Elise. I almost would rather not wait until after dinner to open it."

"Oh, but you must, for we are all famished, are we not?" Elise looked around the room and silently begged everyone to agree. They all nodded, but her grandmother saved her.

"Yes, Heloise dear, if I don't eat something soon, I fear I shall ask cook to roast that goose I saw in the garden earlier chasing the little dog. Annoying creatures geese. Only good for one thing, Christmas dinner."

Christina choked a cough, the younger girls squealed with horror, the older girls didn't react at all, and Michael quietly said, "That won't be necessary, ma'am."

"Oh. Is that what's on the menu?" her grandmother asked. When no one had composed themselves enough to reply, she continued. "Excellent! Goose is one of my favorites. Basted with herbs and butter, it's absolutely delightful."

"Beatrice, please," Lady Richard implored, "I believe that particular bird is a pet."

Everyone followed as the new Lord Camden led the way into the dining hall with his mother on his arm. Once they were all seated and holding glasses of champagne, he met her gaze, then nodded and winked. The younger girls, seated with the adults for the first time, began to bicker. Their mother quickly quieted them by threatening to send them upstairs. Michael stood up and tapped his glass with his spoon, drawing everyone's attention.

"I wanted to be the first to wish my mother a very happy birthday and to give her the first present of the night." Elise thought he looked nervous as he took a deep breath and continued. "A long time ago, a precocious little girl dangled upside down from a tree limb and asked me if I would marry her. Of course, I told her I was too young at the time, being only two and twenty years of age."

He turned an endearing smile her way and she wanted to burst into tears for no reason except that she was blissfully happy. "The problem was, she'd hidden my horse and wouldn't return it until I agreed."

She silently stared into the glass in her hand, watching the bubbles rise in the clear liquid, surface and break. Everyone at the table chuckled except Elise. What was he about? She hated that she blushed so easily, and that the familiar heat began creeping up her neck. Again.

"Then, in January of last year, I became godfather to my best friend's son. And at that time, I was told that the girl who'd been the proverbial thorn in my side for most of her life was going to be Marcus' godmother. My first reaction was to groan, believing that, after a few years of reprieve from her antics, they might all begin again.

"But what I saw that day at St. Paul's pleasantly surprised me. Correction, it was rather more than pleasant. Because, you see, the girl wasn't a girl anymore. She'd become a lovely young lady—full of spirit and charm, beauty and grace. I felt then she'd be important to me one day. But because of her tender years and the fact that she hadn't had that rite of passage due every young lady of her station, I knew I had to wait or risk losing the friend who was more like a brother to me."

Elise felt a tear burning in her eyes and quashed it. *What was he doing? Dear God, was he going to announce a betrothal when he hadn't even asked her?*

Not that she would refuse him, but.... "Oh, good God," she whispered. He was doing this so publicly! Her hand began to tremble and she set the glass down and put her hands in her lap where she could press them on her thighs. Elise kept her head bowed and her eyes closed. She didn't want to see a look of disappointment on Lady Richard's face, and she would as Michael's mother sat directly across from her.

Lia sat next to her and reached a hand to Elise under the table and gave it a little squeeze of reassurance.

"Come forward to this Spring," Michael continued, "and it is now the height of her season. She and I have been thrown together at various events. Consequently, over the course of the past months, I've gotten to know the lady all over again."

Elise heard her sister-in-law whisper, "Open your eyes, dear." She did and avoided looking over to Lady Richard. Michael came to stand next to her, holding out a hand to her. The footman aided with her chair and Elise stood on shaky legs, as her dreams were all about to come true. Michael went down on bended knee before her, holding her gloved hands in his, the warmth of them flowing into her, soothing her trembling body.

"And I would like to change my answer to the young girl who asked me that question so long ago."

She found strength in his hazel-eyed gaze, and the firm grasp he had of her hands. But she knew he was as nervous as she when she heard his deep voice tremble as he said, "I will, if you will still have me."

Tears began to cloud her vision as Elise tried to focus on their hands—hers smothered by his much larger ones. She squeezed her eyes together and the salty drops spilled over. "Of course I will," she whispered. "You have to ask?"

The room instantly burst to life with the joyous chatter of an upcoming wedding, and as Elise found her seat again she observed that Lady Richard alone did not smile. After Michael's sisters and brother-in-law wished them well, and her brother, Lia, and grandmother congratulated them, Lady Richard was quick to remind everyone that nothing should be announced, nor should a wedding take place, until the family came out of mourning.

Michael nodded, saying, "Elise and I discussed it and in August we shall announce our betrothal in all the papers and have the banns read."

Elise noticed that Lady Richard was even more quiet than usual, and hoped she wasn't too taken aback at their announcement. It might not have been the way Elise wanted the engagement announced to the family, but she wanted to have the woman's blessing nonetheless.

After dinner the party gathered in the parlor, and the bride-to-be sat next to her future mother-in-law as the children began to carry boxes for their grandmother to open. One by one she lifted the lids and exclaimed that each item was exactly what she'd wished for or wanted. Elise sent the oldest of Christina's girls, Emily, upstairs to have the basket brought down. Minutes later it arrived, the footman setting it down in front of Lady Richard.

Bending over, Lady Richard flipped the latch and raised the lid. Slowly, two furry faces with orange fur and pink noses, climbed out of the basket.

"Oh my! They're simply adorable little darlings." Lady Richard said, grinning broadly, the first time she'd done so in the four days she'd been at Woodhenge from what Elise had seen. She watched the kittens slowly sniff and investigate the new room, one they'd not yet explored.

Olivia and Sophia, Christina's two younger daughters, caught the kittens and brought them back to their grandmother. She held each one up, inspecting it, and cooing over their pretty blue eyes. She let the younger girls take them and play on the floor.

"Phillipa, Cordelia," Lady Richard called out to her older two granddaughters, "we have kittens!" Lady Richard turned to Michael and thanked him.

Silence fell over the room. Everyone it seemed, but Lady Richard, knew the gift was from Elise. Michael stepped up to his mother and hugged her. "I'm glad you love them mother, but they were completely Elise's idea. I'd been shopping for a broach or some such, and she is the one who found the kittens and fattened them for you."

Lady Richard turned to Elise and thanked her, but the spark of joy she had only moments earlier had disappeared, her smile never reaching her eyes. That was a cutting blow to Elise's heart when she so wanted Michael's mother to like her. She was an odd one, Elise thought. She was happy enough with the gift when she thought it was from her son, but upon learning the kittens were her idea, she became subdued.

Elise decided she would have to ask her grandmother and Lia for advice on how to handle this situation. Not having a mother of her own, she really did want Lady Richard to like her. Or at least approve of their union.

Blissfully unaware of any tension as children usually are, little Sophia came up and told her grandmother what the kittens' names were and how to tell them apart. Lady Richard either did an excellent job of feigning happiness with the kittens, or maybe she actually was pleased.

"Michael said you would like them," Elise said, "or else I never would have given an animal as a pet, because one never knows if it will be well-received."

"Your gift is appreciated Lady Elise,' Lady Richard said. "The kittens will be very spoiled and loved. By all of us, isn't that right Sabrina?"

Sabrina first offered Elise a sympathetic glance, then said, "Yes mama. We shall adore the kittens."

That night before Lady Richard took to her bed, she said a prayer that her son was making the right decision. The duke's sister impressed Heloise as an impulsive and over-indulged girl yet. One headstrong enough that—at this age—she was unlikely to ever change. Her son, now that he had the responsibility of the earldom, needed a countess who would make him proud, and bear his heirs. He did not need an independent-minded, hoydenish young miss in need of a great deal of temperance.

Heloise felt she would be reliving history, yet again.

Chapter Thirteen

On Sunday Ren and Lia prepared to leave for Haldenwood. Ren said he would return to London after a few days, but Lia decided she needed the rest now that she was carrying again and wouldn't return to London, where the heat and smell of the river was becoming more unbearable by the day.

"I've missed Luchino and Sarah these months I've been in London," she told Elise, as she supervised the packing of their things in Lia's rooms. "Though I would not have traded my time helping you get launched, I believe you'll do fine without my assistance. You have Grandmother there to chaperon you."

"I shall be lost without your support, Lia. I'll miss you terribly."

"If you have any questions, write, and I'll reply immediately. I've also warned your brother against being too overbearing, now that you and Michael are betrothed, albeit secretly. This should give you time together to become closer." Lia looked to see if anyone was paying attention to their conversation, then leaned forward and whispered, "and if you need any advice regarding topics of an intimate nature, simply ask."

Elise felt her cheeks flame as she choked back a laugh. "That's not..."

"I'm of the belief that sharing your bodies with one another is a beautiful thing. But only with the man you have committed yourself to. I know how you feel about Michael and from what I've seen, he is starting to return your feelings."

Elise debated whether to tell her about his desire to wait, and that it was *his* desire alone. Not hers. Perhaps she could use her sister-in-law's advice regarding this one thing. "There is something I would like to ask, but I'm not sure how to...."

"Just ask. I promise whatever you are curious about will not shock me."

Elise looked around and noted the closed lids on the trunks and the absence of Lia's maid. "Michael wants to wait until we are married to become... intimate."

"And you do not?"

"No. When I am with him, when he touches me, I feel as if my very body is on fire with want for him."

"That is as it should be when you are in love. Any other man's touch would not be the same."

She shivered involuntarily, and not because of the breeze coming in from the open balcony doors. Elise couldn't envision herself in anyone else's arms but Michael's. And it had nothing to do with the infatuation she'd held for him. This was different, a deeper sensation and truer emotion—for a relationship she instinctively knew was meant to be.

"You are right! When Sinclair touched me, my flesh crawled. He is nice enough, sometimes nice to the point of annoying. But I didn't feel with him or with Captain Wilson that same desire to be as close as I possibly can, the way I do when I am with Michael." She sighed. "I understand Michael's family is in mourning, but now that we are as good as betrothed it is not uncommon to share certain intimacies. Except he wants to wait, and I do not."

"Men. Would that we could share a part of our brain with them," Lia lamented with a sigh. "Though some of what he asks has merit. No. Listen," she said as Elise started to interrupt her. "He has a family of females he must consider. If it is perceived that they are not properly observing the correct period of mourning, they will be thought heathens, or worse, be shunned. He has to think of all the young girls in his family who must eventually be presented at court. Also, I heard Michael tell Ren it is his wish that you wait until they are out of mourning to publicly announce the betrothal, partly because he wants *you* to be sure of your feelings for him."

"How could he doubt...."

"It's not that he doubts, Elise. I think he wants you to be certain that there is no one that will turn your feelings from him. Marriage is for life. He's had years out in society, where if he'd fallen in love before now he'd have settled down. He hasn't, so obviously he's not met that person yet.

"You, on the other hand, are in your first season," Lia said. "I believe he's giving you these weeks to decide that there *is* no one else for you."

"I've told him there has never been anyone else for me. Why does he doubt that?"

"Because, even though he's a man, he has feelings too. They just don't show them as we do. Imagine someone as proud as Michael being made a fool by an unfaithful wife. Not that you would do such a thing, but I think that plays into his fears. And, of course, the story of his uncle's failed marriage still reverberates with his mother."

"I would never—" Elise attempted to argue, but Lia held up her hand, still defending Michael's desire to wait.

"There is also the chance that you might get withchild before the announcement was made. If that happened people might shun you—perhaps only until you are wed, or until the next scandal occurs and their heads are turned to some other titillating bit of gossip. In my experience, the matrons most likely to cause that type of trouble in our society have very long memories and loose tongues when you take the best catch off the market."

Lia held Elise's hands, leaned in closer, then added, "I am not telling you what to do, just that you should be aware of the consequences and decide for yourself. If you are willing to accept the consequences of your *actions*, then by all means, seduce the man. Take him to bed."

The day after her brother and sister-in-law left for Haldenwood, Elise spent the hours after luncheon in the Library, once again going over the previous earl's extensive notes and breeding charts. He had copious writings on the development of this carriage horse he'd been breeding, noting physical characteristics handed down by which mares and sires. She admired the man's dedication to his breeding program.

She placed a lemon wedge in a glass and poured herself more water, then turned the page in the ledger book. The sound of the door opening and closing behind her didn't cause her to lift her head. She and her grandmother were the only two in the house aside from the servants. All the other ladies had gone into the village to shop for ribbons and lace, and Michael and Lawrence out touring the fields with the estate manager.

"Did you have a good nap, Gram?" Elise slid into the affectionate term for her grandmother. After their light repast an hour ago, the older woman had begged off of the shopping trip to rest a while as they'd all spent the previous night playing card games until the wee hours. "You could not have slept long," she said as she turned to see Lady Richard coming toward her.

Michael's mother was beautiful, with delicately graying brown hair and brown eyes. She looked like Sabrina and Michael—only older. She smiled at Lady Richard, wondering as she neared why she didn't return the gesture. Her brain spun like a top. *What could be wrong?*

"I'm certain your grandmother is resting well. Woodhenge is a peaceful estate. It's why my brother-in-law Edward rarely left it. His years fighting in the colonies left him averse to loud noises and crowds of people. Here, he was able to relax and be himself."

Elise nodded, and went to the door to ask the footman to bring them fresh tea. She went to sit opposite Lady Richard near the open terrace doors. "Michael has taken me throughout the property on horseback, and on a walking tour of the old abbey. It is a lovely home, and I would be fortunate to be her mistress."

"It has been a long time since there has been a lady in charge here." Lady Richard stared out on the lawn and garden in the distance. "It is an enormous responsibility. Do you think you are ready?"

"I might be lacking in some household managerial skills, but I am confident I can learn. Admittedly, I have spent more time in barns and know more about managing livestock and kennels than a home. Know that I will do whatever pleases Michael, and if he wishes it, I shall take a more active role in the home, though he knows I shall never abandon my love for my horses." When Lady Richard didn't seem pleased with her response, Elise added, "My horses do not consume so much of my day that I cannot manage a home as well."

The tea cart arrived and after the maid poured and left. "Ma'am? What troubles you?" When Elise got no response, she continued, "Is it that he's asked *me* to marry him?"

Lady Richard stirred her tea and seemed to consider her reply. When she spoke it was without judgment or reservation. "You have had this infatuation with my son since you were a child, I have to wonder if you are marrying him because like a dog you don't want to quit the chase. Or if you are truly ready for marriage, Elise. Please understand, I am not disapproving of the engagement. It is a good match by *ton* standards. But, your tender age and... some of your habits lend themselves to... an image of young lady not ready for such a serious commitment."

"I understand your concerns, ma'am, I do. Please believe me when I say I would never do anything to hurt Michael, or humiliate him. I love him. Have loved him for many years."

"Are you prepared to give him children?"

"As many as Michael wants and God gives us." This seemed to pacify Lady Richard. Elise couldn't believe she was actually having this conversation. Did the woman really think she would marry and not wish to do her duty by her husband?

"His uncle was married to a woman who claimed to love him as well. The minute his back was turned, so were her affections—by the first rake who paid a little attention to her. She died trying to give birth to that other man's child. But Edward loved her until his last breath. He refused to believe his wife was at fault, instead believing she was lured into the salacious affair by someone skilled at flirtation. Someone who knew exactly what to say to a lonely young girl who's husband was away doing the King's business. It doesn't matter what she told my brother-in-law. He was on the continent when the babe was conceived, so everyone knew the child she carried could not possibly be his."

"Michael told me." Elise also remembered what Lia said about it before she left.

Lady Richard nodded. "We have discussed the importance of making a wise decision in selecting his countess. He has known of his uncle's heartbreak for most of his life. It would upset me greatly to see my son hurt in a similar manner."

The older woman set her cup on the saucer, rose and left the room. Elise had a great deal think about these next days. Most importantly, was how she might prove to Lady Richard she was worthy of being Michael's Countess.

Elise spent two more days at Woodhenge with Michael and his relatives. Early on the third morning, with his coaches packed in the pre-dawn hours, she, her grandmother, and Michael left. He'd said he'd been away from work long enough and must return to his office. She was happy to be getting back as well, needing desperately to talk to Beverly.

She required Beverly's assistance in coming up with a plan of seduction now—something she was unable to do when she was cooped up in the country with his family, and hers, all around. In London, with only her grandmother to chaperon her, she stood a better chance at seducing him. To bring Michael to realize he wanted her as much she wanted him. To accomplish this she would need something to spur him along, and as she planned her strategy, she decided she couldn't go wrong with a few new dresses. Perhaps a more daring dress, one made for a woman who wants to entice her lover to her bed.

Elise wanted to insure that Michael's desire to wait to consummate their relationship was as painful for him as it was for her. She also wanted to make sure it didn't last any longer than those two remaining months she agreed to.

While her grandmother slept on the seat next to her, Elise and Michael both read. She'd brought charts and ledgers from the Woodhenge library, and Michael studied papers that had arrived the day before by courier from his offices. After one stop to stretch their legs, drowsiness set in and Elise struggled to keep her eyes open. When she realized she'd read the same sentence several times, she finally she gave in and leaned against the corner of the coach.

She looked across to Michael who raised his eyes from his work, then looked at her softly snoring grandmother. "I'm afraid sleepiness is contagious with me. Would you mind if I napped as well?"

"Not at all." Michael moved his paperwork and

patted the seat next to him, a slight smile on his handsome face. "Sit over here, and lean on me. I promise it will be more comfortable."

Elise moved into the crook of his arm and nestled into his side, curling her feet beneath her. His sandalwood and spice scent was so intoxicating to her she wanted to turn her face up and ask for a kiss, and if not for her grandmother's presence she would have. She yawned and closed her eyes instead. Inhaling deeply, she sighed. "I'm happy Michael."

She felt his arm pull her closer. "So am I, my sweet."

Elise smiled in her half-sleep state, before finally succumbing. Before she knew it, the clattering of the wheels and shod hooves on cobblestone woke her.

"Good afternoon sleepyhead," Michael said softly, brushing her hair from her forehead.

"Where are we?"

"Believe it or not, the outskirts of London."

Bridget entered Elise's rooms the next afternoon followed by Madame Fuichard and her two assistants. Beverly had arrived first thing that morning with her folio and pencils, sketched some ideas for possible gowns, and now Elise wanted to ask Madame if these creations were possible. Especially considering her tall, less curvy form. So as they sat and waited for Madame's critique, Beverly chewed her lower lip, and Elise drummed her fingers on the padded arm of the chair in which she sat.

Going over each drawing, Madame praised Beverly's talent for design and attention to detail. "Oui, oui. These are not just possible, but...." The modiste studied the sketches and lifted her gaze to Elise.

Madame smiled at Beverly, causing her to blush. "They will be magnifique! You have a very good eye, my lady."

She then gave Beverly pointers on design which her friend absorbed eagerly. Since early spring Beverly had been sketching dress designs for herself and Elise, and with Madame's help bringing the designs to life, the two of them had unwittingly become the leading trend setters of the season. Madame commented on the number of women and girls coming into her shop wanting to duplicate her exquisite creations.

"Your designs, my dear," Madame said to Beverly, "are more fitting to the natural form of a woman, bringing the bodice and waistline down closer to its natural curve. I never did like this fashion of hiding a woman's curves behind that empire waistline."

"Yes, Madame," Elise said. "I have very little curve to speak of and need all the help I can get."

"This is why your friend's designs are so suited to your form, my lady" she replied. "They showcase what you do have, instead of hiding what you do not."

Elise spent the next hour selecting fabrics with Madame's assistance, colors, and the various trims for the new gowns. Beverly also selected a few for herself as she was on a similar mission. Earlier that morning she'd confided in Elise that she and Lord Huddleston, were all but betrothed now, though no announcement had been made.

After Madame left, Beverly continued to work on sketches of future dresses at the desk in Elise's suite. Elise sat next to her on her dressing table stool, watching her friend's skill with the charcoal pencil on the sheet of paper before her. "Why has Huddleston not publicly announced his intent for your hand?" Elise asked. "He's already sought approval from your father and received it, did he not?"

Beverly nodded. "It seems my viscount and your earl have one thing in common. They are determined to drive us crazy with this desire to make us wait. Which is why *we*, not just you, are moving on to the next phase. Our men need some gentle prodding. Perhaps attention from other men will make them realize that we are not the simpering little fresh-from-the-schoolroom misses they think we are." Beverly's shoulders sagged as she set the pencil down and looked at her. "I am a woman fully grown. Why, girls younger than we are marrying and having babes. That's what I want, Elise. I want children. Lots of them."

"My sentiments exactly," Elise agreed. "Michael thinks to make me wait. And if he had his way, until the wedding night!"

Beverly's eyes grew comically wide and her jaw fell open. "I just want to get Christopher to make the announcement. I don't mean to incite his jealousy to the point of anger, or... or...."

"The bedroom?" Elise straightened her spine and pressed on, "I do. I want Michael to want me in that way. Because that is the way I want him. There. I've said it!" Elise prayed she didn't lose her friend over her declaration. "You, more than anyone in the world knows this Beverly." She saw the profound concern in her friend's expression. "My confession has likely shocked you, and I hope you do not choose to end our friendship over this, but I just had to say it."

"Elise, have you ever stopped to examine why this rush to intimacy, when you're just months away from a wedding?"

Elise considered her friend's words. "I have not." She mused as she shook her head. "Though...." Elise tried to think of a way to explain the profound emptiness she felt when she thought of life without Michael, a devastation unlike she'd ever experienced in her life. Elise broke her silence, then smiled. "You have brought up a question I shall ponder tonight as I try to fall asleep. When I have an answer, you will be the first to know."

Beverly nodded, then she looked up from the sketches she worked on and asked, "What if something should happen? Such as getting with child? Or, suppose the wedding gets called off for some reason, and you've lost your... your..."

"What? Maidenhead? Virginity?" Elise looked into Beverly's clear blue eyes and said honestly, "Then I will have lost it to the only man I've ever loved and ever will." Elise checked to make certain they were still alone, then leaned in close to her friend and dropped her voice to a whisper. "If I find I am with child, I'll just live out my days in the country somewhere. Scotland perhaps, seeing as Ren's always threatening to send me to that crumbling pile of stone anyway. Maybe in a few years, when the excitement of it all dies down, I could return and live quietly on my mother's dower property. But none of that will come to pass," Elise added while simultaneously praying her words were true. "You'll see. Michael loves me."

Her friend's eyes widened. "Has he told you this?"

"Not in so many words. But in his actions, yes, he has."

She remembered how tender he was with her the

night in the parlor at Woodhenge, when he showed her the wonder of being intimate without taking her virginity. He could not possibly have been so caring with her that night and not love her. And the following morning, there was the fear so clearly evident on his face when she rode the filly she'd since named Zephyr. He had to care for her as more than the sister of his best friend, after all he'd asked her to marry him!

"Of course you know me," Elise lamented, "open book that I am, I told him that I loved him. Though he said he knew, and felt it was a good thing that I have this feeling, he did not..." Elise choked down a knot of emotion. "He could not say he reciprocated yet. He said he needed time to get used to this new relationship between us."

"But he did say he wanted to marry you, correct?"

Elise nodded. "He asked me in front of his entire family and mine. He wants to wait until the family is out of mourning because he doesn't want society to think his siblings and their daughters were ill-bred. After the banns are read, we can marry immediately, if I wish."

Beverly plopped back against her seat. "Except for the proposal with both families present, Michael's plans for the wedding sound utterly *un*romantic," her friend said. "Very much like my own non-proposal. Huddleston and I were riding in the park one morning when he just said, 'I suppose we suit well enough. Perhaps we ought to marry when the season is over.' So casual and unemotional."

Elise rose and began to walk the length of her room, something she did to help her think through things. "If I didn't know any better, I'd think he was friends with

Michael and Ren. They are so alike. both Michael and Huddleston portray cool civility, when under that veneer both have a passionate streak that runs very deep beneath their hardened exterior." She shook her head as she continued pacing, wondering what to do to get their men to profess their love. "It's just a matter of cracking the outer shell, to release that pent-up passion." Both young ladies nodded at that.

"So what do we do?" Beverly asked.

"I don't know about you, but I plan to find the strongest nutcracker possible. Michael is a tough nut to crack."

"I don't think I like the sound of this."

Elise patted Beverly's hand. "All will be well. You'll see."

Within the week, two of the many gowns Elise and Beverly ordered were ready. And after discussing it with both Christopher and Michael, they'd accepted an invitation to the Riddlesworth annual ball. She'd heard those were always *the* most difficult invites to come by, making the Riddlesworth ball one of the most anticipated events each year. And, from everything Elise and Beverly had heard, tonight's ball might even be attended by the King himself. With Lia in the country, Ren worked constantly and said he would pass on attending the affair that evening so as to catch up on some business reading.

Thus, with her grandmother agreeing to act as their chaperon, and having arranged to pick up Beverly promptly at eight-thirty, Elise readied herself with the assistance of the ever-glowering Bridget. Meeting the maid's gaze in the mirror, she said, "Bridget, it is important that Beverly's escort meet us here with Michael and I, and that we all go together. You know she doesn't have a female relation to chaperon her."

"I know you two are up to something, I just don't know what it is yet."

"It's nothing that will get me banished, if that's what you're thinking. I just want to make Michael proud to be my escort this evening," Elise said, hoping she pacified her maid. She hoped their new dresses would show the two gentleman what could be theirs tonight, if they wanted.

The gown she chose to wear was pale peach watered silk, and very simple in design. As had been proven on the night of her own ball, the simple designs suited her more than frills and lace. The wide-scoop neckline with narrow off-the-shoulder straps also created the miraculous effect of enhancing her modest bustline while accentuating her waist. The silk moire fabric then flared out only slightly, enough as to be deemed appropriate, and fell to above her ankles. The scalloped hemline of the gown turned out far better than she'd imagined after seeing it on paper.

And for the first time all season, she and Beverly wore the exact same dress. Intentionally. The only difference in their dresses was her friend's was ice blue with a white silk shawl to match her blond-haired, blue-eyed loveliness. With Elise's darker peach delicate lace shawl to match the silk and plain peach satin slippers, she and Beverly would make a striking pair of friends.

Elise had pulled her short brown hair back with small combs and around her throat she wore a simple single strand of tiny pearls, with earrings to match. The simplicity of her entire ensemble should garner the desired effect from Michael. This was but a first step in her escalating plan to make him insane with desire for her. If this didn't work, she'd have to ramp up her plan to the next level, and she'd continue to do so until he gave in.

She was not going to let him forget she existed, the way her father forgot about her, leaving her out in the country while he lived in Town. She wasn't going to allow that to happen with Michael.

Michael and Christopher Huddleston stood in the parlor with Ren, brandy in hand, conversing amiably while they waited on the three ladies upstairs. If Elise and Beverly had hoped to find he and Huddleston impatient at having to cool their heels in the parlor, they were mistaken. Michael knew the games ladies played.

"I don't envy you, gentlemen," Ren said through a grin. "I couldn't imagine having to go through these games only to end up with a woman who will vex you for the rest of your days. And, believe me these two will do just that." He lifted his glass and downed the rest of his drink.

"Myself, I'm rather looking forward to being vexed," Christopher Huddleston replied. "Can't think of a more beautiful creature to have vexing me."

"Sounds to me like you're in love, Huddleston," Michael teased.

"I'll admit, it's quite possible. I can't think of a feeling that compares. It's almost like drowning, but happily. No, willingly."

"Well, I can safely say, I don't have those emotions," Michael said. "I've known Elise far too long to melt like butter to her hot knife."

Ren choked back a laugh. "Refills, gentlemen? I certainly could use another and God knows how long they're going to keep us here."

"That won't be necessary, brother." Michael swung his gaze toward the doorway and watched Elise and her friend enter, followed by Lady Sewell, the Ladies' chaperon for the evening.

He unconsciously reached a hand to his throat, to pull the cravat loose. The damn thing was cutting off his breath, he thought as he watched Elise cross the room. She was a vision. An incomparable, arousing vision in peach silk, with a style and form to tempt even a monk into sin.

He wasn't sure what they were up to, but he knew something was afoot. Perhaps he'd best prepare Christopher. "When they smile like that Huddleston, be on your guard. The minxes have something up their sleeves."

"Camden, you're blind. They aren't wearing sleeves," noted Huddleston with appreciative awe.

"You would be wise to heed his warning, Huddleston," Elise's grandmother said. "I have done my best to corrupt both of my charges this season. As both are determined young ladies, if you're their targets, be warned I say."

Both young ladies blushed, the warm color so fetching on Elise. Michael watched his future wife lean over to Lady Sewell and say "You're the one who told me I must hook the fish before I can land him. I'm merely trying to get the fish to make the final commitment and 'jump into my pan' as you've so often said." Elise met his gaze and smiled.

Lady Sewell, sharp as ever, quickly replied, "I see I

shall have to teach you to cook soon. Right now you wouldn't know what to do with him once you have him there. But as you learned to fish quick enough, learning the other skills shouldn't be a problem."

After the laughter died down, Michael placed the evening wrap over Elise's shoulders, Christopher doing the same for Beverly, and Ren for his grandmother. Leaving Ren to his work, the duke's laughter behind the closed door was heard by all, as the foursome and Lady Sewell left for their evening out.

The Riddlesworth affair lived up to its reputation as *the fete* of the season. People were crushed together in nearly every room of the spacious home on this late spring evening, making the house rather warm, which caused quite a few party-goers to seek the slight breeze outdoors. The terrace and gardens were appropriately lit with torches to protect the reputations of those seeking fresh air. Michael's gaze never wandered far from Elise, who enjoyed chatting with her friends and dancing. He had to suppress a surge of possessiveness in order to allow her to finish her season unencumbered.

For now, he would just have to satisfy himself with knowing Elise would also end this arrangement if he'd let her. He grinned at the thought.

Each time she took to the dance floor on the arm of any male from twenty to sixty, he wished he could take back those words and make her his officially, right then. And every time a man looked at her as though she were a sweetmeat he wished to devour, Michael wanted to plow a fist into the chap's face.

By the time the evening was over, his innards were twisted in knots, and he knew it would only get worse before it got better. Perhaps he'd have to ask her not to smile so frequently or laugh so genuinely at every funny thing some inane fop whispered to her. Of course, he knew her well enough to know that if he made such a request, Elise would only escalate the flirtation just to spite him.

No, he wouldn't interfere with her fun. Soon enough, they'd be married and she'd be carrying his child. That would settle her, just as it did a high-strung filly.

Milling in the crowd at the Riddlesworth home was one of the two young men whose aim it was to get Lady Elise Halden to the house party they were planning to host for their friends. Marlowe watched as their target flirted with every man who showed her attention. Of course, he could never report this to his cousin. Even before Caversham's lackeys had gotten to him, Sinclair would have seethed just witnessing this gay, laughing temptress flirting with every buck but him.

Since his cousin's beating earlier this week, Marlowe changed his thinking and he now agreed with his cousin. It was no longer just about gaining her sizable dowry for their group. The whore needed to be taught a lesson.

Chapter Fourteen

On a warm sunny morning in mid-June, wearing her new burgundy riding habit in preparation for her morning ride with her brother, Elise entered the dining room to breakfast to find Ren nervously issuing orders for his horse to be brought around immediately and the coach sent to pick up Prescott. Then he instructed Michael on the handling of certain business and legal matters for him while he was away.

"My secretary will arrive at nine," Ren said as he collected several leather-bound folios and handed them to his valet for packing. "He will assist you, Michael. All the files are right there in the office, he knows which ones you should need. Once you've gone over the terms of those contracts and approve them, send them to me for signatures, please."

"Is everything all right?" Concern began to build in Elise as her brother made arrangements for a lengthy absence. The usually collected and normally unruffled Duke of Caversham seemed shaken. The only time she'd ever seen him this way was when someone in their family was ill or harmed in some way. Every possible horrible thing that could befall their kin began to run through her mind, frightening her. "What is the matter? Is it Lia? Are the children hurt?"

He shook his head and took a deep breath, unaware that his upset caused those around him to become distressed as well. "Lia has taken to her bed." His voice quivered noticeably. "She hasn't been feeling well and I'm concerned for the babe. Though she says she's fine and insists I remain in town for your sake, I'm away for Haldenwood and bringing Prescott with me. I'm not sure when I will return."

"I want to go home with you." Turning to a footman, she asked that her maid be notified to pack her things.

Ren motioned to stop the footman. "That's not necessary just yet, Elise. Like I told Grandmother a few minutes ago, give me time to assess the situation. I'll send word if you and she are needed at Haldenwood. For now you can continue with the remainder of the season. You'll have Grandmother with you, and Michael close by, so you will be safe."

Ren left soon after, promising to send word about Lia's health as soon as possible. Elise was too nervous to breakfast, so she proceeded with her ride in the park, with her secret fiance at her side instead of her brother.

Michael Dennis Brightman, Viscount Bellefield, and eleventh Earl of Camden, was nearly unmanned by an innocent slip of a woman. Damn her passion. No, damn his inability to control his desire when he held her in his arms. Her passion for him was a wondrous thing, something he wanted to arouse and nurture for many years to come. Just not yet.

Upon returning from their ride to find Ren's secretary had not yet arrived, Elise had followed Michael into Ren's office. He noticed the despair in her eyes, and his attempt to comfort her turned into a kiss so passionate and intense as to almost make him forget where he was. When the knock sounded on the door, it surprised them both. Elise recovered her senses first and replied to the person on the other side. Only after straightening her riding habit, did she open the door to allow the secretary entrance. She greeted the man as Michael moved uncomfortably to the chair behind Ren's desk, praying the secretary didn't notice his risen predicament.

He had to make Elise see the wisdom in waiting a little longer. In six weeks his family would come out of mourning. After that he would marry her immediately. Except that it wasn't what his mother had asked of him. His mother preferred he have the banns read, and they marry in the chapel at Woodhenge.

Drumming his fingers on the desk as he waited on the secretary to complete a dictated change to the terms of a contract, Michael resolved that his mother didn't order the particulars of his marriage. He'd inform her, and his sisters, of the time and place of the event, and they would be welcomed to attend. Michael wanted his mother to realize their presence wasn't necessary for the sacrament to occur.

He resolved to make quick work of these contracts and be out of here. An afternoon sparring with a suitable partner at Jackson's might help ease this pent up frustration.

Several hours later after reading each contract, making recommendations and changes, then dictating several notes to Ren, he left the packet on the desk for the courier to Haldenwood. After dismissing Ren's secretary for the day, he sought Elise to bid her good day and found her and Lady Sewell in the parlor entertaining Lady Randolph, her daughter Caroline and Captain Wilson. They were partaking of tea and cakes when he entered and they all greeted him warmly. Elise rose and offered to pour him a cup, but he declined.

"Lady Caroline and Captain Wilson have just shared their wonderful news," she said.

"What news is this?" Michael looked from Wilson to Lady Caroline.

"We are getting married in the spring," said Wilson, as he rose from the settee.

The bride-to-be blushed prettily and Michael smiled, genuinely happy for the two of them. "My most sincere congratulations to you both." He walked over to Wilson and shook his hand. After a few moments of exchanging pleasantries regarding the upcoming nuptials, Michael asked for a moment with Elise. "The packet for the courier is on your brother's desk, you and your grandmother can add your letters home to it." He stared at the floral pattern in the carpet. It was the same hand-tied turkey rug he'd seen in this room for years.

Good God, but he felt like a green lad right then! He didn't want to believe it was the kiss they shared earlier causing his distraction. After all, he'd kissed many women, all far more experienced at the art of seduction than Elise, and had never been thus affected.

"In light of the circumstances, I think it inappropriate to go anywhere tonight, as we may get word from Haldenwood soon."

"You're right," she agreed. Then asked, "Would you come for dinner then and keep me and grandmother company?"

"I'm sorry I... cannot. I... have a previous engagement I must attend to." Michael had to leave, he was starting to stutter, something he hadn't done since his school days. "I will see you for breakfast."

Disappointment flickered in her eyes just before acceptance. "Fine. Then I bid you a good evening," she replied and turned back to her guests.

Michael made a last stop in the foyer to speak with Ren's butler. He left only after he checked on the guard and felt certain Elise and Lady Sewell would be safe in the home alone for the evening. Then he was off to Jackson's first and perhaps dinner at his club. He had much to contemplate this night.

Elise heard Beverly enter the house, her long stride sure as she headed toward the dining room, where she and her grandmother sat in quiet contemplation at one end of the long table.

Foregoing a greeting as she entered the room, she asked, "Have you had any word yet?" She refused a place setting, but asked for a cup of tea.

"None," Elise said. Looking at her grandmother, she said, "This was sudden, wasn't it? In the last letter I received from her yesterday, Lia was feeling fine. This morning she is unwell, and it is such that my brother runs home to her bedside. I don't understand, and I admit to being afraid."

"Don't be afraid, girls. I thought she was doing well also," Her grandmother set her spoon down ending her meal with the last of her soup, and backed her chair with the help of a footman. "This is out of our hands, ladies. Prescott is there with Ren. Right now, the best thing we can do is pray for Lia's health." She reached for her cane, and leaned on it heavily, her gnarled and weathered hands aged from years of gardening. Her grandmother looked at them both and said, "Life is fleeting, and to have love in that life is precious. Not everyone does, you know." She closed her eyes, her age and condition showing tonight more than ever. "I have loved twice, and buried both men. If you're fortunate enough to find someone you cannot live without, make sure they know every day how much you love them. Every single day. Because you never know what tomorrow brings." Grandmother turned and began to leave the room. As she walked she added, "And to that end, I am off for bed early. My prayers will be a little longer and more detailed tonight." After she bid her and Beverly good night, she could be heard telling the footman not to hover so closely behind her as she began the climb up the stairs.

She finished her meal in silence, while a plan began to form in her mind. Elise couldn't share her thoughts with Beverly just then. After her friend finished a second cup of tea she said, "Come to my room with me, and lets talk."

"I hope all turns out well with the babe," Beverly said.

"So do I."

Once the bedroom door was shut behind them, Elise searched the room for Bridget or any other maids. "I have been thinking on my grandmother's words," she whispered, "and she's right."

Beverly nodded. "She has seen enough years to speak with authority on most every subject."

"I want to be with Michael tonight. I love him." Elise hoped she conveyed the urgency she felt. Or else Beverly would never understand.

"Your betrothal will be announced in a matter of

weeks, 'Lise. Why rush it now?"

"You heard my grandmother. We never know what tomorrow holds for us, and Lia is an excellent example." She stood and began to pace the length of her sitting room, all while keeping an eye out for Bridget entering through her bedroom. "You see, I have been in contact with Lia these past weeks she's been in the country, on nearly a daily basis. At Woodhenge she was the epitome of maternal good health and beauty. Never once has she mentioned any difficulty with this pregnancy. Rather, it's been just the opposite she says."

Beverly was beginning to look confused. So she clarified, "Lia almost died giving birth to Marcus. Ren was shot at in the field while he was hunting. Grandmother fell down the stairs and hit her head. My father's coach broke a wheel and went down a ravine." At her friend's confused look, she explained, "Beverly, I am done waiting, and taking the chance that all will be well following *his* time table. I want to be the master of my destiny. This is my *life*, and I'm not living it if I'm always following the dictates of others." Elise stood, a new determination spurring her on. "But tonight I'm choosing to live. I'm choosing to be with Michael."

Her friend gave her a disapproving grimace, so Elise tried another explanation. "The other day you asked me a question, and I told you I'd think on it. Remember? You wanted to know why I feel this sense of urgency." When Beverly nodded, she continued. "If my father had loved me as he did Ren, he would have spent more time with me, shown a little interest in me or my life. He didn't. He didn't care about anything I did unless I was in trouble. Perhaps it had something to do with the fact that I lived and my mother died." When Beverly's blue eyes grew round as saucers, Elise reassured her, "Truly, it doesn't matter now. I've reconciled myself to that."

Beverly nodded. "We're finally getting somewhere Elise."

"It's not what you think. I'm not trying to replace my father with Michael. That's abhorrent."

"You are after the affection and intimacy, but not the—" Beverly looked around the room to make sure no one heard her say the next word, and when she did was a whisper. "—Sex."

Elise gave her friend a knowing grin. "No, I assure you I want Michael sexually too."

Her friend shook her pinned-up blond ringlets. "I don't like this, Elise," Beverly said, "I mean, what if you're found out?

"I can be home before sunrise." At Beverly's worried frown, she added, "Before even Bridget awakens. If I get back early enough, no one will know but you."

"You cannot possibly go to his residence," her friend argued.

Elise scanned the room. "Well, I cannot invite him to mine! There are servants here who would report to my brother every detail of my actions while he was away. And what they didn't know for fact, they would speculate upon." She shook her head. "No, I must go to him."

"Oh, damnation," Beverly swore. "I hate it when you get that determined look. It always leads to calamity."

"Yes, but this time you'll not be involved, so you have nothing to worry over. I merely want time alone with Michael."

"Trying to sneak into your house in the middle of the

night is dangerous," Beverly said. "It's too risky."

"Then what do you suggest?"

"Against my better judgment I think.... You should come stay with me tonight," her friend suggested. "Then you don't have to worry when you get home tomorrow morning as you're coming from *my house*. Understand?"

Elise sighed, then gave a slight smile to her friend. "How do I thank you both for giving me this gift?" When Beverly turned a curious glance her way, Elise explained. "You see, in my last letter to Lia, I lamented how Michael never allowed himself to be alone with me. How we were always in the company of others, usually Ren."

"I see," Beverly said as realization dawned. "Brilliant sister-in-law you have there, Elise."

"Yes, I think so, too." Elise went into her dressing room and took out her small valise, and began to put a few of her essentials inside, along with her riding breeches, plain boy's shirt and an old jacket. "Lia presented me with the possibility. You are giving me an option in the execution. So I am taking the opportunity to make my desires known to Michael."

As though Providence itself was shining on her, at exactly the moment she buckled the strap on her valise, a knock on her door brought a footman with two messages from Haldenwood. He handed one packet to her, and said the other was for Lady Sewell. Before he left, the lad said he would wait for a reply if there was one. Anxious for the news, she opened the packet. There were two notes, one from her brother and one from Lia.

She read the note from her brother first. In it, he

stated that all was well for the time being, but Prescott ordered continued bed rest for his duchess and Ren had decided he would stay on for a few days at least, to see how she fared.

Opening Lia's note, Elise released a sigh as she read her words. Her sister-in-law stated all was well and that more than anything she'd missed her husband. She said she hoped that Elise and their grandmother wouldn't be too terribly lonely without Ren there for a few days, but told her she hoped she made good use of her time. She also added a post script.

I thought I would get him out of your way for a few days. – L.

Elise collapsed from relief. "Thank God." Tears blurred her vision as she handed the notes to Beverly before she took a sheet of vellum from her desk drawer. She swallowed a lump in her throat then said, "See? I was right."

She penned a short note to her brother, and another to his perceptive duchess, she thanked them for sending word of Her Grace's condition so quickly. She stated all was well, that she would spend this time with Beverly and Grandmother, and hoped to see them both soon. She added a post script in Lia's note.

Mille Grazie. – E.

Beverly read both missives as Elise wrote her replies. Tears welled in her eyes. "You know, Elise," she sniffled, "You have much to be thankful for. I have no siblings at all, and the only cousins I have are in Scotland."

"Until my brother married, I never appreciated it

enough." Elise sealed the letter and placed it in the leather packet. She handed it to the footman, who assured her it would go back to Haldenwood first thing in the morning, after Lady Sewell had an opportunity to read her letter and reply as well. Lifting her overnight satchel, she led the way down the hall to her grandmother's room and knocked.

Thirty minutes later, after speaking with her grandmother, Elise and Beverly entered the Hepplewhite's carriage and rolled off toward Michael's townhouse. She'd effectively deterred Bridget from coming with her by saying she was going to spend one night and for one night, she could beg the help of Beverly's maid.

When the horses moved into traffic, Elise slid the window shades closed, and opened her bag. She took her breeches out and struggled into them while the vehicle was stopping and starting in London traffic. Beverly helped her remove her day dress and chemise and put on her boy's shirt sans corset. The jacket would suffice to keep her bosom from showing.

"You know," Elise said, "after all these years of complaining about being less well-endowed, tonight, I'm glad I've got little breasts."

"Your short hair also aids in the disguise, don't forget. Can you imagine trying to tame that long mass you had under a cap."

Elise nodded as they shoved the dress and underclothing into her satchel and buttoned it. Beverly knocked on the roof and asked her driver to change direction and drive down the street next to Michael's home.

"I hope he's there," Beverly stated. "What will you

do if he isn't?"

"Why, I'm going to wait for him, of course. Even if I have to sit on the stoop out front."

It took great convincing, but Beverly finally left her off on the corner of Shepherd Street at Hanover Square, down a bit from where Michael lived. Once at his front door, it took twice the amount of persuasion to get past Michael's very skeptical butler. At first, the man did not believe she was a lad from Haldenwood with a message, instructed to wait for Lord Camden's reply. It was only when she confessed who she was that he let Elise into the house. She followed the man, Samuels she learned, down the hallway, to the library, where he said she might be comfortable while she awaited his lordship's return.

"Where is Lord Camden?" Elise inquired.

"His lordship," the man said, infinitely more polite now that she admitted who she was, "is at his club for dinner. Should I send someone around to fetch him, my lady?"

"That won't be necessary, Samuels," she said as the butler held the library door open for her. "I should hate to disturb him. But you will tell him I am here the moment he arrives, won't you?"

"Yes, my lady," he replied.

She gave him what she hoped was an appreciative smile. "Thank you, Samuels."

"Is there anything I can get you?" The butler asked. "Tea? A fire in the hearth?"

"No, thank you. I'll be fine." Once the man left, Elise removed her jacket and boots then sat on the chaise, wondering just how long she would have to wait for Michael to return. After an hour, she stretched out on the lounge. Before much longer, she closed her eyes.

Michael returned home immediately after his meal as he was not in the mood to socialize with anyone this night, much less sit in on a card game. He found Samuels waiting for him in the foyer, a grimace on his already dour face. He hoped there wasn't bad news from Haldenwood.

"My lord, you have a female visitor waiting for you in the library," his butler advised.

Unconcerned for the female waiting for him he replied, "Is there any news from Caversham?"

"Yes, a note arrived an hour ago, and is on your desk. Would you like to see the note first or your guest?"

"I'll get the note. Go on to bed. Whoever the female is, she can wait until after I see what Ren has to say." Michael had no idea who the woman waiting for him could be, but no lady would be in the home of a single man at this hour. Likely it was Juliette, his former mistress, asking to return after realizing the error she made in leaving him.

"Very good, my lord. But...."

"Yes, Samuels?" Michael asked as he walked toward his office.

"I'm sorry, my lord, but the guest waiting for you is not one you will want to keep here for too long. It would not be beneficial to the lady's reputation if anyone witnessed her arrival." His butler then bowed and departed toward the baize door leading to the servants' stairs.

Michael entered his office and immediately spotted the note on his desk. Opening it, he saw it was from

Ren. After he scanned the first few sentences he breathed a sigh of relief. The prayer he'd been repeating in his head all day had been answered, and all was well.

Tossing the note onto his desk, he decided to see who this female was waiting for him in the library and make quick work of dispatching her. Opening the door to the library, he looked around and saw no one. Then a soft snore caught his attention and he went to the leather chaise. At first he thought he saw a boys breech-covered leg. As he drew closer he groaned, especially when he recognized the shapely curve of Elise's thigh and calf and delicate stocking-covered ankle and foot.

"What in the name of all that's holy...." He couldn't believe his eyes. That little minx! His heart lurched when he thought of the explanations needed to cover this up. He wished he could be angry with her, but more than anything he just wanted to wake her with a soft kiss.

He smiled in the dim room. Elise looked ethereal and angelic while she slept. A softly snoring angel, but an angel nonetheless. Reaching out, he touched her to see if she were really there, or if this was—by some odd trick of his imagination—a dream.

Her amber eyes opened slowly and he felt that familiar tightening in his gut when she smiled that soft, sleepy smile up at him.

"Michael," she said, her voice husky from sleep. "I've been waiting for you for ages."

He returned her smile with one of his own. "A man must eat dinner."

She sat up, and pushed her hair off her face. "Don't you have a cook? You seem to eat elsewhere a great deal."

He sat on the ottoman across from her, wondering why she was here. "Are you concerned for your sister-in-law? I just received a letter saying...."

"Yes, I received one as well. I am so pleased, though we should still pray all remains well with Lia and the babe."

Concern began to gnaw at him, now that he understood Samuels' words. "Elise, did anyone see you arrive? Where does your grandmother think you are?"

"Beverly left me off at the corner. No one recognizes me dressed as I am. Grandmama thinks I am staying with Beverly tonight."

He tugged at his collar and cravat, trying to catch a breath. Rising, he went to the sideboard and poured a brandy. "Why are you here, minx?"

She moved to stand in front of him, turning her amber-eyed gaze up to his. "I learned something today. In my worries for Lia and the new babe, I realized life is fleeting. We could be fine one day and on death's door the next. During those hours when I didn't know how she was I prayed for God to spare Lia for Ren, because losing her would devastate him. I am not going to pass up this opportunity to tell you how much I love you. And I will show you this every day Michael because you are that important to me." Lifting a hand to his face, she traced the tiny scar with a finger before cupping his cheek. "At Woodhenge you showed me a glimpse of how wonderful it could be with you. I want more. I want you, Michael."

"Are you certain you do not wish to wait any longer?"

Samuels, the butler at Lord Camden's London

residence smiled as he went down the steps to his quarters next to the pantry. As he sat on his narrow cot, he hoped no one had followed the Lady soon to be his mistress here, or would begin any untoward gossip about her. If that should occur, Samuels would then be forced to spend time on his aching knees begging for forgiveness from his maker, because he would have to lie and say that particular visitor was the courier from Haldenwood awaiting the earl's reply.

It would work, because he would make sure it did.

Chapter Fifteen

"I have never been more certain of anything in my life," Elise said softly, hoping he felt the same way.

He lifted her hand and kissed her palm. The simple action sent a tingling heat straight to her core. He drew her closer and lowered his head, taking her lips in a kiss full of the desire she'd hoped all along he possessed for her. Moaning into his mouth as she opened for him, her hands pulling him even closer as her body mirrored the intensity of his passion. He cupped her bottom and lifted her slightly, bringing her closer to his arousal—something that both frightened and thrilled her. She knew the mechanics of the act and had wanted this with him for weeks now, yet for a moment she thought about fleeing. Though she was curious and aroused, there was a part of her that wondered how the thing she felt against her lower belly was going to fit inside her.

With him so intimately pressed against her and knowing he desired her as much as she did him, she grew bolder. His lips moved down the column of her neck and she arched into him with a rising passion. Sliding her fingers around to his chest, she flicked the buttons open on his waistcoat and pushed both that and his jacket off his shoulders where they fell to the floor behind him.

Michael's palms roved along her back and forward to her breasts causing them to tighten under his touch, and he groaned as he looked at her. "Where are your stays, my lady?"

Humiliated, she blushed as though she'd been caught indecent. "Sacrificed for the sake of the costume. It isn't as though it's needed anyway." She fought the tears that threatened when he didn't reply, and she rushed to apologize for her lack of endowment. "Please...." She cleared her throat. "Please Michael, tell me I do not displease you. It's not as though it's something I can control. I've prayed for a more womanly physique for years now, to no avail."

He cupped her small breasts. "You please me greatly. I've thought of little else since we were at Woodhenge."

She sighed, relieved her body pleased him. "Michael?"

"Yes, minx?"

"You know that I have no experience with what we are about to do and... and... I don't want to disappoint you."

"You could never do that, minx." He kissed her cheeks and forehead. "Never." He tugged the hem of her shirt from her breeches. His hands sought her flesh and skimmed up her ribcage, spreading heat wherever he touched. Her tongue reached out between her parted lips and traced a path from the collar of his shirt to just below his ear, where she pressed a kiss before nibbling on his earlobe just as he'd done to her.

"Michael?" Elise thought she heard a quiver in her voice and prayed he didn't.

He backed away a fraction, just enough for the air to

cool her heated flesh and his eyes to meet hers. "Hmm...."

"I love you, Michael."

He groaned, as he kissed the top of her head.

Elise inhaled his fresh citrus smell and wanted to melt into him. She didn't know any other way to tell him what she wanted other than to come right out and say what was in her heart. "I feel I'm having to beg you to love me in return, Michael. As you've said you wanted to marry me, is it unreasonable of me to hope you might love me?"

His eyes closed and he sighed. "You're not being unreasonable," he said. "I... don't know... how to say the words. They aren't easy for me. But if you'd give me a chance, I could show you."

Her whole body trembled with fear or joy, she was unsure which. But it didn't matter. He *did* love her.

"Then maybe we'd better seek a more comfortable setting, don't you think?"

She nodded and felt heat rush to her cheeks. He lifted her in his arms and moved to carry her from the library up to his room.

"Stop Michael! Put me down. You'll hurt yourself."

"Shh.... You'll wake the staff."

Elise thought he was certainly very strong to carry her such a long way, because she was no petite miss, she was nearly as tall as he. She giggled softly, not wanting to call attention to their antics. For someone about to sleep with her lover for the first time, she wasn't worried that he would hurt her in the bed, but that he might hurt himself on the way to it.

Tucking her face into his neck self-consciously, she begged him not to drop her on the way up the steps. She also stilled her feet under her so as not to hit the wall, stair rail, or heaven forbid knock a bust or vase over.

Until now she fretted about her height and lack of feminine endowments. But Michael's words moments earlier made her feel more desired and wanted than ever.

He adjusted her in his arms to open the door to his bedroom and kicked it shut with his foot. He carried her to the dais where his massive bed beckoned, one corner turned down for him. When he lowered her to stand before him, she didn't have much time to look around because he'd taken her lips again in a kiss that stirred the flame burning in her, causing her to tremble in his arms.

His hands and mouth were everywhere at once. He trailed hot, wet kisses on her face, neck, and most especially in the valley between her breasts, causing the heat to spread down to her lower belly. She felt his hands work the buttons on the side of her breeches. The leather parted and his fingers worked into the waistband, opening them wider. He pushed them down, along with her silk drawers, leaving her bare below her waist. Her linen shirt was next as he raised it and her chemise over her head, baring her to him completely. At first she wanted to hide herself from his molten hazel gaze, and when she tried to raise her hands, he stopped her.

"No," he whispered, his voice sounding as shaky as she felt right then. "Don't hide yourself. I want to see you." Wherever his eyes roved over her flesh, she burned. He sat on the bed and removed his boots.

She stood there and waited, watching him, with nothing to cover herself except her hands, and he wouldn't let her. She watched him hurriedly fuss with his clothing. He threw the cravat and shirt behind him and her pulse began to quicken. When he loosened the top two buttons on his trousers, she gave a little squeak and he chuckled. Without his ever touching her, her entire body felt as though it would combust from the heat of his hazel-eyed gaze.

Reaching out for her, he drew her between his legs and placed his hands on her hips and stared into her eyes and smiled.

"I know you think yourself awkwardly made, but to me you are beautiful. With perfect breasts that are not as small as you seem to think. Hmm...." He held their weight in each palm, his thumbs grazing the tips, causing a moan to escape her. He flicked his tongue over the tips of each taut nipple, and she felt her womb clench in anticipation. "Definitely made for a man's mouth."

"Michael, please," she groaned. "You're teasing me."

He chuckled as he lifted his mouth from her breast. "I don't mean to. It's just I've waited far too long to do this." He moved to the other breast and suckled it as well.

"Not nearly as long as I have for you to do it," she replied, her voice barely a whisper.

His hands roved over her naked form appreciatively. He lifted her foot and caressed her from her ankle to the inside of her knee, causing her to tremble as a flood of desire drenched her core.

"Had I known that was all you wore beneath those breeches of yours, it would have driven me mad when we were at Woodhenge."

"Would you have made me wait this long?"

"Probably not." His fingers stroked the sensitive flesh of her thigh, moving higher, closer to his goal.

Her leg quivered as he neared her apex. "Then I should have told you."

"I'm glad you didn't. Your first time shouldn't have been in a stall or hayloft. It should be—and will be—right here, in my bed." She buckled as his fingers parted her curls, and delved into her wetness.

She held onto his shoulders for dear life as he began to move his fingers between her slick folds. Her hips rocked forward allowing him freer access, and her breaths came short and fast as he stroked her, bringing her to the edge of sanity. She couldn't think, couldn't focus on anything other than the sensations she was experiencing. Then, with a sharp spasm, she fell forward onto him, unable to stand any longer. He rolled her beneath him on the bed, his size and weight causing her to instinctively part her legs to cradle him. As his hands caressed her waist, belly and breasts, she lifted her mouth to his, wanting to devour him again. Their tongues dueled in passionate play. He straddled her, holding her down as he stripped away his shirt. Her hands instinctively reached out to touch the rigid muscles of his abdomen and she could have sworn he shivered as her fingers roved lower to the waistband of his trousers.

"Soon enough, my sweet." He slid down her body to rest between her legs. Lifting her hips slightly he brought her to his mouth, just as he did that night at Woodhenge. Elise stifled a scream with the back of her hand at the enormous jolt of pleasure that raced through her body. She tried to watch, but the delirious ecstasy left her breathless. Her head fell back onto the mattress and she grasped the bed covers as she surrendered herself up to his expert ministration.

"Oh... Michael... yes."

He lifted his head a moment and she felt his fingers enter her. "You like that, don't you? Tell me, do you like this?" he said as his fingers pressed deep into her, making her long for something more. Her body quivered as he kept her on the crest without taking her over the edge.

She met his passionate, heavy-lidded gaze. "Yes!"

"Good, there's more to come."

"Please, Michael, I want it now."

"Patience, my minx. We have all night." Michael smiled, warming her in all the places that were chilled by his temporary absence. "I don't want to tire you out so soon."

"Arrrrgh! Where are you going?" she asked too quickly, then she watched, fascinated by the beauty of his nakedness as he began to removed his trousers.

"Where's the patience I asked for?" He shoved the clothing from his body and came back to her side. His fingers traced a path from her chin over the hollow of her throat to the valley between her firm breasts, downward to her sunken navel and lower to her downy woman's curls. Parting her, he stroked her, applying more pressure. "Hopefully this will ease the sting of your first time. I hear it is uncomfortable and I would take that pain from you if I could."

When she was slick with her own wetness, he moved over her and slid his organ to her entrance. She was so wet, so ready. He rocked forward, introducing her to his body slowly, then backing away. Then moving deeper, and pulling away again.

"Just do it, Michael! Don't think to make it any easier by torturing me."

"As my lady wishes." Taking her lips in a deep kiss, so he could swallow her scream, he drove himself home. But she didn't cry out. He didn't feel any anything that should have prevented him entrance.

His head fell forward, a surge of disappointment stabbed at his heart. His best friend's sister, the woman he'd sworn to marry, kissed his forehead, then his cheek. And when her body relaxed under him, she whispered she loved him.

Bile rose up from her treachery, and something inside him died. She might love him now, but she'd loved someone else before.

Elise felt an extreme stretching and fullness that didn't hurt as she'd been told it would. In fact nothing in her entire life ever felt so right. So wonderful. When he pressed deeper, she moaned from the intense pleasure of it. She opened her eyes to look up to his, wondering if he felt the same pleasure she did. He didn't look nearly as satisfied as she felt. And she noticed he'd stopped moving, holding himself deep within her. She smiled. He was being considerate of her, she knew, by allowing her time to adjust to him.

But she wanted more. Now.

She tilted her hips upward and brought her feet up to his buttocks, intending to spur him onward. The motion seated his great length within her. Her inner muscles clenched him involuntarily, pulling him in, and keeping him there.

He didn't move and she opened her eyes, sensing

something was wrong. He didn't look right. Had she done something to displease him? "Michael? Why have you stopped?"

A myriad of emotions played across his handsome brow. He looked disappointed and at the same time, angry.

"How do you know the act is not over?" She imagined that cool, accusatory tone was one he likely used in the courtrooms.

"Because I was told there would be more...." Her voice began to quaver, but she continued. "And that I would know when the act was nearing completion because it would feel as though I'd fallen from a mountain top and soared on the wind when I climaxed."

"Who told you these things?"

"It doesn't matter, Michael." She didn't want to tell him that she'd discussed marital relations with Lia when she was at Woodhenge a couple of weeks ago. She couldn't bear it if he thought her sister-in-law was involved in her plan to seduce him.

"You're right." He gave her a half-hearted smile. "It doesn't matter now, does it?" He pressed into her deep, moving his hips over her as she began to relax again and enjoy his motions.

His lovemaking took a different turn, no longer slow and kind, but more of a frenzied driving. He sought his release, she knew, because she felt her own building. Elise moved with him, arching up to him holding him with her arms and her legs, wanting to be as close to him as possible. Wanting, for some inexplicable reason, to have him hold her together as she shattered apart.

Then he drove into her deeper than before, repeatedly, pushing her closer to the edge, and finally over the precipice.

And she did soar.

Michael plunged into the deceitful vixen beneath him one last time, his orgasm coming in wave after wave of cleansing release. Realizing what he'd done, he collapsed onto her struggling to catch his breath. He caught a whiff of her lavender scent, and suddenly the smell repulsed him. He pushed away, and rolled from her and covered his eyes with his forearm suddenly overcome by his thoughts, unwilling to look at her.

"There can be no maiden without a head lad," he remembered his uncle telling him one night at Woodhenge when, after several glasses of port, he'd told him of his brief marriage to a woman he loved and adored. A woman who turned out to have a traitorous heart, quite like that of the woman next to him.

Now he was destined to relive history. Except Michael hadn't loved her as her uncle loved his wife. But he could have. He could have loved her, would have given her the world if she'd asked it of him.

She'd lain with another. Perhaps more than one, and that thought rocked him to his core. How could she? After she professed to have *loved* him all of her life, to have been waiting for *him* all of her life. He wondered who it was. Sinclair? Marlowe? No. Not someone in London, he knew, because she'd been under the watchful eye of both him and her brother the entire time. It had to be someone at Haldenwood. Could it have been a stable lad? The thought made him ill.

Whoever it was, could she now be carrying that man's bastard? If so, she had needed to seduce him soon, to make him think this child was his.

God, he was going to be sick. He couldn't look at

her. Couldn't even stand to be in the same room as her.

Too late, he realized the mistake he'd made by climaxing inside of her. Now there really was a chance she might carry his child. What was he to do? He couldn't back out of the promise to marry her now, both families expected a wedding. If she was carrying, he'd pray like hell the child was a daughter.

If she was not carrying, could he refuse to marry her?

No. Doing so now would cost him his friendship with Ren. Just the thought that after all these years he might lose it, because of one deceitful little wench was the knife that twisted in his heart.

Then there was his mother.... He'd had to defend his choice of bride to her before she'd left Woodhenge. She'd warned him that Elise was too independent-minded and perhaps would not make the most dutiful wife. His mother might not ever say out loud that she was right, but Michael would know she thought it.

Elise stretched and turned to her side, her lithe, delectable body so enticing to look at, but her heart so treacherous as to force him to choose between true happiness with an honest woman, and life with a lying wench. One choice meant losing the best friend he'd ever had. The other meant sacrificing the opportunity for real love.

"Michael? Is something wrong?"

Her voice was so innocent, and so deceptive. He couldn't look at her. He was afraid if he did, he might fall prey to her seductive ways and want her yet again. She was a superb actress.

"Have I done something to displease you? Was I not a willing partner? Is there something I could have done to please you more?"

"Yes." The simple word choked him as it rolled off his tongue.

She sat up, bringing a pillow to cover her body. "What is it? What could I have done, Michael, to make it better for you?"

"You could have been honest with me, Elise."

Her soft voice rose along with the growing fear in her expression. "I have never been anything but honest with you, Michael."

He sat up, leaning against his headboard. "Come now, Elise, you know that I am a man of the law. I deal in facts and evidence on a daily basis. You needn't pretend any longer."

Those beautiful amber eyes began to lose the warmth he'd witnessed just minutes earlier. "Good God, Michael, you're frightening me. What have I done?"

"I have but one question Elise, and I want an honest answer from you."

"Michael?" Pulling the sheet around her, she shifted positions, resting back on her ankles and backed away from him, bewilderment marring her beautiful features. "I have always been open and honest with you. I have never lied to you."

"How many others have there been? If it's just one, I might be able to stomach it. More and I might be sick."

Her face blanched. She'd been found out and she knew it. Before he could react, she slapped his face so hard, his head rang like a bell. "How dare you!" she hissed.

He yanked her arm when she moved to strike him again. "I'll tell you how I dare! You had no maidenhead. There was nothing for me to breach when I entered you. Someone else had done the job for me." He tossed her arm aside and rose from the bed. Finding his banyan robe folded on the bench at the foot of the bed, he shoved his arms through and tied the belt.

In an instant, Michael had turned Elise's world upside down. What should have been a beautiful interlude between two lovers had become a sick, disgusting accusation regarding her virtue. Or rather, her lack of it, according to him. Her entire body shook with blood red anger and unspeakable pain, like none she'd ever known before, and she now found herself defending her own honor.

"I have never, ever in my life even kissed a man before you. I cannot control whether you choose to believe me or not. What I can control is being in your presence, for suddenly you disgust me!"

"The facts are the facts, Elise," he said calmly, still rubbing his cheek, her palm print an angry red stain.

She wanted to hit him again. "I don't know how I can prove to you that I've had no lover before you."

"There is a way, Elise," he stated.

"How?"

He threw her a folded and pressed linen from his washstand. "Wipe between your legs and tell me, is there blood?"

As perverse as it sounded, she did so, and she drew forth only the essence of their lovemaking. No streaks of blood at all. His accusations crushed her heart and showed her a dark, unyielding and judgmental side to the man she once loved. But she realized now, as she looked at the linen in her hand, why he made the accusations, and how he'd arrived at his conclusion.

She clenched the sheet tighter around her. "This

proves nothing, Michael. Nothing."

"Quite the contrary, my dear. It proves I am right."

Elise couldn't look at him.

"I rest my case," he said, and left the room through the connecting door without ever looking back at her. She heard the lock click as he shut her out of his life forever.

Elise sat on the bed and cried. How dare he question her virtue? All her life she'd wanted no one but him. Had dreamed of nothing but this night—or rather, how this night should have been.

She hated him. What a fool she'd been all these years. Never had the world seen a bigger fool. She'd been such a simpleton, thinking that by waiting for him and by keeping herself chaste and irreproachable, that one day he would come to love her as she loved him. But he didn't now, and never would.

In fact, he knew nothing of love. She gave him everything she had—her heart, her honor, her honesty. Even her very soul. And what did he give her in return? He broke her heart, maligned her honor, questioned her honesty, and tore her soul from her.

She didn't know how long she sat on Michael's bed but the more she thought, the angrier she got. She had to leave. Leave his bed and his home before he changed his mind and came back to inflict more pain to her now fractured heart.

Her mind made up, she cleaned herself and dressed. She opened the door and looked both ways before entering the hallway. She was certain he'd retreated to his study, so after descending the servant's stairs, she stopped in the library she'd waited in earlier to put her stockings and boots back on, then sneaked out through the kitchens and into the small mews behind his house. She had to give her eyes a moment to adjust to the darkness within, but was soon leading out his big gelding. "Attila," she whispered lovingly. "It's been a long time, hasn't it my friend?" As luck would have it, the horse's bridle hung on a hook near the stall door. She didn't bother with the saddle, Attila went well without one.

She climbed onto the horse's back from the stone block, adjusted her seat and cued the beast forward. He stepped gingerly into a walk and she held the horse back until they were in the park. At this time of night, there would be no one on the track and once there, she leaned forward and gave the beast his head. The gelding flew around the Row with only the fog-shrouded, crescent moon to guide their way.

Elise raced her demons, each and every one bearing the name Michael. Each lap around, she cursed him for something different, for every wound he'd inflicted, every hurtful thing he'd said, until both she and the animal beneath her nearly dropped from exhaustion. And she came to a conclusion.

Her life went on. Without him.

Michael stood at the window of his office and watched her leave on his favorite horse. If anyone other than he could control the beast, it was Elise. She'd be fine, of that he had no worries. Dressed as she was no one would recognize her. In the morning, he'd send a lad to Caversham House to retrieve the animal.

Right now he had a bigger concern than his horse. Or Elise.

What would he say to her brother—his best friend—

to explain what had come between Elise and himself? Knowing Ren as he did, Michael expected he would call him out. He would show, of course. But he'd never raise his weapon toward the man whose friendship meant the world to him. Ren had a family now and a wife who loved him.

No, if anyone deserved to die over the events of this night, it was him, for he never should have taken her to his bed. Never should have believed her when she said she's loved him for forever. Would love him forever. He thought she was different. That what they could have had was different. *He should have known better.*

Yes, there were women who would gladly have married him for the title. Chaste, pure women who would sire heirs in exchange for a position in society. But he had believed that with Elise he had a chance at happiness that had been denied his uncle. Happiness that his parents had but a fleeting taste of. *He should have known better.*

That type of love, that type of happiness, was so rare he was foolish to have hoped he could have a piece of it, even for a short period of time. No matter what she'd said about loving him. No matter that she'd led him to believe it possible.

A soft feminine voice, speaking clear and sure, pierced through the shield encasing his heart. *I have never been anything but honest with you, Michael.* The image, the expression on her face at the moment his accusation registered—the deep pain and anguish he caused—burned in his brain. He couldn't escape the sound of her voice, and the sight of her tears. The sound of her voice grew louder and louder in his head. *I love you, Michael.* She'd whispered the words as he punished her with sex. She loved him and he just broke her heart.

He poured himself a scotch, as a silent cry burst forth. And without taking a sip, he threw the crystal glass against the wall, shattering it and sending shards throughout his study. He just made the most grievous accusation against a lady a man could make.

Dear God, what if he was wrong?

With the gelding beneath her blowing hard, Elise dismounted and walked him back to the Caversham mews, leaving Attila with a trusted stable lad. She slipped onto the property through the alley without anyone in the house the wiser. Elise knew what to do. It was amazing how clarity came easier to her while on horseback.

She was not going to marry Lord Camden. In fact, she prayed for his soul to burn in hell.

However, the morning papers didn't know this.

The next day, the *Morning Post* claimed that according to a source close to the couple, an announcement would be made soon regarding the impending marriage between a certain earl and a sister of a duke.

Chapter Sixteen

Elise's breakfast tray sat untouched on the table in her room. She didn't want to upset her grandmother with her red, puffy eyes and swollen nose. The woman had an intuition like a falcon on the hunt for a rabbit. She'd know there was something wrong, and until she spoke with Beverly and could invent a plausible reason for her upset, Elise thought it better to avoid her.

While she waited for Beverly to arrive, she'd alternately cried and cursed, sometimes both at the same time. Already a footman had returned Michael's horse to his residence in Hanover Square, and delivered her note to the Hepplewhite home. Sitting cross-legged in the middle of her bed, linen kerchief in hand in case tears fell yet again, she thought through her plan once more.

She wiped her nose as Bridget entered with Beverly trailing behind her. Her maid lifted the untouched tray, looked at her again, then left the room shaking her head.

Beverly sat on the bed next to Elise and placed an arm about her shoulders, the sincerity of her action bringing on a fresh bout of sobbing. She cried on her friend's shoulder and, being the dear friend she was, Beverly let her get her new muslin day dress wet with her tears. After several minutes Elise took a shuddering breath and looked her friend in the eyes.

"You look like hell." Beverly never believed in mincing words.

"Thank you," Elise muttered. "I love you, too."

"I take it then, that he refused you."

She wiped her nose as she shook her head. "No. It's much worse than that."

Beverly straightened with a frown, and asked the next question. "What did he do to you?"

"He didn't do anything I didn't *let* him do."

Her friend straightened, a concerned expression forming in her brow. "Did he hurt you? If he did, I'll...."

"Not in the physical sense," she reassured.

"Perhaps you'd best tell me everything." Beverly fluffed the pillows Elise wasn't using and sat against the headboard, settling in for Elise's tale of the night's events.

Ever since they were children Elise and Beverly shared every confidence. Beverly was like a sister to her, even closer than her own sister Sarah, who was still a child. Elise needed her friend's sympathy and wisdom right then. She needed to know what to do next.

But she also felt there was a line she could not cross. It was a line that changed the boundary of their relationship. So for the first time in their years of friendship, she couldn't tell Beverly *every* detail. Elise could only confess so much, leaving out a few intimate details, because to tell another person of the pleasure she found in Michael's arms felt like a violation of her brief happiness. Elise resumed the tale with his disgusting accusation and what he believed was proof of her not being a maid. She told her friend about the slap, taking his horse and racing through the park in the middle of the night, then finally sneaking home in the small hours of the morning.

"That... that... dirty cur!" Beverly stuttered, visibly struggling to find the worst possible names for him. "Why... that... knave!"

"He's worse, Beverly. Much worse." She blew her nose again. "And I never knew. Strange, but I never thought the fantasy of him would be so much better than the reality of him. I truly believed he cared for me, might eventually come to love me, else I never would have offered myself up like a Christmas goose waiting for him to carve out my heart."

"Well, I'm sure there's a way to prove to him that you were, in fact, a virgin when he took you to his bed."

"Not according to him." Elise snorted, and repeated his words with a mocking tone. "'...*I am a man of the law. I deal in facts and evidence on a daily basis.*' He said there was no barrier," Elise whispered with humiliation. "He accused me of having had not just one, but perhaps more before him."

"I can talk to him. No one has known you as long as I, and we truly have no secrets between us."

"It will do no good." Elise stood and began to pace the room. "Besides, we have a much larger, and potentially more disastrous problem than my ruination."

"*What* could be more disastrous than *that*?"

"If my brother learns of this, he'll call Michael out. If that happens, Ren could be killed, leaving Marcus and the new baby without a father and Lia without a husband. I can't be responsible for that." She couldn't say it to Beverly, because she didn't want to shock her friend in such a horrific manner, but before she'd let that happen Elise would just kill Michael herself and hang for the crime. She would rather do that than to have her brother killed in a duel. A fresh wash of tears threatened and she swiped them away with the backs of her hands. How had it come to this?

"The *field of honor*. Ha!" she said, more to herself than to her friend. "He wouldn't know what honor was if it slapped him in the face." She began to laugh, a crazed sounding noise, even to her own ears. "It did slap him in the face and he *still* didn't know what it was!" She laughed through a new wave of tears. She was tired of crying. That poor excuse for a gentleman didn't deserve her tears. "Damn you, Michael," Elise whispered in her empty room. "*Damn you!*"

Realization dawned clear on Beverly's face and her eyes filled with fear. "What are we going to do? Good God, we cannot let your brother learn of this. What about Grandmother? Does she suspect anything?"

Elise shook her head. "I have avoided going downstairs until after we spoke. I cannot tell her. She would be so very disappointed in me. Then she'll say we should tell Ren."

"We cannot have that," Beverly said. After several minutes of silence, she then asked, "So what will you do?"

"I'm thinking I need to talk to Michael, assure him *I* will never speak of last night to anyone, and get him to promise the same. Regardless of what he thinks of me, I don't wish him dead." Elise paced the Aubusson rug. "I'm sure he'll see the wisdom of what I say. If he doesn't, then he deserves his fate."

At that, Elise began another bout of tears, only when she'd settled down did Beverly ask, "Will you go back to Haldenwood now, or see the season to the end?"

"Much as I would love to go home, there are only a few weeks left. I should probably see it through." Elise started to cry again, not that she'd really stopped since she'd gotten home. "I'll..." she sniffled and blew her nose again. "I'll be fine in a day or two. Really."

"You know once word gets out that there is no agreement between you and Michael, you will be hounded by every money-hungry rogue in London."

"Yes, yes. I've been warned. Repeatedly."

Elise sat at her writing desk and took a sheet from the drawer. Lifting her quill, she dipped it and began to scrawl, her hand flying across the paper. She folded it and placed her seal on the back. Elise kissed the vellum and held it to her breast as a tear trickled down her face. *Oh, Michael,* her heart cried. She choked down a lump in her throat. "This should bring him around."

"What did you write?"

"Only that if he didn't come this morning, I would spend my afternoon searching for him, and find him, no matter where he was."

Beverly groaned. "You would, too." Elise nodded. "Your eyes are puffy. Rest while we wait for Michael to either reply or arrive. I shall fetch a book from the library and read."

Elise rang for Bridget and asked for more cold compresses, then reclined on her chaise with the wet material over her eyes. She wished she could cry prettily like Beverly. Instead her nose and eyes swelled like that drawing in last week's paper of Mad Jack Thorne, the pugilist, after his latest bout.

It was imperative to Elise that she appear as normal as possible to Michael when he arrived. Not that she wanted to attract him. No, she wanted him to know she'd not nurse a broken heart for him any longer than it took to change her gowns.

He didn't need to know how shredded her heart really was over his cruel accusation.

Michael looked up from the stack of papers on his desk as Samuels entered carrying a note. "This is for you, my lord. I was told to deliver it to your hands immediately. The messenger is waiting for a reply."

He took the letter and opened it. After reading the short note, written in Elise's scholarly hand, he jotted a reply, handed the note to Samuels and had him send the messenger off. He'd see her, but he had yet to figure out how to apologize to her for his accusation. All night long Michael lay in bed, his mind replaying her expression of hurt and astonishment at his words. He concluded that no one can act that well. Which meant only one thing—he'd truly and deeply wounded the one woman he wanted more than any other. Over the past weeks, he'd fallen in love with her vivacity and charm, her wit and compassion. Michael had begun to look forward to a life with Elise until he'd let his male ego and his uncle's pain from betrayal cloud his vision. He'd made an accusation last night that in another time, or in another culture would be life-ending for a woman.

Just before he'd made the accusation, she'd asked what *she* could have done to better please *him*, had asked what *she'd* done to upset *him*. She'd automatically assumed her inexperience was the issue, when he'd been about to accuse her in a most vile manner.

Michael wiped the moisture that had collected in the corner of his eyes, and exhaled a shaky breath. He'd made a horrible mistake. He knew this now.

And he had no idea how to begin repairing the breach he had ripped between them.

Two hours later, he called for his carriage to be brought around and lifted her satchel. The contents of which he'd memorized, by touch, by sight, by smell. The day dress within was one of his favorites, a pale yellow muslin with green piping that complimented her sun-kissed cheeks beautifully.

He tossed the bag onto the seat next to him, the scent of lavender wafted up and twisted his heart, reminding him of the future he'd so foolishly thrown away. Elise could never have done something as devious as plan to seduce him to provide a father for a bastard by another man. How could he have jumped to such an egregious conclusion?

Michael entered Caversham House, just as he had for nearly twenty years, and for the first time felt... uncomfortable. The condemning stares of the staff were almost tangible, slicing through him like a razor. He was shown into the drawing room, where Elise waited. One look at her and he surmised they knew he was the reason for her red-rimmed and puffy eyes. What they couldn't know was the acute pain in his own heart. Pain multiplied infinite times knowing they were caused from his own actions.

"It took you long enough." She stood and placed the book she'd been reading on the table in front of her, then asked the footman for more tea. Her demeanor was rigid, fortified, not what he'd expected to find when he arrived. She'd built a wall around her heart in the hours since he'd horribly, cruelly wronged her.

He deserved her wrath he thought to himself as a

maid pushed the tea cart in. Elise dismissed the young woman, and poured herself a cup, without offering him one.

"I would have come sooner, but.... I was thinking—trying to come up with a way to say...."

"Please, don't waste your breath apologizing. There is nothing you could say, nothing you could do that can take back the hurt you inflicted upon my person, my honor, my heart. I hate you Michael Brightman. I will hate you forever."

He nodded, stepping forward, thinking if he could hold her, wrap his arms around her, that he might be able to convey the depth of his sorrow at what he had done to her. The more he looked at Elise, the more responsible he felt for her sad, tear-swollen face. He knew his minx could be waspish with her tongue, but over the past few months that side of her had disappeared and he was truly taken by the change in her.

She put her hand up, stopping him. "Do not come near me Michael. And after today, I want you to never enter a room in which I am already in, and I will do the same. Are we clear? I do not wish to breathe the same air as you. Ever again."

Michael shook his head. "We still have an agreement, Elise. Our families still expect a marriage to take place and I am not breaking our betrothal."

"I already have. There is no longer an agreement between us. I called you here to discuss what we are to tell my brother. I don't care what you think of me, but I don't want my nephew growing up without his father. If Ren suspected what you did, he'd call you out. On the off chance that he might get injured or worse, I am telling you, Lord Camden, my brother is to *never* know what you did."

He sucked in a breath, as though he'd been gut-punched in the gym. "I would never hurt my friend," he protested.

She shook her head, mumbling something about fools and men. Taking a deep breath, she straightened her spine and met his gaze directly. "Like you promised never to hurt me, Michael?"

He opened his mouth to defend himself but she cut him off.

"It doesn't matter. If my brother finds out what you accused me of, he'll call you out. It's imperative that we keep this to ourselves. Do I make myself clear?" She crossed to stand before him, a virago so beautiful all he wanted to do was wrap her in his arms and love her again. "Besides, if anyone is to meet on a field of honor, it should be *you* and *me*, because you questioned *my* virtue."

"You're right, I did, and for that I am deeply sorry, Elise."

"I don't believe you, Michael. I'll never believe you again. In fact, I think the only reason you're apologizing is you are afraid of what will happen—not just your relationship with my brother, but with your career. I'm giving you my word that I will never speak of it—and not that I think you believe me, because you made it quite clear you didn't believe me last night."

"After what—" He cleared his throat, his nerves doing strange things to his ability to speak. "—What I said to you, I deserve all this and more," he said.

"You're right," she hissed. "You do." Michael could have sworn the sneer on her face hinted at something deeper. Another emotion besides hurt and anger. Pain.

A pain so deeply entrenched in her soul that it mirrored his. But, unlike him, Elise's pain drove her anger. His pain came from knowing this was all his fault. It was his actions that caused this terrible impasse between them, and it drove him to figuring out how to make amends.

Because he didn't want to live without her. What she didn't recognize yet was he held the upper hand. If he had to, he would demand they marry. He'd already bedded her, and was within his rights to demand they wed as she could be carrying his child.

He could just imagine how she would take being forced to marry. She'd be bitter and resentful, but over time she'd grow to tolerate him.

If he was lucky.

He motioned to the bag on the table. "I've returned your clothing, my lady. Also, I thank you for the safe return of my gelding."

She nodded as she wrung the kerchief in her hands. He could've sworn there were unshed tears swimming in her eyes. Now that he was closer, he recognized the evidence of her crying for it had left its mark on her. Her eyes were red-rimmed and puffy, but more importantly, the life was missing from them. They were flat, emotionless brown eyes. He grasped her wrist as she turned to leave the drawing room.

Wrenching her arm from his grasp, she backed up several steps. "Please go, Michael. I can't believe I was such a fool for so many years. To think I waited for you for so long. Had I known you were such a vicious knave, I would have looked elsewhere and not wasted those years hoping for a fairy-tale ending with you." She didn't give him time to reply, pointing to the door. "Now get out. And if you ever breathe a word or even so much as hint at what transpired last night, I'll kill you."

After the door was shut to his carriage, he thought their meeting went well, considering. She hadn't put a ball through his heart, nor had she sliced his chest open to remove it from him. With a lifetime of groveling and apologizing, he just might win her back.

"Did you hear that?" Elise asked Beverly as she pushed the door open further to the salon off the drawing room. She'd waited to move until she saw Michael was in his carriage and it rolled off into traffic, wanting to make sure he didn't re-enter the house. She then checked the foyer, looking down the hallway and up the steps to see if her grandmother were about.

Beverly stepped through into the drawing room. "It seemed to me he was attempting to apologize and you wouldn't give him a chance."

"He cannot have possibly changed his true opinion." Her voice quavered as she succumbed to the tears again. "I think he fears my brother's anger if...." The painful lump in her throat gave way like a damn bursting, the trickle of tears becoming a gushing flow. "I hate him," she managed between bouts of tears. "No apology he speaks today can undo the pain he caused."

"I agree, but I don't believe you hate him," her friend commiserated. "You can tell yourself that, but you can't fool me."

Elise despised feeling this way. This stabbing pain in her soul could find no relief even in her anger. Any momentary alleviation of heartache she received while lashing out at him, faded the instant he left. Then the tearing, burning feeling of incompleteness rushed back like an incoming tide.

"Someone once said there is a fine line between love and hate, and that you cannot hate someone without having cared first. Think about it, Elise. That would mean the opposite of love is indifference, or the absence of caring."

No longer wiping the tears, Elise collapsed onto the chair and dropped her head into her hands, giving in to wreaking sobs.

Beverly put her arms around her and let her cry. "Oh Elise, you're incapable of indifference because you *are* so full of love. Even if Michael cannot see you for the precious treasure you are, that does not negate the fact that you are—indeed—a most precious treasure."

"It hurts, Beverly. My heart hurts."

"I know it does."

"He's the one that caused the hurt. For that I *can* hate him."

"You can certainly tell yourself that, though I know otherwise," Beverly said. "And in time, you'll get over him. Or, at least the pain will ease."

"How did you get to be so wise about matters of the heart? You're only a few months older than me."

"Remember James?"

Elise nodded, for she remembered Beverly's broken heart over Vicar Evington's son as clear as if it were her very own.

"I'm just repeating everything you told me."

Elise backed away and gave her friend a sympathetic little smile. "Now that I know how you felt, I feel even worse for what you went through."

"Don't. For look at me now. I am very much in love with Christopher, and happier than I ever was with

James because Christopher loves me back. That's not to say I don't ever think of James, for you know I do. But I think of him less frequently, and the pain I once felt is now replaced by new love."

"How do I get to that point?"

"You continue living," Beverly advised. "Live every day as though it were your last." She thought a moment, then smiled and added, "But you already do that."

Elise hiccuped, then gave a hesitant grin. They were silent a moment, while Elise dried her face and blew her nose like a stable hand.

"I do believe he'll keep his end of the bargain," Beverly said finally, "and not say anything."

"He'd better."

Two days later Elise was receiving callers, after her usual early-morning breakneck ride in the park with Beverly. She sat in the drawing room—the very one she sat in the other day when she'd sent Michael out of her life forever—with her grandmother, listening to Lady Digby speak about the plans she had for herself and her shy, somewhat of a bluestocking daughter, Anne, now that the season was almost over. They were likable enough. Lady Digby was an acquaintance of Lia's from one of her charitable committees, and her daughter was a sweet, if shy, seventeen year old, who'd also just come out this year. Anne would make Michael the perfect wife, Elise thought. The quiet, petite brunette with pretty dark eyes, would likely never counter his requests, never argue with him, never refuse him. If Michael asked for two dozen children Elise was certain dutiful Anne would agree, where Elise would tell him her limit was until he had two sons, then argue that she wasn't a broodmare.

While all that went through her head, thankfully her Grandmother carried the conversation. Elise hoped she appeared interested enough in what they said, though for the life of her she couldn't remember who or what they were talking about. She hoped that when she nodded and agreed to their comments that it sounded as though she'd been attentive and that her responses were appropriate. For all she knew she could have just agreed to steal the crown jewels and she would never have known. She really needed to pay more attention to the discussion. She lifted a forkful of cake to her mouth and snapped to attention at the sound of *his* name.

"I beg pardon, Lady Digby, what was that?"

"Lord Camden told Digby yesterday at their club that he would be attending the Holcombe party this evening. As my Digby has a previously arranged meeting tonight, he will be unable to attend with us." Her voice trailed with a querying tone. "And I had so hoped to get an introduction for my Anne," the robust matron finished.

Elise didn't think she could speak. How could they all know already? This was surely proof that society knew something was amiss between them, and Lady Digby was either the bravest or the most desperate of the many who wanted to ask but didn't dare appear so rude.

"Well Adelaide, I certainly hope this meeting is more important than his daughter getting an introduction to the most eligible gentleman this season," her grandmother said. "Why, if it weren't for his family being in mourning he would have been married by now."

Lady Digby nodded her head, the feathers on her hat bobbing over her left eye as she did. "I agree, Lady Sewell. I heard that Camden was using this time to look over this year's crop of debutants and that his decision would be made when his three months were up." The woman's colorful peacock feather bobbed as she lifted her cup and saucer to her lips and sipped. "Of course with less than two weeks left in the season, and no one young lady in the running as his potential bride, I thought surely it's because he's not met the right young lady." The woman puffed her chest out. "Who knows? Perhaps my Anne is the right lady for him," she declared, her voice sounding more like the bird that gave up its feathers for her silly hat, now that Elise thought about it.

She looked to her grandmother and back to Lady Digby. "Why certainly, we can make the introduction, if you would like, Lady Digby," Elise said. "After all Camden is a dear friend of the family." *Where did that come from?*

Elise remembered her plans for the evening didn't involve the Holcombe's but rather the opera, with Beverly and Lord Huddleston. But one look directly into the doe eyes of the meek little brunette in front of her had her agreeing to a diversion first before they went to the theater.

She looked at Anne and smiled. "You'll find that Camden is a dreadful bore, dealing with facts and evidence on a daily basis as he does. Why, all he does is speculate on the innocence or guilt of various parties, whether on trial or not." She forced a bright, if artificial, smile. "But he is a long-time friend of my brother's and if you're certain you want an introduction, I'd be most happy to grant one."

The ladies took their leave soon after, having gotten what they sought. Elise returned to the drawing room, after seeing the ladies out, when her grandmother commented on her behavior.

"That was an interesting visit. With your sister-in-law in the country I would not have expected a visit from Adelaide Digby. She must be desperate to come to us." She raised her gaze to Elise. "But I wonder where they got the idea that Camden was available. The two of you have pretty much made known your arrangement, even though you've had that little tiff the other morning."

"We no longer have an arrangement, and it is for the best," Elise said. She stood at the window watching the ladies get into their closed carriage as the afternoon threatened rain.

"You have asked that I not question you about what has been going on between you, and I have complied as I believe a young person should be allowed a modicum of privacy." Elise turned to her to respectfully protest, but her grandmother lifted a hand to silence her and continued. "But I know your heart, my darling child. And whatever your argument with him, know that no goal that is worth achieving is done so easily. Your grandfather taught me that."

Elise swallowed past the knot forming in her throat. Desperate to leave the room before she began to cry "I appreciate your words Grandmother, but Lord Camden is no longer my heart's desire. And, believe me ma'am, this is for the best." She excused herself and fled the room, hoping to reach her suite before the damnable tears began again.

She told herself not to think of her pain just then because she had a note to write. She had to tell Beverly about the change in their plans. In her note she said that this tiny detour shouldn't inconvenience them over much. They could leave a few minutes earlier than planned, spend less than an hour at the Holcombe's, and still only miss the thirty minutes of socializing before the opera began. Elise reasoned they could be fashionably late and still arrive before the production started.

When Bridget entered the room Elise handed her maid the note for Beverly. "Can you see that the messenger waits for a reply?" Bridget nodded and Elise went to her chifferrobe and flung open the doors. She flipped through the dresses on hangers, looking for a particular dress to wear that night. She had to appear stunning, and make that bloody cur realize what he was missing. No, what he'd thrown away.

Instead of the mint green and ivory dress she'd planned on wearing, she looked for something special. One he was sure to remember. "Bridget? Where is my ivory silk with gold satin ribbon?"

"Downstairs being steamed."

"Thank you." Her lips curved to a mischievous smile. "Have I told you how much I appreciate you lately?"

The maid just mumbled something about good servants knowing every whim of their employer before they asked and left the room.

Elise thought it was more likely she'd been listening at the door of the salon, and thus knew she would see Michael. The ivory and gold *was* her favorite. She'd worn it once, the night of his mother's birthday dinner.

Hopefully, Michael would remember that when he saw her.

Propriety dictated that Elise and her grandmother pick up Beverly and Lord Huddleston at the home of Beverly and her father. From there, the drive to the Holcombe's took longer than expected for so short a distance, as the traffic all through Mayfair was congested. With the season winding down it seemed there were multiple events most nights, which was why there was such a snarl. Their party disembarked from the Caversham carriage and walked a short distance to the entrance. Christopher ordered the carriage to remain nearby, telling the driver they would be out shortly.

But once inside, the crush of people in the modest-sized house almost proved too much for them, especially for her grandmother. She'd had to knock several young men and ladies on the foot with her cane, to allow her to pass. She muttered something about the complete lack of respect the young ones had for their elders and finally gave up, deciding to remain seated near the open windows of the library with two other elderly matrons whose charges were within the house as well. Meanwhile she, Beverly and Christopher meandered through the crowds, managing to find a footman and get drinks. They decided to take their leave having walked through all the rooms and seeing no Lady Digby or Michael, when the matron and her daughter approached and indicated that Earl Camden was in the far corner of the ballroom.

Elise excused herself from her friends. She smiled at Lady Digby and Anne, then followed as they wound their way through the crowd and into the ballroom.

There was no dancing at the moment as the musicians had taken a short hiatus, making it more difficult to cross the room. Lady Digby paused by a pillar and motioned toward Michael. Elise immediately spied him in a small group of men and women.

After two days of not seeing him at all, his handsome visage was like food for her starving soul. She wondered for the thirty-seventh time tonight why she was even in this hot and stuffy room about to introduce the love of her life to a young girl who could never hold the interest of a man like Michael.

She realized now that she hadn't come to make the introduction. It was to see him again, because she missed him and loved him still even after all he'd said and done. Her breath caught in her throat and she cleared it, fortifying the walls of her heart. She took the lead, walking the rest of the way to Michael's side with Lady Digby and Anne behind.

He looked up and met her gaze. His green-brown eyes softened as he skimmed over her form and a slight grin spread over his handsome face. She knew he wasn't immune to her. Elise forced a reserved smile, while inside she wished she could run into his arms and feel him wrap them around her as he held her tight. She wanted to smell his sandalwood spice soap, and feel his whiskers rake her skin as he kissed the nape of her neck.

But it would never happen again. That was a different time. A time when he believed in her, trusted her. Might have even loved her.

"Good evening, my lord," she said to Michael, then greeted the others in his party. Leaning in to him, she whispered, "I was wondering if I might make this introduction so that my party and I can leave for the opera."

He nodded and stepped away from his friends, and Elise invited Lady Digby and her daughter forward. "Lord Camden, may I present to you Lady Digby and her daughter Lady Anne." Turning to the ladies, she reciprocated the introduction. "My lord, Lady Anne has an amazing collection of butterflies she's caught all on her own. They're preserved in glass cases throughout her home. Isn't that right, Lady Anne? She also paints beautiful watercolors and is also a virtuoso on the pianoforte."

She watched as he took both women's hands, kissing the air above their knuckles, and Elise's chest constricted. "I should love to have you come for tea some time, my lord, so my darling Anne could play for you," Lady Digby said proudly.

He smiled warmly at Anne Digby, and Elise wondered if perhaps the other girl *wasn't* more to his liking. That thought send another pain shooting through her breast. "I would love to Lady Digby. Send an invitation soon, as I will be leaving at the end of the term to winter in the country."

"I shall do that. Thank you," the elder lady said.

More pleasantries were exchanged, but Lady Anne never opened her mouth to say a word to the man with whom she'd wanted an introduction. She was such a shy creature. Perhaps Elise ought to take Anne on as a protégé, bringing her under Elise's wing so she could help the girl build her confidence and gain exposure. She was pretty enough. If she had some interests other than paints, the pianoforte, and heaven forbid, those butterflies, she might be able to make a decent match.

But Elise didn't want to stand around and watch as

Michael danced or fell in love with someone else. She had to get out of this room before it choked the life from her. Making her excuses, she left Camden, Lady Ann and her mother behind, and soon caught up with Beverly and Christopher. She had to get out into the cool evening breeze before she expired from the stuffiness of it all.

"Come," she said, "let's get grandmother and go. This house is overcrowded."

To the casual observer it would appear that nothing was amiss between Camden and his lady love. But the man watching was no casual observer. He'd been studying Lady Elise Halden for months now and knew from her stance and attitude toward Camden that something was troubling the lady. There was no spark of love in her eyes and she stood out of the man's reach as she spoke to Camden.

Good. There was trouble in paradise. He had to let his cousin know it was time to visit their favorite apothecary.

Chapter Seventeen

"You should come with us tonight," her grandmother said over their soup, several nights later when the two of them sat down to an early dinner. "If I must play chaperone to Beverly and Huddleston the rest of the season, it would be nice to have you along as well. After all, she is your friend."

"Oh, I'm afraid this case of the sniffles I picked up at the Holcombe's the other night is still lingering," she said. Elise dabbed beneath her dry nose with her napkin as she affected a sniff. "Perhaps it is best that I stay home one more night."

Footmen brought the next course and when they were done, Elise said, "If it is possible, I would like to leave for home this weekend. Huddleston's mother arrives tomorrow, so Beverly will not lack chaperonage for the duration." She lifted her fork and knife absently. "It is a week early, but I think I would recover from this malady far quicker in the country."

She stared at the slice of duck with cranberry sauce on her plate, her appetite now gone. More than anything, Elise didn't wish to run into Michael. The word about town was that he would attend tonight's masque since Lord Whippleworth was a colleague of his.

Already His

As soon as she learned he would attend, Elise decided she'd forego the event, and on her way home from her ride she'd concocted a case of the sniffles, which she'd thought to play out for a few days. If forced to remain in town, she would create another reason not to go about in public for that last week of the season. Two mild maladies should see her through the remainder of her time in Town.

When she thought of that first dance they were to share as a betrothed couple when he came out of mourning, she wanted to cry. She remembered the waltz they shared during Beverly's ball, and the romantic way he'd asked her to dance. He'd taken her out to the private terrace where he'd asked her to come to his mother's party. The party he'd asked her to marry him in front of both families. Elise remembered feeling as though she was finally living her most dearly-held dream. Now there was no longer the possibility of a marriage between them.

A tear threatened again, but she forced it down. She'd save it for later. Elise opened her mouth to again politely decline, when her grandmother, always honest and direct said, "I cannot believe that after all these years of loving him, you're so willing to give him up."

The fork slipped from her fingers and Elise set her knife down, and tried to take a deep breath but wasn't successful. She wanted to tell her grandmother that a happy ending with Michael would never happen now, as he thought her a liar and a woman without virtue.

When the tear began to trail down her cheek, she pushed back her chair, finished with her dinner. From somewhere inside her she found the strength to say, "I cannot be in the same room with him. It would be the end of me."

Before Elise could flee the dining room, her grandmother's voice stopped her. "My darling girl, do not spend another night in your room wishing for something fully within your power to make happen. If it's Camden your heart still longs for, then you should not give up so easily." Her grandmother did not meet her gaze. Instead the other woman focused her attention on cutting a tender asparagus spear. She raised it with her fork and looked at Elise with sympathy. "But if you no longer want him, then it's only right you let him go to find someone who would appreciate him."

Elise fled from the room, and as she ran, she heard her grandmother say, "I plan to leave at half-past eight, if you would like to come along. It would make this old woman happy."

Upon entering her room she ran directly for her water closet where Elise allowed herself five minutes of tears. Five minutes to release the heartbreak, sadness and disappointment over an irrevocable situation completely of her own doing. That realization hurt the most. She'd gone to him that night. He'd not seduced her. Elise went to Michael fully expecting to make love with him. And she got what she wanted hadn't she?

Tonight her grandmother was adamant, in her own subtle way, that she go with her, Beverly and Huddleston. If Michael was going to be present this night, she would show him that she was no love-sick fool. There were other men who might appreciate her. Perhaps there was even one she might eventually come to love.

Her mind made up, she was now going to join Beverly, Huddleston, and her grandmother at the

Whippleworth's masqued ball. The Viscount and Vicountess were old friend's of her father's and her family, and the invitation had been accepted weeks ago.

Upon re-entering her room, she found her maid already standing in front of one of her wardrobes, with both doors opened for her to select a gown. "If ye just pick one out I can get it steamed right quick."

"I swear at times, I think you eavesdrop at doors," Elise said.

Her maid rolled her eyes. "Don't have to. James the footman is sweet on me. He told me when he came out of the dinin' room wit' the untouched dessert tray."

"So that's your secret. Well, what shall it be tonight, Bridget?"

"Green and gold?" Her maid held the gown up with one hand, while at the same time she pointed to one hanging over the door. "Or the apricot?"

Elise didn't want to add that she needed a dress to help her feel pretty this night. Especially after the last few days. "Which do you like better?"

"The apricot," her maid replied. "Suits your coloration better, if ye ask me."

"Apricot it is." Elise went to her jewel case. "Do you think I could get a bath sent up at this late hour?"

"Already ordered, my lady."

"What would I do without you?"

"Oh, ye'd be lost fer sure."

A little over an hour later and only five minutes late, Elise descended the steps to find her grandmother waiting on her, already wearing her wrap. She made her apologies as they climbed into the carriage, heading for Beverly's home.

Their party arrived at the Whippleworths' and

waited in line to come up to the portico to disembark as the evening mist became a light rain. When they entered the ballroom it seemed to Elise that all eyes turned to her. Maybe she was just imagining it, but she was suddenly self-conscious. It felt as though the entire *ton* could see her heart on her sleeve—a heart she'd given to Michael many years ago. Thankfully though, the masque hid her puffy eyes. She smiled hesitantly and with a reassuring squeeze of her hand, her grandmother gave Elise her unstinting support.

Beverly entered on Huddleston's arm directly behind them, and soon her grandmother found her party near some open terrace doors in a corner of the ballroom. All the matrons, it seemed, were desperate for any breeze they could capture in the over-packed and stuffy ballroom. Elise stood next to Lady Royce and watched Beverly and Christopher already on the dance floor.

"Lady Elise." A familiar voice spoke behind her. "What a pleasant surprise."

"Sir Marlowe." She smiled at the handsome cousin of The Not-So-Honorable Mr. Sinclair. "How are you?"

"Very well, thank you." He returned her smile and Elise noticed for the first time how perfectly straight his white teeth were. Even behind the demi-mask she thought him too handsome, with golden-blond hair and piercing blue eyes. For another woman, he would be considered an Adonis come to life. "But, I would be infinitely better if you agree to honor me with a dance later."

She nodded her head, and they conversed a moment before he excused himself promising to return soon.

"Who is that nice-looking young man?" Grandmother asked, turning from her conversation with

Lady Royce and Lady Stone, her face alight with interest. "Do we know him?"

"Beverly and I do. His name is Sir Terence Marlowe, a young Baron from somewhere near Worcester, I believe. He is cousin to Mr. David Sinclair."

"That name sounds familiar. Isn't he the one your brother has warned off you?"

"Sinclair is, yes. Ren thinks the man desperate for my funds, and not interested in me."

"Your brother has excellent instincts when it comes to matters such as those. Please heed his warning."

"Oh, I have. But Marlowe is nothing like Sinclair. He's handsome and has a sweet nature. He also has never pressed me with his attentions."

Her grandmother nodded, then greeted a matron who came up to speak with her. Elise accepted an invitation to a country dance and took the floor with Lord Underwood, then Lord Edgcumbe asked for a polonaise and she accepted. Before long she was dancing nearly every dance, resting only to have a watery lemonade to quench her thirst. At first, her eyes searched the room for Michael. When she realized he was not in this room at least, she began to relax and enjoy herself.

Just as a waltz began, Marlowe arrived. "My lady, I believe this is our dance"

"May I request we sit out this one. I am winded." He appeared disappointed at first, but she offered, "Please, sit here next to me." Elise pat the empty seat next to her as Beverly was out on the dance floor yet again, and Huddleston was in the card room. "You will be my next dance partner. But for now, we can gossip, just you and I."

Elise asked him about his plans for the autumn, and Marlowe began explaining his desire to see the Continent, as he'd never had the opportunity. She confessed, she'd never been, though wanted to go one day. And, as he spoke, Elise breathed a sigh of relief as she was spared dancing a waltz. In her heart, she's promised every waltz to Michael, and even though there was no chance that would ever occur, she still couldn't bring herself to dance one with anyone else just yet.

A momentary awkward silence fell as that piece ended and the musicians began another song. People moved off and onto the dance floor and Marlowe asked, "Have you recovered, Lady Elise?" At her nod, he led her as they followed the others to the center of the room.

Elise rested her hand on top of his and they began to parade across the floor in a polonaise. "I haven't seen you about the past few days. Have you been well, my lady?" he asked. His concern appeared genuine, even if all she could see was the lower half of his face as his mask covered most of his brow. He was such a good-natured and caring young man, with an athletic look about him.

But he isn't Michael, her heart whispered.

"It's very kind of you to have noticed. I have been fighting a case of the sniffles."

"I knew something was amiss." His blue eyes literally sparkled with merriment. "And it had to be something important to keep you from your morning rides in the park."

Elise smiled. She was flattered someone noticed her absence. "Oh, I've been about." With Michael nowhere in sight, Elise relaxed in her partner's arms. She met his gaze and asked him about his cousin.

"He will be glad to know you asked. He is, unfortunately, out of town right now and not due to return for several weeks. He's handling some estate matters." She looked up into his handsome eyes, his affect shy, almost saddened. "We recently lost a relative."

"I am sorry, Sir Marlowe. I didn't know," she said as he whirled her around the floor in the crescendoing finish to their polonaise. He bowed to her and Elise curtsied. She was starting to feel very warm and thirsty. "I think I shall sit out a bit. It's very stuffy in here, is it not? Here, let us go sit with my grandmother, as she is near the terrace doors, and there is a delicious breeze coming through them."

"Of course these silly masks we are forced to wear only serves to heighten the sensation. Shall I get you a lemonade, my lady?" Marlowe asked as he walked her back to her grandmother's side.

"Yes, thank you. I would appreciate that very much. I will catch my breath if you don't mind."

He left, winding his way through the crowd. Elise tried, but couldn't follow the conversation her grandmother and several of her friends were carrying. Looking around the room, she didn't see Beverly or Christopher anywhere and smiled to herself hoping they were finally getting a few minutes alone.

Several minutes later, Marlowe returned with two lemonades. She drank readily of the liquid, quenching her thirst, and he offered her his, saying he would fetch more. This one she drank more slowly, as he left. Elise stood near the doors, thinking it so much cooler outside now that the rain had stopped and stepped out. Keeping her eye on her grandmother, she leaned on the balustrade feeling suddenly very tired.

Shadows in the bushes below caught her attention. She thought it odd that a couple seeking privacy would actually go *into* the bushes as it would seriously muss the lady's dress. Then again, she thought, if the woman *was* a lady she wouldn't be in the bushes would she?

Elise pushed off the railing and made to return to her grandmother's side when a hand stopped her. Marlowe helped her stand for suddenly her knees didn't want to support her weight.

"Could you please bring me back to...."

"Yes, my lady," he said as he wrapped a heavy mantle around her shoulders.

And remembered nothing more.

Michael scanned the room looking for Elise. With any luck, her grandmother would have convinced her to come tonight. He'd been working himself up to apologizing to her all day, and decided the perfect time to do it was while they waltzed. At her come-out ball, she told him it was the dance she would forever save for him alone. And tonight, while they danced it, he would also give her his heart.

She'd said something on that fateful night, before his cruel accusation, that had stuck in his heart. Until now, he'd been unable to actually voice the words, though he'd known all along he felt them. He didn't know why he was tongue-tied over saying them, but that, too, ended tonight. He loved her. He loved Elise with an intensity that scared him. If he didn't love her, he would not be fearful she might refuse him.

After speaking with Martin Whippleworth, he'd

Already His

arranged to have the orchestra play the same piece he and Elise had waltzed to at Beverly's ball—the one he'd taken her out to the terrace to dance. That was the night he knew he had to speak to Ren, or lose her forever to someone else.

Her tall, elegant form always stood out over the sea of average belles. Spying Lady Sewell, he watched as she scanned the room, concern marring her weathered, delicate brow. He excused himself from the party greeting him, and made his way over to the lady's side, intending to greet her and inquire after Elise. The concern on her face began to turn to worry as she looked out toward the balcony. He watched Marlowe enter through the doors and walk to Lady Sewell's side with two glasses of lemonade.

"Is Lady Elise dancing again?" Michael heard the grinning younger man ask as he drew closer.

"No. I believe she's gone out to get air. Didn't you see her?" He saw Marlowe shake his head. Lady Sewell stood, leaning heavily on her cane, then went through the doors. She looked both ways and over the rail. "I am concerned, it's been several minutes and she hasn't returned."

Michael came forward. "Is something amiss, Lady Sewell?"

The light mist changed to rain again as Marlowe set the lemonades down on the balustrade and asked. "Shall I search for her, ma'am? I will take the garden, if Lord Camden will take the inside."

Lady Sewell nodded to Marlowe who left immediately down the terraced steps into the darkened garden. "Camden, find her. Please." There was a plea in her voice that, as close as he was to the family, he understood. Marlowe would not know the seriousness in which they took the threat to Elise. Thankfully, there were three of Cartland's men on the premises, hopefully one saw something. With the heavy mist and light rain that had been falling off and on all night, there weren't any others enjoying the terrace to question.

Huddleston and Beverly finished their dance and seeing the look on Lady Sewell's face hurried over. "Where is Elise?" Beverly asked. "What has happened?"

"I don't know," the older woman choked out. "She was here one minute and gone the next."

Lady Sewell began to get frantic and she, along with Lord and Lady Stone and Lady Royce, quickly moved into Lord Whippleworth's office. Michael asked Huddleston to hurry and fetch Mr. Cartland to them, giving him the investigator's Oxford Street address.

"I would like to do this so that there is minimal damage to my future wife's reputation," Michael said to those in the room. Whippleworth and Stone nodded, as did the ladies. They began to discuss who might have taken Elise when a footman arrived with word that two men were found unconscious in the garden—one just under the terrace behind bushes, and another on the far side of the house.

"Guests?" asked Michael.

The footman looked to Lord Whippleworth for permission to speak freely in front of mixed company. With a nod of Whippleworth's head the man said, "One appears to be a guest, the other is one of the security detail sent over from Caversham House before the festivities began."

"There were three assigned to the ladies," Michael

told Whippleworth and Stone. "Since the third guard is nowhere to be found, I am praying he is following them." He raked his hands through his hair. "How are the men? Can we speak with them?"

The footman shook his head, his expression grim. "They are unconscious."

"Send for a physician quick," Michael told the footman.

"Already done, my lord."

Beverly sat next to Lady Sewell, near tears herself, yet trying to comfort the older woman. "Who could have done this?" Elise's grandmother sobbed.

Beverly looked directly at him and said, "You know she did not willingly leave this property. If you believe nothing else of her, you must believe this."

Her meaning was not lost on him. Elise, it seemed, had confided in her friend. He nodded his head and agreed with Beverly. He knew Elise well enough to know she'd never leave willingly. As to who her abductor was, he had only one suspect. He thought back to Lady Sewell's expression when he'd first seen her after entering the ballroom. He recalled Marlowe entering from the terrace with two glasses of lemonade. Why enter from the terrace if the refreshments were in a room not accessed from the outdoors?

"Lady Sewell, please tell me everything you remember."

She did. Every detail she could recall, she recounted for them—including the fact that the two glasses Marlowe carried in when he saw him after the disappearance were the second glasses of lemonade he'd fetched for Elise and himself in a matter of minutes.

Michael began to understand their plan. He looked at Whippleworth. "Can you ask a footman to bring Sir Marlowe to us for questioning."

"Do you think Marlowe is involved?" Lady Sewell asked, her face white with fear. "Elise said she thought he was harmless." The elderly lady held onto to Lady Royce and Lady Stone's hands. "Think about it, *he* is here while my granddaughter is not."

"He's involved because he gave her both drinks—" Michael said, the attorney in him finding the flaw in Marlowe's execution. "—And didn't drink either one himself. His cousin Sinclair is also involved somehow—" Michael paced the length of the room mumbling to himself as he worked out a possible theory. "—Then when he left to get more lemonade, he slipped out another door and handed over a drugged Elise to Sinclair. Marlowe then returned to the ballroom, secure in the knowledge that he'll never be suspected as he'd gone to fetch more lemonade which he could have had placed ahead of time in a location easy for him to retrieve later, making it appear as though he'd gone for more."

"You're right," Beverly said. "I'm willing to bet, that he got four lemonades the first time and placed two outside to pick up on his way back in."

"If you are correct," Whippleworth said to him, "then Marlowe is long gone. My guess is he's either with—or right behind—Sinclair and Lady Elise."

The clock on the mantle chimed the hour, and Michael surmised at least forty minutes had passed. He felt he should be out searching the streets, but didn't know where to begin. Up above them, the dancing continued because Michael, Lord Whippleworth, and

Lady Sewell all agreed that to call off the event already underway would only draw attention to the fact that something was amiss. As it was, there was a little chatter and speculation as to why their party departed the room *en masse*.

Lord and Lady Stone and Lady Royce all volunteered to return to the ballroom, hoping to fend off any potential rumors. The story everyone in the office agreed to was that Lady Elise had taken ill and was now in the carriage on the way home. It was believable enough because, as most everyone already knew, Elise had been ill earlier this week. Lady Sewell's cousins then left the office, but only after promising to visit her in the morning. Beverly would remain with Elise's grandmother this night.

Huddleston returned with a message from Cartland. "As we were speaking a boy came running up with a message for him. It turns out one of the agents assigned here is following a heavy traveling coach that reportedly left here almost an hour ago."

"Cartland doesn't yet know it, but his other two agents were blackjacked at their posts," Michael told him.

Huddleston nodded. "Cartland said he would meet us at Caversham House."

Whippleworth then assisted their leaving, showing them the way from his office across the lower terrace, then on the gravel path to the back gate where Marlowe or Sinclair likely carried Elise, and where the Caversham carriage now waited. Just the idea that this was where she had been made Michael sick with worry. A small part of him wondered if he'd ever see her smile again. The bigger part of him wondered what he'd do if he couldn't.

Minutes later their carriage pulled up in front of Caversham House and Michael noticed Cartland standing near the lamplight in the fog. He held his horse's reins in one hand, and a glowing cheroot in the other. Their groom came forward and opened the door to the coach and lowered the steps. Once inside, Michael turned over the stunned Lady Sewell and Beverly to the competent care of the housekeeper and maids, while Cartland and Huddleston followed him into the duke's office. He took a sheet of vellum, a pen and ink bottle from the drawer, and as he began to write his note to Ren, he said, "Cartland, I hope one of your men saw something."

In an enclosed, unmarked carriage headed west from London, David Sinclair smiled to himself in the dim, candle-lit conveyance. He peeled the black wool cloak's hood from his guest, revealing her short mouse-brown hair. Then he lifted the mask off her face and saw she still slept. Good. Drinking both glasses should keep her unconscious until tomorrow.

Laying her across the seat opposite him, he knelt on the floor and leaned down to nuzzle her neck, inhaling her scent. He wanted desperately to suck on her delicate flesh and leave the first of the many marks she would receive over the next few weeks from him and his cohorts. The lady would pay for the sins of her brother.

After the beating he took the other day from Caversham's lackeys in the alley behind his club, Sinclair arrived at the idea of stealing away this beauty for their little party next week. He'd show Caversham. The bastard thought his sister too good for the likes of him and his friends. He'll show His-hoity-toity-Grace who his trollop sister wants in her bed—and it isn't going to be that barrister friend of his.

He ran his tongue over the delicate flesh of her collarbone, it was like the finest silk and tasted of flowers. When he reached the area under her ear he began to suck, and the bitch moaned. But when she called out for that bastard Camden, he reached back his hand and slapped her. His signet ring broke the skin on her cheek and a few drops of blood began to mar her milky white complexion. Her eyes fluttered once but still she slept, evidence of the power of the sleeping draught.

Even through closed eyes her tears fell, sliding into the hair at her temples. That angered him further and a familiar stirring began in his groin as the anticipation and excitement of the weeks ahead rose within him. He couldn't wait to brand her, fuck her, then watch her get fucked by his friends. As much as he wanted her now, later when she was awake and struggling would be much, much more enjoyable.

Chapter Eighteen

Niles, the Caversham House butler, entered with a footman bearing a tray with a pot and several cups. The footman placed the tray on his grace's beverage sideboard then was gone from the room. The butler poured coffee for the three gentlemen. Michael handed the sealed note to Niles with the instruction that it was to go at once to Haldenwood and delivered directly into His Grace's hand. Once Niles closed the door to the office, Michael prompted the investigator again.

Cartland closed his eyes as he sipped the warm liquid. Michael did the same, feeling the restorative effects almost instantly. "Yes, my lord, I have had a man leave word that he is following a rented traveling coach leaving London on the Oxfordshire road. Once they are out of the city they will have a difficult time of it, especially with the rain we've been having. You well know that road gets more difficult to travel the farther you get from town. And after a day like today...." The man trailed off, both he and Huddleston nodding.

Michael went to the door and ordered a footman to have a horse saddled. Michael saw Huddleston stand, ready to argue, and changed the order. "Make that two." Turning back to Cartland, he said, "tell us more."

The investigator continued. "That's really all I know,

my lord. My man sent word through one of our contacts, a lamplighter he passed as he left town. The coach was stuck in traffic, and the investigator saw a contact. But don't worry, my man will continue to leave clues for us until we catch up with him."

"How does your man know the woman in the coach is Elise?" Michael asked. He fought the icy void wanting to take over his soul. He cleared his throat and continued. "How do we know that if we all leave for Oxfordshire, Sinclair isn't really moving north to Gretna Green with an unconscious and unwilling bride-to-be?"

"There is no way of knowing for certain," Cartland said honestly. "But my man was stationed at the service gate of the Whippleworth property and he's one of my best. I'm willing to bet this entire fee that if he saw something suspicious from his post at the *rear* of the property, he's got your lady in his sight and will not give up the chase."

"Camden." Lady Sewell had entered the room while his back was turned to the door. He looked at her furrowed brow and worried eyes and his heart ached for her. "You must find her. I feel responsible."

Michael went to her side and took both of her gloved hands in his. "Ma'am this is certainly not your fault," he breathed deeply to calm his own racing heart, and continued.

Elise's grandmother shook her head. "It is my fault, Camden, because she did not wish to go tonight. *I* encouraged her to attend with us as you asked, because *I* wanted the two of you back together and Elise happy again." She took her hands away and dabbed at her eyes with the linen she held. "I swear to you Elise would not voluntarily leave that party. I know my granddaughter." The old woman folded the linen square and tucked it into her glove. Straightening her back she looked straight into his eyes. "At dinner she said she wanted to return to Haldenwood on the weekend. When I asked her why, with only two weeks left to the season, she said she couldn't bear to run into you anywhere these remaining weeks."

Michael winced at that, and deservedly so. Especially when he remembered the callous way he'd treated her. In the days since his cruelty to her, it appeared she'd never said one word to her brother or her grandmother. Apparently Beverly knew something, likely not the entire story, as it was so very like Elise to keep the pain to herself.

It made him feel even more of a brutish ass.

He met Beverly's gaze and said, "I don't believe she left willingly." Turning to Lady Sewell, he said, "I will find her, my lady. I promise."

Huddleston set the cup down and asked of no one in particular, "Why would he be on the Oxfordshire road, when Gretna is in a different direction? What is out west for him?"

Michael's eyes lit with sudden realization. "That property he inherited recently is near Gloucester, in the Cotswolds. I'll bet that's where he's headed."

"You know for certain?" Christopher asked.

He nodded. "I make it my business to know everything about a threat to my family." Michael went to Ren's armoire and opened the cabinet. He took out a pistol for himself. He asked if the other two men needed weapons, Huddleston patted his chest, signifying he already carried his. Cartland did the same.

Niles entered and announced that the two mounts had been readied and all three horses were waiting up front. Michael gave thanks for the rain earlier that day. It meant the coach would not move as quickly as riders could through the mud and with luck they would overtake Sinclair's coach shortly.

"Camden go fetch my granddaughter," Lady Sewell said as they walked from the office and into the foyer where the gentlemen donned their rain gear for the ride to chase down the coach.

Lady Beverly had waited in the hallway for Huddleston, she kissed his cheek to wish him a safe journey. "I have sent a note to my father, do not worry about me. I am safe here."

Michael addressed Lady Sewell. "Hopefully, I shall return before Caversham. But if not, tell him about Gloucester, and the property inherited by Sinclair."

The older woman nodded, and the men were off.

Three men tracked westward through the dark. Michael thought if it weren't for the bloody quagmire the Crown called a road they'd have overtaken Sinclair by now. As it was, they were forced to slow their pace as the horses began slipping in the tricky footing. The only saving grace, if there was one, is that if they were having trouble so was the coach ahead of them.

The drizzle had tapered off, which helped the mounted trio as it made the tracks from the carriage ahead of them still somewhat clear. They would have been in trouble had the rain continued as it would have washed the tracks away. From what he'd discerned from Cartland, who heard from the last informant with whom he spoke, traffic on this road had been scarce all day because of the earlier bouts of heavy rain. The last coach the man saw go by was not more than an hour ahead of them, and by the looks of the wheel tracks in the muck that appeared to be about right.

Once out of town they lost the light from the street lamps, leaving them to ride on in the dark. Their eyes quickly adjusted to what little light filtered through the fog from the quarter moon. He trusted in the fact that horses see better in the dark than humans, and usually know where to place their hooves.

If Sinclair so much as harmed a hair on Elise's beautiful head, Michael would see the man hang. If he did worse, he would kill the bastard himself.

The depth and strength of the emotions he was having frightened him. These were very possessive, deeply primal feelings. Those of a man who loved the woman he wanted to have back at his side. His soul wanted her, his heart needed her.

He didn't think he could live without her. The past few days have proved that. He'd been miserable without her. When he thought about a wife and partner, mother for his children, he could only picture Elise. No other.

He had to find her and save her. Save her from the malicious gossip that would now hound her for years to come because of actions not her own. He knew of only one way to do that. At one time she'd wanted him. Michael prayed there still was a chance she would again, because he was going to marry her.

After helping his horse carefully pick his way through the muck, his party reached a rise where the road improved somewhat. As soon as the footing felt more firm, he urged his horse into a canter. They had to increase their pace or the bastard would harm Elise.

Soon the horses started calling out, and in the distance another responded. He wondered if they could be closing in on the coach. Through the fog they noticed another rider, coming toward them. Michael thought someone perhaps on his way to London on this miserable night. But after traveling a few yards, Cartland immediately recognized his employee and motioned for them to halt.

"They've lost a wheel on the coach," Cartland's investigator said. "The driver didn't want to press on through this mess, but the customers inside forced him along and now they're stuck. The man who'd joined their group on the outskirts of town has taken one of the horses and gone on to High Wycombe to get another carriage, and procure a room at an inn."

"That would be Marlowe," Michael stated.

"The coach is just over the rise, on the left," said the rider. "Two men are still with the coach, the coachman and the suspect. The coachman is innocent in this. From my position in the woods I heard their conversation. He's got the rest of his horses unhitched and tied off at the edge of a field. The suspect inside did not offer to come out to help. Said something about not wanting to get mud on his boots.

"The woman was drugged," the man said. "I saw the whole thing at the house. They kidnapped her, right fast, like it was planned. Dunno if she's come 'round yet. But she ain't makin' noise that's for sure."

God, please let her still be alive. He kept repeating the mental prayer over and over as he spurred his horse onward.

He quickly rode over the rise to the disabled coach, its doors closed and no light coming from within. A stooped over man came forth from the woods, and Michael lifted a finger to his lips, then dismounted his horse, handing the reins over to the man, then motioning for him to move away. Michael cringed as he heard Cartland and Huddleston approach, he didn't want to alert Sinclair to their presence. Drawing his pistol from his breast pocket, he pulled the hammer back to the half-cocked position and exposed the pan. He primed it with powder then pulled the hammer back the rest of the way, ready to pull the trigger if necessary.

Cartland dismounted and silently prepped his pistol, then went to the other side of the coach. Huddleston did the same with his, squatted and crept up to the coach while Michael got into place so that when he opened the door, he could surprise those inside. All three were prepared to shoot to protect Elise.

Sinclair was not getting away without paying for what he's done to Elise. He would see to that if he did nothing else this night.

Standing at the door, he listened for any sound coming from inside but heard nothing. Elise must still be unconscious or everyone in the county would be able to hear her making as much trouble for the cur as possible. He knew this little hellcat well. And he loved her.

At his nod, Christopher simultaneously turned the lever and flung the door open. In the darkened interior it was very difficult to tell where Elise was, but he was able to make out Sinclair's blond hair and white shirt, and the surprised expression on his face as he realized he'd been caught.

Sinclair raised the pistol from his lap but before he could take aim and fire Michael pulled his trigger and placed the ball straight into his chest. The splotch of red quickly spread, saturating his shirt. The stunned expression on Sinclair's face turned to very real concern as he realized what had happened and his approaching demise.

"You never should have touched her," Michael growled, slipping his gun into his coat again. The other man's gun slid from his hand to the coach floor. Unable to speak, Sinclair fell onto the cushioned back of the seat, his expression unchanging as the life drained from him.

The sound of the shot, the acrid smell of burnt powder and now the scent of blood was beginning to rouse Elise. He thanked God he was in time. No matter what had happened, she was alive and he was with her now.

She'd been wrapped in a dark wool cloak, and against the dark velvet of the seat covers, she was virtually indistinguishable until she moved. He needed to see her, make sure she was unharmed, he felt to his left and found the candle holder empty. He climbed into the vehicle and scooped her up, removing her from the dark confines and brought her out into the fresh air. He carried her over to the field where the driver stood with his carriage horses.

The ground was wet, so he knelt down holding her and waited until the coachman set his coat on the ground before setting Elise upon it. She didn't move, didn't speak, and in fact was still deeply asleep. With only the glowing fog as light, he pushed her hood back and saw the bruises and dried blood on her face. When Huddleston came from behind him with the coach's blanket, the other man's sharp intake of breath told

Michael that his friend saw the mark on her neck as well. Cartland came over and stood nearby, not wanting to intrude.

"He's dead," Cartland said. "Is the lady alive?"

Michael nodded.

"My associate and I will ride into the village and search for Marlowe. If we find him close by we shall imprison him there and return him to Town in the morning. We'll send someone for the body and to help the coachman as well."

Michael nodded as the investigators began questioning the coachman with regard to Marlowe's plans. Elise shivered, drawing his attention back to her.

"Can you hear me, sweetheart?" Michael didn't know what to say to her. He wanted to reassure her, but he didn't know how much she could hear of his plea for her to remain with him. He asked Huddleston, "Can you bring me my horse?" Glancing down at the sleeping bundle in his arms, he added, "Please?" His vision was blurring as his eyes filled with hot tears. He recalled the hurtful words he'd said and the naïve look in her eyes as he had to explain his accusation. He should have known she wasn't devious enough to do what he'd accused her of.

"Go back to London and reassure the ladies that all is well," Michael said. He looked down at his still-sleeping bundle. "I will take Elise into High Wycombe and rest there a day or two before going on to Haldenwood."

"You know what you're saying?" Huddleston asked.

Michael looked up at him, "I'll get a special license as soon as I return her to Haldenwood."

Huddleston smiled and clapped him on the back.

"Well, it's not the way she would like to have seen it happen, but Beverly and I are happy for you both."

"Thank you," Michael said as he brushed her hair back with his fingers. The bruising and cut on her face and cheek stabbed at his heart. If the bastard weren't already dead, he'd kill him. Every so often a tear would silently fall, tracing a new path down her cheek. He stroked her forehead, hoping it comforted her.

When his horse arrived Michael stood, then lifted Elise dropping the coarse woolen cloak she wore. He handed her over to Huddleston. "Once I'm up, raise her enough for me to lift her the rest of the way."

Michael mounted the horse and opened his greatcoat. Huddleston handed Elise's unconscious form to up to him and Michael wrapped her in the coat with him, leaving her face and his rein hand out.

"I shall have to do some apologizing, perhaps even groveling. But I realized on the ride here that I can't live without her."

"Then tell her that."

"I plan to." He took the reins from the coachman who held the horse's head. "I will tell her as many times as necessary for her to believe it."

Michael was fortunate enough to get the last room at the inn, but only because Marlowe had it reserved for his party. When Michael informed the innkeeper that Marlowe was headed back to London, and prison, he relented and let Michael have the tiny room.

"With all the rain yesserdy, I'm full to the brim with travelers," the man said. "I'm sorry I can't be gettin' ye the bigger room at the other end of the hall. There's a family of eight in that 'un."

He was thankful they were at the other end of the hall too, because right now he needed sleep. He set Elise on the bed and asked for a tray. "May I get breakfast and hot water for washing? Then afterward five hours of uninterrupted sleep."

"Aye, I'll have the maid bring a ewer of hot water, and the wife fetch a tray straight away." The innkeep stoked the fire in the little hearth. It roared to life when the coals caught, slowly warming the room.

"Soap too, please," Michael added.

"Aye, m'lord. Soap, hot water, a tray and five hours sleep. Anythin' else? Will the missus be needing a lady to help her?"

"No, I'll help her. That will be all. Thank you."

Thirty minutes later, clean and with a full belly, Michael sat in the chair next to the bed and propped his bare feet on the covers, thankful they were finally dry. Once he closed his eyes, it wasn't long before he was sound asleep.

He woke several hours later to Elise's weeping and struggling to breathe. In an instant, he scooped her up and rocked with her while she silently sobbed into his shoulder. It took a while before she relaxed. Throughout, she was never conscious, her eyes were closed and she didn't respond to his request to open them and talk to him. Michael concluded she was likely still under the influence of the sleeping drought Marlowe and Sinclair had given her.

He took the opportunity to peel away the woolen cloak and loosen her dress and corset laces, hopefully to allow her to expand her chest as she breathed. After doing so, he held her close as he relaxed against the headboard and closed his eyes again.

Several hours later, she stirred in his arms. He nuzzled her hair, inhaling the faint scent of her floral soap mixed with the stronger stale scent of old, wet wool. Michael smiled to himself, he didn't care what she smelled like, he was just thankful she was alive. Leaning back his head he looked down at her face, and saw her eyes filled with terror.

"You're fine now, sweetheart. I have you. All is well," he cooed as he caressed her cheek, noting the small cut and darkening bruise on her face and the suck mark on her neck. Last night he'd cleaned the dried blood away, but in the darkness was unable to get a good look at her injuries. The cloak hid the disgusting mark on her neck, and it was a good thing too. He likely would have killed Marlowe as well had he known what they'd done to her drugged body. And he still had no idea to what extent they'd violated her.

Michael lay on his side and drew her into his embrace, holding her close as she trembled. He'd give anything to take the pain from her. She didn't deserve this. He hated knowing he was responsible for sending her into Sinclair's arms by not believing her. "I'm here sweetheart," he cooed as he caressed her cheek with his thumb. She moved her lips as though she wanted to speak,

"Shh, my little minx. All will be well in time." Michael gave her a reassuring squeeze saying, "I will never allow anyone to hurt you again, Elise. Ever." He continued to hold her, trying his best to soothe her.

Elise visibly relaxed under his touch. "Michael," she whispered, her voice hoarse. "I didn't go..." she tried to speak, but was unable.

"I know you wouldn't leave with him willingly. The

guard saw Marlowe carry you and deposit you in the coach. We knew then you had to be drugged or unconscious in some way."

She exhaled and closed her eyes as tears began to silently fall. Elise turned away from him and curled into a ball. He spooned with her while the great wreaking sobs shook her body, and all he could do was hold her as she whimpered softly before she fell back asleep.

Sometime later in the afternoon, Michael awakened again, to a soft knock on the door. When he opened it, Elise's maid, Bridget, and a footman from Caversham House arrived bearing fresh clothing for both of them. The usually dour-faced young woman's brow was creased with worry as she entered the room, took a look at the curled-up form of her lady asleep on the bed, set the clothing down and crossed the room to her mistress' side.

"Lord Huddleston thought you might need these. Since James was coming with yer clothes and the coach to bring ye home, no one was going to keep me from seeing to my lady." She sat on the bed next to Elise and stroked her brow, getting no response. With Elise's unresponsiveness and seeing the cut and bruising on her face, and the mark on her neck, the maid looked at Michael with concern.

"She woke for a moment earlier this morning—only long enough to tell me that she did not willingly leave the ball—then fell back asleep.

"Of course she wouldn't leave the ball with a strange man. She wouldn't leave with you and she loves you." Unafraid of him, the maid straightened her shoulders and came to stand directly in front of Michael. She met his gaze with a cold stare. "Whatever you said to upset my lady you'd better make your apologies. I haven't seen her so sad ever as she has been this past week. So whatever you did, make it right, milord. My lady is good-hearted and don't deserve the pain you put her through."

He knew he should call the red-headed maid on her behavior, but Michael knew he deserved no less than everything she'd said. He cleared his throat of the knot forming just above his breast. "If she will have me, I will spend the rest of my life making up for my words and actions. I swear it."

Feeling relieved to have the maid here, Michael nodded. "I will leave her in your capable hands then. I will take a room of my own close by. Do you require anything from the innkeep?"

The maid stroked Elise's brow. "Fresh bedding," she said, looking at the mud he'd left on the other side of Elise, "plenty of clean towels and hot water. I brought everythin' else."

He lifted the bundle of his clothing. "I will have it sent up immediately," he said, glancing once more over at Elise. "Thank you. For... coming."

Later bathed and dressed, he went below into the public room to wait for the maid to send word that Elise was awake. While Michael waited on his dinner he pulled apart a piece of hard bread, and as he prepared to take a bite he saw Ren stride across the threshold of the building. The look on his face was one of deadly intent. Michael lifted his hand and motioned for him to come over and take a seat.

"How is she?" Ren asked, taking a chair. "Where is she?"

"She is fine, upstairs with her maid, who arrived a

couple of hours ago with a footman from Caversham House. But Elise is not awake yet. Her maid is determining the extent of her injuries now" Michael watched his friend scan the room. "There is no one that I recognize either on the register, or that I've seen. The innkeep and his wife have been sworn to silence on the matter, after I informed them there will be a trial for the accomplice."

Ren sat back in one of the wooden chairs at his table. The thing looked like it belonged more to a little girl's tea service than a seat for two grown men. Their gazes met, and Michael knew what he would ask next.

"Tell me how you killed the bastard," Ren said flatly.

Michael pat his breast, where his pistol rested inside his coat.

"And Marlowe?"

Michael took a deep breath and became the attorney again. He did so because it allowed him to forget his guilt and pain. "Marlowe left in the custody of Cartland and his agent that followed the coach from London."

"Why is she not awake?"

His voice cracked with emotion as his feeble attempts at detachment were useless. Through his emotion, Michael explained everything that occurred the night before. And when he was done, finished the remaining ale in his mug and stood.

"I want to see her," Ren said.

Michael motioned to the innkeep's wife, asking her to check on Elise. "Let's see if that bulldog of a maid she has will let us near her."

The woman returned with a message to give the maids upstairs a few more minutes to finish their tasks, then they could go up.

"The drug is wearing off," Michael said as they climbed the steps to the second level. "Elise knew who I was for just a moment when she opened her eyes, but she closed them again after telling me she didn't go with them willingly." He paused in front of the door to her room and knocked softly. Looking at Ren, he added, "She's been asleep since."

Elise's maid opened the door and let the men enter. She bobbed a quick curtsy, and Michael watched as Ren went to the bed and stood near the foot. Tears welled in Michael's eyes when he saw them in his friend's. His sister's condition, the bruising on her face and neck which had become more colorful as the day progressed caused both men upset and anger.

"I should have stayed in Town," his friend said, his voice a choked whisper. "I would have been there. I should have ordered more guards on her."

"You were with your wife, who needed you as well. You cannot be everywhere." He shook his head and swallowed past the lump in his throat. "No. It was my duty to protect her, and—" He met his friend's gaze for a moment because of the shame he felt. "I failed. I failed, and I will spend the rest of my life making it up to her, if she will let me."

Ren went to her side, and stroked his little sister's head and whispered reassuring words to her. Her eyelids fluttered open momentarily then closed again.

"'Lise? I'm here, Michael's here, your maid's here. If you want to go home, I can bring you."

Michael watched her eyes flutter open, but they didn't seem to focus on anyone. She closed them again and began to move her lips but no words came. He moved closer to the bed, wanting her to speak to him. He had to hear her voice. Wanted to hear her argue with him.

"Thirsty," she said, her voice soft and raspy. Her maid brought her a glass of water. After she drank from it, she smiled. She opened her eyes again, and looked straight at him, and said, "Gun shot," she took another sip from her glass. "Michael... did you... kill him?"

"Yes, minx. Sinclair is dead."

She nodded her head. "Good. Marlowe?"

"He is in custody, and will be charged with kidnapping and assault upon a noblewoman. If I have my way, he will never see the light of day again."

The look on her face was more relaxed now that she recognized he and Ren were there. "I'm tired," she said, closing her eyes again.

"Go ahead and rest darling. Ren and I will be below."

Back in the public taproom, Michael and Ren tried to plan how best to quell rumor and protect Elise.

"When I left I thought all was well between you, and that an autumn wedding was imminent." Ren swigged the dark ale from his mug. "Then I learn from Grandmother and Lia that there was a growing disaffection between you. Before I plan her future, I need to know what your plans are regarding Elise. Is there still an agreement between you?"

"She will tell you no," Michael said, "but we will marry as soon as I can secure a special license."

"Why does she not wish to marry you now, after all these years?"

"Because I was an ass." How many times over the last twenty-four hours had he told himself just that. He was an ass with regard to how he treated her. Michael had to apologize profusely and beg for Elise's forgiveness if he stood any chance at happiness in this life. "Elise *will* marry me. Because she still loves me." Michael thought if he told himself this over and over enough it would make it true. "And I... I cannot live without her."

"You're sure of this? Because I promised her I would never force her to marry someone she didn't love."

"She'll agree, once I apologize and beg forgiveness."

"See that you do then," Ren stood and made for the door, then added, "for I love my sister and she has loved you for years."

If His Grace, the Duke of Caversham, didn't think his friend was the right man for Elise before, he knew now. He'd known Michael for over twenty years, and in all that time he'd never once heard his friend admit to being an ass.

Yes, he must love Elise very much to make such a pronouncement.

Chapter Nineteen

"Elise will not tell me why she does not wish to marry you. She is, however, wanting to return to Haldenwood immediately," Ren said as the two of them sat in Michael's room eating breakfast the following morning. Elise was sleeping again, though did stay awake for several hours as she ate a tiny bit from her tray and spoke with her brother, without Michael present.

This put him a little on edge, not because he feared what she would say to Ren, but because he wanted to be with Elise when she spoke of the night of the abduction, to comfort her, to offer her his love and support. She obviously felt the need to speak to her brother without him. Since Ren didn't come out of her room requesting pistols at dawn, he felt safe she was keeping that part of the story private.

"I told her we could leave as soon as she was ready," Ren said. "Her maid will come with us, and you and the footman can return to Town on horseback."

Michael listened to his friend as he ate the meager fare the inkeep called breakfast. The hard bread, cold eggs, rasher of bacon and unrecognizable pudding would have tasted better hot, he was sure, but by the time it reached them upstairs, the plate with the bacon had congealing grease around the edges. He was so hungry, he pushed the grease aside and dove into the stuff, washing it down with the pitcher of watered down ale the maid brought with it. When he was done with the bland fare, he pushed the tray aside, and began to pace the small room he and Ren shared the night before.

"She will marry me as soon as possible," Michael said, "so that no one besmirches her character, or worse, because of what happened the other night. Even though we did everything in our power to staunch any gossip while we were at Whippleworth's, if her name comes out in Marlowe's trial, she will be ostracized. You know that is the way some in society behave."

His friend nodded. "It will be good for her to go home for a while and let the bruises heal. Too, Lia can talk with her and try to help with this as well. But...." Ren appeared to ponder something serious. "Michael, is that the only reason you want to marry her? Because of gossip, or her reputation? Because if that's the case—"

"No," he quickly interjected. "I'm marrying her because I care for her deeply. I do." Michael went to the rooms only window, and stared out to the stable yard below. "I will be at Haldenwood in a week with a special license. It might take a few days longer for my mother and sisters."

"If she refuses, I will not force her."

"She won't refuse me," Michael said confidently, all the while praying he was right. Because he didn't know what he'd do if she truly would not marry him.

Of course, he did still have the threat card, but knew that was not the way to start off his marriage. He smiled. Elise would cut his heart out if he tried that.

"I will not allow Michael to sacrifice himself to save my reputation," Elise told her brother when she met with him on the afternoon after their return to Haldenwood. "And that is what he'd be doing. You know I am right."

"He *wants* to marry you, Elise," her brother said as he placed his elbows on the desk surface and began to rub his temples. "He cares for you deeply, he's told me so."

"Caring is not the same as loving. He doesn't love me as you love Lia." Elise felt tears threaten to spill over again and she hated it. "How long will it be before he resents his decision? When he realizes he could have made a better match?" She saw Ren's jaw twitch and knew he fought his rising frustration with her.

"That will not happen with Michael. I know him. Once he makes a vow of commitment, he will honor it."

She was tired of discussing this. "He might honor it, but he will not be happy. And I'll not do that to him. I've already put him through enough over the years. He deserves happiness."

It made Elise sick to think that had she not been abducted he would never have offered to marry her. Michael was only doing this out of his devotion to her brother. And she was doing what she was doing for the same reason.

Now it seemed she would have to tell Michael this in order for him to recant on this plan to make himself a martyr because he felt guilt over the other night's events. The nerve of him.

"Is it because of this... argument you had. Can it not be worked out?"

Elise shook her head.

"What is it you wish to do if not marry?"

Her brother's tone was taught, as though he were conducting an uncomfortable interview. Elise felt his voice was cool, and not his normal grumbly ogre self. She wondered why he was being so solicitous after what she'd just had happen. "I want to live the quiet life of an eccentric aunt to my nephew, and hopefully a new niece. To that end, I've decided I would like to live in mother's dower house. It's a beautiful place, and I can see being happy there."

"It's yours, so you may certainly live there. With a proper companion, of course." Her brother drummed his fingers on the desktop, not because he was thinking, but because he was restraining his upset for her sake. "We would have to give the tenants notice. It could be... six months to a year before you were able to move. "

"I expected as much. Thank you, brother," she said as she fought down a painful lump in her throat that threatened to bring up tears. But she wouldn't cry again. The past was over and done with, and the future lie ahead.

"Are you sure you are well? I wish you would let me call in Prescott."

She nodded. "The bruises are fading, and this...." She fingered the cut on her cheek. "This is healing nicely. The good doctor would not be able to do anything for me, except perhaps give me laudanum. And I've never been fond of that stuff as it tastes horrible."

"As you wish."

Eight days after parting ways with Elise and Ren at the inn, Michael took the seat across from his friend in the ducal office at Haldenwood. "Were you able to convince her then?"

Ren shook his head. "We have had two discussions, and she has remained adamant. She thinks you would be sacrificing yourself for her honor, and said you deserve better. She thinks to live in our mother's dower house and become an eccentric spinster."

Michael laughed, for the first time in days. Elise had too much passion to closet herself away from the world the rest of her life. "She's already eccentric. It's one of the many things I love about her. And, if I have my way, she'll not become a spinster."

"Don't press her, Michael. Give her time. She'll come around eventually. Especially with Beverly here with her."

"I don't want to wait."

"I don't understand," his friend said. "Why the rush to marry?"

Michael turned away and stared into the glowing remnants of logs in the hearth. He didn't want to tell his friend there was a chance, even through it had only been once, that his sister might be with child.

"Michael, Lia asked Elise if she felt as though Sinclair might have...." Ren cleared his throat, the topic uncomfortable for them both. "Abused her...."

"Stop." He lifted his hand, stopping his friend before Ren spoke further. "I don't care." Once the realization came to him that this feeling he had was more than just need or want, more even than desire—because it was all that and so very much more—*that's* when Michael felt the words rushing from his mouth as never before. "I... I love her."

"Then you have some groveling to do," Ren said,

shaking his head in confusion. "Because I sense that's what she's wanting from you."

He could only nod. He planned to find her and apologize. Michael had to start making amends right now. If she truly needed time to get over the trauma of the abduction, he'd give her all the time she needed—after they were wed.

Elise dismissed Bridget after the maids finished carrying in the hot water. Alone in her bathing chamber, she dropped her robe and stared into the pier glass. She was thankful that the bruises on her face and neck were fading quickly, though her breasts were still tender. She wished she knew what that heathen had done to her, how she received the cut and bruise on her cheek, what he'd done to her breasts to make them so very sore. If only she could remember all that happened that night over a week ago. But try as she might she could not. Both Grandmother and Lia thought it was a good thing she didn't remember, then it wouldn't interfere with her finding pleasure with a husband later they told her, should she marry one day.

She remembered the night she met Sinclair, how his touch made her skin crawl. Had she trusted that instinct a little more none of this would have occurred. Thinking back on those few encounters with him, Sinclair never gave any clues of his true nature. He had been quiet and introspective at times, but she didn't think.... She even remembered telling her grandmother once she thought him harmless.

"Ha! Harmless," she said to the empty room.

As she sunk deeper into the big brass tub, she relished the feel of the hot water as it relaxed her sore muscles. Evidently in her unconscious state, she must have fought him because the muscles in her arms and legs still ached.

She wished she could turn back the hands of the clock and undo all that had occurred. But who could have known that Marlowe would do something so dastardly as to lace her drink with a sleeping drought, then hand her over to Sinclair? Why did he do such a thing? What had she ever done to him, to either of them, that they would do this to her?

Did they want her inheritance? If so, they could have gone about it in a different way and not inflicted this harm on her person. She'd heard stories of heiresses being abducted and taken to Gretna Green where they would be coerced into marriages, but she'd never met any. Had Sinclair done so, she never would have signed a certificate, and secondly, her brother would have contested it and had it deemed illegal.

Then there was Michael.

Why had he suddenly become so solicitous toward her? *Now* he believed in her virtue? She wondered what had changed his mind, for something obviously had.

And why did he all of the sudden want to marry her? Especially now. It had to be because he pitied her. She didn't want a husband who felt sorry for her, and that was all he felt right now. Whether he realized it or not.

The pain of knowing that this was all Michael felt for her, hurt almost as much as the physical pain she felt due to Sinclair and Marlow's actions. She'd told Ren the truth when she'd said Michael would come to resent her should she marry him. But she could never tell her brother what Michael believed of her. Refusing to marry him was the right thing to do. Eventually Michael would come to think he could have made a better match with a woman more virtuous than he thought her to be. One who didn't have shame hanging over her from being compromised.

She wished she'd never been abducted, and that Michael loved her.

Conversely, if Michael had loved her, she never would have been abducted.

It was a vicious circle, she knew, and one not likely to change her current predicament. Nothing would. Except maybe the passage of time. Time for her wounds, both emotional and physical to heal. Time for someone else to do something equally if not more reckless than she, making them the next target of the gossip columns and scandalmongers.

Michael grew tired of waiting in the hallway outside Elise's rooms. The chair he'd moved in front of her door two hours and ten minutes ago had become impossible to remain in. Thus he began wearing a path in the carpet. By his estimation, there was one hundred and twenty feet of runner in the hallway. At two and a half foot strides, it took him forty nine steps to make it from one end to the other. And if he shortened his stride mere inches, he could get fifty steps.

This was bollocks, pacing the hall and sitting outside her door waiting for Elise to come out of her room so he might catch a moment with her.

Elise was being obstinate. She'd skipped coming down for dinner the past two nights and had, in fact, taken to having all her meals brought up. She even skipped her morning ride once she learned he was in the barn waiting for her. In fact, since Michael had arrived, she'd not come out of her rooms at all.

Which is why he waited in the hallway.

Lady Beverly went in to visit Elise on his behalf, and returned with a message for him. "My lord, she does not wish to see you, and asks that you please go from her home so that she may continue with her life."

Elise's words were like a blow to the gut, but he quickly recovered, replying, "Not until I have two minutes of her time, in private."

Beverly went back in Elise's room, and quickly returned with another reply. "My friend has begged me to convey to you that she said all she had to say to you the morning after at Caversham House. She also asked me to remind you that honorable men keep their promises."

"Lady Beverly, I know I've been a boorish ass, but in my deepest heart I pray Elise still loves me. And I am not—" He paused and took a deep breath, collecting himself. "She must care. She must, or she wouldn't be acting this way."

He lowered his frame into the under-sized, impractical chair he'd put in front of her door earlier. Crossing his legs at the ankle, he reclined as best he could. "So, tell the lady I will wait no matter how long it takes."

"Well," her grandmother said as she entered Elise's sitting room an hour later with her stitching in hand. Both Grandmother and Lia had taken to doing their stitching each afternoon with she and Beverly in the better light of her west-facing sitting room. "Michael said he is not leaving his spot, and that he will in fact sleep across your threshold tonight." Elise watched her grandmother's maid set her stitching on the table, then helped her grandmother onto the sofa under the window in Elise's sitting room. "You know your brother will not allow this silliness to continue much longer before he says something, either in your favor or his friend's."

When Elise sniffed and refused to comment, her grandmother continued, "If His Grace were to ask my opinion, to help him make a decision, I shall be completely honest with him." The maid handed Grandmother her hoop frame and threaded needle, then set the pin cushion holding the other pre-threaded needles for later use on the side table. Without ever looking at Elise her maternal relative continued, "My opinion is that Lord Camden will make a wonderful match for you. Whatever tiff you feel you have will work itself out in time, and..."

Beverly raised a startled gaze and sucked in a breath at Lady Sewell's words.

Elise was fighting tears again, just when she thought she'd dried out. She looked at the penciled pattern in the taught fabric of the embroidery hoop in her lap and watched the first of several tears fall onto the cloth. When the maid departed, she said through her tears, "It will never work. He doesn't believe me and will never trust me."

"What are you talking about? He's obviously ready to apologize for whatever caused this spat between you. He stands out there a man in love, wanting to grovel! I say make him grovel a bit, then put both yourselves out of misery and marry the man."

"I have said the same ma'am," Beverly chimed in. "They are obviously still in love, no matter what he's said in the past."

Elise could feel her lower lip begin to quiver and she pressed them together. She didn't want to go into detail with her grandmother, but she had to know the situation was hopeless. "He thinks I've been with another man."

"Didn't Ren tell him what you and your maid concluded?"

"It doesn't matter, Grandmother," Elise whispered, unable to look at her and feeling the familiar knot begin to rise in her throat, the one that usually preceded her tears. "This was before the Whippleworth's masque."

Elise watched as her meaning became clear to her grandmother. The older woman's wrinkled brow rose with concern and her gray eyes widened. "What made him think this?"

"If I tell you, will you promise not to tell Ren or Lia? I could never live with myself if my brother died in a duel, leaving Marcus with no father, and Lia with no husband." Only when her grandmother promised did she begin. Elise had not yet finished when they both heard the door to her bedroom open.

Lia entered her sitting room with her embroidery, to work on baby linens, while Elise and Beverly worked on cradle bedding. Her sister-in-law looked from one to the other, realizing she'd interrupted a conversation. "Shall I leave the room so you can finish?"

Elise's grandmother looked at her and said, "Why haven't you come to us with this before now? We could have taken care of it without your brother learning of it."

"What are we keeping from my husband now?" Lia asked.

Elise's story came pouring out of her again, this time with a remarkable amount of control over her emotions.

She told them both the reason for the estrangement from Michael in London and her animosity toward him now. She did not hide her shameful part in the tryst—the fact that she had gone to him. She then confessed her fear of a duel, and her unwillingness to see him. "I'm afraid that he is feeling pity for me, or doing this to prevent gossip, as it might affect him or his legal practice. Or perhaps he's doing it out of loyalty to my brother." Elise wiped her eyes and blew her nose again. "But I am certain it is not because he loves me.

The four of them sat quietly for a while as her grandmother and sister-in-law digested her tale. Elise and Beverly exchanged worried glances, then Elise heaved a trembling sigh when she realized there were no more tears. It felt good to have shared the weight of this burden with the women she loved most. And it didn't appear—at least not yet—that they were horrified at her pronouncement.

Her grandmother set aside her stitching and lifted her cane. "That scoundrel! He needs to hear a piece of this old lady's mind." She rose slowly, her joints aching more in recent days. "Elise, fetch that no-good rapscallion and tell him to get in here." Elise looked to Lia who nodded, then back at her grandmother. The woman waved her hand at her in a shooing fashion and added, "Then the two of you go to the barn or something."

Elise did as she was told, not meeting Michael's gaze when she opened the door. "You're presence is requested in my sitting room," was all she said as Michael crossed the threshold into her rooms. Elise motioned through the door at the left, and stepped out of his reach when he put a hand out for her. Beverly excused herself and went to her old room, she said, to write a letter to Christopher.

Taking her pelisse from the footman, Elise threw it over her shoulders and walked out the front doors and began to walk across the expansive lawn with no particular destination in mind. Not dressed for a ride, nor a long walk, she turned towards the Summer House. She loved going there to read, though hadn't done so in months. Not since before she went to London for her season. The one that started with such promise and ended so disastrously.

At least Beverly would have love. She and Lord Huddleston seemed to have found true happiness in each other's company. For that she could be thankful. And although she'd always wanted children of her own, she would just have to be satisfied being an aunt to Lia and Beverly's children, and one day even Sarah and Lucky's.

She bypassed the Summer House and went down to the lake, and sat on her swing. The one she begged her father for when she was a child. He'd had the swing installed, but Elise could never recall a time when he pushed her on it.

In fact, she could not remember anyone ever pushing her on the swing. Sarah and Lucky enjoyed being pushed, so Elise couldn't wait for Marcus to get big enough so she could push him. She could imagine the smiles on his face now. And later, her new niece or nephew....

She heard footsteps behind her and turned to see who it was coming toward her, though she really didn't need to. Her heart told her who's footfall came down the gently sloping hill toward the lake. For a moment she considered dropping her pelisse and climbing into the tree, but he'd only come after her. Elise had to, for her sanity's sake, make it clear to him that she wanted no future with him. She wanted him to go away and let her get on with her life.

He stopped some feet away and they locked gazes. She fought tears and lowered hers, speaking first. "I am begging you Michael, to leave here and let me be. I have promised I will never bother you again, and I shall keep that promise. Go. Find a bride and get to work on your nursery."

He moved closer still, holding the ropes above her hands. "The woman I want to marry is right here, and there is no other that I want as the mother of my children."

His nearness caused her choke on her words. "I will not... I cannot marry you, Michael."

"Why not, when it has been your dream since you were ten?" His voice was not accusatory, but more inquisitive and gentle. As though he spoke to someone fragile.

She tried to control her emotion, to remain calm, but she still trembled as she spoke. "That dream turned into a nightmare. One of my own creation. I will forever regret the harm I have done to you, for all these years of thinking myself in love with you."

"Your animosity and disaffection are warranted. I have broken your heart and treated you abominably. But, minx, if you let me, we can...." His sympathetic tone and gentle stroking of her head made her feel pitied, and that was the last thing she wanted from this man.

"Don't call me that," she hissed. "Never, ever call

me that! That was a name given to me by a man I thought had an intimate affection for me in his heart. We will never share that kind of intimacy again."

"We can if you will let me apologize, Elise."

Elise tried to stand, but he stood in front of her, effectively keeping her on her swing. "We can do nothing, Michael. Go home. I will not marry you."

He got down on his knees before her and held the swing steady, keeping her prisoner on the seat. Since she would not look at him while he stood, he looked up at her from his position at her knees. "I am sorry for everything I said... everything I did... that night you came to me. I don't know why I let the memories of my uncle's drunken ramblings cloud what I knew to be true in my heart."

"This coming from the man who deals in facts and evidence on a daily basis?"

He dropped his head to her lap. "I deserve that."

"Yes. You do."

He turned to look up at her again, his hazel eyes full of the love she'd always wanted from him. "I was an ass. An ass who also feels responsible for what happened the other night. Because of what I said, because of what I did, I sent you into the arms of someone who harmed you."

She didn't want his pity! Elise tried to shove him away and rise, but he held her down on the swing. "Oh, so you come to me to ease your guilt now? Leave me, Michael. Go away!"

"No. I come to you because I love you."

"You don't know what love is." She lashed out at him. Angry that he thought pretty words would buy his way back into her good graces. "Loyalty, for certain.

Devotion, maybe. But not love."

"I don't care if you believe me or not," he argued. "I want to marry you because I was never more afraid in my entire life than I was that night Sinclair and Marlowe stole you away. I was afraid I would never see your smile again. Never hear your voice."

He rested his head in her lap again, and Elise thought she felt him shudder, which caused her damn to burst. "I love you," he whispered, his cracking voice raw with emotion. "If you refuse to marry me, then the title dies with me because I will never marry another."

She tried to get him to see reason. Using the same tone of voice she used when trying to convince someone of the rightness of an idea she said, "You might love me, but you don't trust me, Michael. In the back of your mind you will always wonder if another came before you. Then you'll wonder who he was. And that type of obsessive and possessive thinking will eat at you and our marriage until we will no longer be able to stand each other—even if I did bear your heirs. Jealousy isn't something you can just will away."

"It is, Elise. I knew I was wrong as I watched you ride off with Attila. I tried to tell you this the next day but couldn't find the words. I had planned to apologize again at Whippleworth's, while we waltzed. On my honor Elise, I am telling you the truth. I had planned to ask you to marry me again while we danced to the same piece we danced to at Beverly's ball. It is why your grandmother encouraged you to go. She knew this, Elise. I swear it." He wiped her eyes with a kerchief as he stared up at her. "Please don't cry anymore. Tell me you accept my apology. Tell me that you will marry me. If you will, I promise each day I will wake determined to prove my love for you."

"Why Michael? Why do you want me now?"

"Because I cannot live without you, Elise." He read the uncertainty on her face. He was winning her over, he could tell. But still, something held her back.

He wasn't so proud he wouldn't use every argument at his disposal either. He'd given this considerable thought, not knowing how she might react, and said, "Have you considered that you might be carrying our babe?" Her eyes widened in surprise and he added, "It is a possibility, Elise."

Michael could tell it wasn't something she'd considered because the expression that crossed her face just then was unpracticed and unseasoned. She could never have prepared that look.

"If I am, what makes you think it's yours?" she asked him.

"My words and actions that night hurt you deeply, and I deserve your backlash," he offered humbly. "But I also know that you have never attempted to deceive me in the past and I had no right—none at all—to assume you would. Your faith that I would one day return your affections never, ever wavered. That is how I know for certain if you are carrying, it is my child. It could be no one else's.

"I do not deserve your love after what I did, but I promise to try every day to win it back. But I can only do that if you marry me." When he got no reply, he had to ask one last time before walking out of her life forever. "Elise, will you marry me?"

She lifted her gaze from her hands resting in her lap, to meet his troubled hazel eyes. She smiled, relief visibly flowing through him. She nodded. "Only if you swear to me you will never again question my devotion to you."

"Never," he whispered, placing his head on her lap again. "Never again." Michael sighed deep and she could see the tension leaving his body, and she smiled.

After Michael left the ladies in the sitting room to search out Elise, Lady Sewell shook her head and mumbled something Her Grace could not hear clearly. The duchess then asked if the older lady was well. To which she replied, "Men are all the same. Every single one fancies himself Captain Cook, wanting to be the first on virgin ground."

Chapter Twenty

Because of the events at the Whippleworth's ball, both Elise and Michael decided that their wedding should be a small, intimate affair with only family as witnesses. And seeing as it would take place in the country, with only family present, they both agreed sooner was better.

"Tomorrow afternoon, you have everyone you need here," he argued.

"No. We will wait until your family arrives. There is no rush, Michael," she countered.

Elise sat with Michael in the library composing a letter of invitation to Michael's mother and two sisters. Elise reiterated yet again, that she would, indeed, marry him, but not the very next day and *not* without his family present.

"Michael, do you really want to start our marriage knowing we've broken your mother's heart? You are her only son," Elise chided. "It's only right that she should give her blessing and be at our wedding."

He shook his head, chuckling softly. "Forgive me but just a few weeks ago, you wanted to marry me as soon as possible, and I wanted to wait. Now that I want to marry tomorrow, you're the one making us wait."

"It is only fitting that they be here, Michael." She

looked at the sheet of vellum in front of her on the table, then glanced up to him. "Besides, I never would have gone through with a wedding if my family was not present."

"But you said...."

"False bravado. Pure and simple." She grinned, then winked at him. "I'm full of it." Lifting the quill and dipping the tip, she told Michael, "Work on your sister's letters." Elise put the date on her page. "I shall write to your mother."

"Are you sure you want to write *her* invitation?"

She smiled. "Of course. She will be the closest thing to a mother I've ever had. Mine died after I was born and Amelia didn't really like me much, and avoided me unless Papa was around."

"If you need help with it, I'll be right here," he offered as he began working on his first invitation.

Haldenwood, July 1, 1823

Dear Lady Richard,

If I promise not to climb a tree or trellis will you come to Haldenwood? It is my fondest wish that you come as soon as possible, ma'am. Michael has decided he does not want to wait until he is out of mourning to marry. In fact, he wishes to get married tomorrow, but I have told him I will not stand in front of the minister until you arrive and give us your blessing.

Please say you'll come. We await your reply.

With all our love,

Elise and Michael

She sanded, then folded the page. As she pressed her seal into the wax, she said "There. This should do it!"

Next, Elise went to find herself a pair of attendants to stand with her. She found Lia in the nursery, rocking Marcus to sleep. The sight of the sleeping babe in her arms sent a pang of longing through her. She wanted a babe of Michael's one day, and hopefully by this time next year she would have a son or daughter to rock herself.

Elise asked her sister-in-law if she would stand up for her, and Lia readily agreed, saying she would be honored. Then she went to Beverly's room and found her sitting on her settee before the hearth, the ever-present book in hand. She sat next to her friend and said, "I wanted to ask you if you would stand with me at my wedding as my maid of honor." Seeing Beverly's expression change from one of shock to one of fear, Elise wanted to reassure her it wasn't something to be frightened of. "You will have Lia to guide you, she's already agreed, and I promise you will not have to sing or speak in front of strangers."

"That's not it. I...." Her friend stuttered, something she hadn't done in years.

Elise continued, unaware of her friend's reasons for her nervousness. "I told Michael I wanted you and Lia to stand with me, and he is going to ask Huddleston to stand with him along with Ren."

"That's not it. Elise, I... will have to stand up in front of the Bishop as your *maid* of honor, and I will surely be damned for eternity if I did so. Because.... Well, you see..., 'Lise, I'm no longer a maid!"

Elise stared at her friend, a smile forming as she came upon a most perfect solution to their predicament. "Your father will be here, as will Christopher's mother. I think we should do this as we've done everything else since the day we met. Together."

"That would be p—p—perfect! But..." Her friend began to stutter and her cheeks turned bright pink from excitement. "Oh, d—dear. I came here the morning after. And we were going to c—come up with a date when I got back to town. How do I convince Christopher?"

"You could always just ask him," Elise said. "Since you were both going to stand up for us, wouldn't it be wonderful if we stood up for each other?"

"Yes," Beverly said, sounding more confident that she looked. "That's what I shall tell him."

Four nights later, a celebratory dinner was held at Haldenwood. Michael's family had arrived from Bath and Plymouth. Viscount Huddleston, his mother, and Beverly's father were also in attendance. Before dinner the men congregated in the library waiting on the ladies to come down.

Michael, Christopher and Ren stood near the sideboard, sipping some of Caversham's incomparable stock of wines. "It's a pity the rest of your family cannot be here to watch you marry," Michael told Christopher while they waited in the drawing room before dinner, "but at least you have your mother."

The other bridegroom's grin faded. "As am I, but they would never make it in time. Besides," he added, "the opportunity to marry in a way that is special to Beverly and Elise seemed more important than having my six sisters, and their families, scurrying for gowns and finery to attend our wedding here at Haldenwood." Michael must have had a comical look on his face, for Christopher continued, "They aren't heathens, I promise, though I cannot say the same for my two younger brothers. But, if that flock of hens suspected I was marrying here they would would break the bank on new gowns, shoes, pelisses and hats. So not only am I saving myself a headache but also a small fortune for I have a very large family."

Michael took a sip of his wine, still nervous about the missing license. He asked Ren, "Are you certain Christopher's license will be arriving before the wedding?"

"If I had known before leaving Town," Christopher said, "I would have picked one up. But..."

"The license will arrive, I assure you," Ren said. "In fact, it should be here any minute now, as the special guest we are waiting dinner on is the man bringing it."

"How do you know he will make it?" Michael wondered what he would do if the courier didn't arrive. He hated the thought of waiting until a piece of paper got here.

"My special courier sent an outrider ahead," Ren said. "He is on Haldenwood land as we speak."

"You're being very secretive, Your Grace," Christopher said.

"And have you taken care of the ring?" Ren asked them, skillfully changing the subject. "There is a fine goldsmith in our village who can fashion a band should you need one."

Christopher patted his breast pocket. "When my mother came down to Town, I requested she bring several rings from the family collection for Beverly to choose from."

Michael chimed in, "I've had one for a few weeks now. Had to buy one as my uncle sold most of the more valuable pieces when he needed funds."

The Caversham butler stood at the doorway of the drawing room and announced the arrival of Archbishop of Canterbury. Michael watched as Ren stepped forward to greet the gray-headed gentleman as he entered the room with a flourish. Michael and Christopher shared a bemused glance before following their friend to the Archbishop's side.

"Charles, it's good to see you. I'm glad you finally arrived. My friend here was getting nervous." Ren said, as he motioned toward Christopher.

The older man accepted a glass of wine from a footman, and greeted all the gentlemen in the room, including Lord Hepplewhite and Lord Vance. "I'd not miss a week of fishing your streams and lake for the world," the Archbishop replied. "And if I get to officiate Camden and Huddleston's marriages, all the better."

"I thank you, sir," Christopher replied, and Michael seconded.

"See, you two? I told you I had the minister and missing license covered." Ren chuckled as he shook his head. "You were worried for nothing."

"When the invitation arrived, I had my secretary clear the calendar," the Archbishop said. "Haldenwood has always been one of my favorite places to visit. The last time I was here was to marry your father and my cousin, Amelia. I had a wonderful visit then. If I remember, the trout in your stream are fat and delicious."

"Haha! They still are, Charles," Hepplewhite said. "Why Vance and I caught three just today, and plan to go out again tomorrow. You should come with us."

"I think I will," the Archbishop said.

As the three of them began a conversation about fishing, Michael pulled Ren aside and asked, "How did you manage to get the Archbishop here?" Christopher nodded, wanting to know as well.

"I've upheld the responsibilities of the title for a few years now, without ever taking advantage of the perks of my position," Ren said, his grin spreading. "It was time I asked for one of those perks."

The ladies soon joined them in the drawing room, having been in the Duchess' morning room discussing wedding plans, which the men had earlier decided they wanted no part of. The butler returned and announced dinner, and the guests followed His Grace and the Duchess into the massive dining hall reserved for special occasions at Haldenwood. After everyone had taken their assigned seats, and the footmen filled the wine glasses, toasts were made starting with Ren's to both brides and their grooms, then Michael squeezed Elise's hand under the table reassuringly and stood. "If I might have everyone's attention please, I would like to make a toast." He looked to his future bride, who appeared near tears, and said, "To my darling minx, I look forward to spending the rest of our lives together. You are my heart, my home. From you I gain my strength as a man, to you I give all that I am in hopes that we may one day see our children and grandchildren grow to follow in our footsteps. I want to be your mounting block in this most adventurous ride we call life. May our nursery be filled with as many children as God wishes us to have, for I shall adore them all as they are part of you."

His gaze never left hers, as a blushing Elise wiped a stray tear, and thanked him. Huddleston, arose and toasted Beverly as well, thanking her father for raising the most perfect woman in the world for him. Then Lord Hepplewhite rose and toasted the young couples, and also thanked the duke and duchess for all that they have done for he and Beverly since the death of his wife. Without them, he said, his daughter would not have found the love she had with her future husband.

When dinner was done and the children were sent to their beds, the ladies congregated in the salon, while the men went back to the library to enjoy his grace's finest port and cigars. Michael was deep in conversation when he notice Elise coming toward him. Moving over to her, he smiled. "Care to try port and cigars, minx?"

"Not hardly," she whispered. "Meet me in the music room in five minutes." After she left the room, without appearing too hurried, he downed the rest of his port, and set the glass on the tray on the sideboard. He wanted to see just what his future wife was up to.

Elise closed the door to the darkened music room and went to the back, near the wall of beveled-glass windows which provided a modest amount of moonlight from the partial moon overhead. She got there before Michael and waited for him. There was no balcony on this level, and no other entry or exit from the room.

Footsteps in the hallway announced Michael's arrival. Elise's heart began to race with excitement.

"'Lise?" she heard his whispered call in the

cavernous room.

She stepped away from the curtains and into the light, so he could see her. When he got close she closed the distance and wrapped her arms around his waist and lay her head on his chest. "I've missed you, Michael. We've been so busy with the arrangements for the wedding, that I haven't had time to let you know how happy I am. Your toast tonight reminded me how very lucky I am that you want me for your wife. Throughout dinner I was thinking of a way to get you alone so I could tell you this."

He placed a finger under her chin and tilted her head to face him. "I'm the lucky one, sweetheart," he whispered as he brought his lips down on hers.

She opened readily for him, giving him everything she'd been unable to for nearly a month. With this one kiss she shared all of her heart and soul, her body and life.

Her tongue danced with his, tracing the peaks and valleys of his teeth, and beyond. His hands came forward to caress her waist and up to her breasts. She broke away from his mouth and traced along the line of his jaw back to behind his ear with light touches of her tongue.

"I love you, Michael. I have loved you forever."

He pulled backed and looked into her eyes with his own passion-filled hazel depths. "I know you have, minx, and I love you, too. Why have you asked me up here to meet you?"

"You'd asked earlier why we chose an afternoon wedding, and I wanted you to know so that you do not panic in the morning if you hear we've left. Beverly and I are going for one last ride together as unwed ladies."

Elise felt a tear spill over her lashes and she swiped it. "It's something we will never be able to do again, as I leave with you after dinner, and she with Christopher the next morning." Another tear spilled over, opening the damn. Elise removed her kerchief from her pocket and dried them. "We don't know when we will see each other again, and until we do we will have tomorrow morning to cherish."

Michael kissed the tip of her nose, the simple act reassuring her he didn't mind. "Enjoy yourselves, minx." He led her to her bedroom and left her at the door. "Goodnight, sweetheart. I will see you at the altar."

At precisely three in the afternoon the next day, Michael and Christopher stood with the Archbishop in front of the altar in the small family chapel at Haldenwood. Roses of varying shades of pink and white, all cut from the Duchess' garden, mixed with greenery bedecked the altar and entry way to the small stone structure. Christina's three little ones came toward them spreading flower petals from their baskets on the aisle before them as they walked. They made excellent flower girls as they prepared the way for the Duchess, who would stand as Matron of Honor for both brides, as each bride would also stand as Maid of Honor for the other.

A collective sigh reached the men at the altar as everyone turned to watch the first bride stand in the doorway with her father.

Lord Hepplewhite and Beverly began their walk up the aisle and Michael heard Christopher's intake of breath as he saw his bride for the first time in over twenty-four hours. Beverly was beautiful in her ice-blue watered silk gown. He knew that she and Christopher would be very happy together.

When Ren and Elise made their entrance in the doorway, it was his turn to gasp audibly. He smiled as he realized he should have suspected they'd do something like this. They always did everything together. And just as they had the night of the Riddlesworth ball, the friends wore their matching dresses. Elise wore the exact same gown of watered silk, only in the palest peach color, to match her creamy pink complexion. Around her neck rested perfectly-matching tiny seed pearls in a necklace that grazed just below the collar bone, and on her earlobes she wore the matching earrings.

Elise. His bride. Until a few months ago, he'd never have thought this would come to pass. But here she was. A vision of bridal loveliness. A simple, vivacious, yet ethereal beauty to which none could compare—and she was his. There'd never been a more exquisite and enchanting young lady ever created. He felt as though he'd been kicked in the gut as he watched her come toward him for the last time as an unmarried girl. From this moment on she would be his wife, the Countess of Camden. Michael held out his arm for her, and she placed a trembling hand on his, her brother having taken his place next to him as best man.

"You are breathtaking, minx," he whispered.

Through a blushing and tremulous smile, she replied, "Thank you."

The ceremony was blessedly short. He didn't think he could take it if it had been any longer. As soon as the rite was done, Michael could barely recall anything about the entire service except for how radiant and lovely Elise looked. He obviously said and did the appropriate things at the appropriate times, else the Archbishop wouldn't have pronounced them man and wife, which he blessedly did.

She was finally his, and he couldn't wait to take her to his home, to their bed, and love her properly. As she should have been loved on that first night a month ago.

He held her close as they walked as man and wife together out of the room and into the great hall where a sumptuous dinner awaited them. Their families congratulated them with handshakes, hugs and kisses, everyone wishing them a lifetime of happiness as they walked by. Because family was so important to everyone in attendance, the older children were welcome at their celebratory dinner, with only the infants upstairs in the nursery.

Dinner seemed to take forever to Michael, who wanted nothing more than to spirit his wife away to Woodhenge, a good three hours carriage ride away, to begin their wedding night. They'd already sent Elise's maid and his valet ahead, along with Elise's belongings.

He noticed Elise barely touched any of the plates that were brought out, including dessert, which was usually her favorite course. "Are you nervous, minx?" She nodded her reply, not looking at him, but rather at the nut-covered spiced custard she pushed around the tiny plate. "I am, too."

"You are?" she asked incredulously.

"Of course. I've never been married before."

"Oh. I was thinking about what comes next, and you have done that before."

"Yes, but never with my *wife*." He stressed her

newly changed status, a reminder that she was his truly now.

"Michael you're making me blush," she admonished, as she stared at her dessert.

He leaned in and whispered to her, "I'm about to take you to your new home and make you blush all over."

"Then let's get on with it," she whispered in reply, "because this waiting is only making me more and more anxious."

Minutes later, Michael stood and thanked everyone for attending, and thanked his friend for not only hosting the wedding, but giving him his sister. Michael also wished Christopher and Beverly well, and before leaving both girls went up to Elise's rooms to have a few moments alone to say goodbye to each other and to Lia. Soon Elise and Michael were both enclosed in his carriage on the way to their new home.

The three hour ride to his home only served to tighten her already taught nerves. She didn't know what she was so afraid of. There was nothing different about what she was about to do tonight than what she'd done the night she went to his town home. Still, the fact that she now knew what to expect didn't ease her fears.

When she examined her worries earlier in the day, she realized they all came from wanting Michael to be happy with her in all ways. So she sought guidance from her insightful and wise sister-in-law, who enlightened her about several techniques sure to thoroughly please a man.

Now here she was, about to enter her husband's home and her new bed. She decided then she would be mistress of both, giving him no reason to seek satisfaction elsewhere.

The carriage rolled to a stop in front of Michael's home. No. Their home, Woodhenge. Michael assisted her down once the footman placed the steps beneath the vehicle. Upon entering the foyer Elise saw all the servants lined up, including Bridget, who chose to follow her to her new home. Turning her in his arms, he greeted the staff, then announced to all, "I present to your new mistress, my countess." Cheers and clapping echoed under the stone ceiling, reverberated through her. As Michael led her past the line, he introduced her to each person, informing her of their position. She nodded and smiled, and hopefully said the appropriate things as they worked their way up the few steps slowly. Lastly, they came to her maid, who ushered her in and told her all was in readiness upstairs.

"Thank you, Bridget."

Michael turned to her, and admitted, "There's one thing I forgot to warn you about—a task I must now perform."

"Which is?"

"There's a tradition with the Earls Camden going back to the very first one."

"What are you about Michael?" she asked as he scooped her into his arms and ran with her into the house and directly up the stairs as though she weighed no more than a sack of feathers.

"Michael, stop. You'll hurt yourself!"

"Not hardly, minx."

Only after the door to his rooms had shut behind them did she hear the cheering continue, ringing through the hallways and corridors of the home. He set her down on his bed as though she were delicate and fragile, then straightened and stared at her in wonderment.

"Michael, you could have gotten hurt."

"Afraid I'd be unable to perform my duties, minx?"

"No. More afraid that you'd drop me and I wouldn't get to ride in the morning." She sat up in the deep comfort of his mattress. "What was that about?"

"Something I had to do. If I'd kept to the letter of the custom, I would have thrown you over my shoulder and ran with you, but I didn't think that would be very dignified."

"That's not really a tradition, is it?"

"On my honor, it is. And, if I had not done so, then our marriage would be fated as unhappy and unfruitful. Just look at what happened with my uncle."

"And how did you learn of this 'tradition'?"

"I was informed by Uncle's ancient butler, Renfro."

She absorbed his words, and decided he was telling the truth. "You don't seem winded in the least, have you been practicing?"

"Yes. I've been running up and down the stairs daily in town, carrying a scullery maid for practice."

Even though his eyes crinkled in the corners from his broad grin, she had to ask, "Are you joking with me?"

"Of course I am." he said, as he worked at the knot of his cravat. "Not about the tradition, for that is a fact, but the scullery maid bit, yes."

"Michael?" Her voice cracked from her nerves, something she had no experience with until the past week.

"Yes, minx?"

She swallowed hard as he met her gaze in the mirror. His beauty did things to her insides, and she didn't know to say that, so she told him the words that burst forth from her heart right then. "I love you."

"And I love you, my sweet, gullible, wife."

She threw a pillow at him, hitting him square in the head.

Elise rose from the bed, looked about his bedroom. None of her belongings were here, nothing to show that his room was also hers. She didn't want to keep separate rooms even though she knew it was an accepted custom among their peers. "Michael," she met his gaze in the mirror, "I notice that my things are not here, and I was wondering... did you wish to keep separate rooms?"

"My wish is whatever you desire, minx." Elise watched him lower his massive frame on the sofa before the marble hearth which had an inviting warm fire glowing within. He poured them two glasses of wine from the decanter on the tray table before him. Her husband held out her glass to her.

She took the glass and sipped, taking the opportunity for reinforcement. "I don't want separate rooms Michael. I want to be with you every minute I possibly can."

"Then we shall not keep that practice," he replied. "I don't wish to be separated from you any more than necessary either. But I did instruct that your things be placed in the countess' suite simply because you have so many clothes, my dear. There isn't enough space in here for my wardrobes *and* yours."

She took another sip of her wine, suddenly too nervous to meet his gaze. "I should let Bridget help me change. She'll be waiting."

"And I'm sure my valet is waiting to assist me."

He took her glass from her and set it on the tray for later, then showed her the door that connected their rooms, and the hidden door to her dressing room where Bridget waited. He left her in the capable hands of her maid, saying "When you're done, come back."

Michael returned to his room, to find his valet standing near the chifforobe, ready to do his bidding. "If you'll just pour me a brandy, Connor, you may go. I'll not require your assistance tonight."

"If you're sure, my lord."

He nodded. More than anything Michael wanted time alone before Elise returned. He wanted Elise with an intensity he would never have imagined a mere four months ago. It would be his undoing, but he had to proceed slowly with her. Not just because of the ordeal she'd gone through two weeks prior, but also because of his own boorish behavior. If he held any hope of having a satisfying sexual relationship with her, he had to help her forget his actions from her first night with him.

She needed soft kisses, sweet words and gentle touches. And if it killed him, he'd be considerate of her needs tonight. Downing the last swallow of brandy, he glanced at the clock on the mantel and wondered what was keeping her. He rose and crossed the room, intending to check on her, to make sure she hadn't suddenly grown fearful or unwilling. Before he reached her door, she'd turned the knob, drew the door open and stepped into his candle-lit suite. A tremor of nervous excitement surged through him as he got the first glimpse of her.

Michael felt the breath leave him. She wasn't wearing what a man might think a newly-married young miss would wear on this most auspicious occasion. For his bride wore no typical *peignoir*. His beautiful minx was clad in the sheerest ivory silk pantalettes and tunic, with gold chain riding low on her waist and a fine gold bracelet on her left ankle above bare feet. She appeared more an Arab princess on her wedding night than a noble Englishwoman. The outfit was made to entice a lover, with strategic embroidery concealing her genitals and breasts. But the rest alluded to her flawless beauty, revealing the curves of her waist, hips, thighs and calves.

He forced himself to remember to be considerate of her needs. Her heightened color told him she was uncertain—either shy of revealing herself in the outfit, or of his approval of her appearance. With his own voice quivering, he reassured her immediately.

"Minx, you are so very lovely, I find myself speechless."

She closed her eyes and exhaled, obviously relieved. "Thank you. I was afraid you might not...."

"I do," he whispered. "Whatever you thought I didn't," he extended his hand to her, "I do." Elise came forward into his embrace, and he just held her while he forced his boiling blood to cool before he frightened her.

He led her to the sofa before the fire, and handed her the glass of brandy he poured earlier. Lowering his frame onto the deep cushioned sofa, he made himself comfortable in the corner, then drew Elise down to sit on his lap. He lifted the glass from her fingers, and sipped before handing it back to her. She put her lips to the rim and took one, then two sips, and handed the snifter back to him to place on the table.

"Michael, I'm nervous."

"So am I, minx," he confessed, while his right hand lightly stroked her back. He could feel her entire body tense and quiver as his fingers feathered tiny circles on her flesh.

Her position made her face level with his, and he raised his hand to rest behind her head, twining his fingers in her short light-brown hair, and bringing her close for a kiss. He parted her lips with his tongue and coaxed her to open for him, which she did willingly. Their tongues mated and danced as they explored each other with hands as well as mouths.

Elise shivered as she felt his erection growing beneath her. She shifted, afraid she was hurting him. Kissing his eyes and temples, her lips then traced a path to below and behind his ear, where his pulsed thrummed wildly. Her hands parted his robe and she caressed his chest. Resting her hand over his heart, she could have sworn it beat so hard it would burst from his chest. Moving her hand again, she felt the tip of his nipples harden under her palm. She stared into his hazel eyes, filled with an emotion she'd always longed to see there. Her husband loved her. He tugged at the chain around her waist, and she rose from his lap and unfastened it. He took it from her and dropped it to the floor. Then she felt his hands slip beneath the tunic and slide upward to cover her breasts, which ached for his touch. He toyed with her nipples, sending sharp rivulets of fire to her core.

When he lifted the tunic, she raised her arms for him allowing him to remove it from her. His hands were everywhere at once, caressing her back, her waist and shoulders. She felt his tongue tracing a path down the nape of her neck, and rest at her collarbone, her head fell backward giving up her breasts to his mouth. As he laved her nipples, his hand had worked the drawstring free from her pantalettes and she felt his hand reach in and stroke her bottom. She tried to turn on his lap without hurting him, and eventually stood to reposition herself. As she did, the pantalettes slid down her hips, falling silently onto the floor. She stepped out of them and stood before him, naked, except for the fine chain around her ankle. Fighting the instinct to cover herself, she let her hands fall to her sides while she awaited his touch.

It wasn't long in coming. He reached out and lay his palm across her womb, and looked into her eyes. "I cannot wait to see you grow with our child."

"I want that more than anything, Michael." The voice that came from her body sounded so different to her ears. So sultry and seductive, she didn't think it was her speaking.

He stood and lifted her in his arms and carried her to the bed, where he lay her on the turned-back sheets. Elise boldly watched as he unbelted his robe, and let it slide from his body, his large, muscular frame finally as naked as she. His manhood stood pulsing and she glanced up to his face, to see his desire for her burning in his eyes. She welcomed his warmth as he lay next to her, his arms wrapping around her, his hands stroking her softly.

His lips took hers again, kissing her deeply and provocatively. She enjoyed his touch, and began to caress him as well, one hand moving across his back, and the other boldly traveling to his erection. Taking him in her hand, she heard him suck in a deep breath as she began to fondle him, stimulating him in the up and down motion she was told he would enjoy. As she did this, his fingers dipped in her woman's curls causing her legs to fall open for him. When he slid a finger into her, touching her on her sensitive core, she nearly leaped from the bed. Drawing forth her moisture, he then began to stroke her gently. But only for a moment. She whimpered when he removed his hand and rose up on his knees before straddling her. Leaning over he took first one nipple and then the other, into his mouth to suckle. The sensations as his tongue moving over the tender peaks caused a coiling tension within her womb and she called out to him. He chuckled and roved lower with his mouth, kissing her navel, and lower still, until his tongue traced the slit covering her nub.

Even though he'd done this for her before, she'd forgotten the how wonderful it felt. His expert ministrations brought her to a level of passion she hadn't experienced since her first night here at Woodhenge, all those weeks ago. Her breathing became rapid. She felt unable to inhale deeply, almost as though a vise were clamping her around the waist. The pressure within her intensified, and she begged him for release.

Raising his head, he lifted himself over her and before taking her lips with his, he said, "Not just yet, minx. There's more."

Michael slid into her slowly at first, to allow her to acclimate to his invasion. Once fully within her, he held still a moment before beginning to move. When she wrapped her legs around him allowing him deeper access, he sighed, knowing there was nothing more right and more perfect in the world than being with this woman, like this. His thrusts were slow and deep at first, but before long she was again pleading with him for relief.

Her breaths matched his movements as her walls surrounded him, pulling him in, squeezing and releasing rhythmically. He tried to keep his passion in check, but her sweet body demanded release, and after fighting it for only a moment, he decided to give them both what their bodies wanted, promising himself he would take more time later.

Driving into her deep and fast, he felt her nearing her peak. He pushed her over the edge first, as her sheath tightened, the contractions drawing him forward to his own climax. Unable to control his body any longer, his orgasm overcame him and he poured himself into her depths.

After a few minutes, he lifted from her, intending to roll over, when she stopped him.

"Please don't. I've wanted this for so long. Stay with me for a moment longer."

"I'm afraid to hurt you, sweetheart," he replied.

"You're not hurting me, I promise. Just hold me this way."

"I'm going to roll over onto my back and bring you with me, so I'll still be inside you, just not on top of you." Then he did so. "I weigh twice what you do, minx. I'd smother you."

"No you wouldn't," she said as she rose to sit on him, still impaled on his shaft. She shifted slightly feeling him within her depths. "Mmmm. Now this is interesting," she said as she gently lifted and lowered herself on him, slowly at first, then picking up her speed. The motion was similar to posting a slow trot. "And it feels good, too."

"If you keep that up, you'll not get any rest," he warned her.

"You're the one that thinks I need rest. *I* think I want more of *this*," she replied as she flexed the muscles inside her, drawing a smile and muttered curse from her husband.

Close to sunrise, laughter was heard coming from the earl's suite by a maid passing by in the hallway. She smiled and went about her morning chores.

Epilogue

Woodhenge, May 1823

Michael pushed Attila as hard as his conscience would allow. As a result, he turned onto the long drive leading to Woodhenge in almost an hour under what the ride from London normally took. The message from his sister Sabrina stated simply, *It is time*.

If his partner hadn't insisted he be the one to present the closing argument before the high court, he would never have left Elise's side, and would already be here for her. He'd hated the thought of leaving his wife so near her time, but the case was one sure to bring about reform in the banking industry if the court ruled in their favor, and perhaps avert a mass financial crisis in the country.

Before the stable lad had even reached him, Michael had dismounted and threw Attila's reins to him. He ignored the footman who stood awaiting his arrival, and ran through the open doors and up the stairs. The scene that greeted him when he bounded into their suite was a surprise. His wife stood, albeit hunched over and holding both her distended belly and her back simultaneously. And with the help of his mother, Elise was attempting to walk.

"Shouldn't she be in bed?" he asked her.

"No. The delivery will be easier if she walks as much as she can before taking to the bed. It is something I wish I knew when you and your older sister were born. By the time Christina came along, old Magda had passed away and her assistant was a young girl by the name of Piper, or Poppy, I cannot remember. She's the one who told me to walk while I labored before your younger sister was born. As a result, her birthing was a much easier, much faster process."

"Where's Prescott? Has he been notified? I didn't see his coach."

"He's sent word. The good doctor will come as soon as he is able."

"Where on earth is he when my wife is having my child?"

"Beverly is in labor as well," Elise replied, "and she has no female relatives to sit with her. Since I have your mother and sister here, I thought it best the doctor go to Beverly's side before coming to mine." She grimaced, before taking a sharp, deep breath and doubled over.

He ran to her side and held her as she cursed the very ground he walked on. His mother looked over Elise's head and said, "She doesn't mean what she's saying. It's the pain talking."

"Maybe it's time to put her in the bed," he said, concerned only for his wife's well-being.

"Not yet. We've got hours more of this. Why don't you go downstairs and have some brandy and a cigar. You'll be a father before the night is through."

"I'm not leaving my wife."

"Michael, go away!" his wife shrieked.

"I'm sorry my love, I stay. This is my child as well."

Elise looked to his mother, "Make him go away. Please."

"Michael, leave us for a little while."

Reluctantly, he left the room, but only after vowing to return. He passed through the connecting door to his rooms, and stripped away the coat, cravat and waistcoat, tossing them on the bed. After pouring a whiskey, he fell into the chair before the hearth. Connor arrived and offered to help him freshen up, but Michael refused. He listened to the sounds coming from the room next door, and prayed all was well with the babe and his wife. Perhaps he should send for a mid-wife from the village as well. He felt helpless and uncertain for the first time in his thirty three years.

He heard Sabrina and Elise's maid entering and talk of hot water. At the sound of Elise's very pained groaning, he rose and re-entered her room, but only after knocking and awaiting permission. He found his wife lying on the bed, and a sheet thrown over her. "Is she alright?"

"Michael, you can ask *me* how I'm feeling, you know." She sounded tired and annoyed at the same time. "Quit speaking as though I'm not in the room."

On trembling legs, he stepped closer to the bed and asked, "How do you feel, minx?"

"Horrible right now, though everyone says I'll feel better by morning."

His mother looked to him and said, "This babe is coming quickly for a first child. Please go see what's keeping that hot water."

"But she's fine, isn't she?" His mother nodded, and Michael sighed, only somewhat relieved. "Right. I'll go fetch the hot water." He strode from the room and ran down the stairs, nearly knocking into two maids carrying pitchers, presumably of hot water. Taking one, he sent the maid back for another, unsure how much the women needed.

He poured the water in the basin beside the foot of the bed then went to sit next to Elise's head. Stroking her sweat-covered brow, she grimaced and groaned through another painful contraction, and his mother again ordered him from the room.

"No," he said firmly. "I stay."

After looking to Elise, who nodded her head, his mother then lifted the sheet and checked her progress. "Everything is coming along just fine. Your babe is eager to be born, my dear."

"And I am eager to have her out of me!"

"Or him," Michael stated.

Elise grimaced again, and he helped her sit upright, as his mother directed. Soon Elise began to bear down hard and scream. The sound wrenching his heart. It was almost enough to make him never get her with child again.

"It's a girl," she panted. "Lia said it's a girl." More panting. "And I feel as though it's a daughter." Grimacing again, she screamed as she pushed now harder than before.

Thirty minutes later, his mother said, "I see the head, Elise. At the next contraction, push as hard as you can." That next contraction came sooner than Michael thought, and as he supported Elise, she squeezed his hand until he felt his fingers going numb. "Good. Keep pushing. Don't stop pushing, dear." Then his mother looked up and said, "We have a head, Elise. Now at the next contraction, give me the rest of my grandchild."

Elise relaxed a moment, then began pushing again. This time she pushed with a renewed vigor, and screamed louder and longer than before. Sabrina went to her mother with the twine and a pair of scissors, set them down and opened up the folded towels, holding one ready in her hands. And in a moment Michael will never forget, he saw his child for the very first time as his mother lifted the babe and handed it into Sabrina's toweled hands.

All scrunched up and coated in a grayish-white wax, streaked with blood, the baby began to wail from a very healthy set of lungs. It was the most beautiful sound he'd ever heard. Elise relaxed and lay back against his chest, encircled in his arms, exhaling as tears began to fall from her closed eyes.

"I have a grand-daughter," his mother said.

Michael dropped a kiss on his wife's damp brow. "Don't cry, sweetheart."

Sabrina took the infant to the large table brought in for the occasion and began to wash the babe with clean cloths and warm water. His mother continued working with Elise, and soon had her covers drawn up over his resting wife. Sabrina carried the babe over to him and handed him his clean, blanketed daughter. Elise opened her eyes and smiled. He lowered the babe to her, and she took the infant from his arms.

"She's beautiful, sweetheart. Almost as beautiful as you."

Grandmother and aunt quietly left the room to spread the joyous news, leaving the proud parents alone with their newborn daughter.

"I don't feel beautiful right now," she said. "I feel very tired."

"Take a nap. You deserve it. I'll be here with you."

Exactly six weeks from the date of baby Charlotte's birth, three couples gathered in the chapel at St. Paul's, for the christening of three infants. And each of the three infant girls, had two sets of godparents. The minister gathered the six adults and their infants around the baptismal font, and read off the names of the children, and adults, asking for the godparents to respond with "I will" only after reading all the names because, he said, he only wanted to read through them once.

Thus it was that the little ladies Charlotte Simone Brightman, Isabel Agnese Halden, and Penelope Heather Fenwicke, became baptized into the Church of England.

In the first pew behind the attendees at the font, Lady Sarah Halden—the youngest sister of the Duke of Caversham—sat next to her grandmother playing with a doll she named Prudence. The child spoke, her loud whisper echoing through the cavernous cathedral. "Grandmama, I'm going to have lots of babies one day." She set the doll on the seat between her and her grandmother. Turning a blue-eyed gaze up to Lady Sewell the child added, "But not until I have some adventures first."

The End

Author's Note

Putting our work "out there" makes most artists feel vulnerable in some way. But, for a few of us, there is nothing in the world we would rather be doing than creating stories that touch the heart, no matter the fear of scrutiny. I hope you enjoyed reading about Michael and Elise as much as I enjoyed writing their story. If you did, please leave a rating or review at the vendor where you purchased this book. Because I truly believe all constructive criticism helps writers better themselves at this craft we love so much.

Loving Sarah

SANDY RAVEN

Here is the first chapter preview of the third book in **The Caversham Chronicles**. In **Loving Sarah**, Lady Sarah Halden craves adventure and wants to see the world. And London's just not satisfying this need in her. She wants to be a Grand Eccentric Spinster Aunt to her nieces and nephews, thinking she can have her adventures if she was officially 'off the shelf.'

Sarah plans for her new life to begin at the start of the Atlantic Crossing Challenge. Which she intends to participate in with her brother-by-marriage, Lucky Gualtiero. Sarah meticulously plans her escape from home, and even arranges for a cabin boy to row her out to Lucky's boat.

But the lad brought her to the wrong boat, and that's where her new life begins.

Coming, Summer 2013

Chapter One

Liverpool, June 1835

"What about her? She looks fast doesn't she?"

"Hmmm... *Aurelia*," Ian Alexander Ross, grandson of the Earl of Mackeever, mused as he strolled alongside his friend Lucky Gualtiero, brother of Lia, the Duchess of Caversham. "She may look fast, but she's not built the way I like. Something about her shape... too curvy if you ask me. It looks like she might fall apart before the ordeal is over."

"What about that one? *Evangeline*," his tanned, olive-skinned friend asked.

Ian turned his gaze to where Lucky motioned. "Too top heavy, and her bottom's too narrow to support her. She'll tip over in a stiff wind."

"What about that one?"

"Her bottom's too broad. She'll be too slow to tack."

"Well, you can't say the same about that one over there. She has a nice, well-proportioned hull. At least what I can see of it."

He didn't need to consider the vessel in question, for he knew her design well. He should, it was very similar to, if not exactly, a design of his father's. "Yes. Nice curves, sturdily built, and I think I know her owner. If it is who I think, he has a load of money, but no skill at the wheel." He gazed at *Ann McKim* longingly. "She was launched two years ago from the very yard my father helped found and has already broken records for fastest crossing times for the Atlantic and Pacific in both directions. But a ship like that could do far better with the right man at the wheel." Sighing, he turned to Lucky. "What that lady needs is a man with a knowledgeable, soft hand and the experience to coax her on when she wants to give up."

"So, do you think we stand a chance?" Lucky stopped and turned toward him.

Ian looked over the competition once more, and nodded. "Oh, I'd say the odds are very good. Next to McKim's lady out there, we've definitely got the best boats in this race. A little smaller, a little aged, but well broken in. More importantly, both of them are lovingly maintained and handled." They walked away from the dock and the preparations for the next day's ceremony. "I believe everything is ready for the morning. God willing, we'll have good wind."

"The weather will hold until we're well out," Lucky said as he scanned the sky and horizon around them. Ian didn't question him. He knew better. Like an old sailor, Lucky had an instinct for forecasting weather just by looking at the clouds. "Remember, my sister's throwing us a dinner party to see us off. Be at the house around seven."

"I'll be there. You know I wouldn't miss an opportunity for real food. Anything is better than the grub Mick throws into a kettle," Ian said as they neared a waiting hackney.

"You need to find a better cook," Lucky replied. "So you stop trying to take mine away."

The driver tipped his hat and opened the door for the men. "You go on without me. I'm just going to get cleaned up, make sure the watch is in place, and I'll be right behind you."

"Fine." Lucky gave a quick nod to the man holding the door, then asked Ian if he needed the address again. Ian shook his head, and asked the hackney driver to simply return for him after dropping off Lucky. "Then I'll see you soon."

The hackney door closed on his friend. After the driver cued the horse to move on, Ian turned back to the dinghy tied below, and rowed out to the *Revenge,* his best hope for victory in this race. Their supplies had been loaded earlier in the day, so he'd moved his boat away from the hustle and bustle of the dock. And any potential sabotage. Not that he suspected his fellow competitors of such underhanded behavior, but one could never be too careful when the stakes were this high. Tying off the dinghy, he climbed onto the deck and double-checked to make sure all was in readiness for the start of the race.

Normally, he wouldn't have even considered wasting their time entering a race, but the twenty-five thousand pound purse was far too large to ignore. More importantly, if he and Lucky were serious about succeeding in their joint venture, the newly chartered British Tea Import Company, they needed more ships. Two retrofit Baltimore schooners, though a respectable beginning, wouldn't turn the kind of profits necessary to expand their business in the manner they wanted. The one tea run they'd made last year left him with barely enough to live on after paying the note—a full half of what they'd borrowed—and their crews' salaries. Lucky might not need the money as much as he did, but he'd be damned if he'd let his partner pay their way until they could turn a profit. Lucky had done enough already by paying the shipyard bill for the retrofit of the two boats over the past winter.

His dream, and Lucky's too, was to have a fleet of at least a dozen clippers, preferably designed and built to their specifications. After carefully studying Colonel Beaufoy's publication, *Nautical and Hydraulic Experiments*, where Beaufoy tested and found Newton's hydraulics theory unlikely, Ian had begun drawing his own hull designs. In order to maximize hull space for valuable cargo, Ian's idea was first to streamline the design of the hull; next to make her longer and deeper in the keel; then, thirdly, to eliminate the complete dependence on ballast and use lead plate on the keel in conjunction with minimal internal ballast for stabilization. He was excited and anxious to test his theory. If it worked, he knew it would forever change the way hulls were designed and built. And his father, wherever his soul rested, would be proud.

Having grown up with a naval architect for a father, a man who designed clipper hulls and constructed them, Ian knew that shipyards in New York and Baltimore were more willing to build experimental designs; whereas in Aberdeen and Halifax, they were more likely to insist the time-tested and proven designs they have been very successful building for the last twenty years were better. Ian knew his design held promise, and so did his partner. But, he would amuse Lucky and have the Aberdeen yards look at the designs, but Ian knew they would likely have to go back to America to have them built.

Ian made his way down to his small cabin, stopping to take a bucket of fresh water from the barrel near the companionway. He ladled some into the metal basin, set the bucket down near the washstand, then stripped. He dunked his head into the bowl and began washing. One day, he'd like to have a house with a proper bathing chamber. There would be no more tossing water out of the aft windows and refilling wash basins. No more bathing with cold water except when at sea. Worst of all were the times he had to bathe with salt water, because it always left him feeling sticky and itchy. For that reason, he understood why some of the crew went without baths during those times.

Life at sea wasn't the romantic, adventurous dream he'd imagined. But, this had been his reality for the past three years since leaving university. He supposed he could have lived on credit and taken rooms somewhere, as did others in his financial situation. But Ian was too American for that, as Lucky reminded him on those rare occasions he complained out loud. He might be the nephew of the current Earl of Mackeever, but he was still the American-born son of a Baltimore naval architect who designed ships for the Americans in their war for independence. A fact not lost to most of his classmates. Except for Lucky, who was as much of an outsider because of his foreign title and swarthy appearance as he for his American blood at a time when most still remembered their deceased loved ones. In that atmosphere, he and Lucky had become fast friends; then immediately after university, business partners.

Now, at age twenty-five, Ian had the entire world

before him.

And no place to call home except this ship.

Opening the cabinet, he remembered the cedar lining still needed replacing as he took out his good clothing. Repairs inside his cabin had been low in priority during the renovations, but now as he looked over his best trousers to make sure they weren't moth-eaten or torn somewhere, he decided it needed to get moved up on the list. He checked the coat and linen shirt also for tiny holes, saw none and smiled. Lifting the only waistcoat he owned, he noticed the stitching at the edge of the wool where it met the satin was coming apart, but knew it would remain hidden by the coat if he kept it on.

If he ever planned to take his place in society, he would need to pay more attention to his dress. Ian owed it to his father's sisters not to be an embarrassment when he did. Especially after all they've done for him over the years, from taking him in when his father sent him over for a formal education to sponsoring his entrée into society. Events like this dinner with Lucky's family were sure to become more common as they became more successful. He had to get over the gnawing hatred of his two uncles, and think of tonight as an opportunity to polish his manners, and become more accustomed with the world he'd not been born to, but found himself in now. To do so would make those little old ladies proud.

Lady Sarah Eileen Halden dropped her gaze as her brothers discussed the upcoming race, lest they see the delight in her eyes while her final plan started to form. The rented home in Liverpool the family had taken for the next several months was nowhere near as large or opulent as Caversham House or Haldenwood, but it had something that would serve her well this night, as she'd spied it right after arriving and looking over her temporary bedroom. She had a balcony, that was a mere ten or twelve feet above ground. Sarah could quite easily climb over the railing and ease herself down. The drop, after lowering herself as much as possible, wouldn't be much more than the jump from her favorite tree at home.

She saw it as a sign that she was meant to go with Lucky on this race.

"Ian and I have gone over the charts several times, and already plotted our course." Lucky pointed to something on the map Sarah's brother Ren, the Duke of Caversham, had spread across the table in the drawing room where they all gathered while waiting for the last of their dinner guests to arrive. "Both crews have been with us since last year. They made the tea run with us, and they're all veteran sailors. Most have crossed the Atlantic at least once, some several times. So we're very confident in everyone's abilities."

"Good," her brother, Ren, said, "I know this is an exciting challenge for you, but remember do not push your boat any harder than she can handle. Even if you don't win this race, you know I'll finance you."

"I appreciate your offer, Ren, truly. But this is something I want to do on my own, and Ian feels the same."

Just then, the butler announced the arrival of Ian Alexander Ross, Lucky's business partner and long-time friend. When Sarah looked up and met his eyes, she could have sworn her heart skipped several beats and her mouth went dry. His brown-eyed gaze met hers and she quickly turned away and took a sip of her sweet wine.

It had been over a year since she'd last seen him., the night he'd come for dinner at Caversham House before leaving on their trip to China. She remembered it was right as the season was getting underway, and she'd thought it was a shame he wouldn't be around to amuse her and her friends. After all, he was certainly handsome enough then. But now he was Adonis come to life. The last year seemed to have matured him even more. He'd become broader in the shoulders and his face bore a healthy sun-kissed glow. His dark blond hair was liberally streaked with gold in a manner that could only have come from working out in the sunshine on the open sea, like hers had when she was a girl sailing her little sloop around the pond, pretending she was a great explorer.

Rugged and handsome. Those were the only words she could think of as she glanced at him again. Without a doubt his viking god-like looks caused tiny tremors to course through her body when she just looked at him. She felt perhaps, if given time together, there would certainly be a curious plethora of emotions and feelings to discover.

Sarah had to stop thinking of him this way. As attractive as the man was, she had no time for flirtation. She had a race to sail with Lucky.

From her position, half-turned from him, she covertly watched him greet some of the other guests as he slowly made his way toward where she stood with her brother Ren, and her brother-by-marriage Lucky. As he did, she noticed his evening wear was somewhat outdated, but it did nothing to detract from his intense vitality. Before she embarrassed herself, she took her leave from her Ren and Lucky and sought her sister-in-law's company as she sat with a group of ladies, including her sister Elise.

Talk among the women soon turned to the goings on in town now that the season was almost over. Lady Vance smiled and shared some of the interesting events they'd attended over the past months. "My girls are still in Town with their aunt," she said, "and they were loathe to leave. Now that my two nieces are married, my sister is relishing taking my elder daughter through the season's events."

Sarah traveled in a different set than Miss Vance, the younger girl's friends being more the blue-stocking type. Just the same, she smiled politely, remembering how exciting that first season had been for her as well. She'd truly enjoyed her first and even her second season. Then her friends began to marry, leaving her to start their own families. And with each successive year her tolerance for the superficiality that was the season grew thinner. In her head and heart she was always elsewhere. Her friends knew it, and the men she'd met sensed it. Which is why she was twenty one and still unwed, without a prospect on the horizon.

Sarah had long grown bored with what was her lot in life. She craved adventure. Needed to see the world. Growing up, she'd always questioned why it was that men were respected when they successfully ventured outside the boundaries set for them by society, but never women. Why was a woman's reputation in tatters when she did something bold and adventurous, and not a man's?

The year before she'd thought to stowaway with

Lucky to China, but was afraid. That fear was the only thing keeping her inside her comfy, gilded cage—the fear of not being accepted after she'd gone to seek her grand adventure. But not this year.

With only a few weeks until the end of this—her fourth—season, Sarah was beginning to feel her fate might lie in spinsterhood because of these ideas. She knew she was choosy, but wasn't about to compromise in her requirements for a husband. Not only did he have to desire adventure as much as she, his kiss should leave her weak in the knees and curl her toes—something her friends told her was how they knew their husbands were the ones for them.

So, unless and until she found that man, she wouldn't consider marriage. She'd rather remain the eccentric relative to her family. Because she would never compromise those two requirements.

Her decision made to take this chance for adventure, she would turn her back on caution and grasp this one opportunity for adventure. And worry about what might happen upon her return tomorrow.

"You're quiet little sister," her sister Elise said as she sidled up to Sarah, who stood on the fringe of the group of ladies. "You have a wistful look about you. What are thinking about?"

"Wondering why I couldn't have been born a male. I envy Lucky."

Elise stifled a giggle. "You would have made a very effeminate male, and not very attractive to the ladies I dare say."

Sarah shrugged. "You know what I mean. I have to return to London after they start their race, and finish out the season. And I'll do so, wishing the entire time I was racing with them."

"As ladies our rewards are in the home—in caring for our families, friends and neighbors. Our legacy is the children we raise to carry on after we're gone. I never thought of it that way until after I had Charlotte and needed to be a role model for her." Her sister turned her gaze to her, and seemed to study Sarah's face. "I think next season we should concentrate more intently on finding you a match. A man is what you need now that the social season holds no more charm for you. A family will settle that adventurous spirit of yours."

The dinner bell rang and all the guests proceeded into the dining room, taking their seats. Sarah discovered her dinner companion to her right was Lucky's partner, Mr. Ross. At first, having the handsome, seafaring adventurer beside her caused her pulse to race. But it wasn't long before she knew it wasn't that he'd sailed around the globe, but the man himself who stirred her senses.

The faint scent of cedar and citrus wafted from his direction and she inhaled a shaky breath before looking his way. She smiled.

"So Mr. Ross, you must be excited. Lucky was when we spoke just before your arrival. And it must feel good to return to your home. Even if it is for only a day."

"I wish I had time to visit Baltimore but, in all honesty, there is no reason for me to return there yet."

"Oh. Then you plan to eventually?"

"If we win this race, I will likely return to have my father's friend build our two new clippers. There is no finer shipyard on the eastern seaboard."

"You could have your ships build here. I'm sure His Grace can make the necessary introductions in

Aberdeen. It's where his import company was based before he bought out his cousins and moved operations to London. I'm certain we have relatives that likely know a shipbuilder or two."

"That was one of the places we intended to query about building custom clippers."

Footmen began serving the soup and Sarah listened as the men continued their pre-dinner discourse on the opportunities for trade and import now that the East India Company had lost its monopoly as sole importers of tea to Britain. Talk of finance, trade, and the importance of diversification floated about the table. Much to her surprise, some of the women participated as well.

But not Sarah. Her breast quivered under her skin in the presence of Lucky's partner. Or was it the excitement of the race? She was unsure. She pushed her fork around the plate as she listened to their conversation, trying to hide her anticipation. Sarah wasn't quite sure if her titillation came from her plan to stow aboard Lucky's clipper, or her close proximity to this man who had a strange effect on her senses. Because of this, she tried to make certain not to bump her arm into his, especially when she noted he was left-handed. But when she dropped her napkin, she bumped his arm, causing him to spill the spoonful of soup on his cravat and waistcoat. When she lifted her head, she turned her gaze to his and was mortified, but at the same time wanted to drown in his gold-flecked brown eyes. Or lick the warm, creamy onion soup from his chest.

Where had that thought come from?

"I'm so sorry. I...." Her face burned at the images racing through her head, and the entirety of the table staring their way. She immediately took her napkin and began to dab at his waistcoat, until the footman hurried over to take care of it for her with a clean damp linen. Mr. Ross waved the man away, blotting what little remained of the soup on his waistcoat.

"There wasn't much soup left, as I was nearly done." He showed her the bowl. "See? All is well, my lady," he said through a smile. "No harm done."

"Thank goodness," she whispered, "I'm not normally so clumsy, and I sincerely apologize."

Conversation resumed around them, when Mr. Ross asked her, "Where you going to come out to the dockyards in the morning and watch the ships jockey for position at the starting line?"

Sarah kept her eyes cast downward, unwilling to have him see her excitement as she spooned her soup. She took a deep breath to collect her emotion, and replied, "Yes, Mr. Ross. I wouldn't miss that for the world."

Her dinner partner was turning out to be very charming for an American. She had to admit her earlier perception of him as cocksure and bit self-absorbed was wrong. He was gracious to everyone with whom he spoke.

"Your brother said you are very much alike in that you are as adventuresome as he."

Sarah sighed, again regretting her gender. "Lucky is right. One would think we were true brother and sister, rather than joined by the marriage of our siblings."

"I'm fortunate to have your brother as a friend and partner. I've never met a more honest, intelligent and unprejudiced man before. I consider myself honored to call him friend."

Sarah smiled as she held another spoonful of the hearty onion broth in mid-air. "He can also be annoying and stubborn, but that's coming from a sisterly perspective."

"I never had a sibling to annoy, or I'm sure I would have been the same."

"Don't say so! It would ruin my image of you," she teased.

"Oh?" Mr. Ross laughed, the sound warm and pleasing to her ears. "What image is that?"

"One of a kind gentleman who is understanding, and not as rigid and straight-laced as my older brother and Lucky."

The next course was served, and the topic changed to the two schooners, *Revenge* and *Avenger*, and the remodeling done to the sister ships. Lucky and Ian were obviously proud of the modifications made to their boats, and felt they stood a solid chance of winning after sizing up most of their competition earlier that afternoon.

"On first glance," Lucky said, "the *Ann McKim* looks to be the best boat in the race, but looks can be deceiving. She's long and sleek all right. But without knowing how she carries her ballast, or the type of keel she has, there's really no knowing how well she'll do. She's a brand new design, built in Baltimore, at Ian's father's very shipyard and while the American owner will captain her, my opinion is he doesn't have half the experience necessary for an undertaking such as this."

An uneasy quiet came over the table, when everyone realized that in an endeavor such as this, not everyone survived. "Unfortunately," Ren said, "there will be lives lost during this race. But I have every confidence in the two of you. In fact, were I twenty years younger, I might have entered myself. Not for the purse so much as the thrill of the adventure."

Sarah pushed the vegetables around on the plate and kept her eyes downcast, for that was the very reason she planned to stow away aboard Lucky's boat.

Sarah shoved the packed canvas bag she'd brought with her from London under her bed. She was going to be on that boat when it sailed in the morning. There was no way she was going to allow Lucky to have this adventure without her. She was tired of reading about everyone else's voyages and missing out on the ones right before her!

She'd spent the last five years the embodiment of a well-mannered young lady because that was what was expected of her, the sister of a duke. And, for the past four seasons, she'd smiled and swallowed her envy as Lucky lived the adventures of which she could only dream. First he and his partner sailed to America to buy the two American-made schooners they required for their newly chartered import company. Then last spring she forced herself to feign interest in the upcoming social season while Lucky sailed to China to make their first tea run now that he and Ian were officially in business. She smiled and wished him well, all the while wishing she were with them.

Well, the balls, musicales, dinner parties, morning calls, and rides through Hyde Park would still be there when she returned. She was not going to sit in her room and cry as he sailed away. Not this time. This was the chance of a lifetime—and she wasn't letting it pass her by.

By tomorrow night, she would feel the salty spray of the ocean on her face and the motion of the vessel under her feet. For some inexplicable reason she just knew her heart would soar as she heard the snapping of the sailcloth in the wind and the shouts of the men as they performed the tasks ordered by their captain. It would be just as Ren described when he told her of the adventures he had when she was a babe. Sarah smiled as she remembered forcing her brother to repeat each voyage every evening he was home.

When she was older, she read the journals and ship logs that lined the shelves of her brother's office, finding these far more stimulating reading than the historical or scientific tomes or romantic novels in the library. These were log books with descriptions written in the hand of her relatives, who had seen and witnessed each act and event she'd read.

It was those tales of adventure, and the uncertainty of success that started this desire within her to travel and see the world. They were food to her adventurer's mind and soul.

Yes, without a doubt, Lucky would be angry with her when he discovered she'd stowed away, but he'd soon get over his anger when he realized he couldn't very well return her to dry land. Her older brother would be furious as well once he realized what she'd done. But by the time anyone noticed her missing, she'd already be somewhere in the Atlantic and there'd be nothing they could do about it. She'd write a note to Ren explaining what she'd done and leave it on the *secretaire.* They'd find it when they looked through her room for clues, though they should know she'd seize the opportunity to sail the Atlantic and see New York City when it presented itself. After all, she talked about her desire to see the Americas her entire life.

The devil take her, but she'd happily face Ren's anger upon her return for an adventure such as this!

A soft knock on her door preceded her maid, who'd come to help her undress for bed. While Trudy braided her thick mass of unruly waves, Sarah contemplated the timing of her escape. She had to leave well before breakfast and do so without setting up an alarm. Darkness was her ally. With the mound of pillows on the bed, she would fashion a suitable form under the covers that hopefully upon first glance would appear human, thus intimating to her maid she still slept. Then once at the docks, she'd need someone to take her out to the boat. That was why she'd thrown her coin purse in the satchel. She didn't doubt that she'd find someone to take her. In her experience, when you offered someone enough coin, they'd willingly do just about anything.

Like the summer she was ten years old, when she mapped the entire estate over a period of five weeks while the rest of the family enjoyed their season in London. She had been studying geography at the time and Ren had joked about her mapping the American continents one too many times. Sarah had wanted to prove her map drawing skill to her brother and set out alone to accomplish the task.

Of course she was found out before she'd gone one hundred yards from the stables. Theo the stable lad had discovered what she was up to as she led her pony, loaded with all her supplies, plus a rolled napkin with some pilfered crusty bread and fruit. At first, he refused to keep quiet about her expedition. Until she offered him her collection of Roman coins she'd dug up near the old church ruins.

On her brother's birthday, she proudly presented him with a rolled, charted map of Haldenwood, current up to that date, with boundaries and elevation changes. When asked how she'd accomplished the task, she proudly regaled to the entire family of her solo adventures in mapping.

Sarah waited until her maid had gone, then opened the drawer to her desk and took out a sheet of vellum, quill and ink.

My dearest family,

First, please do not be upset. Rest assured, I am safe with Lucky. And please, for pity's sake, do NOT interrupt the race because of my desire to not have another adventure pass me by!

I have decided that since it is highly doubtful that I shall ever marry, there are a few things I would like to do before I settle into my spinsterhood. One is seeing if the ocean really is as clear and blue as I've always heard; and another is to see America.

Also, please do not fault Lucky in this. He knew nothing of my plans.

Love, and etc.,
　Your Sister,
　Sarah

With the note written, she placed it inside the old ship's journal she'd been reading. The only thing she waited for now was for the house to go quiet for the night.

Slipping past the fire boy as he slept in the kitchen proved easier than she'd expected and once outside she made her way to the street, keeping to the shadows alongside the house as much as possible. She walked briskly and with intent toward the port a short distance away. She entered the area cordoned off for the morning ceremonies and began to look for someone to ferry her out to *Avenger*. Pulling the gray coarse-knit cap down lower over her brow, she took on a stooped posture and with the bag slung over her shoulder she looked very much like any other young sailor. She raised the collar of her coat, hiding her face and any trace of the waist-length braid tucked inside.

A scrawny lad sat with his feet dangling over the side of the dock. Glancing over the edge, she saw a dinghy tied below. Sarah dropped her voice, hoping she sounded masculine. "Can ye ferry me out to me boat, lad? I shoulda been on it hours ago and th' cap'n will be missin' me come sun-up."

The lad shook his head. "Can't do it. I'm waitin' on me own cap'n."

"There'll be coin in it for ye."

The boy looked more interested now that money was mentioned. "'Ow much ye got?"

Sarah fished two half sovereigns from her pocket and showed him. The boy looked at the money in her hand, then around the darkened pier.

"Fine. But I gotta be quick, don't know when me cap'n's comin' back." Sarah tossed the bag into the dinghy and stepped down into it. Once the boy shoved away from the pier with the oar, he asked, "Which un's yer boat?"

"*Avenger*."

"Aye. I knows where it is."

They rowed out about a hundred yards into the darkness with only the light of a cloud-covered sliver of moon. Gentle waves lapped the side of the tiny craft.

This was it. There was no turning back now. She was on her way to see the ocean and America. Well, at least one city in America. She told herself that she would return later to see more of the country later. Perhaps once she found a traveling companion.

She practically trembled with anticipation when the lad brought the dinghy along-side Lucky's boat, near the rope ladder. Sarah asked, "Are ye sure ye got the right boat? Don't want me cap'n lashin' me back."

"Aye, she's the right un. I'm right alongside ye on *Evangeline*."

She handed the lad the two coins, tossed her satchel over her shoulder, and grabbed hold of Jacob's ladder.

"Good luck to ye."

"Aye. And to you too," she replied as she began to climb up the port side.

She peered over the rail and saw no one about. Silently climbing onto the deck, Sarah wound her way toward the bow and prayed the hatch to the forward hold would be open. If so, she'd climb down and hide there. If it wasn't, she knew she couldn't lift it easily or quietly. In that case, she'd have to find the lazarette, or dry goods storeroom if there was one, and hide there.

Seeing the open hatch, she thanked God and knelt to look inside. It was dark out and even darker below in the hold. She'd just have to take her chances. She lowered her bag in and dropped it. It didn't make a sound so she assumed her landing, too, would be soft and silent. She sat in front of the hold, grabbing the lip of the hatch opposite and scooted her bottom forward, then dropped herself feet first into the abyss.

As she'd suspected, she landed on folded canvas duck cloth. Yards and yards of the stuff. Spare sails, she thought. Wonderful. Moving to the far corner of the cavernous dark hold, she lay on the folded material and using her satchel as a pillow, forced her racing heart to calm and tried to sleep.

Grayish-pink light filtered into the forward hold from overhead. Day was breaking. Footsteps alerted her to at least one crewman awake above deck. The man drew closer to the bow, and her hideout. Sarah quickly lifted a fold of sailcloth and ducked under it, then remembered her bag and covered herself and it thoroughly. The hatch overhead slammed shut, echoing in the hold and reverberating through her body. Trapped. Truly shut-in. The time to cry off, if she were going to do such a thing was now past.

She threw the stifling sail off her and thought about the adventure ahead. Soon, the race would be underway and Lucky wouldn't be able to send her ashore. That's when she would come out of hiding. There was no way she'd spend the entire voyage down here. She wanted to see the ocean teaming with fishes, feel the salty wind and sea spray as it whipped over her face and through her hair. She wanted to see no land, because she'd never sailed anywhere before where you couldn't see or swim to land nearby. She wanted to experience that sense of vulnerability that comes with being at the complete mercy of a force greater than any she'd ever known—

that supreme force of nature described by her relatives and the other captains of whom she'd read. They were the same men who established trade with countries around the globe, men whose bravery and skills brought almost every boat and man home.

The darkened hold became stifling, the smell of pitch stronger now that no air entered from the hatchway. Removing her coat, she tossed it to the side along with her hat and satchel. Sounds coming from above told her the crew was weighing anchor. The boat began to move, now free from its mooring. Sails were raised and the vessel surged forward. The boat pitched hard to port as it turned and Sarah was thrown into the bulkhead, striking her shoulder on a beam. Thinking of a way to keep from getting tossed about while she was down here, she resigned herself to lying close to the center of the hold, under several folds of sail, even though it was more than a bit warm. The additional weight kept her relatively padded and safe.

She tried to get situated once again and settled in with the comforting rocking and rolling motion of a ship at full sail. Smiling in the inky blackness, she wondered if her maid had noticed her gone yet and if her brother had found her letter.

He was sure to be angry, but hopefully not so angry that he'd delay the start of the race to search Lucky's boat and haul her back home.

No, he wouldn't do that. That would cause a scandal. And if there was one thing the Duke of Caversham detested more than lying, it was the mere thought of the family name tangled up in a scandal.

Sarah knew the precise moment they'd hit the open

sea. The boat began to pitch unlike anything she'd ever known before. Of course it didn't help being in the farthest front compartment as the bow sliced through the waves. Perhaps that was why people didn't sleep in the bow, and only sails were stored up here. Sails couldn't get beat up, like stupid, impulsive ladies who don't think before they get themselves locked in the forward hold.

Thankfully the sailcloth provided her some protection, but she still got tossed about the small compartment. Once she'd even hit the solid oak rafter of the deck above her. Sarah heard a voice issue orders above, and the scurry of footsteps as the command was carried out.

This went on for quite a while, as Sarah contemplated banging on the hatch to have someone let her out. She was thirsty and hungry, and needed to relieve herself. She had no idea how long she'd been down here, nor how far out of Liverpool they were. Another pitch and she felt weightless again, and braced herself for another hit against the rafter.

This was insane. She wanted adventure, not broken bones. When the boat turned hard over, Sarah flew into the right bulkhead. She vowed that the minute she heard footsteps above deck she would scream for the man to let her out. Having no idea how long the seas were going to be rough, or when anyone might open the hatch so she could get some fresh air, she decided she just could not wait any longer. Oh, what was she thinking? No one even knew she was down here. It was then she realized spare sails don't need fresh air, just protection from water.

It seemed an eternity before she heard voices and

footsteps headed toward the bow. But as soon as she did, she let out with the loudest, longest scream she could muster.

Ian stood at the wheel, with his eye on the fore-and-aft sail and foresail. Scanning the horizon once again, he caught sight of *Avenger* and knew she followed his lead. He had approximately a six minute lead out of the box, which meant nearly a mile separated the two vessels. Ahead were three square-rigged vessels at full sail and the *Ann McKim*. By luck of the draw, nineteen of the thirty-two boats entered left the box before him. Ian allowed himself a smile of satisfaction as he realized all that stood between him and the lead were the four vessels ahead. Especially since the *Revenge* was a three masted topsail schooner, which at first glance didn't look nearly as fast as *Ann McKim*, with her long jibboom and four headsails. But was, in fact, much quicker.

He knew a race such as this wasn't won on the number of sails or masts. A skilled captain was essential, but what some sailors tended to overlook was the one thing Ian considered most important. The hull and keel. And these had been retrofitted specifically to his design. If he was right, and he won, then his entire fleet of schooners would be designed the same.

As he set a course to the next coordinate, Ian pondered the things he could do with that winning purse. During his musings, one of the crew shouted something to him from the bow. Looking out at the flying jib, and seeing nothing awry, he motioned for the man to speak up.

"There's a lad stowed away in the sail locker!"

Ian handed the wheel over to his second, and strode the ninety odd feet to the hatch in the bow.

"Did I hear you correctly? You said there was a stow-away?"

"Right, Cap'n, sir. He's a hollerin' up a storm down there."

"Are you sure you heard correctly?" Ian asked as he held onto the brass railing. Just then he heard it too, a voice, bellowing from below.

"Get him out of there and lock him up. We'll turn him in when we return. He gets minimal ration, too. I'm not feeding some little whelp a full three squares if he's broken the law and stowed away."

"Aye-aye cap'n," the man said as Ian turned back to his post at the wheel.

A few minutes later, the crewman shoved a scrawny kid in front of him. His oil cloth slicker, two sizes too big was buttoned to the chin, and the knitted cap covered his head. "Cap'n, sir, he says he's your brother."

"I don't have a brother," Ian said without needing to look down at the scamp. "Lock him up in the lazarette. I'll deal with him later."

"Where's Lucky?" the definitely female voice squeaked with fear.

Just then Ian looked down into the deepest amber brown eyes he'd seen only once before. He didn't need to see the color of her hair, or the slender feminine form that plagued his dreams the night before to know who it was. "Holy Mother of God," he swore, unable to take his gaze from hers. "What have you done?"

"Obviously stowed away onto the wrong boat."

About the Author

Sandy Raven has a husband who spoils her rotten, and kids that are just a hair's breadth away from perfect. She's addicted to House Hunter's International and has *never* missed an episode, though she acknowledges that she could never live in most of those countries because the houses are just too small. She is also addicted to Starbucks' Chai Latte, and never passes up an opportunity to have one.

Sandy grew up on the Texas Gulf Coast with sand between her toes and perpetually frizzy hair. Which is why she now lives in the middle-of-nowhere Virginia, in a place with minimal to moderate humidity (for perfect, non-frizzy curls,) rolling hills and farmed forests. The only downside to that is the temperamental satellite internet and the closest Starbucks being a thirty minute drive away.

Home is a renovated old farm house she shares with her hero husband, in the foothills of Blue Ridge Mountains, where she's owned by more cats, dogs and horses than she cares to admit to. She's a long-time member of RWA, and is a member of VRW and the Beau Monde. Second to writing is her love for her horses. She practices natural horsemanship, and loves to ride her barefoot Tennessee Walkers on the trails and in the woods around her home.

You can visit her at
Website: SandyRaven.com
On Facebook: Facebook.com/SandyRavenAuthor

Printed in Great Britain
by Amazon.co.uk, Ltd.,
Marston Gate.